THE
GEOMANCER

ALSO BY
CLAY GRIFFITH AND SUSAN GRIFFITH

The Greyfriar

The Rift Walker

The Kingmakers

THE
GEOMANCER

VAMPIRE EMPIRE

—⋙—

A GARETH AND ADELE NOVEL

CLAY GRIFFITH
AND SUSAN GRIFFITH

an imprint of **Prometheus Books**
Amherst, NY

Cover design by Grace M. Conti-Zilsberger
Cover illustration © Chris McGrath

This is a work of fiction. Characters, locales, and events portrayed in this novel either are products of the author's imagination or are used fictitiously.

Inquiries should be addressed to

Pyr
59 John Glenn Drive
Amherst, New York 14228
VOICE: 716–691–0133
FAX: 716–691–0137
WWW.PYRSF.COM

19 18 17 16 15   5 4 3 2 1

Library of Congress Cataloging-in-Publication Data

Griffith, Clay.
The geomancer : vampire empire: a Gareth and Adele novel / by Clay Griffith and Susan Griffith.
pages ; cm
ISBN 978-1-63388-094-8 (pbk.) — ISBN 978-1-63388-095-5 (e-book)
1. Vampires—Fiction. I. Griffith, Susan, 1963- II. Title.

PS3607.R5486G46 2015
813'.6—dc23

2015023534

Printed in the United States of America

PROLOGUE

"**T**his city is dead. Stop jumping at shadows."

"It's not dead," came the return mumble. "I hear things at night; whispers, hissing."

Ruins of jagged stone surrounded the two soldiers as they made their rounds. Once grand streets overflowed with dark foliage and twisted vines that had reclaimed their territory. Narrow alleys buried in perpetual shadow led to dim warrens and long abandoned courtyards. Debris that littered the ground included long discarded garbage, crumbled walls, and piles of bones covered in ash.

"There are no more monsters here in London," the sergeant insisted sternly in Arabic. "They're all gone. We're here now to see that it stays safe. What you're hearing is just the remains of the vampires' human herds. They've taken refuge in what's left of these old buildings."

The second trooper held up a lantern to ward off the shadows that appeared to creep closer. The trembling lantern barely illuminated five feet in front of them as they walked the darkened path. Both men clutched pistols.

The sergeant kicked a skull that hosted sharp canine teeth. "I was at Grenoble. I saw with my own eyes vampires turning to dust before the might of our empress. And she did worse here. None of those monsters can set foot on these consecrated lands."

A low moan sounded from ahead and the lantern's light caught a pale white shape. The young private gasped and his pistol swung toward the ghostly figure as it shuffled out of sight. "Was that one of them—the herds?"

"Probably. Let's make sure. The damn fool wasn't wearing a stitch of clothes. It will die of the cold for sure on a night like this."

"Why bother? If it's stupid enough to stand out here, maybe it isn't worth saving."

"It's been a slave its entire life. It doesn't know any better. But it's still human. Sort of."

The two soldiers weaved toward the spot where they had seen the figure. Thin footprints in the light snow led them further down an alley. Amidst the rubble stood a building. The door was nothing more than a plank of wood, but that had been shoved to the side. Shining their lanterns into the dark structure, they called out in English, "We are Equatorian soldiers. We've come to check on you."

Low whimpers answered, along with some shuffling sounds. The lantern light penetrated a corner where dirty blank faces stared back. Five pitiful human forms huddled together, their bony arms clutching one another. Rationed blankets lay crumpled at their feet.

"Bah. They are even too stupid to know what a blanket is for," muttered the nervous young trooper.

The sergeant stopped his companion's grumble with a hard hand on his shoulder. There was another noise coming from the dark. A high-pitched keening and then grunts like an animal foraging.

Trying to keep his hand steady, the private swung his light. The yellow beam illuminated a lone woman standing with head bowed. She was nude, swaying on her feet. She was young, maybe twenty. Strands of unkempt blond hair lay in a tangled curtain about her face. This was the pale figure that had led them to this place.

"Here now," the young man spoke, his tone suddenly softer, feeling ashamed for his prior scorn. "You're safe."

It was then he realized that the grunting wasn't coming from her. The shifting light caught the sudden reflected glow of an animal's eyes just behind her.

"Something's in here with them," he shouted.

A clawed hand stroked the naked woman's hair, almost affectionately. The creature smiled a rictus grin, sharp canines flashing, and licked her bare throat. The woman moaned and bowed low.

The sergeant's lantern struck the same corner just as three new figures rose from the floor. Long arms dangled from thin pale bodies. They quivered and twitched, their muscles caught in some sort of palsied excitement. At their feet, four others crouched over a pile of prone bodies. Their heads jerked up and their grunting quieted as gazes locked onto new prey. Gaping mouths dripped black with fresh blood suckled from the torn throats of their victims.

The monsters had lured them here. The soldiers lifted their pistols, and gunfire boomed in the small chamber. The vampires lunged from the circles of light. Screams erupted as weapons and lanterns tumbled to the floor. The naked woman stood motionless, caught in a fallen beam of light, her expression slack as she watched the sickening feast at the doorway. She didn't even blink, but stood waiting.

Then the lantern lights flickered out and the charnel house went dark.

CHAPTER 1

Adele walked through the weedy grounds of Greyfriars kirkyard. She found comfort in the long rows of funerary markers and in the crumbling church. Her fingers drifted across grave markers that were no longer legible. Mossy stone skulls stared at her as she passed. Heavy gates lay askew and black iron cages sat on the ground, mortsafes intended to keep out grave robbers.

A bright moon shone through the leaves, giving her a shadow on the grass. The air was warm and Adele wore only a nightgown, which she briefly thought odd. Buttercups swayed in clumps below the tombs. Crocuses grew along the walls of the church.

Footfalls through the grass brought Adele around. A figure in a long kimono of green silk came through the moonlight. Short, compact, powerful, the man strode toward Adele with a smile on his face.

"Mamoru." Adele was excited to see her old teacher. It seemed like it had been a long time. His presence usually brought something new and fascinating. He didn't speak, although she longed to hear his deep voice. It was always reassuring.

She held out her hands to take his as he approached. "I'm so glad to see you. I was reading the last book you gave me, and I have a question about the permanent positioning of rifts in the Earth." Adele felt his strong fingers intertwine with hers and a familiar warmth spread through her. "I have questions about crystallography as well."

Her hands hurt. Mamoru was squeezing them. He stared at her with eyes like the iron gates on the graves around them. He sneered and twisted her hands. The pain drove her to her knees.

"Don't," Adele cried in confusion. "What have I done?"

He dragged her toward a stone sarcophagus. She struggled but found herself shoved flat until her back pressed against the cold marble.

She didn't move even after he released her hands, her limbs strangely numb. Bewilderment turned to terror.

Suddenly Adele stood beside Mamoru, looking at him as well as down at her own body where he had placed her atop the sarcophagus. She looked so young lying there. She watched as he produced crystals from his robe and placed one on her supine form.

Mamoru turned away and walked about the kirkyard. He carried an instrument that was something like a maritime sextant with crystals at principle points. He took readings with the scryer, set a crystal carefully on the ground, and then proceeded to chart a place for another.

Adele followed him as he went about his complex task. She pointed back at her body lying on the crypt. "I beg you, don't do this. I'm your student. And you taught my mother before me. I have honored you for all these years."

Mamoru stopped with a yellow crystal in his hand and regarded her. He then set that stone on the ground. Without another glance at her, he returned to the tomb where she lay. Adele could feel the power of the Earth awaken under her feet. The life force of several rifts roared in her ears like the sound of water rushing through hidden pipes.

"Get up!" Adele shouted at her immobile self on the moss-speckled tomb. That version of herself looked so young and innocent. "Don't be afraid. You have the power to stop this!"

Mamoru made one final adjustment to the crystal that rested on the chest of her younger self. Adele stiffened as if she were stone too. Fire from the hungry Earth reached up and seized her. She was dragged down through the graves of Greyfriars. The skeletons stared as she fell far below their loamy houses. She felt the hellish heat and smelled a sickening mélange of scents from across the world. The normally melodious crystalline tones clanged and smashed around her. The burning silver rifts swept her along.

The power tore at her flesh, eating its way inside. It swirled through her, using her as a lens to focus itself. Then it ripped out, surging back into the rifts, spreading like flaming blood in the veins of the Earth.

Far to the south of Edinburgh, across the border into northern England where the vampires lived, the dying began. The creatures sensed the coming wave only seconds before it struck. From the ground came silver fire that poured over them. They screamed with a horrible agony that none had ever known. They writhed and fell. Their flesh turned to ash leaving white bones scattered across the countryside.

Adele turned her horrified eyes from the spreading extinction she had begun, and suddenly she was back in the kirkyard. Dread filled her. She knew what was coming. A familiar figure dropped like a meteor through the branches and smashed to the ground. Gareth. He rose with a face like death for Mamoru. Adele tried to shout at Gareth to run. The fires of the Earth struck him and he too twisted in agony, just as all his brethren had. Mamoru slammed him to the ground. Gareth fought to rise and Mamoru battered him again. Gareth struggled up once more, his sharp fangs bared.

Adele's younger self finally stirred on the tomb, kicking crystals away. Swinging her feet over the edge, she sat up, shoving the stupor and the pain aside. She had her mother's khukri in her hand. She walked unsteadily across the graveyard toward Mamoru, who pressed his boot on Gareth's throat. Gareth grasped the man's ankle, but couldn't find the strength to shift it.

The young woman plunged the glowing dagger into Mamoru's back. He didn't cry out. He simply turned and looked at her as if he was disappointed. Then he vanished in the moonlight.

Adele ran over to her younger self, who stood over Gareth as he writhed in agony in the dirt. Geysers of silver fire erupted across the cemetery. Gareth's flesh turned red, then black. His face cracked and tore away. His outstretched hand shriveled. His horrible cry faded and his bones dropped smoldering in the grass.

Adele grabbed herself, trying to shake awareness into her stunned face. "Stop it! Don't let Mamoru turn you into a tool of extinction. It's *your* power, not *his*. It isn't his choice." She pointed at the charred skeleton of Gareth. "Save him!"

"I can't," she replied in a cracking voice Adele remembered from years ago. "It's too late."

An overwhelming helplessness gripped Adele. She fell to her hands and knees in the ashes of her lover and screamed.

The dark timbers of Edinburgh Castle abruptly hovered above her. Adele gasped and felt sweat dripping along the sides of her neck. Her heart pounded, nearly shaking the bed. She reached across the mattress to find it cold and empty.

Gareth had died. She hadn't saved him in the kirkyard. He was gone. Adele couldn't remember the days between that terrible night and this one. She could only remember the way he held her in his arms. If only she could go back to sleep and live in a dream where they were together.

A blast of cold wind scattered thick photographs from the bed. A tall shadow entered an open window. Gareth stood silhouetted against the grey skies. His blue eyes reflected in the dim lamplight. He stared at Adele for a long moment before swinging the glass shut.

"Adele." His voice rumbled in the quiet.

Her hand gripped the covers beside her, along with the pictures she had been studying before she dozed off. Gareth stepped down from the windowsill. He wore his usual black trousers and white shirt. His long black hair was tousled from the wind.

"You're alive." Adele hadn't wanted to say it out loud in case it might wake her up again.

His brow furrowed and he smiled. "I was only out for an hour or two." He moved to the bed with a silent tread and took her arms in his firm grip. He was tall and elegant, but well-muscled. His lips were soft when he kissed her.

Adele clutched him tight.

"Another nightmare?" Gareth asked.

"Yes." She pressed her face against his chilled chest. "As always, I couldn't use my geomancy to save you, and I couldn't stop the death that Mamoru started."

"But you did."

Adele pushed back against her pillows and pulled her knees up. The truth didn't assuage her. Every time the nightmare struck, she was left in fuming helplessness. Over the months since the horrors of that night, the frequency of the dreams had lessened. However, when they came they still brought the same rage and she needed a moment to calm herself.

Taking long breaths, she was surprised to see her face across the room in a wall mirror. She was olive skinned with voluminous brunette hair and the Persian features of her mother. However, this face was different from the one in the dream. Adele was only twenty years old, but her girlish features were overlaid with lines creasing the corners of her eyes and grey streaking her hair. She looked away from the face that had been born that night in the kirkyard and hastily changed the subject. "Were you writing, or out thinking?"

"No. I was feeding."

"I thought your people came to the castle for you to feed."

"With your troops here in Edinburgh now, they're uncomfortable passing by your soldiers."

"Have there been any incidents? I'll have Major Shirazi deal with it."

"No, but they feel the Equatorians look down on them for providing me with blood. So I go to them now to spare them the embarrassment."

Adele felt a twinge of sadness at his discomfort. "I'm sorry. My troops don't understand yet that your people give their blood willingly. It's so foreign to them."

"I understand. They've never seen it before because it's never happened before." Gareth gathered the papers that had flown around the room. He looked at each of the pictures as he picked them up. Most of them were shots of Greyfriars kirkyard. "Perhaps you shouldn't go back there."

"Why?" Adele asked with alarm as she crossed to the fireplace to be away from her reflection in the mirror.

"If you stayed away maybe the nightmares would stop."

"I don't want to stay away. Taking pictures has helped me over the last few months. It's therapeutic." She knelt to toss in several chunks of coal and jostled them with an iron rod. "I keep taking pictures of it expecting to see . . . something. Something from that night. Burns. Fire. Some proof that it happened in the real world. I know what I did that night, but the pictures all look normal."

Gareth came up behind her, holding a stack of photographs. "We know it happened. We were both there. All the vampires were scoured from Britain. I died—"

"Stop." Adele stared at the glowing embers. That night in the kirkyard, she had done more than just destroy all the vampires and make the island uninhabitable for them; she had silenced the power of the Earth here forever. Anywhere else in the world, the rifts would sing to her. But not in Britain or Scotland. It had taken several months before she stopped trying to find the rifts again, to touch the warmth that she was used to flowing at her fingertips. Adele knew that power was still available to her if she left the island, but she had grown oddly content at its absence. Now she was almost used to the silence and the cold that surrounded her in this place. A part of her felt like any other normal human being. Her thoughts were interrupted by the sound of Gareth flipping through the photos.

He said, "Pet is very photogenic."

Adele smiled and rose. He was looking at a picture of a grey cat stretched out on his back, looking coyly into the camera. There were many other pictures of the cat and of the many other cats who lived around the castle. Gareth continued to shuffle through the photos. Many showed Edinburgh's inhabitants at their daily chores. A pretty young woman smiled into the camera in a few of the shots. And there were other pictures of the stone city of Edinburgh in various seasons and sunlight. Soldiers of her personal guard lounging or training. Townspeople drinking, laughing, flirting.

Gareth nodded with approval. However, there was something curious, a little disappointed, about his expression. He obviously noticed an absence among the photos. Adele took the stack from his hands and went to her desk. She pulled open a drawer and removed a box.

"What's that?" Gareth asked.

"Pictures of you."

He tried to look surprised, but he couldn't keep the satisfaction off his face. "I have my own box?"

Adele pulled out a pile of photos and set them on the desk near a flickering lamp. He joined her and saw an extraordinary variety of pictures of him. Some he posed for, but most she had taken when he was unaware. Sitting before the fire. Staring out the window. As a distant shape in the air above the castle. There was a picture of him on the battlements surrounded by a veritable herd of cats, with his hand resting idly on the back of one that arched happily under his touch.

He flipped through a series of close-up pictures of his hands. His fingers were long. His fingernails were sharp and capable of being extended into claws. The photos showed his hands draped along the arms of chairs, holding books, settled on a tabletop, holding a pen, and grasping Adele's hand.

Gareth looked up at her. "You seem fascinated by my hands."

"I am." She placed her own over his, relishing the roughness of his hands. "They're wonderful."

"They are just hands."

"No. They belong to a vampire. You have a diminished sense of touch compared to humans, and yet, look. Holding a pen. Writing. You use tools, unlike any of your kind. Your hands are subtle. Facile. Elegant. Powerful." She kissed his fingers. "And yet gentle."

His lips skimmed over hers, light as the air itself. "Let's go back to bed."

Adele took the photos and dropped them back in the box. "I'm not sleepy."

Gareth swept her up off her feet. He clutched her tight against his chest as he leaned down and blew out the lamp. "Who said anything about sleep?"

CHAPTER 2

Adele woke the next morning with Gareth beside her. He stared at the ceiling with one arm looped over her shoulders. Pressing into his side, she enjoyed the warmth for a few minutes longer. The position of the sun on the floor told her that it was long past mid-morning.

"I could stay in bed all day," she told Gareth.

"I should get up."

"Eager to be at work?"

Gareth gave a huffing breath that could have been agreement. He sat up, taking the heavy quilt and allowing the frigid air to assault her body.

"Oh God, it's cold." A furry form shifted and complained at the foot of the bed. Then a huge grey cat stretched and padded over to Adele. With a groan, she lifted the feline deadweight into her arms. Adele buried her face in his luxurious fur. "Oh my God, Pet. You're like the best bed warmer ever. When Gareth isn't about, that is."

She grabbed for her robe and raced for the coal grate to prod the embers. A faint orange glow throbbed, and she tossed several new pieces on the fire. Tending her own hearth would be forbidden at home in Alexandria, but there were few true servants in Edinburgh Castle and she kept them all out of this wing so she and Gareth could be alone. The nature of their relationship was kept secret, although no doubt rumors of all sort likely circulated around the city and beyond. Adele had little time to worry about that. This time together was the only common domesticity she and Gareth had ever shared, and she relished any touches of normalcy.

Adele noted the wonderfully rumpled Gareth sitting on the side of the bed with his muscled legs stretched out. She found it alluring that he was so unaware of himself at all times. She wanted a picture. Her camera rested on a nearby table. It was a box several inches square with a lens on one side, a viewfinder on the back, and a single button on top. A simple but wondrous device that created instant memories and history. When Adele lifted the camera, Gareth gave her a mild warning glance. She shifted her focus to a yellow cat sitting outside the thick window. She pretended to click the shutter and gave Gareth a charming smile. When he looked away, she took a photo of him.

As she dressed, Adele remarked, "I'm starving. I wonder what Morgana made for breakfast."

"Whatever it is you'll declare it delicious."

"You sound jealous you can't taste her magnificent cooking."

"A vampire's curse." He tucked in his shirt. "I'm thinking a scouting mission to the Continent might be in order soon."

"That's dangerous, isn't it?"

Gareth fumbled briefly with the knob, then pulled the door open for her. "Yes, but we want to be ready for the offensive when the weather warms."

"We'll plan something." Adele knew he was right, but didn't want him going off alone.

Breakfast was laid in a front room along with a roaring fire. Coffee, tea, and orange marmalade shipped in from Egypt. The Scottish farms provided eggs and bacon and neeps, or turnips, which the locals never seemed to tire of. Adele piled food on her plate, having pushed away the terrors of the night. Gareth didn't eat, so he spent his time fighting curious cat paws away from the plate of bacon.

They both heard footsteps coming rapidly down the hall and looked up to see Morgana in the door. She was the pretty young woman seen in so many of Adele's photographs. Her face was red from exertion. Her normally soft eyes were wide. The young servant was barely twenty years old and quite pretty in a vigorous farm girl sense. Her brunette hair was long and nearly as uncontrolled as Adele's. The two women had become fast friends and Adele trusted her implicitly. Morgana carried a sheet of paper in her hand that Adele recognized was a yellow tear-sheet from the telegraph pad.

Morgana swallowed. "Miss, this message came this morning from Governor-General Condorcet's office in London. It's in code." She held up several sheets, with her handwritten scrawls of letters that made no sense.

"You have the code pads."

"It's in Arabic, miss."

"Really? Arabic and in code?" Adele took the sheets from the servant with an unwelcome sense of apprehension. Arabic was used for more private messages, and although Morgana had mastered translating the English codes, Arabic was as yet beyond her. "Morgana, send for Major Shirazi."

Morgana paused at the door with a shocked look. "But miss . . . I don't . . ."

"I'm sure it's nothing," she assured her friend with as warm a smile as she could muster. "But best to take care of the usual protocol. Hurry now."

Adele began working alone. Several minutes later Morgana returned with the commander of her Home Guard, a unit known as the Harmattan. In his heavy winter serge, Major Shirazi stood at the door, his worried eyes staring at the coded sheet, and then up at Gareth. Adele and Morgana sat at the table and worked together with the codebook. Gareth paced, pausing to study the women conversing, running their fingers down columns of symbols, and writing. He failed to notice that Pet had captured an entire plate of bacon and carried it off piece by piece until the cat collapsed by the fire unable to move.

The room was deathly quiet but for the scratch of the pencil on the paper and Adele's quickening breath. The words fell into logical place. Finally, she scrawled out the last Arabic word and sat with pencil trembling.

"This is impossible." Adele studied the sheaf of pages. "There must be a mistake."

"What is it?" Gareth stood at her shoulder. He spoke Arabic fluently, with several regional accents, but he couldn't read it.

"Vampires." Adele's voice almost broke.

Gareth relaxed. "Oh. An attack of some sort on the Continent?"

"An attack in London."

"London?" He looked down in confusion. "I don't understand. There are no vampires in London, in the entire British Isles."

Shirazi offered Gareth a baleful glare. "Present company excepted."

Adele gave her commander a warning glance before continuing, "Governor-General Condorcet reports there have been murders by vampires in London, the most recent on several of our soldiers."

"It must be a mistake." Gareth waved a dismissive hand and walked to the far wall where ancient weapons of war hung. "I wouldn't be surprised if Cesare's old human soldiers, the Undead Legion, were committing acts designed to look like vampires. They all dreamed of being vampires in any case."

Adele looked hopeful. "Is that possible?"

Gareth appeared doubtful. "I thought that between your forces and the vengeful populace, the remnants of the Undead Legion had been hunted down. But it's *possible*."

She threw the paper on the table and slammed her hand down. "Damn it!"

Only Gareth didn't flinch. "Even so, you knew your geomancy might not keep them out forever."

"But not even a year." Adele put her head in her hands before realizing Morgana and Shirazi were there. She sat up straight, but her eyes sought out Gareth. "All that torture and death for a few months of freedom."

Shirazi asked, "Can you not renew it? Whatever it was?"

"No," replied Gareth sharply. Adele saw the flash of fear in his eyes. He continued, "That's what *you* said."

She turned slowly from his gaze. "I can no longer touch the rifts here in Britain. It's as if the Earth is scabbed over from the damage I caused that night."

"And," Gareth asserted firmly, as if she had missed the more important point, "you said that if you attempted activity of that scale again, it would kill you."

Shirazi stared at Gareth, clearly suspicious of the vampire lord's emotional outburst about Adele's well-being.

Adele let the moment pass, taking a deep breath. "I said it's *unlikely* I could endure another such bout of energy moving through me. But if it's necessary—"

"Don't," Gareth said quietly. "It will never be that necessary."

"Prince Gareth," Major Shirazi clutched his hands behind his back, "do you know anything about your kind returning to these shores that perhaps you've neglected to tell us?"

Gareth spun with such fury that Adele bolted to her feet, fearful he was about to fly across the room and attack the soldier.

"Major!" Adele stuck out her hand toward Gareth, whose eyes flicked to her and grew slightly less brutal. She glared at her commander. "Your accusation is outrageous. Would you care to withdraw it?"

Shirazi's stern face was unchanged. He slid his hand from the butt of his revolver. He bowed toward Adele. "I apologize, Your Majesty. I meant no insult."

Adele resumed her seat to calm the room. "Morgana, ask Captain Hariri to prepare my airship. I will embark for the south as soon as possible."

"Yes, miss." Morgana's voice lowered with disappointment at the political tone of Empress Adele, now sounding as if she was again at war.

Adele glanced around the table with resolution. "I'll send for Greyfriar to meet me in London. Major Shirazi, I'll want you and the Harmattan with me." She gathered her papers together. The soldier saluted, stood aside for Morgana to exit, and then went out himself. Adele slumped and said softly to Gareth, "Will Greyfriar meet me in London?"

"Indeed he will." Gareth slid a strong hand across her shoulders. "As always."

CHAPTER 3

A shadow crossed the starry sky over London and fell upon an old man. His strangled cry broke the silence. The nearby crowd shifted away from him and huddled closer together.

The shadow lifted its face from its prey's neck, sharp teeth glinting white in the light of the swollen moon overhead. Its head dipped down again to drink from the moaning victim. Blood pooled in the hollow of the man's gasping throat. The horrible shape rose from the bleeding man and moved to stalk a fresh meal.

Suddenly a blade flashed bright and struck the vampire in the base of the spine. It let out a screech as it arched backward and twisted. Adele lifted her sword high to strike again. She was dressed in supple leather and rich cloth, unlike the ragged herd that stood placidly watching. Determination tightened her face as she struck. Steel sliced through the muscle of the vampire's left arm. No scream of pain fell from its lips. Instead it lunged at the woman, the claws on its hand ripping her thick skirt, tearing it at the knees in an attempt to cripple her.

It was a clumsy attack. Adele's dark eyes flashed with confusion. This vampire moved more sluggishly than its kind typically did, but not from the wounds she had given it. Such cuts should've been paltry to the creature; hardly felt by a vampire. But in this case, its motions were slower than usual. It almost writhed with some sort of palsy affliction.

Adele spun aside, bringing out a second weapon. The dagger's wicked curved blade glowed green and sizzled as it drove into the vampire's arm, cutting it straight to the bone and carving out a fair chunk of flesh. The beast staggered and stumbled over the body of its victim. It recovered and ran. Adele sped after the vampire and the milling humans broke apart like a wave, letting the combatants pass without lifting a hand to help or hinder. These remnants of the vampires' herds remained the easiest of prey. It made sense that this was the area where the creature had been hunting. It didn't make sense that the vampire existed here at all, but Adele put that out of her mind.

She raced through the overgrown woods of old Hyde Park, leaping over chipped, ivy-covered marble benches in an attempt to match speed with the vampire. It dove for the shadows of the deep woods and Adele plunged in after it, pulling her arms close to avoid the tangled and overgrown branches. She hacked at some that loomed too close to her face. Then she was through to a clearing and the vampire spun to a halt, facing her.

Adele's lips held a grin of victory until she saw numerous glowing eyes behind her quarry. A pack of vampires crept forward to join their brethren. She only had time for a shocked cry at the impossibility when they surged at her all at once, their tattered clothing flapping like ghosts.

Adele raised her blades to meet the snarling horde. Dodging under the swipe of the first one, she thrust up into the heart of the second. Her other arm swung backward and cut deep into the back of the vampire that had overshot her. Others reached for her with fierce claws and gaping jaws. She kicked one in the face and heard teeth shatter. Each thrust of her weapons drew blood, but she knew she would soon be overwhelmed.

From high in the canopy of trees, a silhouette dropped, barely visible against the forest of deep shadows. There was a definitive shudder among the vampires. They threw themselves away as a cloaked swordsman alighted next to Adele with rapier and pistol clutched in his hands.

One of the vampires whispered, "The Greyfriar."

"I found them!" Adele exclaimed, gasping and grateful for the respite.

"You have a singular knack," came the man's calm response.

"What can I say? I attract them."

If the man returned her grin, it was hidden. A grey wool scarf was wrapped around his head, except for his eyes, and they were covered by mirrored glasses. He wore the outdated jacket of a Napoleonic rifleman, with its gold piping across the front, and the high black boots of a dragoon. He seemed an odd mishmash of adventurers' costumes.

The vampires regained a bit of nerve, or realized their desperate plight. There was no escape now. It was fight or die. They summoned their nerve and growled at the two interlopers.

"We need one alive." Adele warned.

"As you wish." Greyfriar waded into the mob. His blade moved with a speed that Adele could not match even on her best day. Every story written about him couldn't capture his graceful killing strokes that rose and fell with a fluid system of iambic pentameter. Greyfriar dispatched one of his attackers, obliterating the creature's heart with a twist of his blade. It wasn't out of cruelty but because he knew such damage to a major organ was virtually the only way to assure it would stay down. As the vampire fell backward, another came in its place. This one too was dropped, with a bullet to the brain. One by one, the beasts fell in the face of the onslaught. Creatures moved to attack from behind, but Greyfriar didn't react. Either he didn't see them, or he trusted Adele implicitly.

Adele contented herself by dispatching the stragglers that scrambled out of the way of Greyfriar's deadly blade work. Her own weapons aimed for the heart.

Finally, only two remained. Adele doubled over, sucking in breath. The vampires saw their salvation and fled.

Greyfriar cursed and raised his pistol, but stopped when he saw a knowing smile on Adele's face. "Did you allow that?"

"I am a little winded, but yes, we need to know if there are more of them in the city, and where they are hiding. So don't lose them!" Adele lurched after the vampires.

Greyfriar darted on her heels, easily keeping pace. Their boots crunched along the streets of London. Grass and roots pushed up through the cracks in the ancient pavement.

The two vampires took to the air, drifting up above the trees toward the largely deserted buildings to the south. Their flight was erratic, as if struggling to control their quivering limbs that threatened to steer them off course.

Ahead of Adele was the ruin of a memorial arch and, beyond, another heavy, nearly impassable forest that had once been charming Green Park. She ran along the only open path available, the old broken road of Constitution Hill. On her right was the scorched, cratered wasteland where Buckingham Palace had once stood.

Adele and Greyfriar continued west down the center of a stately tree-lined avenue, now overgrown and wild. Greyfriar raced ahead. Then he veered to the right, shot through the trees, and leapt to a ruined building, scurrying effortlessly up its side. He was on the slate roof in seconds and legging after the sailing vampires across the jagged landscape of peaks and chimneys.

Forced to take a slower path, Adele ran all the harder to keep them in view. She was truly laboring now, hardly in prime fighting shape. A razor sharp pain cut into her side with each ragged breath. She lost sight of her quarry in the high spires of steeples and towers, but then glimpsed Greyfriar's fluttering cloak against the stars.

She stumbled over a large mound of garbage and her boots kicked into a pile of burnt bones. A blackened skull rolled ahead. Her stride stumbled as the face turned toward her, showing the sharp needle canines grinning at her.

Adele recoiled. In her first trip to London nearly two years ago as a captive of the fearsome British vampire clan, the pile of cadavers would have been human. Now the dead scattered around were all vampires, all members of that very clan. Gareth's clan. Slaughtered by her. Forcing herself past the telltale bones, Adele pushed west with legs pounding, but the horrific image of the countless charnel piles across Britain haunted her.

Greyfriar appeared suddenly in front of her. "Gareth!" she shouted as she clutched his arms in relief, unmindful that she had used his true name in human territory.

"Are you all right?" Greyfriar's head tilted in concern as his hand lifted to hold her.

"Did you lose them?" Adele prayed he didn't feel her shaking, She immediately regretted her accusatory tone.

"Of course not," he offered calmly. "They disappeared into a ruin on the far side of the river. I came back to get you. Against my better judgment."

Adele's regret at her sharp response quickly fled. "We've discussed this already."

"Discussing and agreeing are two different things. Your geomancy is useless here."

Adele shook her head. They moved past the dark bulk of Big Ben and Parliament onto Westminster Bridge. Finally, she had enough wind to say, "They're real, aren't they? Vampires in Britain again."

"Yes."

"We need answers. People are scared, and I don't blame them. They'd just gotten used to the idea that they were free. I promised these people safety." Adele hissed angrily, "Vampires shouldn't be here. They shouldn't be able to set foot in Britain without withering. There's only one vampire who should be able to live here, and that's you."

Greyfriar had no answers for her, and he wasn't prone to abstract speculation. They left the bridge for the bleak landscape of Lambeth. He hardly glanced at the scattered bones of his clan that littered the streets. Adele wondered how he could remain so impassive.

They rounded a corner and Adele stopped at the sight of a dome rising above scraggly trees. Beyond a partially tumbled wall, and through the twisted trunks of a gloomy forest, she could see a sprawling building. It was a heavy institutional pile, devoid of art, thick and immobile, with an air of anger. She got a chill.

"They went in there?" Adele asked.

"Yes." Greyfriar shoved aside the ruined metal gate and slipped among the trees.

"Shouldn't we find a less obtrusive way inside?" Adele quickly followed. She studied the dark woods for more shining eyes. Their feet crunched in the gravel as they approached the portico.

Adele looked up at the heavy pediment. In carved letters discolored by moss, she read *Royal Bethlehem Hospital*. She suppressed a gasp.

"Bedlam," she whispered.

"What?"

"I've heard of this place. It was a famous asylum."

"Are you still going in?"

"Of course."

Scowling, Greyfriar gave a cursory glance around, then lifted his head as if scenting the air. "Be ready." He wrenched the doors open as quietly as he could, creating a narrow gap. A horrible stench crowded their nostrils.

Adele put her arm across her nose. "Decaying flesh."

"They probably brought some of their meals here," was Greyfriar's quick assessment.

Adele grimaced. "It will be their last supper."

Together they entered the darkness of the madhouse.

CHAPTER 4

The halls of Bedlam were silent and surprisingly free of detritus. In some of the corners, bodies lay torn and bled, tossed aside like so much trash. They were all relatively fresh, hence the stench. They passed a few rooms filled with objects of domesticity, such as tables and chairs, lamps and curtains, an indication that humans had lived here recently.

Greyfriar's attention was drawn to the distant end of the hallway. He pointed into the darkness and then put a finger to his lips. Adele nodded. They crept down the hall until she saw a double door. They slipped up to it and she put an ear against the cracked wood. Adele heard nothing, but she trusted Greyfriar implicitly. If he said their quarry was inside then they were inside. There was no telling how large the nest was. They had chased only two here, but it didn't mean there weren't more lurking inside the defunct madhouse. Greyfriar gripped the door handles and made ready to yank them open at Adele's word.

She sheathed her sword and pulled a revolver. She lifted her glowing khukri with its Fahrenheit blade, coated in a terrible burning chemical that could do significant damage even to a vampire. Adele nodded. Greyfriar's shoulders bunched and he flung open the doors. Adele rushed in. She immediately spotted six hunched figures perched on a long mahogany table. All of them writhed and quivered like the vampires in Hyde Park. They rose to their feet to face Adele and Greyfriar.

The mob rushed forward. Greyfriar leapt ahead to meet their charge. Adele shook her head at him, but then joined the fight. Two struck at her with their claws, but their shuddering limbs made their aim unreliable. Her dagger deflected the attacks easily. Her pistol fired at the forehead of one and its head snapped backward. Adele ducked under the swipe of the other, thrusting the khukri into its chest. Its brain tried to register why it suddenly couldn't kill the smaller woman in front on it. Then it died as she yanked out the steaming steel.

Two vampires surged past their crumpling companion and Adele backpedaled for more room. The ornate blade arced in front of her, slicing through the throat of one. The other lunged and she fired her revolver, but claws dug into her shoulder and flung her across the floor. Weapons flew as she landed hard. Her hands grabbed for purchase to stop her slide. The vampire leapt for her, mouth open, fangs extended. She scrambled to her hands and knees, searching for her dagger. The body of another vampire slammed into her attacker, sending them both tumbling away. She laid a hand on her pistol.

Greyfriar grabbed one of the last two vampires and threw it to the floor in front of him. His foot jammed onto its stomach, restraining it so he could stab its heart. The thing died clutching his blade.

Adele's arm extended and she shot the last one as it recovered to fling itself at Greyfriar. It flopped to the floor with a shattered leg. It hissed wildly and tried to crawl away.

Greyfriar went over to it, drawing a short sword, and ran both his blades through its forearms, pinning it to the floor. The male vampire writhed on the ground, unable to free itself. It glared at Greyfriar with blazing blue eyes.

"That was too easy," Adele said.

"Glad you think so."

"They aren't as fast as they should be. They feel pain more than they should." Adele retrieved her khukri from the corner, where its glow was growing fainter. She returned it to the sheath that would replenish the chemical charge. "Is that all of them?"

"Yes."

She rounded on the vampire and snapped, "How can you survive here?"

The creature spat at her, which earned a kick in the face from Greyfriar. "Answer her."

The vampire cursed at them in a guttural human language.

"You have seconds to live," Greyfriar replied in the same tongue. "Tell us what we want to know and it may buy you minutes instead."

"What did it say?" Adele asked in Arabic, which was not a language well-known among vampires, who could readily pick up most human ver-naculars if exposed to them. "I don't recognize its language. German?"

"Flemish," said Greyfriar, also in Arabic. He leaned over to study the vampire closer.

"Does it speak English?" Adele asked in that language.

The creature cast spiteful glances at both of them.

"He does. He's just being difficult, but he'll use it or I'll kill him." Greyfriar pointed at Adele. "Do you know who she is?"

The vampire sneered. "My next meal."

"Hardly." Greyfriar laughed. "She is Empress Adele of Equatoria."

The vampire froze with a fearful moan, "The Death Bringer."

"The Death Bringer?" Adele whispered in shock. She felt a sick-ening slap from the name. Still, she sneered aggressively to prevent the creature from knowing it. Adele replied in an offhand way she didn't feel, "That's catchy in a horrific way."

Greyfriar turned to her, but his limited expression betrayed no reac-tion she could discern, because of his garb.

Adele stepped closer to the vampire, lifting a hand that held no power here. But perhaps the vampire didn't know that. "Your death will be long and agonizing unless you answer our questions. Where are you from?"

It tried to press into the floor, struggling to move away from Adele. It shook more violently, limbs twitching. "From Bruges."

"Why are you here?"

"I was sent here by my prince."

Adele's brow furrowed. "Didn't you know that was a death sentence? Britain is a burial ground for your kind. How can you even be here?"

"Your power no longer harms us!" the vampire shouted defiantly, even though it was clearly in pain and had been for some time.

Adele noticed a glint of something metallic around its neck. When she reached, the vampire screamed, struggling to get away from her.

"Be still." Greyfriar stomped on the vampire's chest. He asked Adele, "What is it?"

"Look at its throat."

Greyfriar used his rapier to flick open the creature's shirt revealing a gold chain.

"Are vampires prone to wearing jewelry?" Adele asked, though it was directed at Greyfriar and not the vampire. Greyfriar lifted the gold links up with the point of his sword. Dangling from the end of the chain was a crystal talisman.

The vampire shrieked, "Don't take it!"

Adele crouched next to the immobilized vampire, peering at the pendant that had a blue crystal at its center.

Greyfriar said quietly in Arabic, "I recognize that. My brother Cesare had one to protect him from your power. A human crafted it for him. He called the man his *Witchfinder*."

Adele's mouth went dry. She knew the story from Gareth. Cesare's so-called *Witchfinder* had claimed to know something of geomancy and used those principles to create the talisman. In the early days of the Equatorian forces landing in Britain, they had searched for the Witchfinder, as they had for all of Cesare's human servants, but with no luck. They assumed these collaborators had died, or been killed in retribution by the British humans. Adele assumed the talisman had been a unique object since no others turned up.

She cursed and turned to the dead vampires around them. She checked them all, and each wore an identical talisman. Adele yanked one free and that vampire's corpse immediately burst into silver flame. She gave out a strange sigh of relief. "At least we know the geomancy barrier is still active. It isn't my power breaking down that allowed these vampires to come here. It's these talismans."

Adele brought her attention back to the prisoner. Her hand felt the heat that still lingered on the crystal as it rested in her palm. She held out the pendant. "Where did you get this?"

The vampire cringed, terrified to be the center of attention once more. "From my prince."

"Where did *your prince* get it?" she demanded. "It couldn't have made one. Your prince is just a vampire. Your kind doesn't make anything."

"I don't know. We were ordered to wear them and come here to Gareth's Grave."

Greyfriar flinched at the name it used for Britain.

"And we survived." The vampire's voice rose with newfound boldness. "Your powers will soon mean nothing to—"

"Enough!" Greyfriar stepped on the vampire's throat, silencing the ranting to a strangled gurgle. "Where did an idiot like the prince of Bruges get amulets such as these?"

"I don't . . . know!" the vampire choked out as Greyfriar eased off its neck.

Adele remarked once again in Arabic, "I think Cesare's Witchfinder is on the Continent."

"I'm dubious. Cesare was unique, even visionary. All vampires use humans to do certain tasks. *Bloodmen* hold doors for us, dress us, and help manage our herds, even fly airships to carry our wealth. *Bloodnurses* provide food for our children so they don't kill their own mothers by overfeeding. But slaves are hardly more than our version of tools. We don't hold humans in enough esteem to listen to them. No other vampire prince but Cesare would have the genius to use humans for strategic value."

Adele scoffed. "Even if one of us comes bearing gifts?" She stared deep into the crystal's facets, fascinated that it somehow worked to reverse her power. A thrill of discovery swelled at the thought of diving into the crystal to see how it functioned, but that would have to wait until they were well out of Britain. "Though not a very good gift. Some of my power must be getting through the talisman's barrier. From the way these vampires move, you can see they're in constant pain."

Greyfriar reached out to touch the talisman, but Adele pulled it away.

"Stop! We don't know what it will do to you!"

His head tilted with amusement. "Probably no more than it's doing to you."

Despite his levity, Adele couldn't keep anxiety from her face. "When I saved you from the event Mamoru triggered, I changed you in ways even I don't understand. I have no idea what geomancy does to you now because I've hardly practiced since that day."

Greyfriar's gloved hand brushed at her cheek. "You worry too much."

"And you not enough," she pointed out quickly. "At least let me examine the bloody thing before everyone and their mother touches it."

Gareth gestured to the prisoner. "What should we do with him?"

"We can't let him go. I don't want this prince of his to know the experiment was a success."

"Assuming, of course, there aren't other vampires in Britain with other talismans."

Adele's stomach bottomed out at the thought of more of these protective amulets flooding out to the vampire clans.

"We won't kill him." Greyfriar grunted with disgust as he stared at the vampire lying on the floor clutching the crystal. "You'll wish you had died with your friends after you're delivered to Sir Godfrey Randolph in Equatoria for his anatomy lessons."

Adele felt a twinge of sympathy for the whimpering creature, although she knew it was without pity. She stared into the blue facets of the talisman in her hand. "I can't believe this Witchfinder is capable of such things in the north, with no schools or teachers or books. How can he do it?"

"There's only one way to find out," Greyfriar replied. "I'll go to the Continent and visit Bruges."

"*We'll* visit Bruges."

"It's inside enemy territory, Adele." Greyfriar crossed his arms with a stance of defiance. "General Anhalt won't like it."

"No. I suppose he won't. Fortunately he's in Alexandria. Would you care to cable him and tell him how you can't keep me under control?"

Greyfriar paused, staring down into Adele's expectant face. "No. Let's not tell him until we're back."

"Coward."

Greyfriar snorted. "I prefer *tactician*."

Laughing, she headed toward the door. "Come on, let's finish searching this place so we can deliver our friend there to the army."

CHAPTER 5

Adele's rooms in the old Montagu House overlooked the Thames
River. Despite the many coal grates throughout the large
mansion, kept glowing hot, the house was damp and cold. After more
than a century of misuse and neglect, it was remarkable that it was
as livable as it was. Still, it was a suitable abode for the empress-in-
residence, close enough to the seat of the government at the old windy
parliament building.

London was something of an armed camp, with Equatorian troops
patrolling the streets. For nearly a year, Britain had been a de facto province of Equatoria, thanks to two events. General Anhalt and the American senator Miles Clark led the bold attack on London in the great
American steamnaught USS *Bolivar*. The airship had crashed into Buckingham Palace, killing nearly everyone aboard, but wiping out several
vampire clan lords who had gathered for Cesare's coronation. At the same
time, Mamoru forced Adele to trigger the event that swept the vampires
away. She had since brought several regiments of her soldiers to control
an island full of humans who had lived generations under vampire terror
and tyranny. Britain would become an important test case to show how
the territories ripped from vampire rule would be re-integrated into free
human society. At the moment, it was still an open question.

Adele walked the dim corridors, clanking with each step because of
her photography equipment and several lanterns she carried. The door
to Gareth's private chamber was open, as always. He sat in a chair near
the window staring out into the winter bleakness, his long legs propped
against the sill. He shifted enough to let her know he had heard her;
there was no way she could take him unaware. She stood watching him.
He still wore the accouterments of the Greyfriar, rifleman's jacket and
trousers with high boots, but his scarf was pulled down, lying loose
about his shoulders. His dark glasses were set aside.

"Gareth," she said, her breath misting the air. "Am I disturbing you?"

"Of course not." He glanced over his shoulder at her, eyeing the camera and tripod in her hands.

Adele saw the pile of paper on the ancient desk across the room. She silently chided herself for interrupting him at work. Sitting atop the ream was his heavy leather gunbelt with twin pistols. "I just don't want to interrupt you if you're trying to make progress before we leave for Bruges tomorrow."

"No. I'm not making much progress as Gareth." He sat up, placing his feet heavily on the floor. With a tug on his rifleman's tunic, he said, "Perhaps the other fellow will have more luck."

Adele laughed nervously. "I wouldn't mind reading what you've written. At some point."

"Shouldn't take you long." Gareth raised his hand toward the papers. "Have a look."

Adele went to his desk, barely containing her excitement. She had flown reams of stationary up from Equatoria along with the finest pens and inks, which were scattered across the desk. She flipped through the stack of paper. Sheet after sheet of blank white met her eyes. Her brow furrowed. "I can't find what you wrote. These are blank."

"Oh sorry. Look next to the empty pages."

Beside the pile of stationery was a single sheet of paper. Adele picked it up and flipped it over. There were several lines written in Gareth's natural, spidery hand: *I am Gareth, son of Dmitri. I was born south of Kili-whimin in the Great Glen of Scotland. My father taught me to hunt humans and drink their blood. That is what I am. I am a monster.*

Adele stared at the page. Her face flushed with shock. She couldn't find any words to reply.

Gareth took the paper from her and looked at it with a nod of mock satisfaction. He set it down on the desk. "It says everything, don't you think? Is it long enough to be a book?"

"Gareth," Adele forced herself to speak calmly, "we decided that you would write this book to explain to humans that vampires aren't what they think. To show them your humanity."

"It turns out I have none."

She put her hand to her head.

"Adele, don't worry about my foolishness. You have so much to do. Compared to that, this is exactly what it looks like, a pile of nothing." He thumbed through the stack of blank paper. "This was a ludicrous idea in any case. The price is too high."

Adele regarded him with confusion. "What price?"

"Surely you've considered that this book will have ramifications that will ripple across the world. Everything would change. You are Adele the First, Empress of Equatoria. You fought hard to achieve that. Do you think you could continue in that role once our relationship is known? Your people will have both our heads on stakes."

Adele stared at him evenly, as if she had already accepted that complication. "I'll accept whatever happens."

"I won't."

"This book means a great deal. To both of us. To both our kinds. The future can only—"

"The future is only what we find in Bruges. After that, we'll have to see what it is." Gareth jutted his chin across the room, eager to change the conversation. "I see you brought your camera."

Adele understood his weak ploy, but was content to move on for the moment. "I have one more undeveloped piece of film until the next supply ship from Equatoria and I was hoping you'd let me take our picture. Finally."

"What do you mean *finally*? You have a box full of pictures of me. And there are thousands of pictures of the two of us." Gareth shuffled more papers aside on the desk to reveal several cheap paperback novels. They were in pristine condition because Gareth valued books, any books, above all else. Adele recognized these potboilers from the penny dreadful presses in far-off Equatoria. They all featured the great freedom fighter of the north, the Greyfriar. Each book sported a garishly colored cover with the cloaked swordsman killing vampires with blade or gun, his face swathed in his trademark scarf to hide his mysterious identity from the world and instead of his actual mirrored glasses, the artistic Greyfriar wore more adventurous goggles. *Swords Against the Bloody North. Carpathian Hellscape. The Crypts Open Tonight.*

He pawed through the books and held one up. "Here! This one has both of us. *Two Against the Legions of Hell.*" The cover was a full-color painting of the Greyfriar. He was tall and muscular, which was easy to see because his shirt had been torn away. He had an exquisitely chiseled chest and abdomen, and his arms were corded and thick with veins. His rough hands clutched a sword and pistol. He stood in the snow wearing abnormally snug trousers. His face was partially shrouded with a scarf, but his eyes shone hard and fierce, and his long dark hair flew in the wind. Crouched next to the Greyfriar was a ferocious buxom wench in a state of undress. Her heaving bosom was barely contained in some sort of tiny metallic cups. She clutched the Greyfriar's muscular thigh as if it would save her from drowning.

Adele smirked. "That woman is supposed to be me?"

"I assume so. She seems . . . capable."

Adele stared at the picture for a long moment, eyes lingering on the dynamic figure of the Greyfriar. "I may need a copy of this one when we get to Alexandria." She set the distracting cover face down on the desk. "And you know what I mean. Yes, there are thousands of pictures of *me* and Greyfriar. Some even look like me. But I want one with *Gareth*." She pressed her hand next to his on the stack of blank paper. "That's the whole point of this exercise, isn't it?"

She returned to the door where she had leaned the tripod. She set up the camera near the door and spent a moment framing the desk in the dark. She pulled a long flexible trigger cable from her pocket and screwed one end into the camera. As she was making final adjustments, a large grey cat appeared. He curled about her legs and leapt onto the table to inspect the strange new contraption, rubbing his chin along the side of the camera. She swore that Pet could sniff out something new in mere seconds. Adele shoved the cat to the floor and repositioned the camera. She took the trigger cable and dragged the other end to the desk. She positioned the lanterns to provide enough light for a moody exposure.

Adele grabbed Gareth's arm and pulled him next to her. "Stand here and we'll have a real picture together." She poised her thumb over the button.

He continued to watch her.

"Don't look at me," she chided. "Look at the camera. And smile." Adele gave a wide grin.

Gareth turned back to the camera, attempting to please Adele.

"Hold that smile because it's dark and I have to leave the shutter open for a minute." She thumbed the trigger and the lens clattered open. After a long moment, it closed. She exhaled. "There. That wasn't hard."

"It seemed stressful for you."

Adele went back to the camera. She worked a switch to open a door on the rear of the box and removed a metal plate. She hummed idly, waiting for the picture to develop. Gareth watched her while leaning against the desk. After a minute, she opened the hinged plate and pulled out the still-damp paper photograph. She studied it with a critical huff. In the photo, Gareth towered over Adele. She was well lit, unfortunately, but he was nearly in shadow. Gareth's eyes glowed unnaturally and his *smile* appeared more like a menacing snarl of a predator. Adele abruptly tore the picture in half.

Gareth watched the pieces flutter to the floor. "What are you doing?"

"It was horrible. I looked like death warmed over. We'll take another one when I have more film. I'd prefer a photo where I look human."

"Isn't it more important that I look human?" Gareth laughed oddly. "But I can only manage that when I wear a mask."

CHAPTER 6

In the days of King Louis XIV, the palace of Versailles had hosted a man who considered himself the most powerful man on Earth. Now it did again, in the long gallery called the Hall of Mirrors that ran the length of an upper floor in the rear of the main palace. The mirrors were long since smashed, and shards lay cracked on the floor. Sunlight streamed in the vast windows where a man stood overseeing the grounds below.

Nearby, a small clutch of vampires waited for him to do whatever it was he was doing. Waiting on a human was unusual behavior for their kind. It was particularly odd given they were the elite of their clan, the rulers of Paris since the days of the Great Killing over a century ago.

The queen of the Paris clan, Caterina, shuffled her feet with annoyance. She glanced at her eldest son who stood at a noticeable distance. Honore was the heir to the clan. As such, he bore the title of Dauphin, which vampires had appropriated with gleeful mockery of the humans who had come before them. Honore preferred to be closer to another figure, a slender willowy female who was pale and blond where Caterina was dark and commanding. He exchanged whispers with the female, eliciting intimate nods and quiet replies seemingly meant to exclude the queen. Having her son ignore her created a sense of indignation in Caterina that was uncommon.

"Lady Hallow," Caterina said with growing disdain, "how long will we wait here?"

The human at the window dared to glare at the queen, annoyed by her loud voice and the interruption of his reverie. He was tall and old, with a long white beard. He wore a fine suit of clothes with a long white coat. His dark and piercing eyes held none of the usual fear when regarding vampires. It disturbed the queen.

Hallow replied evenly, "The Witchfinder must prepare, Your Majesty."

The queen shook her head and looked out the window. Once an open promenade sectioned off by topiary, the vast grounds were now overgrown and ragged. Hints of carefully planned walkways remained. Clumps of ivy revealed where statues lay hidden around fetid pools. Among the riotous foliage humans stood, perhaps a hundred of them, spread across the decrepit grounds of the palace. They shifted from foot to foot, nervous or bored. Vampires drifted in the air overhead, watching the herd to insure none moved too much or tried to run away.

Caterina also saw flecks of color dotting the wild landscape. Crystals. Throughout the entire day, the human—the Witchfinder—had spent hours positioning the stones just so. Carrying some sort of weird hand-drawn maps and scurrying about the overgrown paving stones, he would peer around with some sort of brass device. He consulted the device's needles and numbers, and then would set a crystal on the ground. He continued in that manner for hour after exhausting hour. The herd of humans had wondered at the man who moved between them without speaking. Caterina with her son and Lady Hallow had stood watching from the windows before growing intolerably uninterested.

Finally, the Witchfinder had joined the three vampires in the palace, where he began the equally tiresome activity of replicating a smaller version of the same pattern of crystals in the Hall of Mirrors. He paid little attention to the vampires as he went about his business. His calm demeanor couldn't hide the scent of excitement that Caterina could smell on him. The Witchfinder grew more eager by the second as he built the complex crystal pattern on the floor around him.

Finally, overcome by boredom, Caterina asked, "So this man came from London?"

"Yes," Honore replied with annoyance, his normal state of being. "He was in the service of Prince Cesare, as was Lady Hallow. Now they are in *my* service."

Lady Hallow's pale blue eyes flicked with amusement.

Caterina smiled cynically at her son. "Prince Cesare? He's dead now. Perhaps we should look beyond *his* former servants for our saviors."

Honore snarled, "Cesare is dead because he was betrayed by his own brother! By your old friend, Gareth. The great traitor."

Lady Hallow regarded Caterina as if the queen was a misinformed child. At the same time she put a soft hand on Honore's arm. "Your Majesty, Prince Cesare was brilliant. Perhaps the most brilliant mind I have ever known. He knew that a war with the humans could be disastrous. But when he tried to forestall it, his efforts were blocked by Prince Gareth. Then with war forced on him, Cesare conceived unique ways to win, yes, including using humans to serve him. And again, it was Gareth who ruined those plans. You and I have both known Gareth for a long time, Your Majesty. And we both know he is mad. It is because of his insanity that the human armies could be outside Paris this spring. Therefore, I have brought the last of Cesare's weapons to save you. We must hold the line here." She looked at Honore. "And *we* will."

Caterina wanted to respond sarcastically. The queen knew that Hallow had, in fact, been Gareth's lover more than a century ago before turning her allegiance to his brother, Cesare. Now Hallow was shifting her *allegiance* to yet another prince.

Honore brushed Hallow's pale cheek with his strong fingers. When he turned to his mother, he didn't see Hallow scowl in distaste at his touch. The Dauphin said, "The Equatorians are coming. There's no doubt. Do you think King Lothaire could do anything about it?"

Caterina snapped, "Don't disrespect your king."

"Where is he? We arranged this demonstration, and he isn't here."

"I came," Caterina retorted in defiance, "in his stead."

The Dauphin sneered. "With the children, no doubt. He spends more time in the nursery than I ever did."

"He is still your father."

"So you say. He's soft and weak. His failure to our people makes me sick. Cesare always said father was worthless, just like Gareth, and he could cost our people the war. But once I destroy the Equatorians, I will be the face of the Paris clan. I will take our power around the world to put the humans back in their place. I am Cesare's heir, not Lothaire's."

Caterina fought to control herself. "You do realize that your hero, Cesare, lost everything. His clan is dead." She pointed at Hallow. "Except for a few refugees who were lucky enough to be outside Britain when the fire came, and who now come looking to rule another clan with an army of homeless mercenaries to displace our own packs." Caterina looked at the vampires who floated over the helpless humans outside. She knew these were all gathered from the clans of southern France and the Balkans that had been smashed by the Equatorian armies. They owed allegiance to Lady Hallow alone. "But no matter what refuse Hallow brings us, the Equatorians have the Death Bringer. What do we have against that?"

Honore's visage went red with anger. "We have *me*, mother. I am the war chief now. Father's old relics from the Great Killing have been set aside and I am in charge. Lady Hallow is my right arm, and she has brought the Witchfinder."

The Witchfinder himself paid no attention to the bickering vampires as he knelt to place a crystal on the floor. He stared through his brass sextant before nodding to himself in satisfaction.

Honore reached inside his shirt and pulled out a blue crystal on a chain. "He can stop the Death Bringer. We have sent forces back into Britain wearing these."

Caterina stared at the object. "Is that true? We have set foot in Britain?"

Lady Hallow pressed Honore's hand down, slipping the talisman back into his shirt. "We certainly saw them reach the island, where none of our people have gone since that night the Death Bringer killed everyone."

"Even so," the queen retorted, "is your human going to make those stones for every living vampire?"

"No, I'm not," came the voice of the bearded man as he finally turned to the trio of vampires. He came forward, stepping carefully through the complex pattern of crystals he had arranged on the floor. "Those talismans are merely tests of my theory on how the empress exploits the power of the Earth, what we scientists call geomancy. I had made one of those baubles for Prince Cesare because he was afraid of the empress, rightfully so it appears." The Witchfinder chuckled. "In any case, those talismans are minor applications of my grand theory. What you will see here today is another application. This will win the war for you. In terms of the empress, I'm not too concerned about her. She can be dispatched with a bullet or a knife. Cesare almost succeeded in that. In any case, once I win the war for you, I will move on to more interesting theoretical work."

Hallow cleared her throat and glared with menace. "Your theories won't help you if we don't defeat the humans first, Goronwy."

"Yes, ma'am." The Witchfinder nodded with unexpected deference to the pale female. Then he held a green crystal between his thumb and forefinger. "If you will look out the windows, you will see the first step on that road."

Caterina felt Honore and Hallow join her. They watched the scattered crowd of humans standing restlessly or squatting with fatigue. The cold sun sinking below the distant tree line illuminated the scene with a sad light.

The Witchfinder found a spot on the floor and set the green crystal into the larger pattern. He made one final check with his brass instrument before letting it fall to his side on its leather strap. He gently moved the crystal a quarter inch clockwise.

Outside in the winter shadows, hundreds of humans screamed. They flailed and tried to run, but few made it more than a couple of steps. They dropped to the ground, screeching, wide-eyed, fingers grasping at nothing. One after another, they fell writhing, then went still. In a few seconds, hundreds of humans were dead.

Caterina stared in disbelief. It didn't seem real, but she knew it was. She had sensed the terror in the herd and she smelled the death wafting through the shattered windows before her. Next to her, Honore had lost the pretense of a hardened warrior. He grasped the edge of the window in shock. His face was a mask of incredulity.

Lady Hallow laughed.

Caterina watched the last of the spasms play out below her. She had certainly seen death before, and on a large scale, but never without violence and bloodshed. This was stunning in both its suddenness and in its mystery. The Witchfinder had merely set a crystal on the floor and hundreds of humans died. He hadn't laid a hand on them. There were no weapons. She backed away from the window, disturbed by the unnatural field of death below her.

She crossed the gallery toward the Witchfinder. As she grew near, she felt a painful slap of heat and drew back with a hiss.

The human remained calm. "Oh, I'm sorry. I'd advise that you don't get too close, Your Majesty. I carry many traditional talismans on me which serve to repel your kind." He reached into one coat pocket and pulled out a yellow crystal, and from inside his waistcoat he withdrew a small gold cross. When the queen pulled back farther, the Witchfinder slipped the talismans back into his pockets. "Nothing personal. One can't be too careful. There may be some vampires who may not realize I am the clan's science advisor."

"Science advisor?" Caterina realized she was likely the only vampire present without a protective talisman. She gathered herself, eyeing the disturbing human before returning to the window. "What happened to those humans out there?"

Goronwy leaned against the far wall with his hands clasped before him. He didn't move toward the window to view the carnage. He seemed satisfied with the screams as proof of concept. "The power of the rifts. I used the Earth to kill them. It's the very same principle that killed the British clan, but frankly much more complicated to accomplish. You vampires are susceptible to such energy. It's actually very easy to kill you by overloading the rifts. What the empress did was impressive only in its scale." He smiled with pride. "Humans are hard to kill with geomancy, but I have grasped the principle. They are vulnerable to having their energies drawn out of them and into the Earth. Next I will test a long-distance event. I have prepared a site in the north that I will attempt to trigger from here in Paris."

Lady Hallow looked back eagerly over her shoulder. "So you could kill everyone in Alexandria just like that?"

Goronwy rolled his eyes. "That's a little simplistic, I'm afraid. In practice, it's always more complicated than you might like. I would have to arrange the target pattern, those crystals you see on the ground, around the rifts of Alexandria. And then if I could create a complementary pattern, such as you see here on the floor, I could trigger the effect. But as it stands now, it would be quite difficult."

Hallow grew cold. "So as a weapon, your value is limited?"

"Honestly, Lady Hallow, yes. At the moment. However, I'm confident I can simplify and amplify the process you just witnessed. I merely wanted to be sure that the principle works before I go to the trouble involved in overcoming the field limitations. For instance, I could eliminate the need for the target pattern as long as I can replicate the complementary—"

"I don't want to hear your nonsensical blather any more than Cesare did." Hallow narrowed her eyes. "What does it mean for me?"

Goronwy sighed, marshaling his patience. "In day-to-day terminology, Lady Hallow, it means you will have the power to kill whomever you wish, whenever you wish. I assume that is the sum of your scientific curiosity."

Now Lady Hallow purred with pleasure. She eyed Honore with what passed for lascivious desire in a cold-blooded creature. The two of them were lost in their moment, no longer caring that the queen was even present. "I don't need to have scientific curiosity, Goronwy. That's why I have you. Do whatever you need to do to make it happen. The resources of the clan are at your disposal."

Caterina instinctively wanted to upbraid Hallow for her bold distribution of the clan's largesse. She looked to her son to say something since he was the clan war chief, and Hallow only his personal advisor. He didn't react. It angered Caterina to see the pathetic falseness of Hallow's blunt sexuality aimed at her son. It was so lifeless and fabricated that Caterina couldn't believe Honore didn't shove the pale female away out of self-respect. However, judging by the hungry look on Honore's face, he had no notion he was being used. Hallow had him on a leash.

On some level, the queen respected the cunning of her rival who had come to Paris as an exile from dead Britain. In less than a year, she had scanned the likely candidates who could serve her, selected the Dauphin as her tool, fanned the lad's disdain for his father, worked her way into a place of power, and made herself invaluable to the clan's survival. It was no surprise Cesare had trusted her as his chief political advisor.

Caterina knew better than to fight here in the moment of Hallow's triumph. In addition to her son, Hallow had the Witchfinder, who not only seemed to hold the key to saving the clan from the human armies, but also had powers over life and death, perhaps including Caterina's. The queen had no choice but to stand by quietly and keep her mouth shut.

CHAPTER 7

Adele could feel the Earth again in its full glory. Her geomancy had returned in force as soon as her airship, HMS *Edinburgh*, cruised out over the Channel. The barrier over Britain that had muffled her as if her head was wrapped in thick wool, fell away in a marvelous rush. Warm tendrils reached for her, slipped into her. This was what she remembered from her wonderful days learning geomancy when Mamoru was still her trusted teacher and the world was a source of constant wonder. The comforting colors and pleasing sounds called to her, eager to pull her deeper.

She surrendered to the call and walked the rifts, those avenues of power that some initiates called ley lines or dragon spines. She saw the veins of the world stretching out, pulsing with life, intersecting, intertwining, and tunneling off to do their unfathomable duties. They roared around Adele, bombarding her with the scents and crystalline music of the world. She tasted the chalky shores of Europe and slipped beyond to the rich loam of the Rhine Valley. With a thought, she shot even farther to the delicious dry salt and lemony aftertaste of her own home of Alexandria.

Adele reveled in the fact that this was a sensation most people could only experience when overwhelmed by the colors of a sunset or the sounds of the ocean or the smells of a fir forest. This was geomancy on a level that Adele was born to dominate and trained to understand. There may have been others around the world who could do the same, she had no idea exactly how many, but likely there were none who could do it as naturally as she did. Her mother had possessed similar skills, but Adele long surpassed her. She needed no preparation, no tools, no crystals, no meditation, no site of power. That was why she had been chosen and trained by her mentor to be the greatest of geomancers and his ultimate weapon in the war against vampires.

Adele streaked back toward the Channel. She pushed north, intent on testing Britain, to see what had become of it. The energy swirled on the outskirts of the island, sinking and twisting in odd directions, seeking paths to travel. The rifts of Britain looked gnarled and agonized. The lines of power had frozen into dark cracks, gaping wide down to the cold depths. Those rifts had been ravaged by geomancy. Her geomancy. That devastation was the reason why she couldn't access the glory of the Earth inside Britain, and Adele nearly wept at it. She wondered if Britain would ever be the same. There was no telling what the ramifications would be for many years to come. Had Mamoru known? Had he cared? Adele felt uneasy and confused. She realized that the energy swirled around her with ever greater insistence. It had been so long since she had ventured so deep. Adele didn't trust herself, constantly feeling that she could easily be dragged into the miraculous and lost.

It was more of a struggle than she expected to detach herself from the seductive comfort of the rifts. Mamoru had always warned that the heart of the rifts, the Belly of the Dragon as he called it, was a dangerous place. It was vast with landmarks that were deceptive. She had to be careful not to be fooled into thinking its warmth and comfort meant it cared whether she lived or died. It was possible to lose yourself in your own sense of power.

With a terrific shudder, Adele reeled herself back to the cold flinty Channel. Greyfriar's gaze was on her, studying her, and she forced a smile instinctively to signal him that all was well. She adjusted her khukri and a pistol on her belt as if she had merely been daydreaming, but the sheen of perspiration on her face betrayed the truth of the struggle she had just experienced.

Breathing out a slow shaking breath, she was relieved to see Greyfriar apparently unaffected. In the past, any use of her geomancy would have inflicted pain on him. She had obviously altered him the night of the event. Still, Adele had no confidence in how safe he would be if she unleashed her power in a massive storm.

Greyfriar settled in to watch the two boatmen who directed the small pilot cutter toward distant Europe. *Edinburgh* had carried them all more than halfway to the Flemish coast, then lowered the boat into the dark sea. Adele and Greyfriar had climbed in with these two trusted sailors and set off. Above them, the airship drifted silently into the night and vanished.

They all remained quiet as the boat labored for hours through the winter swells. The wind was frigid. A thin coating of ice formed on the quivering lines. Greyfriar settled close to Adele, placing his cloak around her. She relished the warmth he offered but his gaze occasionally shifted uneasily to the dark waters around them. He was never comfortable on or over water; his kind had a natural apprehension of it.

She was reminded of their long journey north to Scotland in a boat half this cutter's size and a fraction of its seaworthiness. It seemed so long ago, although it was barely two years. Greyfriar had been just what he appeared—a masked adventurer from a storybook, a silent scythe among the vampire hordes of the north. Now she could see the man beneath his disguise. And yet, here with the creaking planks and cracking black sails, with the stars reflected in his glasses, he seemed to be no more than the fairy tale again. For a moment they were back to the days of flying headlong from the merciless pursuit of Cesare's war chief, Flay. Only Adele would describe those days as a more carefree time.

She and Greyfriar were together with a mystery, a mission, and a goal. Where it would lead, she had no idea. For the time being, no matter how dire their task, they could at least focus on that and work toward something together. She could forget her long unsettling walks through Greyfriars kirkyard searching for photographic evidence, some truth. She could ignore his manuscript lying unfinished and hated. Adele took his gloved hand and squeezed it.

Adele thought she saw a wave blotting out low stars on the horizon, but it proved to be the coast of Europe. Greyfriar rose to his feet, steadying himself in the rocking boat. The closer they drew to land, the more likely they would fall under the sharp eyes of hunting vampires.

Water slapped the gunwales, accompanied by the sound of crashing surf. One sailor wrestled in most of the sail. The cutter rolled in the waves and Adele took a line in hand, enjoying the wild motion. The instant the bottom scraped stones, Greyfriar vaulted the side, splashing into the knee-deep water. He took two heavy packs from the helmsman and looped them over his shoulders. Then he reached out for Adele.

"It's not deep," she gently chided his unremitting chivalry. "I can make it."

"I don't want you any wetter. We may be hours from a fire."

Adele felt silly but slipped into his powerful arms. He waded to the beach carrying her high against his chest. She clutched a rucksack, careful to protect it from the water since it contained one of her prized possessions, her mother's notebook on geomancy. Adele needed to study quickly and learn more about her science. She had once thought herself an expert, but the specter of the Witchfinder forced her to face her own limitations.

Once on dry land, Greyfriar set her down, dropped the packs, and returned to the surf to push the boat off. The two sailors poled out through the breakers before giving a quick silent gesture of farewell and setting sail for the open sea.

Adele reached into her pocket and retrieved a small clear stone. The uncanny sense of the Earth filled her body. She felt the strange vibrations of its twin that rested in the possession of Captain Hariri aboard her airship over the Channel. When she and Greyfriar needed retrieval, she would shatter Hariri's stone and he would send the cutter, or the airship itself if necessary.

Greyfriar strode out of the water and snatched up the packs. Adele hefted her rucksack, following him off the stony beach to the grassy dunes. Both of them stayed silent and scanned the skies. They walked for hours through the soft marshy terrain until Greyfriar spotted a dark blot on the landscape and pointed. Then Adele saw it was a small cabin. No light. No scent of smoke. It was clearly abandoned, which she preferred. Too many of Greyfriar's friends and allies had died helping her in the past.

Greyfriar moved toward the roughhewn home. The door was unlocked. Once they were inside, he paused, pulling the scarf from his nose and sniffing the air. "This place is one of my safe houses. No one has been here for a long time."

"Is that bad?"

He shrugged. "The house is open to all. But it's not uncommon for it to be empty. Set your pack down. We'll rest."

Adele remembered she was still lugging the heavy rucksack, so she dropped it with a sigh of relief. Greyfriar slid an old chair across the floor to her and pulled open one of the packs. He removed a block of cheese and some crusty bread. Jamming his dagger into the cheese, he handed it to Adele who had sunk into the damp chair. She was so tired the foul fabric didn't alarm her.

"I can start a fire." He unbuckled his sword and gunbelt. He proceeded to doff his cloak and tunic, beginning the transformation from Greyfriar to Gareth.

"Don't risk it." Adele scrabbled in her pack and pulled out a leather bottle. "Morgana sent along some Edinburgh whisky. Should warm me up."

Gareth raised an eyebrow. "I'll fetch water. I smelled a fresh stream nearby."

"You're better than a camel."

"Thank you." He found an old bucket in the corner and headed out into the night. "I think."

So much of northern Europe was sparsely populated, with no industrial activity to speak of, that the streams and lakes were often clear and fresh. Adele wouldn't dream of drinking from any body of water in her Egyptian homeland. She ate a few bites of cheese, preferring to wait for Gareth to return out of politeness even though he didn't eat. She dozed until an odd sound slipped into her fuzzy thoughts. It was an ill-defined, distant whisper as of laundry on a line in a faint breeze. But it was insistent.

She sprang up and drew Greyfriar's rapier and her own revolver. Easing back the door, she paused in the frigid air. Her breath misted as she stepped onto the frost-covered grass. She looked up. The sky was lightening with faint sun seeping up in the east. Against the dying blue night sky, a swarm of dark figures floated over the far side of a hillock.

A whisper of movement behind her gave an ambush away. She spun around and took aim at four plummeting shadows. Thunderously loud shots punched bullets into two of the plunging vampires, sending them cartwheeling through the air. The other two creatures dove toward her. One hissed in its language, cursing her as a human. She fired again, but missed. The vampires dropped lightly in front of her, content in their ability to cow a mere woman, even an armed one.

Adele eyed the vampires with an expectant smile. The creatures paused, confused by strange sensations that suddenly pierced their body. She dropped her pistol and reached out. Laying her hand on the face of one vampire, smoke rose with a sizzling roar. The creature screeched. Adele focused on her glowing fingers, driving more power into the vampire and she actually felt its flesh melting under her touch. She pulled her hand back in disgust and the creature flailed to the ground. The second vampire stared at its stricken companion and, realizing it was alone, backed away.

Adele stuck out her hand toward it, with silver smoke curling off her fingertips. The vampire hissed something that might have been her name and vaulted into the air. She left the wounded things wriggling in the dirt; reaching Gareth was more important.

Adele staggered on. Every inch of her ached suddenly and her muscles shook as they protested supporting her. Even such a minor use of her power was draining. She fought against her own weakness because of the sounds of distant fighting. Adele ran through the damp grass and stumbled to the top of the hillock.

The air still swirled with dark shapes. Below her, beside an icy stream, Gareth fought with five vampires, eight already lay dead and gutted on the ground. He was a melee of limbs and feet, smashing against the five things. Adele hardly had time to wonder why they had attacked him; he was unmasked and clearly a vampire to his own kind. She raced down the hill.

"Gareth!" she called and lobbed the rapier toward him.

He slammed a foot into the chest of one of his attackers, ducked a clawed swipe from another, and vaulted into the air. He caught the sword and landed, lunging with the glinting blade. The rapier plunged into a vampire's chest, piercing the heart and causing the creature to seize. Gareth drew the sword free and spun calmly to another.

The black cloud of monsters descended upon them. Now there was little room to maneuver and it was all Adele could do to swing her glowing khukri, cutting with its searing Fahrenheit chemicals. Silver tendrils wreathed her limbs. She grabbed the vampires that came near enough. Her touch burned worse than her blade, raising smoke and the stench of seared flesh. But her endurance was near its end. Already she could barely catch her breath with each strike. Adele knew that they were faltering. Gareth's strength was not unlimited, not against so many.

Their eyes locked for a split second. Adele knew she had the power to destroy this horde. She could fall on her knees and press her hands on the ground. Her arms would sink into the soft soil up to her elbows as she touched the network of green and white. Living tendrils would sing. Adele could bend the dragon spine toward her so she could grasp it. The shadows of the vampires would melt before her gaze, turning to dust and bone.

But then the image of Gareth burning flashed through Adele's brain. She feared the greedy power of the rifts would seize her and drag her deep into its seductive grip, urging her to unleash it all, to unlock the vast system of fiery circulation around the world. She might be unable to resist. She might be unable to save Gareth again.

An arm slammed hard against the side of Adele's head. A vampire reeled away, smoking from even that small touch. Adele collapsed on the ground near Gareth's feet. A constant roar filled her ears and she wasn't sure of anything save her attempt to shake off the encroaching blackness as a horrific dark swarm surrounded them.

Through blurred vision, Adele saw what appeared to be vampires striking their own. Lean wolfish figures, moving with preternatural speed, dug their claws into others of their kind. Wounds opened. Limbs tore. Bodies dropped heavy to the grass all around her. Some of the creatures wore expressions of shock. Others were fierce and brutal.

When Adele's vision cleared she saw that Gareth stood over her, blood dripping from his rapier as well as his wounds. She gained her feet with his help. With an unsteady arm, she raised her pistol at the five last remaining vampires as they stared around searching for more victims, and finally turned to her and Gareth. Something caused her to hold her fire. Gareth stood with sword ready, facing the last vampires. They backed away from him with faces of shock.

"The sword," Adele said in Arabic. "They're confused you're using a sword."

Gareth grinned with disdain. "Idiots."

The five vampires drew in their claws and held out their hands in a sign of supplication. Then they fell to their knees.

Fearful of a ruse, of some sort of ambush, Adele looked around but only saw the bodies of the slain. She exchanged a glance with the bewildered Gareth.

Without lowering his sword, he demanded in Dutch, "What is this? Why are you groveling?"

"Forgive us," one of the vampires, a young female, said in poor English without raising her eyes. "We couldn't know you would come."

"Aren't you from here? Why do you speak English?"

She replied, "We speak the tongue of your clan out of respect."

"What do you mean respect?"

The female looked up. Her eyes glistened with terrified tears. "You are Prince Gareth. You are the way."

—⁂—

The five vampires, one female and four males, sat in the grass staring at Gareth. They all seemed young to Adele, although age was difficult to determine in vampires. Gareth paced before his audience. He seemed unnerved by the rapt faces following his every move. His sword rested casually on his shoulder.

"Why did you come to my aid?" he asked.

"We had heard the Greyfriar had landed on our shores."

"And sought to win a name for yourselves by killing him?"

"No! We came here to save him!"

When Gareth regarded them incredulously, the female vampire quickly continued, "Some months ago, a servant of the Greyfriar was taken captive in this area. He was tortured and admitted that this cabin belonged to the Greyfriar, and he would come at some time. So the packs of Bruges have been watching. We could not allow them to harm him. Earlier today, when scouts came into Bruges with news of his arrival on the coast, we followed the pack here. But it was you, not the Greyfriar."

"What possible reason do you have to help the Greyfriar?"

"We know he often took humans from Europe and brought them to Prince Gareth's realm in Scotland."

"How do you know that?" Gareth snapped. That was certainly nothing a vampire should know.

She quailed at his tone. "We hoped that the Greyfriar could find a way to let Prince Gareth know about us. But we find you instead. It's a miracle."

Gareth exchanged a glance at Adele who shrugged in confusion and blew into her frigid hands. He directed his question back at the female prone before him. "How do you know anything about me? How did you know Greyfriar ever brought refugees to Edinburgh?"

The female bit her lip. "You should speak to Kasteel."

"I'm speaking to you!"

She cowered. One of the males glanced at Adele with concern and then whispered to his female companion. The two of them began a hushed argument in their own unintelligible tongue.

"Shut up, the both of you," Gareth snarled, swinging his sword through the air barely inches from their noses. Then he knelt to retrieve his gloves which he had tossed aside when he was attacked.

Adele asked, "What did they say? I couldn't hear them."

Gareth responded to her in his perfect Alexandrian Arabic, "He is concerned that you will kill them and then kill this Kasteel, whoever that is, if they bring us to him."

"Oh. So the whole *Death Bringer* thing again?"

"Exactly." He offered her a humorous nod. "They referred to you as the Empress of the End."

"How nice that I have so many apocalyptic nicknames." Adele again tried to ignore the distressing implications of those epithets. She wondered if the vampires would be so terrified if they knew Adele was likely incapable, and certainly unwilling, to wield such genocidal power any longer. "How do they even know who I am?"

"They know I made myself the last king of Britain through the power of my terrible consort, Adele of Equatoria. Since they saw you incinerate some of their brethren, it's simple to assume you are the terrible Adele."

"Consort?" Adele raised an amused eyebrow. "You are *my* consort, not the other way around."

"Please leave me with a little stature among my own kind, imaginary though it may be." Gareth tapped the female vampire with the flat of his rapier to bring her attention from Adele, and asked in English, "What's your name?"

Her eyes were wide. "Nadzia."

"Well, Nadzia, who is this Kasteel I should talk to?"

"He is our teacher. And a disciple of Prince Gareth. Of you."

Adele stiffened in shock. "Your *disciple*?"

Gareth said to Adele, "I have no clue what she's talking about. Apparently Bruges has many mysteries. I look forward to visiting now." Gareth laughed and ran a hand over Adele's cheek, and she leaned into it. The vampires gasped as if they were witnessing a revelation.

CHAPTER 8

Gareth drifted on the wind with Nadzia and the others. He could see Adele's small form below, afoot, using her remarkable ability to mask herself from the attention of vampires. All vampires but him because of the event. Any humans would see her, of course, but likely care little.

Gareth wore dull clothes he had brought from Britain and sported a cloak with a hood to obscure his face as much as possible. He had removed his gloves again to avoid anything that might attract attention from vampires. If he was recognized as Gareth, he would likely be killed as a traitor to his own kind. The irony that he had to go masked in clan territory to hide his true identity, rather than to create the character of Greyfriar, was not lost on him.

The old city of Bruges nestled inside a circle of canals in the dim daylight. Corpses bobbed in the stagnant, slushy water. The ruined buildings were covered in rank winter ivy. Decaying spires and crumbling step gables oversaw filthy streets and alleys littered with dead bodies. Dark shapes floated in the sky above the medieval cityscape. Human figures moved about the streets, hunched and furtive, knowing they could be seized and killed at any moment. Gareth and his group gave a wide berth to the many vampires swarming around a great brick belfry before they settled onto a nearby square.

Nadzia started toward a building with a high step gabled front and many smashed windows. It looked like it had been a private mansion once. Gareth hissed at them to stop. They froze, mortified by his censure.

"We wait for her," he ordered. "And stop staring at me."

Nearly an hour passed and they were watching the figures floating overhead, noting those who came and returned. Finally Gareth straightened because from the far corner of the square, Adele strolled out of the shadows. She stopped to gain her bearings, then saw Gareth and the others. When she reached their side, she said, "Sorry it took so long."

The five vampires jumped in alarm, suddenly hearing but not seeing Adele. Nadzia stared about in awe. The males backed away, growling deep in their throats.

"Easy," Gareth murmured. "You'll attract attention to her."

Adele's face glistened with a sheen of perspiration. Hiding in the ley lines was taking a toll on her. It never had before, not to this extreme at any rate. She looked up at the vampires clutching the rooftops and circling above. None had altered their course or attention. They hadn't seen her.

"Can we get inside?" she said. "I don't know how much longer I can stay hidden from sight."

Nadzia nodded and led the way into the grey building, stepping over the shattered wreckage of a heavy door. They found themselves in a vast hallway. It was plain and unornamented, with columns and arches along the walls.

Several other vampires slouching inside looked up at the arrival. They were all young. They offered nods of greeting and stares of interest at the hooded Gareth. Not one of them had the stature or the fierce stare of a warrior. None of them spared a glance for Adele, so she was obviously invisible to them. Her teeth were clamped shut from the strain of staying concealed.

"They're no threat," Gareth whispered, into empty air to everyone's view. "You should release your cloak."

With a shuddering breath, Adele let the shimmer fall away. The vampires yelped with shock at a human woman suddenly appearing before them. One of them cried out and claws appeared.

"No!" Nadzia shouted. "Don't! You don't understand!" The vampire with claws out glared at her.

Adele grasped the pommel of her dagger, but Gareth touched her sleeve, urging her to stay her hand. He shoved back his hood and the other vampires stared at him without recognition. Gareth was a little disappointed that his dramatic gesture fell flat. He had grown embarrassingly amused by the expressions of veneration that his mere presence generated down by the coast.

"Nadzia, is that you?" came a voice from the shadows. "What happened? Did you find the Greyfriar?" A figure descended a wide staircase. The male vampire wore black trousers and a white shirt. His auburn hair was long and tangled. There was something strangely familiar in the shape of his youthful face, the curve of his chin. His blue eyes were like gemstones as they darted across the scene. He squinted with concern at Adele, but then he saw Gareth.

The young vampire froze.

After a long moment, he looked at Nadzia, who gave him a beautiful smile of confirmation. His feet slipped out from under him and he fell hard onto the bottom step as if his legs would no longer support him. He gaped at Gareth, but couldn't force his mouth to make sounds. He pushed himself forward, sprawling on the floor. He pressed his face against the stone and breathed, "Prince Gareth. My lord."

All the vampires in the chamber scrambled to kneel. Fifteen dark shapes on the dusty floor. Adele stepped closer to Gareth, surveying the strange tableaux around them.

She asked, "Are you *sure* you don't know these people?"

The young male on the floor murmured, "We're not ready."

"Ready for what?" Gareth asked, then barked, "Stand up! I don't want to speak to your backs."

They all remained locked in place except Nadzia, who rose slowly and pulled the young male off his face. He resisted at first, but finally struggled begrudgingly to one knee.

Nadzia said, "This is Kasteel."

The young male, Kasteel, looked angry or afraid, as if disturbed that his name had been spoken in Gareth's presence. He glanced quickly at the great lord to determine what insult had been done.

"Kasteel." Gareth reached out. "I am Gareth of Scotland."

Kasteel stared at the proffered hand without understanding.

Gareth realized that shaking a hand was a human trait he had absorbed. Vampires had no use for it. So instead he took the kneeling figure by the arm, eliciting a hiss of fear from the lad, and drew him to his feet. "You seem to know me, but I fear I don't know you. Do I?"

"No, my lord."

"Why do you address me as *my lord*? Are you attached to Dmitri's clan?"

"No, my lord. I never had that honor."

Gareth scowled. An *honor* that would likely have seen the lad dead along with all the other members of the British clan. "Then why—"

"I'm sorry, my lord," Kasteel interrupted weakly. "I wanted to accomplish so much more before you judged us. How did you even know of us?" The vampire looked horrified and fell on his knees again. "I'm sorry, my lord. Forgive me! Of course you know. There is nothing you don't know."

Adele gave a bemused grunt but remained otherwise still.

Gareth settled onto an embrasure shelf inside one of the arches. "Kasteel, stand up. Again. Explain yourself. Who are you, and what are you doing here?"

Kasteel took several steeling breaths and launched into what seemed a prepared speech. "We serve your goals. We believe, like you, that the days of the clans are at an end. They are bloated pathetic cadavers that have no use." The young vampire clenched his hands into fists. "It is the only way forward for us. You have shown us the future."

"Have I? How did I do that?"

Kasteel smiled as if being tested on a subject he knew very well. "You left the court in London. You abandoned your clan and their polluted ways. You lived alone in Scotland, treating your humans not as disposable herds but as reliable sources of nourishment."

Gareth again regarded Adele. She was watching the fervent Kasteel with fascination.

Kasteel stood with mounting enthusiasm. "You saw the problem with our kind. And you acted."

"I did?" Gareth sat forward. "What did I do?"

"You destroyed your clan." Kasteel's eyes shone with messianic fervor. "You raised the Death Bringer and used her like claws to tear Cesare from the Earth."

Gareth steadied himself against a sudden rush of anger. Somehow he managed to speak in an even tone. "You find that admirable, do you?"

"Not admirable but necessary. The clans must fall. We must return to the dark. As you teach."

"I've never taught you anything," Gareth spat. "Are you mad?"

Kasteel lowered his eyes at the rebuke. "We know of you through your works. We know something of your mind, granted only the glittering tip, from he who was at your side over the years."

"Baudoin," Adele breathed, staring at Kasteel. "He looks like Baudoin. He could be his son."

Gareth saw it too now. That was the flash of recognition he'd experienced when he first saw the young vampire. Baudoin had come to Britain in service to Gareth's father, King Dmitri, and had become Gareth's servant. In the end, he had become less of a devoted manservant and more one of Gareth's most trusted and valued friends. His loss still cut deep. Baudoin had been slaughtered by Flay during his final act of saving Gareth. "Baudoin had no offspring. He raised Cesare and I as if we were his children."

"Baudoin was not my father," Kasteel said. "My father was the revered Baudoin's brother."

"Conrad? You're Conrad's son? So you are from the Aachen clan, as Baudoin was?"

"I am."

"Where's your father now?"

"He is dead. Killed last year fighting the Equatorians near Budapest."

Despite himself, Gareth flinched. Both brothers had died the same year. He asked quietly, "So Baudoin talked about me to you?"

"He rarely spoke of anything but you. He spent most of his days up in Edinburgh at your side, but over the years we saw him a handful of times. Baudoin knew that most of our kind viewed you with scorn. Some believed you were mad, as your father had gone mad."

Gareth shifted uncomfortably at the reference to his father, but he stayed quiet.

Kasteel dared a step closer. "Baudoin loved you like his own son and he defended you against any criticism. He admitted you were different, but he felt that was a trait of strength not frailty. You understood things that no other of our kind did."

The memory of watching Baudoin die stung Gareth anew. He had a hard time imagining this ebullient praise from his stodgy old manservant, the one who quarreled with all Gareth did and derided his ridiculous Greyfriar fancies.

Kasteel looked worried that he wasn't explaining the doctrine properly. "We believe, as you do, that our kind have grown lazy and wasteful with walking skins full of blood at our fingertips. We must set the humans free and return to the hunt. There is no need to kill to feed. We should leave humans alive, because that grants us a constant meal."

"That's philanthropic," Adele muttered. "Speaking as a walking skin full of blood."

Kasteel paused, fretful he had misinterpreted Gareth's life lessons. His companions were equally worried, looking among themselves for reassurance. "Those are the lessons of the old days."

Gareth found Kasteel's innocent pleading bothersome. He rose and paced. "How would you know? All of you are too young to remember the times before the Great Killing."

Kasteel swept his arm before the tense faces of his companions. "That's why we need you to help us."

"And is this all of you?" Gareth asked.

"No," Kasteel began hesitantly. "There are a few others, but most are . . . resistant to your teaching."

"Shocking." Gareth gazed about the room at the starry-eyed young crowd. "I'm surprised you've gotten this many."

Adele looked over at him with a triumphant grin. "I told you that you weren't the only one."

Gareth grunted with doubt and turned his attention back to Kasteel. "If you believe so strongly in the *old ways*, why do you all live here in this comfortable house? There are plenty of empty caves out in the woods if you wanted to go as your fathers went."

Mortification swept across Kasteel's face and his head bowed. "I would certainly love to live in a cave or an old tomb like our forefathers once did, but it's hard enough getting this lot to even understand the danger of the clans, and the need to change our ways, without throwing in a life of constant damp." His head lifted and his eyes met Gareth's directly. "And correct me if I'm wrong, but you live in a castle. My lord."

Adele couldn't help but laugh. "He has you there."

CHAPTER 9

Adele blew into her chapped hands. She settled in a patch of sun on the floor of a large room upstairs. The fixtures here were lavish and Gothic, the ones that were still unbroken in any case. There were even a few remnants of thick glass in the windows and paint on the walls. The floor was littered with trash, but there were no bones or human remains of any sort that typically littered vampire dwellings. Rummaging through her pack, Adele pulled out the cheese and bread that she hadn't had time for at the safe house. "So, what do you make of them?"

"What *can* I make of them?" Gareth paced before the windows with his head down. "Baudoin's nephew, here, thinking of me as some sort of leader."

"More than a leader. Nearly a prophet."

"Yes. A prophet." Gareth laughed angrily. "Truly, what is wrong with the younger generation?"

"So you're not a prophet?" Adele arched an eyebrow with a playfulness that belied the seriousness of the question.

"Speaking as my own biographer, I can assure you I'm not."

"But Kasteel does have a point, of sorts. You have always felt that your people were going in the wrong direction. You told me yourself that their day was near an end, like mayflies, you said. A great dying off would soon occur."

"That's just the cycle of our nature. I didn't intend to start it off myself by killing my entire clan."

"That's not what I meant, Gareth," Adele said gently, through the hurt she felt. "And you had nothing to do with it. I killed them all." She did her best to conjure any thoughts to replace the vision of thousands of living creatures, vampires to be sure, but still young and old, some likely blameless, swept to their sudden and terrifying destruction by her geomancy.

She always asked herself the same question. Why had she stopped it? She risked her life to halt the wave of death at the edges of Britain. Vampires had plagued humanity for millennia before the creatures rose up in that horrible winter of 1870 and obliterated human civilization in the northern hemisphere. Those humans that escaped the Great Killing fled with their guns and science to the tropics, where vampires couldn't easily survive because they were susceptible to heat. The refugees clashed and then blended with the indigenous populations to form new societies like Adele's own Equatorian Empire.

The vampires crouched on the ruins of the north and kept herds of humans for food. The world would be a better place without those creatures, wouldn't it? Adele was the ruler of an empire that was fighting a war to liberate the northern humans from the vampire clans. She could have wiped every one of the blood-drinking monsters out of existence. She would have been the savior of humanity.

Instead Adele had risked her life struggling with the Earth to save one man, one vampire.

She felt Gareth taking her hands. The confusion that had filled his eyes about the rebels was now replaced by worry for her.

"There are reasons why men or women become leaders," Gareth said. "You are born to it. You took a chaotic nation on the verge of civil war and brought it under your control. You understood your options and your enemies. I am not that person. I hardly know what I'm going to do in the next hour, much less what path my people should take in the future."

Despite the truth of that statement, Adele shook her head. "Not all leaders are planned. You've obviously sparked something, whether you wanted to or not. This group wouldn't have sprung up around you for no reason."

"There's a reason. It's called madness. Vampires are losing the war. Not just in Europe, but in North America too. But it's more than that. Our society was reforged by the Great Killing less than two hundred years ago. We think of it as our ancient birthright, but it's very recent.

And now it is flying apart. We know we're failing, but we don't know why or how to stop it. The signs of madness are everywhere. Cesare used humans to fight his war. This little band of ridiculous outcasts here. Even me. I dress up like a character I saw in a children's storybook and fight my own kind." Gareth laughed without humor, his agitation growing as he talked. "That's all madness, isn't it?"

"As usual, you underestimate yourself. Your actions have inspired these rebels here to question the cruelty of your people."

Gareth pursed his lips and his eyes moved back and forth, as if searching with puzzled resentment. "Rebels? No, they find me temporarily fascinating because I seem to stand against authority. Prince Gareth is a hated figure in every court. So, that makes me a hero to this lot. All youth rebels against their parents' values."

"Even vampires?"

"Of course. That's why most of us leave our clan and wander for years when we come of age. Sometimes we don't go back. It isn't as common with the new clans these days."

"Are the clans different now than they used to be?"

"Very. My kind has always lived in clans or tribes. And there have always been kings or queens. Kasteel calls me *lord* even though he hates the clans, because we've always had rulers. But in the old days, clan identity was fluid. It was more common to move and choose your place. Power was limited. Then as we approached the Great Killing and ever since, we've had more rules to protect the powerful and preserve their herds. The hierarchy grew more rigid. Territories became more defined. Vampires have become sedentary and suspicious of one another."

"Like humans?"

Gareth let the comment lie with a disagreeable nod. "These children here are just exploring some of the old mentality. It's all very romantic and mysterious and exciting. Like donning a cape and mask."

Adele kissed his cheek to calm him. "The mere existence of vampires who express some concern for humanity is a remarkable phenomenon. You're not alone anymore."

"I believe I said I was the only one with an interest in human history and culture, and none of these children show any of those interests." Gareth wrapped a grateful arm around her waist. "They only want to play vampire, what they perceive as *real* vampire."

"They seem eager to learn from you."

"I have nothing to teach them. I'm not their father."

A sound came from the stairs leading from the lower chamber. Kasteel and Nadzia stood watching.

"Yes?" Gareth asked in English with an imperiousness that came naturally.

"Do you need anything, my lord?" Kasteel asked.

"No. Thank you."

"Perhaps." Adele's hand went to her neck. She touched the chain that just showed above the top of her rough tunic. She eyed Gareth. He seemed concerned, but then nodded. She pulled out the blue stone talisman taken from the vampire in London. It glinted in the faint light. The two young rebels exchanged glances of recognition.

"You've seen one of those before," Gareth said. It wasn't a question. "Tell us about it."

"Yes." Nadzia swallowed. "I can show you."

Kasteel nodded toward Adele. "She won't like it."

—⁂—

"There." Kasteel crouched behind a rocky outcropping. Down a snowy slope and two hundred yards across an open glade, stood a small gathering of tumbled huts and cottages.

Gareth helped a lagging Adele to the top. They studied the area. She used a brass spyglass; his natural eyesight was superior to her enhanced optics. There was no sign of occupation, either human or vampire. Adele felt a wave of nausea and dropped the telescope. Cold sweat broke out on her forehead. She took deep breaths, fighting the urge to vomit.

"Adele!" Gareth took her arm. "What's wrong?"

"I don't know. I've been feeling sick for the last few miles." She fought the dizziness, and bringing the glass back to her eye, she said to Nadzia, "You saw vampires here with crystals like the one I have?"

"I did." The reply was meek.

"We're twenty miles from Bruges. You just happened across them?"

"No. We saw strangers in town from another clan. They had those blue crystals and gave them to the prince of Bruges. Then a whole group came out here, some from Bruges, some of the newcomers. And there was a human with them, but he didn't act like food. So I followed them."

"The Witchfinder," Adele growled. "How long ago was this?"

"Within the last month."

Gareth asked, "Have these foreign vampires returned to Bruges since?"

"To Bruges? Not to my knowledge. But out here, I don't know. I haven't been back here since that day. I didn't care about some lord's private herds."

Adele labored to push herself up. "Let's have a look around."

Gareth rose too. "I think it's safe, but it's hard to tell with the wind swirling."

Adele and the others climbed over the rocks and slid down the hill. Snow fell in thick wet flakes, slapping against her face. Another bout of vertigo sent the white nightscape spinning around her. She stopped to steady herself, but felt another strange sensation picking at her brain as if a ferocious headache was starting. Her eyes dropped to her feet. Something made her lean down and sweep the snow away. Her fingers hit something hard that skittered aside. Adele reached into the snow pile and came out with a stone the size of a hen's egg. It was a faceted crystal. She needed only her practiced eye to tell that a skilled craftsman of geomancy had worked it, not simply a jeweler.

Kasteel and Nadzia watched in confusion as Adele tugged a glove off with her teeth. Gareth merely stood by with interest. Taking the cold crystal in her bare hand, crippling light flashed behind her eyes. She felt as if a horse had kicked her in the stomach. Adele toppled face first into the snow.

"Adele!" Gareth pulled the stone from her clenched fist.

She rolled away from him to retch.

He put a strong hand against the back of her neck. "We should go back."

"No." Adele wiped her mouth. "There's something here. I've never experienced anything like that."

Gareth's head suddenly jerked to the side. "There is death here."

Adele reached for her dagger.

Kasteel scented the air. "I don't smell blood."

"Not blood." Gareth pointed toward the shadowy huts. "Death. All around us. Look at those mounds in the snow. Corpses."

Adele could detect only slight rises in the fresh clean snowfield. If Gareth hadn't called attention to them, she would've assumed they were the natural rise and fall of the ground or clumps of grass. She trudged toward the closest one, her unsteady legs whooshing through the deep powder.

Gareth slipped in front of her and knelt by the mound. He cleared the snow until there appeared a human face framed by glittering ice. The skin was bluish and the features slightly bloated. The expression, however, was inhuman and ghastly. Eyes were wide and his jaw was distended as if frozen from a scream too ragged to escape a normal mouth.

"Good God," Adele hissed, again fighting against a wave of sickness. "What happened to him?"

Gareth continued to brush snow away from the cadaver. He checked for wounds of feeding, but there were none.

Adele spun in the snow to another lump. Frantic fingers swept snow off what turned out to be a pair of feet. She worked her way up the body, white spray sparkling around her. Soon another face was revealed, this one also contorted in terrible pain or fear.

Adele staggered to yet another snow-bound body. She cleared this one and found a woman with long blond hair. Something fell when Adele pried open the cracking fingers. It was a small cross woven from simple grass.

Adele took the artifact and held it carefully in her hand. "Nadzia, how many humans were out here?"

"Perhaps thirty." Nadzia was quiet, as if fearful of being the target of Adele's righteous anger at the slaughter of her kind.

Adele set the simple cross on the dead woman's chest. "There's a sickness in the Earth here." She took several breaths to prepare herself. She didn't want to contemplate her next step, but she had to. "I'm going into a rift to try to understand better."

"No," Gareth said emphatically. "It's too dangerous and you're not strong enough. Just being here sickens you. If you try to engage it, there's no telling what could happen. These bodies are human, and whatever happened here killed them."

"That's what frightens me. First we've seen vampires able to resist geomancy. Now humans, killed by some unknown force. I don't think there's any other reasonable possibility except that Cesare's Witchfinder is still alive and active. We have to find him and stop him. Looking at this place, I can't conceive of what horrors he could set in motion."

"So you're doing it no matter what I say?"

She touched Gareth's hand. "If it gets too dangerous, I'll withdraw."

"What if you can't?"

"Then remove me bodily from here." She turned to Kasteel and Nadzia. "You two should move far away. Gareth, you too. I don't know what your limits are."

"I've been burned before." He stood rooted. "Do what you're going to do, I'll be here."

Adele shook her head at his obstinacy but in the wake of her own there was little she could argue against. Then she tossed him the talisman before sinking onto her knee. Fighting down growing apprehension, she pressed her hands onto the frozen ground.

Immediately, she tasted bile. The colors and sounds that wafted from a nearby rift were different, muted. She felt a surge of rage at the foul stench and garish blasts of light. Instead of warm comfort, she was met by raucous pollution. A stain of black sludge undulated in a turbulent sea. With teeth clamped, Adele pushed deeper into the disturbing mire. She couldn't keep her sense of direction. The anchoring cold air from above was gone. Lances of light seared her skin and her ears throbbed with the beating of her heart.

Battling the cacophony around her that threatened to pummel her senseless, Adele reached out for the lines of the Earth's power. She could sense them around her, but they were jagged and twisted into a thicket. She took them in hand, and shouted with pain as the lines cut deep into her palms. The threads jerked away, quivering and rabid, dripping with her blood.

Adele dared another step deeper into the terror. She saw a rift slashing back and forth, fearful of her approach. She seized it and it jerked against her grip. A razor sliced deep into her hand, tearing through the flesh and muscle and wedging against the bones. Adele nearly blacked out from the agony, but she traced the line even so. She could feel its wildness, its lunacy. It was dying and fighting against whatever was killing it, and failing.

She followed the line, walking the rift in spite of the cuts that appeared in her hands and up her arms and across her body. Her feet were drenched in blood. The rift ran south until Adele saw a city in the distance. The line in her hand tugged slightly as if someone on the other end felt her presence. She wondered if this was what a fish experienced just before a sharp hook plunged through its cheek.

Adele released the rift and struggled to move away from the city. Noise and smells buffeted her, trying to push her ever downward. Adele swam up, ignoring the pain and exhaustion, focusing on getting back to Gareth. Then she saw white and felt cold. The near silence deafened her and frigid air seared her lungs.

Adele felt the frozen dirt between her fingers. The snowy landscape stretched out before her. She searched for Gareth's face and gave him a comforting nod as he took her sagging shoulders. Adele sat back in the snow, ignoring the wetness. She rubbed her face in exhaustion. "Gareth, you told me that your friend was the king in Paris. Lothaire? Is he still the king there?"

His curious gaze showed that he was concerned she was still rattled from her trip into the rift. "As far as I know. Why?"

She looked into his eyes. "The Earth is polluted here and that's obviously the source of this slaughter. I followed one of the distressed rifts and it ran toward Paris. That's where we'll find the Witchfinder."

"That's not possible. Not Lothaire."

"I hope not."

Gareth was no longer looking at her. He was staring off to the south through the snow.

CHAPTER 10

Adele had settled into the upstairs room in Bruges to continue her study of her mother's notebook while Gareth went out to feed. The sickness she had experienced out at that death camp had finally faded, except in her angry memory. Her muscles ached, but she didn't show any of the wounds that had occurred in the rifts. Nadzia had helped by bringing food, bland but serviceable, plus a local beer that was quite good.

Adele did her best to pierce the aspects of the blue crystal but found it murky going. There were few stones that didn't open their secrets to her with only a touch and a minimal amount of study. Her natural skills allowed her to penetrate crystalline surfaces and explore the lines and internal facets that channeled and reflected energy. Normally Adele could determine any number of things from even cursory examinations, from a stone's place of origin to its age. If a crystal had been carved or altered, particularly by a geomancer, she could typically determine for what purpose.

This blue stone remained a mystery to Adele. She couldn't extend her power into it. She knew it had been altered, quite skillfully too. The Witchfinder had cut the raw stone with stunning precision. He had used normal tools because it was a rare geomancer indeed who could modify a stone with pure energy, as Adele could. Even so, she was unable to fathom exactly the result of the alterations. She didn't understand the feel or sound or smell of the crystal's energy. So she took whatever time she had to turn to her sources, limited as they were, for some hints. She wished she had her texts in Alexandria, or the great arcane library of Sir Godfrey Randolph. Alas, she had only her mother's notebook, but it would have to serve.

The time for study would be short because she and Gareth were leaving for Paris in the morning. Gareth was nervous about what they would find there. He held King Lothaire in unique regard and feared what had become of him under the pressure of the Equatorian war from the south. Adele was nervous too, but her concerns seemed to have a simple answer, to a certain extent. Find the Witchfinder and put an end to his activities, one way or another. Adele might not comprehend how he did his work, but she knew it was dangerous and had to be stopped.

"Empress?"

Adele spun to see Kasteel peering at her from the stairs. His face was pale and he trembled.

"What's wrong?" Adele asked quickly, sure that something had happened to Gareth. There was no other reason for the rebel leader to look so distraught.

"Nothing." He shrank back and muttered, "I'm sorry for disturbing you."

She frightened him. The Death Bringer. The Empress of the End. She suppressed a scowl and waved him up. Her examination of the blue crystal cast waves of geomantic power in the confined space. It had to be painful for Kasteel. Adele set the stone aside and concentrated on bringing even these faint hints of energy under control. The vampire's English was fair so she said, "Come, Kasteel. I won't harm you. What do you want? Gareth isn't here."

"I know." He crept to the top step again. "I want to see you."

"Me?" Adele stood her ground, careful not to make any aggressive moves that might spook the vampire. "Speak."

"Was the food satisfactory?"

"Yes, thank you."

Kasteel nodded silently, standing there like a shadow.

Adele leaned forward. "Anything else?"

He didn't raise his head. "Lord Gareth is going away soon."

"Tomorrow. We're off to Paris."

"To pursue the blue stone?"

"Yes."

"Will he return?"

"I don't know."

There was another long pause. Kasteel ran his hand along a stone column. Adele waited and watched the nervous vampire struggle to find words.

"What does he want?" Kasteel met her eyes in desperation. There was true questing pain in them that vampires never showed, at least not to a human. It was the same unquenchable desire and curiosity she had seen in Gareth when he asked questions about the inscrutable nature of human life. "I want to help him as he saves our kind, but he doesn't seem pleased with us. How can I aid him?"

The catch in his voice touched Adele. "You're asking *me*?"

"I'm sorry, Empress. I know you could burn me to ashes for asking, but that doesn't matter. There is no one else. Baudoin is dead. I've tried to understand Lord Gareth from his actions. I've tried to teach others. If he leaves without telling us we're on the right path, we'll have nowhere to go. We'll be adrift once more."

The amazing vision of Kasteel standing before her, struggling with ideas, trying to plan and define behavior rather than simply feeding and killing, caused Adele to smile.

"Why is that funny?" he snapped and turned away.

Adele almost blurted out an apology before realizing she dare not show any weakness deep inside vampire territory. Still, she held up her hand to stop him from charging back down the steps. "Kasteel, wait! I'm not mocking you. Believe me. I'm merely overjoyed you're trying to learn. I wish I knew how to help you, but it's not my place to explain Gareth's mind to you."

The vampire's anger passed and was replaced with a sudden look of alarm. He had just shouted at the Death Bringer.

She came forward with calm words. "It seems to me that you're doing the most important thing. You're showing others that change is possible. That's incredibly powerful."

"Yes!" Kasteel brightened with pride, but then his expression fell again. "But why does he not see that? What have we done wrong?"

For a moment, Kasteel looked as young as Simon when he was scolded by their father. "You've done nothing wrong. You're just a surprise to him."

"I've tried to spread the word. I've tried very hard. And there are more of us than you know. There will be many more once others realize what Lord Gareth is."

"I'm sure you've tried." Adele was eager to collect more hints of what these rebels believed, but she had to be cautious. It was difficult to bridge the gap between Death Bringer and confidant. "What exactly is Lord Gareth to you?"

"He is the prince who abandoned his rightful place to live alone among his humans . . . and cats apparently; I'm not sure how to judge that. But I know how he fought to free himself from the grip of his father, Dmitri, the despot of Britain."

Adele looked doubtfully at the youthful face. "You'll forgive me, but the Gareth I know is different from the one you seem to see. Gareth has said many times that it was Dmitri who formed him. His father believed that vampires should live in the night and leave humans to the sun. Dmitri preached against the Great Killing. All that, Gareth gained from his father."

"But they say Dmitri was mad," Kasteel said, confused. "And Lord Gareth abandoned him."

"The madness came later," she replied gently. "After the Great Killing. And it broke Gareth's heart."

Kasteel watched Adele with glowing eyes. He sank to sit cross-legged on the floor, listening rapturously to the words he craved to hear.

—⁂—

Gareth crouched in an alley, waiting. Hunger was gnawing at him; it had been several days since he fed. A huddled shape passed the opening and Gareth struck. The attack wasn't particularly artful, but he seized the man quickly and took him in an unbreakable hold. Wrenching the man's wrist up to his mouth, Gareth bit and tasted warming blood. The victim was healthy and frightened. He resisted, trying to pull away. Gareth found that unexpected, but heartening. After taking just enough blood to dull his hunger, he released the man. The large fellow rounded with a look of terror.

Gareth narrowed his eyes. "You're free to go. Take the road."

The man took a few halting steps, then turned and broke into a run. He vanished into the dark.

With a satisfied breath, Gareth walked to the far side of the street and looked down at a frozen canal. He paused at a bare willow tree with its long slender tendrils draping down to where they were trapped in the ice. He heard the whisper of vampires floating past so he lowered his head, sinking deeper into his hood.

A dark figure swooped in front of him, landing on the frozen white surface of the canal. Gareth angrily tensed for a fight until he saw it was Kasteel. The young rebel smiled up at him.

"May I come with you to Paris?" Kasteel asked.

"No."

Kasteel pushed off along the ice with one foot and slid a few feet. "I can serve you there, my lord. I have places you can stay safely."

"I work alone. Well, with Adele."

"You may need help. The Paris clan has become brutal."

Gareth turned away. "What do you know of that?"

"I have been there several times since the war in the south began. Old Lothaire has lost his grip. Power resides with the Dauphin."

"Prince Honore?" Gareth spun back to see Kasteel skating gracefully from one bank of the canal to the other.

"Yes. Honore. Do you know the king's son?"

"We've met. He was an acolyte of my brother's."

"Cesare." Kasteel's voice dripped with venom. "It's hard to believe that you are of the same clan, much less the same blood. Are you happy he's dead?"

Gareth was surprised by the pain that rose in him over Kasteel's callous mention of Cesare. The young vampire spun on the ice with his arms out. It was a peculiar sight to see a vampire playing, almost like a human child. The carefree moment annoyed Gareth. "Have you never been back to your clan at Aachen?"

"No." Kasteel slowed his rotation and rose into the air while still spinning.

"You claim a lot of wisdom for one so young." Gareth watched the vampire drift toward him.

Kasteel set his feet lightly on the stones in front of Gareth to stop his spin. "I know the most important thing, my lord. There are two paths to the future. Yours or Cesare's. You're standing here, and he's dead."

"So if you're so wise, tell me, after the clan lords fall, what next?"

"We return to the night, as we were before the Great Killing."

"And the humans?"

"They return to the day. They thrive. We feed. As it always was."

"Happily ever after?"

Kasteel narrowed his gaze in confusion. "I don't understand."

"You believe the humans will suffer to be our food source?"

"Some may, like your humans in Scotland. Ultimately it doesn't matter. We will take what we need from them. We need not rule them to do it. That only corrupts us. They'll live their lives as they wish. So will we." The rebel eyed Gareth, sure this conversation was merely another test of his interpretation of the philosophy.

Gareth lifted his face upward and watched small snowflakes drift down like stars dropping from the sky. "That's one dream you can have, I suppose."

"It was King Dmitri's dream too, wasn't it?"

Gareth felt a jolt run through him at the mention of his father, but he didn't look away from the sky.

Kasteel dropped his shoulders, his voice despondent. "Baudoin always admired Dmitri. I feel as if I don't really understand his legacy. Perhaps I never will. But I wish to."

"You have a safe place in Paris?"

"Yes," Kasteel answered eagerly. "We have already found a few new brothers there. Lothaire's rule creates open minds. Honore's not as much."

Gareth gave the rebel a warm smile. "Very well. Gather the most trusted you have. I may need you in Paris after all."

Kasteel clenched his fists in triumph. "Yes, my lord! I would die for you!"

"Good. Just don't do it until I tell you."

Kasteel kicked off and sailed into the air. He rolled away on the wind and vanished behind a clock tower. Gareth shook his head. He appreciated enthusiasm because it was such a human attribute, but he was wary of it too—because it was such a human attribute. Kasteel's type of focused hero worship was very questionable, particularly since Gareth was intimately acquainted with the failings of the rebel's hero.

He stared down at the icy canal and saw the chaotic traces in the light snow that Kasteel had made. He glanced around for anyone who might be watching. He felt an odd surge of exhilaration, similar to his early days donning the Greyfriar costume. Childish, he knew. Gareth climbed down the sheer stone wall. Just before his foot touched the frozen canal, he stopped himself. The ice had seemed solid enough when Kasteel had been on it. Gareth had no desire to fall through.

Grasping the rocks of the canal wall, he let his toes touch the ice. Then slowly he put his weight down. The ice creaked, but stayed firm. He went to stand free. His left foot slipped and flew up. Strong fingers crunched into the stones to keep him from falling. Then the right leg jerked aside. He desperately clung to the wall to keep his balance. Gareth pulled himself up and lightened his frame a bit. Once his feet were again planted, he straightened. A quick pause for balance and he pushed off.

It was a strange sensation floating across the surface of the canal. He barely felt the ice under his feet. It was like flying. As he made a slow glide, he raised his arms in front of him and fell into a crouch for no particular reason. Then he went into an unplanned spin. His back slammed against the opposite wall, and he grasped thick rooted vines covering the stones. His feet flew out from under him, but he held himself up.

Pleased with his first attempt, Gareth shoved off again with a cavalier kick. The ice seemed more hospitable now. This wasn't difficult at all. Suddenly he crashed onto the ice with an undignified grunt and skidded along the canal with his legs splayed around him.

A rhythmic sound rose over his breathy muttering. He saw a figure standing at the railing laughing.

Adele.

He collided with the bank near her. She stood with a brilliant smile and one foot up on the low stone curb overlooking the canal.

"That was very graceful," she called down.

Gareth tugged on his cuffs and wiped snow from his legs. "It's what I wanted to do."

"I have no doubt. It was beautiful. You could have a career in the ballet."

He rose, slipped down again, but then dragged himself to his feet. "I suppose you are skilled at this, as you are at everything," he said, a gentle challenge in his tone.

"Don't be cross." Adele pulled her scarf up over her nose, obscuring her amusement, except for her bright eyes.

Gareth reached up. "Here. Let's see."

"No. I'd kill myself down there."

He remained motionless with his arm extended up to her.

"Gareth, stop playing games. I'm not going to . . . Gareth, seriously, I'm sorry. I wasn't making fun of you . . . listen . . . I'm from the desert . . . Fine. Fine. But if I break my leg, you'll have to carry me home." Adele dropped awkwardly and clambered down the jagged frosty wall, kicking snow as she went. Gareth took her hand and helped set her feet on the glassy ground.

Adele waited breathlessly for disaster. She stood frozen, as still as a statue with her eyes wide and hands outstretched. When she spoke, she whispered, as if even the motion of her jaw would throw her off balance. "Will it hold both of us?"

Gareth drew her close.

Adele slipped and she clutched him tight. "Whoa! Don't just move without warning me." She looked down at their feet and hesitantly inched one of her boots. Then she brought it back. She chortled like a child, pressing her forehead against his unmoving chest. "You know what you're doing, right? You've done this before."

"Not at all." Lightened by the clean ring of her laughter, Gareth pushed off suddenly with Adele in tow. "Shall we!"

Adele let out a shriek before clenching her mouth shut. Her legs quivered as the ice flashed beneath them. She squeezed Gareth around the waist, his solid frame steadfast despite their perilous glide. High walls of stone and the wooden sides of abandoned houses flashed past. Snowflakes swirled around them.

Gareth spun out in front of her and took the brunt of the impact when they bounced off a bank. Despite the bump, they remained upright and continued skating along the glistening surface.

"Are you cloaked?" he asked.

"I think so." Adele let out another peal of laughter. "I was anyway, before this started."

They left their world behind, flying across the canal, and in this moment, it was just the two of them, free of obligations and moralities. Gareth turned to her and found her bright gaze upon him, sheer joy written upon it.

Adele hesitantly released her death grip on Gareth's body. They moved apart slowly. She drifted out until the length of their two arms, fingers entwined, separated them. They glided down the center of the canal, crouching to pass under a bridge and then back out into the open.

Gareth laughed too, wondering at the spectacle any vampire was witnessing. A madman skating with a nonexistent partner. While human watchers might only suspect two lovers stealing a dangerous moment on the ice.

Adele gave a spirited snort and kicked off to increase their speed. Gareth let her pull him faster down the canal. He watched her cutting the snow in a crystalline swirl about them. The flakes landed on their dark attire and sparked like gemstones. Her intense eyes were not looking at her feet any longer; they were focused ahead. She was bent slightly at the knees, luxuriating in the wind and cold and speed.

A dark wall loomed up suddenly. Gareth moved quickly and swept them into a precarious right turn. Adele moved with him. Together they each leaned wildly onto one leg. They managed stay up and kept racing down the ice.

Adele crowed with exhilaration. She came back to his side and he looped his arm around her waist again, pulling her close. She sighed as his warmth encircled her. "Did Kasteel find you? He went looking for you."

"Yes. He is coming to Paris with us."

"He is? Are you starting to enjoy having disciples?"

"Hardly."

Adele let her head rest against his shoulder. She reached out and let her fingertips patter along the wall to slow them to a walking pace.

Gareth said, "I've grown immune to pointless admiration. Whether ridiculous stories about the Greyfriar or now misplaced confidence in Prince Gareth. Humans and vampires can both create a figure in their mind and make it mean what they wish."

"You're wrong." Adele clutched at the stones and brought herself to a stop while Gareth continued slowly on and made a wide loop to return toward her. "Kasteel respects you as a leader of your people. And, my God, you know how humans love the Greyfriar, and it isn't for nothing. You did great things."

Gareth stared into her questioning eyes and sighed. "We should go back."

"Fine, but I wasn't the one who started this skating party," Adele reminded him, climbing toward the street. "Maybe seeing Lothaire will cheer you up and remind you of better days."

"The only better days are the ones with you."

"Oh, don't put the whip to your gallantry now. It's not finishing this race." She labored onto the street and brushed the snow off her coat.

He took her shoulders, making her look up at him. "The truth is the truth." His lips brushed hers, warming her with his breath. Her eyes closed and her arms encircled him under the drape of his cloak. The embrace did not last long, in case someone spied them. They parted reluctantly. The fire in Adele's eyes had shifted from irritated to something decidedly more passionate. She adjusted her coat and sauntered off. Gareth smiled and drifted up into the air, floating just above her all the way back to their once-grand lodging.

CHAPTER 11

General Mehmet Anhalt walked across the large public square toward Victoria Palace. Lines of carriages streamed through the ornate gate leading to the palace grounds. The crowds in the square showed many combinations of long white thobes or grey morning suits, full gowns or embroidered jalabiya, top hats and fezzes and hijabs. Greetings and close conversations swirled in English, Arabic, Swahili, Hindi, and various other languages from around the Equatorian Empire.

Anhalt was short but powerfully built, dark and grim of face, with the solid military bearing of a Gurkha. He walked with a cane and carried a heavy leather attaché. His general's uniform caused no great stir here near the palace where generals were plentiful. Most of the other officers striding the area were bedecked with glittering chests full of medals and citations, but Anhalt's tunic was plain except for his emblems of rank. Still countless officers and enlisted men recognized him and saluted. He struggled to return the greetings as he limped along.

"Good morning, General!"

A carriage halted beside him. An older man, cadaverous and whiskered, appeared at the coach window above the embossed emblem of the sirdar, supreme commander of the Imperial Army. It was an emblem that Anhalt once had on his carriage, a carriage that he had never used.

"Would you care for a lift, Mehmet?" Sirdar Field Marshal Maxwell Rotherford opened the door.

"I am enjoying my walk, but I thank you."

"Come now. It's unseemly for the former sirdar to be afoot." Field Marshal Rotherford stroked his impressive mustache.

Anhalt noticed that the carriage's horses were stopped in the palace gate. Already, impatient coachmen around them were shouting and heads craned in search of the blockage.

The field marshal slid his lanky form away from the open door. "I insist."

Anhalt sighed and climbed into the carriage. As he sank into the soft leather seat, the door was slammed shut and the coach rattled into the courtyard and stopped almost immediately. It settled into the arrival line for the palace only a hundred yards away and continued to inch forward. Anhalt could have beaten it on foot even with his hampered stride.

The field marshal held up a newspaper. "Have you seen this?"

"I have, yes."

"Too far! They've gone too far!" Rotherford read: *"Young men, far from their balmy homes and warm families back in Egypt and Tanganyika and Bengal, tighten their threadbare coats and choke down their miserable cold meals. Their eyes strain ever skyward with the failing of the sun, knowing that the dark hordes will soon sweep down on them. Many of them will not see the spring. Their very dying blood will feed the war machine of an enemy as invisible as the night, as numerous as the stars, as invincible as the cold itself."*

Anhalt nodded appreciatively. "Not bad writing."

"I call it treason! Invincible! Threadbare coats! He makes it sound as if we're rounding up a schoolyard full of boys and tossing them into a meat grinder with no training or support. It's unpatriotic!"

General Anhalt remembered very similar nights in the frozen trenches below Grenoble. He remained silent and gazed longingly at the palace.

"No opinion, Mehmet?" the field marshal insisted. "We must drive the monsters to extinction. I shall take Paris in the springtime. And likely Vienna by mid-summer. We're exploring a fresh alliance with the Americans and talking to the Japanese Empire about an Asian offensive." He threw the newspaper across the carriage. "But judging by the papers, you'd think my army had been pushed off the Continent!"

Anhalt felt the man staring, and he knew what was coming.

Field Marshal Rotherford pointed out the window toward Victoria Palace. "There is no coordinated rebuttal from the Court. Honestly, Mehmet, in your personal opinion, just between us, don't you believe it would be better if the empress were here in Alexandria? Why is she still in Britain? She's been there since it fell to our forces last year."

The general straightened his aching right leg, wincing at the effort, a wound that he acquired crashing an airship into Buckingham Palace. He nodded just to show he was listening.

"Mehmet, there's no secret of the depth of your admiration for the empress," Rotherford continued. "Your years as the commander of her household guard bound you to her. That's understandable. We all agree she is a remarkable figure. Her handling of Lord Kelvin's coup was extraordinary. Of course, she had precipitated the crisis in the first place by running off rather than marrying Senator Clark, but that's neither here nor there. I'm sure I'm not telling you anything you haven't heard before."

"You are not."

Rotherford seemed unaware of the deep rumbling anger in his companion's voice, or didn't care. "We all admire the fortitude it required to survive the ordeal after she was captured by Cesare and Gareth two years ago. That said, many wonder why she maintains this relationship with Prince Gareth, of all people . . . if I can call him *people*." The field marshal paused and shook his head. "You would think she would never want to see that creature again once she was free of it. But she's drawn back to the north always."

Anhalt recognized genuine bewilderment in Rotherford, and he understood it. "Prince Gareth is an ally, like it or not. You may recall, we were losing the war before the empress brought him to our side. He provided us with the intelligence that allowed us to kill Cesare and break the vampire alliance."

Rotherford pointed at Anhalt. "So she feels some sense of gratitude to this Gareth creature? He may be manipulating her to his own ends."

"Rubbish. No one *manipulates* Empress Adele."

"Can you be sure, Mehmet? What if she is under the sway of a vampire prince?"

"Sir, you clearly have no concept of what our empress is made of, nor the sacrifices she has made for Equatoria, nor the horrors she has witnessed, nor the hardships she's endured. There have been numerous attempts on her life, by *humans*, not by vampires. She preserved this empire against traitors and then took it to war against an implacable enemy. And all the while she had to endure the pointless, petty carping of small-minded bureaucrats and technocrats who couldn't survive a day in her world. So kindly spare me your beliefs on what the empress should or shouldn't do about the war or the press or her hairstyle." Anhalt kicked open the door, barely feeling the shock that ran up his leg. "Good day. Thank you for carrying me twenty yards closer to the palace."

General Anhalt dropped to the cobblestones and limped toward the wide portico. He reached the large doors opening into the palace foyer before he felt a tinge of regret for losing his temper. Not that he was wrong, but keeping the good graces of the high command was critical. Even so, he felt a selfish undercurrent of calm, having unleashed his anger on Field Marshal Rotherford.

At the foot of a curving staircase up to the royal residence, soldiers snapped to attention, presenting rifles with a clatter. The general walked up slowly and continued down an ornate corridor. He passed through a hurriedly opened door into a huge office where a woman stood before a chalkboard. She was small and covered completely in a burka, except for her piercing eyes and her hands, which were laced with delicate henna tattoos.

"Nizami is accessible in translation, but we want to study the original Persian sources," the woman was saying. She paused and turned to the newcomer at the door. "Ah, General Anhalt. Have you come to contribute to our discussion of poetry?"

"General Anhalt!" cried Prince Simon, a lad of fourteen, from behind a desk where he listened to the lecturer, or supposedly listened. He sounded as if he was adrift at sea and calling for a rescuer.

Anhalt inclined his head. "I should like nothing more, Sanah. I am a devotee of Nizami. I'm sorry, though, I didn't realize you were still in session."

Sanah set down a piece of chalk and brushed her hands together with a cloud of white dust that settled onto her black burka. "Our lesson is done for today, General. Tomorrow, Your Highness, we will discuss *Eskander Nameh.*

You should like that; it's about Alexander the Great, so perhaps there will be many battles and great carnage." The woman gathered her books and papers. She regarded young Prince Simon, who quickly scrambled to his feet and bowed to her. She paused by General Anhalt. "Have you heard from Adele recently? It's been nearly two weeks since my last letter."

"Just yesterday, ma'am. Your niece, the empress, is well. Most recently taking some refuge in Edinburgh."

Sanah hummed quietly in contentment. "Good. She seemed taxed in her last note. She used to write to me frequently to ask questions about her mother, and her mother's notebooks on geomancy, but that has dropped off in recent months. Do you know if she's coming back to the warmth of Alexandria anytime soon?"

"She didn't mention it, ma'am."

"Thank you, sir." Sanah admirably covered her disappointment. She turned back to Simon with a wagging finger. "Study your Persian, Simon." She laughed over his exasperated explanation of how difficult the language was, and she went out.

General Anhalt closed the door and deployed his own paperwork in practiced fashion on the opposite side of Simon's desk. "Are you benefitting from Sanah's instruction?"

"It's dull," said the prince of Bengal, as he threw one leg onto the arm of his chair.

"Poetry dull?" Anhalt peered over his spectacles in genuine surprise. "You might as well say life is dull."

The lad snorted with amusement and drew his own red folder from a desk drawer. He slapped it on the desk and shuffled through it. The way Simon rifled the dispatches, glancing at them with eyes that could already absorb their essence quickly, made Anhalt proud. It also gave him a slight twinge of regret that the rambunctious lad he loved might soon be gone for all time. He watched the boy, although he was hardly a boy any longer. His once chubby cheeks, while still ruddy, were hardening into the features of a young man. He was beginning to show the handsome looks of his northern-featured father while Adele was an image of their Persian mother, Pareesa. One had to look beneath the skin tone and nose shape to the steel that came into their eyes when challenged as the sole way to determine that the empress and the prince were siblings. Simon shut his folder and looked at Anhalt with an expectant smile.

The general lifted his top sheet. "The Americans have been driven from their positions along the Ohio River."

"Hah!" Simon re-opened his folder and showed that his copy of the exact memo was on top of his pile too. It was a game they played to see if they agreed on the issues of the day. "Vampire packs are raiding the outskirts of St. Louis. I've told you, we'll be in Paris long before the Americans can reach Chicago or Philadelphia. They were so smug with their early victories."

"Why has their offensive faltered?"

"Because they stopped slaughtering everyone in their path."

"Care to elaborate?"

"When Senator Clark was their commander, they just gassed all the herds in vampire territory to kill off the enemy food supply. Of course the vampires retreated. When Clark died, the Americans stopped doing that. They found out that true war is harder than they thought. They were bragging about exploiting their eastern coalfields last year." Simon returned to his files with satisfaction. "Number two?"

Anhalt flipped to the next page. "Concerns over the rise in what is called *fanaticism* here in the homeland because of Empress Adele's open embrace of faith and magic."

Simon pulled his hand from his folder. It was empty. He shifted angrily in his chair.

The general said innocently, "We disagree on number two, I take it."

"I saw it. I tore it up."

"Your Highness, you don't have to agree with troublesome opinions, but you must hear them." Anhalt hesitated, remembering how he had lashed out at Sirdar Rotherford and kicked his way out of the carriage. He cleared his throat. "There is genuine concern that your sister is undermining the rational foundations of our society."

"That's crap!" Simon stood abruptly and went to the wide window.

"There are many beliefs in the world, and they're changing quickly. It was just a few years ago when most people still thought vampires were undead humans."

"No one thinks that anymore. No one smart thought that for years. I read Sir Godfrey's book on *Homo nosferatii*. Well, most of it. But I know that vampires are just a parasitic species that lives off human blood. They don't turn to dust in the sunlight; they just don't like the heat. That's why they don't live in the tropics, and why we do. They're fast and strong, but you can kill them with a bullet. Adele knows that too."

"Better than anyone."

"Right. So if she wants to believe in religion too, that's her affair. Isn't it?"

"It goes beyond religion, Your Highness. Geomancy posits that there is energy in the Earth and that vampires are susceptible to it. Adele tells me that the old myths about vampires being repelled by holy objects or places have a basis in fact. I admit I have seen evidence of it as well. Most religion and mystical thought has been scorned here in the south since the Great Killing because it failed to save the north from the vampires. There are those technocrats who fear it is returning and that your sister is leading the movement."

Simon leaned against the glass, staring down at the vast harbor beyond the palace grounds on the Ras al Tin peninsula. The waterfront was thick with ships and machinery. Large groups of soldiers marched up gangplanks onto steaming troop carriers for the voyage to Europe. "I know that, but why does it matter what I think? She's not crazy. Right? Why does everyone want me to have an opinion on her? Isn't it enough that Adele has the support of Greyfriar? And you!"

Anhalt shifted uncomfortably. "Our opinions are suspect. Greyfriar is the empress's consort. And I am merely an old soldier with little left to give."

Simon's tempestuous face suddenly turned to stern maturity. "Never say that again! Do you hear me?"

Anhalt was jarred back into his chair. He fumbled with the sheet of paper and cleared his throat in surprise.

Simon stalked back to his desk and yanked open a drawer. He pulled out a handsome teak box. "Do you know what this is?"

"No, Highness."

The prince opened the box and lifted out medals. One after another. Simple or gaudy. Gold, silver, bejeweled. Ribbons of various colors. He laid them carefully on the desk, barely glancing at them while calling out their names. "Mandalay Offensive. Nagaland Defense. Zulu Campaign. Imperial Order of the Nile. Zanzibar Revolt. Equatorian Crescent. Ptolemy Incident. Badge of the Sirdar. Grenoble Conquest. London Invasion. Wounded in Line of Duty. Wounded in Line of Duty. Wounded in Line of Duty." He stared at Anhalt with uncharacteristically adult directness. "Do you know what they are now?"

The general looked down and adjusted his reading spectacles. "Yes, Your Highness."

"Yes. These are *your* commendations. I know you don't like to wear them or boast about your accomplishments."

"A lot of young men died in those actions." Anhalt tried not to sound pompous or scolding because that wasn't his intention. "I don't care to boil them down to a piece of metal and ribbon."

Simon softened his expression and picked up one of the medals. "I understand that, but these represent your life. You have given everything to the army and Equatoria, to Adele, and now to me. Even if you don't value that, I do."

General Anhalt sighed and nodded silently for a moment. "You honor me, Simon. Thank you."

Simon's shoulders slumped as if embarrassed by the moment. He turned to gaze again toward the full-sailed airships crowding the skies. He brightened with a genius idea. "Let's go to Britain!"

"Go to Britain?"

The boy grinned. "To see Adele. And I want to see the place before we civilize it."

"Your Highness, I fear any extended trip away from the capital, particularly one so distant and treacherous as Britain, is impossible. The people require at least one of the royal siblings to remain here."

"The *people*? They want something different every day."

"Then the Privy Council. Commons. Her Majesty's government. The sirdar and the army high command. Any or all want you here."

"Come on! If I was Adele asking you to fly off somewhere, you'd already be packing."

"Perhaps. Once." Anhalt closed the red folder and smiled wistfully. "Your sister entrusted me to stand by your side, and I shall. But we will do our standing here in Alexandria."

"I could command a ship to take me."

"No, you couldn't."

"Why not? Adele used to order people to take her everywhere!"

"No, she didn't. She just went."

"That's not fair!"

General Anhalt shifted in his chair with a pained hiss and stretched out his crooked leg. "No, it's not. But it is your duty." He noticed that Simon's eyes had fallen on the back of Anhalt's hand resting on the red folder. The skin was scarred from terrible burns and his fingers were gnarled, hardly capable of holding his pen. Anhalt pulled his hand away and dropped it beside his chair. "Shall we continue?"

"Forgive me, General. Do you want anything? Tea?"

"A glass of water, if you don't mind." Anhalt suddenly realized it that it sounded as if he had asked the prince to serve him. He groaned with effort as he pushed off the arms of the chair. "I'll get it."

Simon raised his hand to stop the general. Ignoring a bellpull that would have summoned a servant, he went to a tray on the sideboard and poured water from a sweating silver pitcher. He brought the glass to the desk.

"Thank you." Anhalt sipped and looked down at the folder. "We still have a great deal to get through before your fencing lesson at eleven."

Simon moved around the chair, placing a hesitant hand on General Anhalt's shoulder. He returned to his own seat and opened his red folder.

CHAPTER 12

Paris smelled of blood and fear.

Gareth sensed a suppressed mania in the air. The vampires of the great city were normally assured and sedate, but now they were on edge. Their calm languid style had been replaced by a near frantic sense, and they were perturbed by it. They took out their annoyance on the humans. The streets were full of dead, and some not quite dead, squirming among the cadavers without hope. Vermin stared boldly from curbs, and packs of dogs wandered the once-green gardens. More bodies littered squares and courtyards than any time since the Great Killing. The vampires of Paris were coming apart because the Equatorian Army was sleeping in its winter quarters to the south, waiting for spring when it would rise hungry.

Gareth paced nervously before a wall of bones and skulls. It had been hours since Adele had left the catacombs to make her way to the Tuileries Palace to find Lothaire. She shouldn't have gone. There was just too much unknown about the current situation. Numberless empty eye sockets watched him pass to and fro in the underground cemetery. He needed to cultivate a sense of strategy. It was always Adele who conceived their plans, and she always reserved the most dangerous role for herself. Gareth knew he would have to become brighter or risk losing her at some point.

Light footsteps came from the passageway to the surface. Too light to be Adele's. Vampires. Two figures appeared from the shadows; Gareth recognized the scents.

King Lothaire and Queen Caterina came into view. They both stopped to stare at Gareth as if he was a stranger. The royal couple wore very plain clothes, which added to the dismaying sense that they were lost or out of place.

"Lothaire!" Gareth rushed forward with relief, grinning out of habit at seeing the companion of his youth. He quickly saw the hesitance in Lothaire's eyes and drew to a stop. With more reservation, he turned to the queen. "Caterina. I didn't expect you too."

"Gareth." Lothaire greeted him quietly, saying the name as if for the first time.

Lothaire was the same age as Gareth but looked much older and was even a bit stooped. The king had lost weight in the year since Gareth had seen him last, but instead of looking healthier he seemed sallow. There was a sad weariness about him. Caterina had changed little. Strong and beautiful, dark skinned with nearly black hair. However, her expression was harder. The warmth that had always flowed from her toward Gareth was missing. Its absence here in this cold grave of a meeting place chilled him.

"Adele found you then?" Gareth kept a respectful distance. This was not the reunion he had naively hoped for. "Is she with you?"

"No," Caterina answered. "She said she'd make her own way here."

"Ah, good. I'm sorry for the mystery, but it's wonderful to see both of you."

Lothaire remained stoic, almost confused and unsure how to proceed. He was content for the queen to speak.

Caterina asked, "Why are you here, Gareth?"

"I need information."

"Why should we give you anything?" she asked with ferocity and hurt. "Why should we do anything except kill you? You're a traitor. Aren't you?"

Her accusation was like a savage blow. Gareth took a step back. He had known Caterina for centuries and a harsh word had never passed between them.

"Yes," he said.

"And now," she continued hotly, "you've come here with that monster to drag Lothaire into your insanity. You know he would never refuse you anything, but this is too much. They say you've lost your mind, which I believe, but for some reason I never thought you would lose your honor. How could—"

Lothaire interrupted softly, "My dear, I should like to hear what Gareth has to say. I've known him forever, and you have too. Are we to give him up for lies and rumors?"

"What lies?" Caterina's desperate tone indicated that she wanted her husband to take away her doubt and anger.

Lothaire touched his wife's arm. "Look at all the stories flying about. Some say he's dead. Clearly he's not. Others say there are lunatics in the forests who worship him as some sort of avatar of a new age."

Gareth tried not to react.

Lothaire held up a finger as if he had finally lit on a point to prove his assertions. "They even say he was the Greyfriar." The king eyed Gareth. "Are you the Greyfriar?"

Gareth stared at his old friend until Lothaire laughed. Gareth laughed along, a bit loudly.

Lothaire said in triumph, "So with all those fables about him, we can at least learn the truth. We owe him the courtesy of an audience."

"Why? It's our family we must protect." Caterina's eyes flicked toward Gareth almost apologetically.

"I owe him then," Lothaire said gently. "If you love me, you will consent. Why did we come here otherwise?"

Caterina closed her eyes. Gareth could see the struggle in her. The mother versus the wife. But eventually the latter won out. She nodded.

"Thank you, Caterina," Gareth said.

Lothaire moved closer to his old friend, his posture altering perceptibly into a younger, more eager version of himself. "Gareth, you know that if you're seen in Paris, you'll be killed? There is no clan that will offer you sanctuary."

"I assumed so."

"I couldn't save you, even if I dared try, which I won't."

"I know that, Lothaire. But I had to come."

"Very well." The king raised questioning hands. "I can't assume you've come because you miss me. So why?"

"I have missed you, but I need to know about this." Gareth reached into his pocket and drew out the blue crystal talisman.

"What is that?" Lothaire eyed the stone.

"I was hoping you might know."

"It's a rock on a string. Nothing particularly interesting about it, except that you're carrying it around like a human."

Caterina stared at the talisman. Her gaze darted to Gareth's before she looked at the ground. Gareth continued to watch her, but said nothing. She clearly knew something about the talisman.

Lothaire noticed his wife's reaction too. "Do you know that thing, my dear?"

"No," she answered quickly.

The king tilted his head in doubt. "Does it have something to do with Honore and—"

"Be quiet!" she flared. "He's still our son!"

Gareth said, "I have no quarrel with Honore."

Lothaire took his wife's hand. "Caterina, Gareth didn't come to threaten our son. He obviously came to Paris because he knows Hallow is here."

"Hallow is here?" Gareth exclaimed.

"Or perhaps he didn't know." Lothaire shrugged. "Yes, Lady Hallow was in Europe when . . . when your clan was killed. She came here because Honore had been a supporter of your brother's. She's become Honore's chief advisor."

"Lothaire, please!" Caterina gripped her husband's hands. "Stop telling him everything until we know more."

Gareth stood stunned. Now that he'd heard Lady Hallow was alive, it didn't surprise him. It was possible that he had loved her once, although that seemed increasingly unlikely as the decades passed. No matter what he thought of Hallow personally, her political acumen was unquestioned. She had built the grand alliance of vampire clans that nearly allowed Cesare to smash the Equatorian war before it began. And when Hallow's clan was obliterated, she was resourceful enough to escape and apparently thrive elsewhere. Gareth smiled coldly at her skill. "I suppose if there's anyone who could've avoided the destruction of the clan, it would be Lady Hallow."

"Or you," Caterina said, almost in accusation. "Were you on the Continent as she was?"

Gareth leaned against the wall of skulls. "No. I was in Edinburgh. Adele protected me."

"Tell me, Gareth," Caterina asked with trembling words, "did the Empress really kill them all?"

He took a breath. "Yes."

"Did you command her to do it?"

"No. She was betrayed. If she hadn't stopped it when she did, all of us would be dead now."

Lothaire's eyes widened. "That seems impossible. How could any human do such a thing?"

Gareth caught the subtle flinch from Caterina. "Remember the old days and how the power of the stones and the churches and prayer could burn us? She can wield that power. Humans call it geomancy. I don't understand it, but I've seen it and felt it."

Caterina's lips tightened in rage. "You knew she had that power, and you let her live? Why, Gareth? Did you want her to kill us all?"

He was quiet for a moment, his chest tight. "Perhaps."

"When you were in Paris last year, you were so happy. You told me you had finally found someone you truly loved. Gareth, you didn't mean *her*, did you?"

"Yes."

The queen put a hand to her mouth in shock.

"I can't fully explain it," Gareth said, relieved to finally be honest. "At first, she was no more than a way to foil Cesare. But from the first time I met her, I sensed something about her, something incredible, powerful, even terrible, but I could see the future in her eyes when I had never seen a future before."

He had hardly finished speaking when he heard a strange noise from the entrance. He broke for the shadowy corridor. Shapes scrambled in the darkness and fled. He seized one. Claws raked at him, but he ducked the blow that shattered skulls in the wall.

He heard Lothaire and Caterina coming up behind him. "Go after them! There are at least three more."

The king and queen raced past. Gareth grabbed again for the vampire who still fought to escape. He slammed the struggling thing into the wall of bone. Shards of white flew. Gareth flung him back into the far side. The vampire snarled and struck out. Gareth barely dodged again, his feet clattering through skeletal remains. He then crashed against his opponent with his forearm crushing the vampire's windpipe.

Gareth drew a long bone out of the wall behind his struggling enemy. He pressed the bulbous end of the femur against the ground and stomped, snapping it in half. He thrust the jagged end up under the vampire's ribs. He pushed it in deep. The vampire tried to claw, but only swiped helplessly as his heart was destroyed. Gareth dropped him and ran toward the shaft of light from the catacomb entrance high above.

He lightened and pulled himself up through the center of the collapsing spiral staircase. Hand over hand, he rose to the surface. Once clear of the gates, he came out into the street. Gareth caught a scent of Lothaire, but saw no trace of him in the sky, so he ran down the gravel path in front of him. He stopped at a crossroad and the slight sound of shuffling feet and heavy breathing propelled him into an alleyway.

He burst out into a courtyard to see Lothaire struggling with a vampire who looked terrified to be fighting with the king. Lothaire's attacks were slow from years of disuse. A competent fighter could have taken the king easily. Instead his opponent was more interested in flight than victory. Lothaire seized the vampire and threw him down. His opponent kicked the king's legs out from under him, sending Lothaire tumbling.

Gareth leapt in before the assailant could get to his feet, but the vampire landed a solid blow. Tasting his own blood, Gareth slammed his fist into his adversary's face several times.

Lothaire surged in with a roar, sinking his teeth into the stunned vampire's neck. With a shake of his head, he ripped most of the assailant's throat away. The vampire fell limp in Gareth's grip.

Wild-eyed and bloody, Lothaire murmured, "Caterina" and raced off.

They lifted into the air, leaping crumbled ruins and half-collapsed walls. Lothaire tried to scent frantically, but his face was drenched in blood. Gareth listened and again heard the sounds of combat. They raced over a rooftop, coming to a halt at the eaves. In the street below, they saw Caterina standing with her gown covered in blood. She stood over a vampire that was kicking in his death throes. Lothaire laughed, more one of relief than anything else.

A shape moved near Caterina. The final spy bounded for the queen, screeching angrily about the dying body at her feet. Lothaire and Gareth shouted and leapt off the roof. The queen turned in surprise.

A shadow wavered into sight between Caterina and the charging vampire. There was a flash of green. The vampire screamed and arched in agony. Adele pulled her Fahrenheit dagger free of the vampire's ribs and swept it across his throat. The creature staggered and fell in a dusty tumble.

When Gareth landed, he and Adele instantly spun outward, ready for more attackers. Lothaire hit the ground hard with a grunt. He struggled up and went to his wife.

"I'm fine, I'm fine," she assured him, eyeing his bloody face.

Satisfied that they were in the clear, Gareth touched Adele's arm and gave her a nod of gratitude. She slipped her dagger back into the sheath.

"Either of you recognize any of them?" Gareth slid a foot under one of the dead vampires and flipped him over. He saw that the royal couple were staring at Adele in wonder or fear. Gareth gave a sharp whistle and nodded down at the cadaver. "Lothaire? Recognize him?"

The king jerked out of his fascination with the empress. He narrowed his eyes at the dead body. "I've seen him. With Honore." The king spat blood and looked at Caterina with determination. Then he turned to Gareth. "We need to go somewhere that will be safe from Honore's spies."

"I know a place," Gareth said.

The queen pulled Lothaire close. "We can't. He is our son."

"Open your eyes. Our *son* sent his mercenaries after us. And that one would have killed you but for the empress coming out of nowhere." Lothaire scowled angrily. "No, Caterina, I'm sorry, but I am through being his prisoner. It's time to tell Gareth about the Witchfinder."

CHAPTER 13

Gareth, Lothaire, and Caterina walked north toward the river and the signs of death grew thicker as they moved closer to the center of the city. Gareth whispered for the sake of Adele who walked beside him, hidden from vampire sight, "This isn't the Paris I saw last year. It looks more like London under Cesare."

Lothaire grumbled at the insult. "Not surprising with Hallow leading Honore by the nose." He angrily kicked at a large crow picking at a rib cage. The bird screeched into the sky, only to flutter back down to its meal after they moved on.

"I'm sorry, Lothaire. I wasn't implying that you would sanction this butchery." Gareth pulled his hood tighter.

"It's worse than you know, Gareth. The city is full of mercenaries that Hallow brought from packs all across Europe, most of them from the clans that were allies of Cesare and whose leaders are dead now. My old war chief, Fanon, whom we both fought beside has even turned."

Gareth didn't reply to keep from forcing his friend to air more of the failures he was experiencing. They slipped through silent warrens until they reached the Rue de Lille, strewn with garbage and mounds of bricks from tumbled buildings. Shapes flitted overhead, but none seemed to be following or even noticing.

Finally ahead of them was the Quai Voltaire and an unremarkable building overlooking the Seine where Kasteel had said they should rendezvous with his nest of rebels. Gareth eyed the area and scented the wet air, trying to uncover any sort of peculiarity in the setting. An unnecessary second glance from a figure drifting overhead. An impatient glare from a shadow on the corner. A furtive slip of claws. Anything to tip him to a potential ambush.

Gareth waited until the skies seemed relatively clear, then he nodded quickly to Adele before lifting off the ground. He rose up along the wall to an attic window in the grey tile roof. He gripped the glassless window frame and listened. The voices inside were distant, but he recognized the authoritative boom of Kasteel. Gareth counted seven different voices, but smelled more waiting silently.

He slipped in the window and landed lightly on the floor. He crept to the door, hardly touching, pushing himself along the wall. On the floor below, he heard the sounds of heavy strides, probably Kasteel's, and the rebel leader was muttering impatiently. "He should be here today at some point. I left them just north of Senlis with directions."

"Is *she* still with him?" came an unknown voice with a quaver of fear.

"Yes," Kasteel said gruffly. "She is always with him."

"What is she like?"

"She's quiet and calm. But she looks through you as if she sees your weakest trait immediately."

"You saw her kill some of us?"

"Stop!" Kasteel cried. "She doesn't matter. She is nothing more than Lord Gareth's claws. She is an emanation of his will."

Gareth smiled. Let them believe as they would. For now it worked in his favor.

"She won't destroy Paris, will she?" asked the first quavering voice. "I mean, she'll tell us first so we can leave, right? She'll let us live like Lord Gareth lived, since we follow him."

Kasteel growled with a touch more dread than anger. "With Lord Gareth, we have nothing to fear from her. Paris is falling apart, but we have to stay together. That is our strength."

Gareth had glided down the decrepit staircase and stood outside the large room where Kasteel paced from end to end with others following his every move. Kasteel went to the front window, searching the street and darkening sky.

"Waiting for someone?" Gareth asked.

Kasteel spun in shock. The other vampires in the room, perhaps twenty of them, leapt in alarm. They were all dressed in a poor fashion, even for vampires. They looked at Kasteel for confirmation and the rebel leader tried to overcome his embarrassment at being taken by surprise in his own lair.

"My lord." Kasteel bowed. "Yes, we were waiting for you. Welcome." He craned his neck to peer past Gareth into the hallway. "Is the Death Br—the empress with you?"

"You'll see her when she desires it." Gareth pulled back his hood, glancing at the others. "I brought visitors."

—m—

Adele watched the dumbfounded faces around the room when Lothaire and Caterina entered. It had been a momentous few days for the young rebels. First Gareth, then the Death Bringer, and now the lords of the Paris clan. Kasteel was speechless, unable to grasp the events that were piling on top of him. The rest of the rebels looked to him for guidance, but found none from their chief.

Gareth threw off his cloak and said to Kasteel, "Post guards. Put someone on the roof and on each floor. Anyone could walk in, as I did."

Kasteel sent several of his group scurrying up the stairs, all of them staring back at Gareth as they went. Nadzia went without orders to a front window where she alternated studying the street outside and the rarefied company in the room.

Then Adele let her protection fade. All the vampires saw her suddenly appear in their midst. Some shouted in alarm. Caterina suppressed a startled shudder and glared with suspicion. Adele remained placid, trying not to smile at the childish prank.

The queen asked her, "How do you do that?"

"Magic," Adele replied without cynicism.

"Why can't all humans do it? Why are you special?"

Lothaire nervously cleared his throat. "My dear, don't interrogate the Death Bringer. She need not answer to us. We're here to answer *her* questions."

Caterina raised her eyebrows in challenge. "I'm sure the Death

Bringer doesn't mind. She is traveling with vampires after all." She looked toward Gareth. "She obviously holds us in some minor esteem."

"I hold some of you in high esteem." Adele was direct but not cold. "However, call me Adele. Death Bringer puts a damper on polite conversation, I think."

"Very well." Caterina nodded in bemused acceptance. "What would *you* like to know?"

"Tell us about the Witchfinder."

"I know very little," Caterina said and paused, but when heads turned to Lothaire, she added, "He knows even less."

"True, I'm afraid." The king grinned with embarrassment. "I've never even seen him. I only know he exists because I've been told he does."

"But *you've* seen him?" Gareth asked Caterina.

"Only once or twice. He's an older human with a long white beard. He seems quite at home among vampires. In fact, he acts as an equal." She said the last line with natural haughtiness. She couldn't keep herself from glancing at Adele, but there was a touching flash of shame. She wandered the room as she talked, pausing next to Nadzia and, with a remarkable hint of unconscious motherhood, she cupped the young female's cheek with a hand and smiled down at her. "You're the same age as my oldest daughter Isolde." Caterina brushed hair from the surprised Nadzia's face before turning back to Adele. "He came to Paris with Lady Hallow."

"Who's this Lady Hallow you've been talking about?" Adele could tell immediately that the name was familiar to everyone, but she had never heard it, and that struck her as unusual.

Lothaire and Caterina both glanced with silent amusement at Gareth, who said, "She is a member of my clan. She was one of Cesare's chief advisors. Second only to Flay in importance at court."

Caterina gave Gareth a chiding glance over something unsaid. "Lady Hallow came to Paris where she offered the services of the Witchfinder as a token of goodwill."

"What services does he perform?" Adele let her curiosity about Lady Hallow drift away because of more important issues.

"I'm not sure," Caterina said calmly. "We were never privy to those discussions. I did see those blue stones handed about, but I have no idea what they're supposed to be."

Adele didn't want to accuse the queen of lying or holding back information. Certainly Gareth didn't appear suspicious of her. "You'll forgive me, but you are the king and queen. How is it that this man can operate without your full knowledge?"

Caterina frosted over. "He is the tool of Lady Hallow, who is involved in the defense of Paris against your armies. She has given him liberty to pursue victory as he sees fit."

"I see." Adele gave Caterina a hard stare. "Do you know where the Witchfinder is now?"

"No. He left Paris days ago in a bloodman airship, with some of our packs. Honore says he was off somewhere far to the east, and was going to be gone for several months at least. He is supposed to return before your army tries to destroy us in the spring."

Lothaire blurted out, "Honore granted him an estate south of the city. That's where he stays most of the time."

"Good." Adele dropped her pack on the floor. "I'll have something to eat and then we'll have a look there."

Caterina continued to study Adele. "We wouldn't be averse to this Witchfinder being removed. We consider him to be a vestige of Cesare's reign, and therefore he belongs to Gareth. Do with him as you will."

Adele nodded with acceptance and offered a smile. She patted the hilt of her dagger. "That's the plan."

—m—

Gareth's face was partially covered, similar to his Greyfriar garb. It was an easy enough explanation to tell the wagon driver that his face had been disfigured by a vampire. The farmer hadn't shown much interest in Gareth or Adele as he drove out of the city. He had taken them within a few miles of their destination before dropping the pair on the rutted path with the muttered words, "None who enter Versailles ever return."

Adele and Gareth made their way through the deserted village. There was no sign of recent habitation. Tree roots broke and tumbled the cobblestone streets. Adele stumbled, hoping for an instant that it was only a loose stone, but knowing it was an attack of vertigo. She pressed her hand against a rough tree trunk, trying to keep from sinking to her knees.

"Adele!" Gareth grabbed her.

"It's the same thing," she gasped. "Like outside Bruges."

"Go back. I'll search the area."

"No." Adele straightened with a deep breath, focusing on a nearby window pane to calm the dizziness. "You won't know what to look for. I'm fine now. It just hit me by surprise. It's not as bad as before."

As they slipped quietly through the ivy-covered rows of gutted buildings, more waves of nausea washed over Adele. She took long wet breaths, willing herself to ignore her body and focus on the outside. Stone after stone underfoot. Noting each tree they passed. Every time she looked up, she saw the roof of the grand palace of Versailles that loomed over the squat buildings grow larger. She extended her mind into the putrid malaise that saturated the area, scouring for any sweet scents and clinging to faint hints of rhythm amidst the screaming cacophony.

Adele felt Gareth's worried gaze on her, even while he kept an eye on the skies for challenges. The wind shifted and she grew ill again, but not from the repulsive aura of twisted geomancy. Rather it was the sadly familiar stench of dead bodies.

They worked their way to the rear of the palace where formerly precise arrangements of arbors were wild tangles of brush. The decrepit gardens fell away and engineered terracing was now just a rolling natural landscape recaptured by the forest.

Adele stared up at the massive yellow stone edifice with row after row of high rectangular windows, most broken. Sections of the roof appeared to be caved in and the walls were strangled with vines. "Do you believe the queen when she tells you the Witchfinder isn't here?"

"I do."

"You trust both of them, don't you?"

"With my life. Those aren't the true Lothaire and Caterina you saw. Lothaire ran a fairly enlightened regime. *Enlightened* by vampire standards, in any case. Other clan lords took that to mean Lothaire was soft, which he was. But he was thoughtful too. He was never satisfied with cruelty as a belief system." Gareth grew quiet. "He has no idea what to do. Watching his son grow up under my brother's specter must be horrible for him."

In the past, Adele had only seen Gareth express such deep emotions about two others, his father and his old retainer, Baudoin. He was a singular person, preferring his own company, with the exception of Adele. However, she had watched him with Lothaire and saw the way he interacted with the king. It was unlike the way he had interacted with anyone else. Gareth immediately fell into a posture and language of easy familiarity that Adele had never seen before. Even with the tension of the situation, he and Lothaire acted like old friends. She had never seen Gareth with a *friend*. That strange, new Gareth was fascinating and attractive. She would have liked to have seen Gareth as he was in those days, exploring Paris with Lothaire. Watching the grim figure before her, it was almost impossible to imagine him as an adventurous young man. She smirked cynically when she realized that he wouldn't have been a young *man*, and his adventures would've included hunting humans for blood.

Adele put a comforting hand on his back. "I trust them too then. But perhaps we should still go in through the roof to be a little unexpected."

Without question, Gareth slipped off through the heavy brush. Adele followed, keeping low. They reached the wall that towered above them and he stooped slightly as a sign for her to wrap her arms over him. She shifted the pack on her back and took hold of his strong shoulders. He leapt high, seizing the stones and ivy with powerful fingers, and scrambled up the side of the building like a lizard with Adele clinging to him. He swung from window embrasure to ledge, pushing upward, and kicked off a crumbling cornice. He snatched the low railing at the eaves and vaulted over it onto the flat grey roof. They crouched silently, waiting and searching.

"Can you smell anything?" Adele whispered.

"Just death. Again. We need to get under cover. I can see vampires in the distance, so they could see us." Gareth gave Adele a sign to proceed with great caution on the creaking rooftop and slipped along the eaves until he reached a jagged hole in the slate. He knelt by the edge and quickly inspected the interior. He snatched Adele around the waist and dropped to the floor far below. All around them the flaking remnants of paintings covered the walls, showing only staring eyes or random lacy sleeves. Gold leaf peeled from ceilings to fall unheeded with dead leaves on the filthy floor.

They moved cautiously through a series of chambers. Every room was a forgotten remnant of the old world, the failed hubris of the human north. They found no sign of life, only the occasional skeletons of long-dead vampire meals.

Adele and Gareth came to a small room that joined the north wing with the main part of the old chateau. Pausing to listen and smell, Gareth glanced ahead. Adele felt a rush of nausea. She put a hand on Gareth's shoulder to stop him moving forward until it passed as quickly as it had come. At her nod, they started off again.

Before them a vast gallery stretched the length of the main chateau. Rows of windows looked out over the feral gardens. The space glittered in the late-day sun because of the remnants of endless mirrors. Light reflected off the walls and from shards swept into piles on the floor. The clearing of the glass here was the first sign of human attention to order.

Something sparkled oddly and caught Adele's eye. It wasn't a sliver of mirror. It was a crystal lying on the floor in the center of the long gallery. Near it was another, and another. Numerous crystals were scattered throughout the mirrored corridor. No, not scattered. They were placed in a very specific pattern. It was a geomantic arrangement marking a complicated quincunx design on the floor.

Adele ventured out into the great hall of mirrors. Gareth followed, tense to their surroundings. She studied the pattern of crystals. This sort of applied geomancy wasn't her strong suit. Even so, she could sense the crystals before her were burned out of their power. Likely all their unique facets were shattered or melted. When she went to step inside the quincunx, Gareth grabbed her.

"It's fine," she said. "These stones are spent. They're harmless, like an exploded bomb."

Adele moved inside the geometry of crystals, but she felt nothing. She gazed out through a partially broken glass door that overlooked the vast piazza below. A new wave of nausea washed over her. An expansive gravel yard stretched out below her. Dark shapes dotted the pale stones, lying around stagnant pools.

Dead bodies. Hundreds of cadavers littered the grounds near the palace and many more were barely visible farther out, collapsed amidst the brush of the overgrown gardens. They all lay in different positions, as if they had simply fallen dead while standing in formation. Most were partially decayed from exposure. Some had been half-eaten by predators, and there were marks in the gravel where some bodies had been dragged off by dogs or wolves.

Adele saw more crystals down among the dead. She couldn't see the full extent of their placement because of distance, failing sunlight, and the overgrowth. However, from what she could view, she knew those crystals were organized in the same geometric patterns as the ones in the gallery where she stood. She knelt and picked up one of the crystals on the floor. Its empty touch chilled her, but she could acquire enough of a sense to know it was local. It was a stone from here in Paris, from virtually under their feet. She tested the others and found the same thing. She realized she had been crouching in the center of the quincunx for some time when she looked up to see Gareth staring anxiously at her. She tossed the sad cold crystal down, and then swept the pattern out of existence with her arm.

"He murdered all of them." Her voice was rough with frustration and rage. "All those people out there."

"How?"

"He seems to be drawing on the power of the rifts with his crystal arrangements." Adele pointed to the field of the dead on the grounds of Versailles. "And then he is replicating this same pattern out there, on a larger scale."

"But those are humans."

"I know. He is doing the same thing to humans that I did to vampires."

"How is that possible? Is that something you could do?"

"No," Adele replied bitterly. "I have no idea how he's doing it. Damn it. I can't believe he is self-taught. He knows more about geomancy than I do, and I went to school for ages."

Gareth kicked a crystal aside and pulled Adele to her feet. "I smell traces of him. This way." He led them out of the mirror gallery toward the front of the chateau. In these chambers they found evidence of cooking, and there were clothes strewn about.

Gareth put objects to his nose and smelled deeply. He tasted the handles of spoons and pencils that he found scattered about. "It's been a week or so since he's been here."

They stepped into a small room off the bedchamber and Adele's eyes immediately went to a table covered in crystals. Some of them had been smashed by a hammer and chisel that sat nearby. A strong hand lens rested on the table too.

She took one crystal in her hand and it pulsed with life. Even the revolting pall over the area couldn't completely block her out from the stone's essence. She tasted bright sun and a hint of lemon. She squeezed that crystal in fury. "Alexandria. This stone is from *home*. Why would he have it?"

Adele put a trembling finger into the coarse dust of one of the shattered crystals. This stone was as dead as those in the mirror gallery. Only the faintest hint of place slipped across her tongue.

"Bruges." Adele brushed the cold dust from her hands. "This crystal is from Bruges where that death camp was located."

She turned away from the table and noticed a stack of large, thick paper lying on the floor. When she approached, she saw it wasn't paper; it was canvas. Paintings. Portraits of kings and queens. Still lifes of fruit and wild game. Battle scenes. Most of them were heavy oils painted hundreds of years ago, long before the Great Killing. The paints were faded and the canvases ill-used from age and lack of care. They all had been cut or torn from frames and now lay on the floor of the Witchfinder's room. How odd that he had a penchant for old art.

Adele sorted through the paintings. Then she noticed something odd. There were marks on the backs of each canvas. They were strangely familiar lines and symbols, seemingly chaotic and random.

"Damn!" Adele shouted with recognition, as she flipped over canvas after canvas. "No. No."

"What's wrong?"

"Look at this." She held up one of the canvases so he could see the scribbles on the back.

"What is it?"

"Ley lines. The Witchfinder is mapping the lines." Adele continued to shift the thick sheets. "Look at these labels. Carnac, in Normandy. Incredible. I've never seen the rifts so thick. And here's what looks to be a complete map of Britain. And here's Paris and southern France." She went rigid with shock and gripped one of the canvases so tight it tore under her fingers. "Alexandria."

"Are they accurate?"

Adele made a quick study of the Alexandria map, trying to orient her knowledge with the peculiar style the Witchfinder used. "I think so. It's hard to read this, but I think he has the gist of it. I can't believe it."

"What does that mean?" Gareth joined her to look at the canvas.

Adele caught a glimpse of the book he was holding. "Where did you get that?"

He pointed to a small shelf in the corner, where three old tomes rested. He held it out to her. It was well-worn and roughly used. The spine read *On Concentrative Reflexes*.

"It's a seminal geomancy treatise by the great scholar al-Khuri. It's very rare. I've never seen one; only read excerpts." Adele opened the volume. "Oh God!"

"What?"

She placed a finger on a bookplate pasted on the inside cover. "This book belonged to Sir Godfrey Randolph."

"The surgeon?"

"Yes. The very one who saved my life when I was stabbed in Alexandria." She opened the three other books and found the same plates inside them. "He also has one of the greatest libraries of the esoteric in the known world. He was a close ally of Mamoru's, until Mamoru went insane."

"How did his book get to vampire Paris? Is Sir Godfrey a traitor?"

"No, I can't imagine. Sir Godfrey told me that a number of his books had disappeared from his home in Giza over the last few years. We know his brother, Lord Aden, collaborated with your brother, Cesare. I'll bet Lord Aden stole the books and sent them to Cesare to deliver to the Witchfinder. Sir Godfrey had a complete set of Mamoru's ley line maps; it's possible Aden copied those as well." Adele sighed and flipped through the tome. She drew in a sharp breath.

Gareth looked at her expectantly.

"Look at these notes in the margins," Adele said. "I assume they're written by the Witchfinder, and it looks as if he had conversations with another man, a skilled geomancer."

"So he did have a teacher. His skill isn't so mysterious now."

"Perhaps. His teacher was Selkirk."

Gareth gaped in alarm. "Are you sure?"

"Yes. The Witchfinder writes here in glowing terms about *Doctor* Selkirk and his extensive knowledge of geomancy. And how much he learned from him." Adele shut the book with a cloud of dust. "First, we're going to burn all these charts. Then it's time to go home and have a chat with *Doctor* Selkirk. He should be easy to find. He's been in prison in Alexandria since he tried to kill me."

CHAPTER 14

The warmth was heavenly. The hazy sun rejuvenated Adele even though it was late winter and hardly the balmiest day in Alexandria. The thick salty mist rolled into Victoria Palace, where she stood on a balcony overlooking the choppy Mediterranean. If only it had been summer and she could have ventured into the desert to bake in the shimmering sun. Only then Adele realized how the damp of Britain kept her from healing as much as she should.

Gareth's young enthusiasts in Paris hadn't been happy with his abrupt departure, but Kasteel believed Gareth would return. Adele wondered if he would. She believed that the potential those young vampires offered could not be forsaken. Gareth had seemed less enamored of their importance in the grand scheme of history.

However, it was not an issue they could pursue at the moment. It was the Witchfinder who had to be pursued. He had the power to blunt Adele's geomancy, but more, he could kill in ways that Adele couldn't understand. So she and Gareth had rushed back to the coast, signaled the *Edinburgh*, and set sail for Equatoria.

There was a knock on the door to Adele's private office. She felt a surge of girlish excitement and grinned like a fool as she dropped her mother's notebook onto her desk and waited for the door to open. Simon stood with his own giant grin on his incredibly grown-up face, but before he even shouted her name, the lad froze. His features melted into disbelief. General Anhalt stood behind Simon, but Adele was locked on her brother's surprising reaction.

"What's wrong, Simon?" Adele forced a chuckle and inspected her dress as a nervous joke. "Am I so far out of fashion already?"

The boy didn't try to cover his distress. "You're so old. You could be thirty."

"Oh." She exhaled in relief. Simon hadn't seen her since the event in Edinburgh last year. She came to the door and embraced him. "Well, look at you. You're like a young man now. I see father in you." She reached out one hand toward the hallway. "Dear General Anhalt. I'm so glad to see you again."

The general kissed her hand. "Forgive me, Your Majesty. I did try to prepare him."

"Yes, my appearance has changed a bit." She tightened her arms around her brother, realizing that he wasn't hugging her back.

"A bit? You've aged a decade in a year!" Simon pushed back from Adele with a gasp of terror. "Oh no! Is Greyfriar old too?"

"No. He's still delightfully youthful. You two can play together while I huddle beneath a shawl."

Simon exchanged a sour glance with the expressionless Anhalt. "Well, getting old hasn't made her *less* cranky."

"Prince Simon." Anhalt clapped a firm hand on the lad's shoulder. "I pray you control your hyperbole. Your sister is the empress and has the army under her command."

Adele inclined her head and tried to stare down imperiously at her sibling. "Listen to him."

Simon rolled his eyes and then regarded her a bit more softly. Grinning, he wrapped his arms around her and gave her the enthusiastic embrace she craved. "All right. I suppose it's not that noticeable. I *am* happy to see you. It's horribly dull when you are not here."

She relished the feel of his oddly strong arms around her neck. "Oh how I've missed you!"

"I've missed you too." He looked past her into the office with typical boyishness. "Where's Pet? Did he come back with you?"

"Thank you for putting me just before the cat at least." Adele drew her brother and General Anhalt inside. "He's around somewhere. I brought him to the palace, but after that he's on his own."

"Where's Greyfriar?"

"I don't know. I brought him to the palace too, but neither he nor the cat will abide a leash."

Simon laughed and pulled at his stiff uniform collar. He passed to the open French windows and drew in a deep breath even with the tinge of chemical haze and coal smoke. His gaze tracked an airship that was beating against the wind above the harbor. "I really am glad you're back because now that you're here, I can go off. General Anhalt said I could go to Britain."

"Did he indeed?" Adele looked sharply at Anhalt, who shook his head firmly.

"Yes." The boy turned inside. He settled in a chair and took pleasure in waving at the piles of files and folders on the desk. He noted with a sour look the stacks of peculiar notebooks and occult tomes stacked on top of the official documents. "The empire of paper is all yours now. Along with the votes and factories and favors and money and poetry."

Adele tapped one of the crystallography texts as she took a seat behind the desk. "Did you read the materials I suggested to you about geomancy?"

Simon's blank face showed that he had not. "Yes."

"That's why I found them still dusty on the shelf in the library? And did you meet with Sanah and Sir Godfrey while I was gone?"

"Yes." The prince bristled. "I have been pretty busy. Plus going to school. Plus training with the navy. Maybe you don't realize what responsibility means now. You're off with Greyfriar."

Silence sat thick in the room. Simon sulked at Adele across the stacks of books. He wasn't sorry; he wasn't prepared to take anything back. Ever the peacemaker, General Anhalt surveyed the glum boy, then offered a silent plea for Adele's understanding.

She sat back in her chair. "Simon, this past year has been difficult for you. I do appreciate your efforts more than I can say. I am enormously proud of what you've accomplished."

"Yeah?"

Adele felt her brother's frustration; she remembered the same emotions in herself. She worked her thumb anxiously across the blue crystal in her hand. "Yes. I'll tell you what, why don't we postpone our conference until tomorrow? We've obviously gotten off on the wrong foot today."

"Tomorrow I'll be training on HMS *Nur Jahan*."

"All right." She took a breath. "I'll have my staff contact your staff for your next available time before your departure for Europe."

Simon gave a sullen sneer until he processed what she had just said. "Wait. You mean I can go to Britain?"

"Yes, you may."

Simon's eruptive whoop of joy startled Adele. He rushed her and threw his arms around her in an exuberant display of delight. "I can't believe you said yes. I'm going to Britain."

"With an armed escort," she said. "A *large* armed escort."

"I don't care. Just so long as I can go. Deus vult! I have packing to do!" He kissed her wetly on the cheek and ran from the room. A second later he darted back in and delivered a well-practiced formal bow. His wide boisterous grin made it far less formal than was intended, and it made Adele laugh. Then he was out the door and racing down the hall toward his quarters.

Adele regarded General Anhalt, waiting for him to chide her. He was moving a chair into place.

"Just say it. I placated him." Adele sighed with self-criticism. "I've been looking forward to seeing Simon for months. I just didn't realize he resented me so much. I wish you had let me know."

"He doesn't resent you. Prince Simon is under enormous stress. May I speak plainly?"

"Always."

"He has worked very hard, very hard indeed, certainly since last summer when you sent me back from Britain to help him. He is energetic, but not well-focused."

"Like me."

"Like you were, but worse. Perhaps because he's unsure what his purpose is, short of pleasing you."

"He feels that he's the one actually ruling the empire, but I'm still the empress. He's doing the work and I get the bouquets."

"He doesn't begrudge you your position, but some discouragement is natural."

Adele gestured. "General, please sit down. It hurts *my* hip to see you standing."

Anhalt lowered himself into the padded chair. "Prince Simon doesn't want to be emperor. However, he doesn't want the work of one for no reason. He's young so he's easily bored and frequently annoyed."

"Like me."

"Like you were." Anhalt smiled. "The fact is, in many ways, he is an effective leader. He is very well-liked by the Council and by Commons."

"I'm not surprised. He's a likeable boy." Adele paused with a sad smile. She thought back to the cherubic little tornado of a boy whom she had bundled off to Katanga after spreading the rumor he had been killed by vampires. It was all part of her war strategy, and all so long ago. "He's not my little brother any longer. He's a young man."

Anhalt shifted uncomfortably in his seat. "He will always be your little brother. You are doing the right thing sending Prince Simon to Britain. He has earned it. And, quite frankly, it's not a bad idea to send him. It is an imperial province now. He handles himself quite well, and he is extremely affable with soldiers and politicians."

"He's only *unaffable* with me then?"

"You're his sister. He loves you and he worries about you, but he is jealous of the freedoms you take. Prince Simon is a young man and he wants a bit of adventure."

"That's entirely reasonable." Adele looked pleadingly at Anhalt. "I do want him to experience more of the world. It's good for the empire, and it's his right. But the idea of him in danger chills me."

"Time away from Alexandria would benefit His Highness. Here in the capital, he is naturally prone to fall in with the technocrats who surround him and who are not friends of the occult sciences. Prince Simon is torn between their views, views he was raised to believe, and his love for you." Anhalt hesitated, eyeing the blue crystal that Adele worked unconsciously between her fingers. "There has been much . . . talk."

"Then I was right to send you home to guide him."

The general pushed himself to his feet. He gave her an under-standing smile. "I will make the arrangements for his trip."

Adele nervously shifted books into new piles. "If one of our ironclads is available, he may take that. And he must stay inside it at all times."

"Majesty?"

Adele laughed quietly. "I'm only joking. Just keep him out of Scotland."

Anhalt looked curious at the command.

Adele continued, "You know damn well he'll try to sneak up there to see the mysterious Prince Gareth."

"Like you?"

"Don't be fresh. Just make sure the governor's staff in London keeps him away from anything to do with Gareth. He's not ready for every secret."

"Yes, ma'am. And thank you." Anhalt leaned on his walking stick. "And now that Your Majesty is officially in residence, I become your chief-of-staff. What are your plans?"

"This." She laid a hand on one of the piles of reports. "I have to digest all this information before speaking to Commons in a few days. Oh, and I'll want to speak to Selkirk."

General Anhalt reared back in surprise. "Selkirk? That would be most unwise. He attempted to murder you last year."

Adele tapped her pen against a pile of folders. "Oh, who hasn't tried to murder me? We'll arrange for proper security, but I want to see him."

"Of course, Your Majesty." Anhalt stared with a glint of wise suspi-cion. "Don't take this as an expression of less than my sheer delight that you have come home, but why have you come home? Simply to have a chat with an assassin?"

"No. There were a few interesting events in Britain and Europe that sent me here. I'd be happy to tell you about them." Adele smiled sheep-ishly. "But only if you promise not to be angry."

"Dear Lord." General Anhalt sank back into his seat with a deep breath. He took a firm grip on the arms of the chair. "In that case I may need a glass of brandy."

Adele crossed to the sideboard and poured a hefty glass. She handed it to the general and settled herself again behind her desk as he downed it in a single swallow, then stared evenly at her.

"Very well," Anhalt said. "You may carry on."

CHAPTER 15

Adele waited inside the Victoria Palace classroom where she had taken her lessons as a child, including many hours of instruction from Mamoru on geomancy and other forbidden, or at least frowned upon, subjects. She had prepared the room with books on geomancy and crystals scattered on tables, as well as recognizable paraphernalia for the testing of crystalline structures and the mapping of ley lines. Perhaps disguising the interrogation as something familiar would put Selkirk at ease and make him talkative. Four knocks on the door signaled that the time was here.

Adele made a quick adjustment to the equipment display and then went to sit in a hard chair in a bright corner, her usual spot for class. The door opened. General Anhalt glanced inside to make sure she was ready. Adele nodded.

The general entered along with Major Shirazi, followed by Selkirk. The geomancer had grown shockingly thin and pale. Adele remembered him as robust and tanned. His long flaxen hair was now unkempt and growing grey and wiry. His clothes were presentable but hardly palace style. He clutched his jacket together as he stared at Adele. Clearly he sensed his relative shabbiness, even though his eyes were hazy and unsure.

Greyfriar's commanding figure pressed in after Selkirk, and he had to nearly shove the hesitant prisoner deeper into the room. He closed the door as the Harmattan took up their places in the hall. With a hand on the pommel of his rapier, Greyfriar stood watch from the corner.

Anhalt gestured toward a padded chair opposite Adele. Selkirk shuffled across the floor. He glanced with confusion toward the crystals and books.

"Mr. Selkirk." Adele stood and, out of habit, extended her hand. The man just stared at it, so she lowered it. "Won't you have a seat?"

The door opened again and servants carried in trays of fruit and cheese with pots of tea and bottles of wine. They laid the food on a table and silently filed out. Adele went to pour tea, but Anhalt hobbled over and assumed the serving duties.

She begrudgingly surrendered the teapot to the general. "Tea, Mr. Selkirk? Or a glass of wine perhaps?"

Selkirk was focused completely on a stray thread hanging off the cuff of his jacket. Anhalt poured a cup of tea anyway and set it near him. The general gave Adele a disgusted glance, indicating Selkirk. She nodded him away.

Adele drew a yellow crystal from her pocket. It was a stone she had brought from London, specifically from the area around Bedlam in the southern part of the city. She took Selkirk by the arm, creating a ripple of tension in Greyfriar and Anhalt. It was difficult to pull the man's fingers away from the loose thread. Finally, she wrenched his hand toward her and placed the crystal between his thumb and forefinger, hoping he would take to it. He froze, not looking up. And then slowly his fingers rolled the crystal. His brow furrowed with attention.

Adele sat back casually and sipped her tea. "Do you know me, sir?"

He lifted his head, staring into the distance. She reached over and took the crystal away from him. He jerked with surprise at his empty hand.

"Do you know me?" Adele repeated clearly.

"No." Selkirk flexed his fingers. "But I met your daughter in London."

"My daughter?"

"Yes, ma'am. She was very pleasant. Even though I imagine she was frightened, she didn't show it." He bit his lip in concentration as he pulled at the thread on his cuff again. "My condolences."

"Condolences for what, Mr. Selkirk?"

"Her death, ma'am. I'm very sorry I killed her."

Adele glanced at Greyfriar, who rose slightly on the balls of his feet, ready to strike at the twitching man in the chair. She looked him back down and politely addressed Selkirk, "Why did you kill me . . . I mean, her?"

He breathed out through his nose. "Prince Cesare wanted her dead."

Adele sat back. "Do you know Prince Cesare is dead?"

Selkirk rubbed his eye with a bemused huff. "Good."

"Do you know that Mamoru is dead?"

"Good."

"The Witchfinder is alive."

Selkirk's eyes flicked to Adele, but he quickly recovered his bland demeanor. "Good."

Adele reached over to a small table and retrieved the copy of the al-Khuri book she had brought from Versailles. She held it out to Selkirk. He took it and read the spine. Then he set the book in his lap with a hand resting on the leather cover.

Adele pointed at the book. "Would you turn to page three hundred and twenty-four, please?"

Selkirk immediately opened the tome with mild interest and flipped the thick pages. He finally found the right place and lifted it toward Adele.

"Oh no," she said. "You look at it."

He glanced down at the section about energy conservation and crystalline geometry. The margins and blank spaces were filled with ragged scrawls.

"You'll note," Adele said, "several comments written there about *Doctor* Selkirk. Is that you?"

He smiled wistfully. "Yes. He always referred to me as *doctor*."

"The Witchfinder, you mean?"

"That was his favorite title. Silly." Selkirk pursed his lips and studied the notes with greater interest. "Although he found me out right enough."

"What was his real name?"

"Goronwy. Doctor or Professor or Reverend Goronwy, depending on his mood."

"Where was he from?"

"Wales." Selkirk paused uncomfortably. "Mamoru told us to avoid the locals while we were mapping ley lines, but I couldn't. It was so cold and horrible up there. Vampires everywhere." He looked up at Adele. "When I found a village where the creatures didn't go, I wanted to stay there. Just for a rest. Can you understand?"

Adele held his eyes with sympathy. "Tell me about Dr. Goronwy. Did you know him well?"

"Not really." Selkirk returned to leafing through the book, stopping and reading certain passages. "In Wales, we would discuss various topics. He was interested in my opinions on geomancy." He looked around the room, peering toward the filtered sunlight of the draped French windows. The vague shadows of soldiers on the balcony were visible. "I lived at his institute."

Adele glanced again at Greyfriar and mouthed *Bedlam*. Then to Selkirk, "Did you assist Dr. Goronwy mapping the lines?"

"I believe we did work on that. I had my maps of Britain, and some of the original set from Equatoria and Asia that Mamoru had made."

"I see." Adele produced the blue talisman she had taken off the vampire in London. "Is this one of the projects you two worked on?"

Selkirk eyed the crystal. "It looks like something he was toying with. Cesare wanted to protect his people from your daughter. Goronwy fashioned crystals that could negate her energy, technically diffuse it, I suppose. I must admit I never fully understood what he was doing, but it was simple for him."

"Why was Dr. Goronwy interested in the subject?"

Selkirk sighed patiently and shut the book. "Let me see if I can put it in simple terms. Your daughter was trying to kill vampires."

"Yes."

"Well, the primary patron for Dr. Goronwy's research at the time was Prince Cesare."

Adele waited.

Selkirk tilted his head condescendingly. "Prince Cesare is a vampire, you see. He wanted to find a way to stop your daughter from killing his people. We were close, successful on a small scale to blocking her geomancy with those crystals you have there. It wasn't enough for Prince

Cesare. Typical impatient patron. So I was assigned to just kill your daughter. Sometimes the simplest solution is the best."

Adele tried to tamp down her rising anger. She remembered that day she was surprised by Selkirk's blank face down in the family tomb. A hand lifted to her chest as if she could feel the pressure of his cold dagger sliding into her. Her legs had grown weak and she had fallen to the hard floor of the crypt. She could still remember the frantic, muffled cries of Greyfriar as all she could do was stare at the cold tomb of her father where she lay bleeding.

Selkirk continued as if giving a casual lecture. "What was actually more exciting than our work to stop your daughter was Dr. Goronwy's belief that her power could be reversed, or I should say, altered to work in an opposite direction."

Adele forced her attention back to the present. "What do you mean?"

"What she did, in effect, was to accelerate the energies of the Earth, which served to burn up the vampires." He leaned forward with excitement. "What Dr. Goronwy discovered, with my help, was that the process could work the other direction. The energy of living beings could be extracted. Geomancy could be used to kill anything. Or, in theory, everything."

"*Everything?*" Adele felt the blood seeping from her brain and extremities. The air suddenly turned very cold on this warm afternoon.

General Anhalt muttered, "Utter rubbish."

"Theoretically." Selkirk raised a finger to punctuate his word. "Of course, theoretically, you could also kill everything with poison gas. But practically speaking you can't manufacture enough gas, and it spreads and weakens. You see? It's possible to theorize anything, but in the real world, there are boundaries."

"So this application of geomancy to killing humans is limited, yes?"

"Of course." He was calm and reassuring. "It would be very difficult and require complicated crystal arrangements to draw and focus the rifts. Under normal circumstances, the geomancer's reach would be very limited. To achieve real value, we required an amplifier of sorts."

"Did you have one?"

"No. Such a thing only exists in legend."

"What *legend* are you referring to?"

Selkirk sat back, taking up his cup of tea now. He was settling into shop talk. "Years ago, when I was a student at Mamoru's academy on Java, there were a few teachers who would talk about concepts and applications of the science similar to those that interested Dr. Goronwy. Of course they only did it when Mamoru was far away; he had no patience for anything that didn't apply to his mission of removing vampires from the Earth. He had committed himself to his search for the perfect tool in human form. I think it had to do with his late wife and her view of geomancy, which had shaped his own. However, I was very interested and did all I could to learn about those fringe studies. In any case, these instructors used to talk about a particular artifact, quietly and without much seriousness. But I started to wonder. When I finished my lessons, I conducted my mapping practicum in the Himalayas." He stopped as if that explained everything.

"Why the Himalayas?" Adele poured another cup of tea, hoping that her hands didn't jangle the spoon against the cup.

"That's where the Tear of Death was said to be."

"The Tear of Death?"

"Yes, it took years of following clues, but I finally worked my way to the northern face of the Himalayas, where I visited a village that claimed knowledge of the actual artifact. The elders said it was locked away in an ancient monastery in the mountains above them. There was no way for me to climb up there, so I never tested their theory. I had to return to Java, but hopefully I'll be able to return at some point and search for the Tear. I wanted to find it and bring it to Mamoru in case your daughter's discipleship didn't work out."

Adele was fascinated and frightened by his calm professionalism, but confused by his words. She had no idea what he was talking about. She wondered if he had strayed off into lunacy. "What exactly is the Tear of Death?"

Selkirk gave another condescending smile, warming up to his role as expert among the ignorant. "The easiest way to explain it is that it's a *catalyst* of some sort. That's what your daughter was, which is why Mamoru wanted her. But supposedly, with the Tear of Death, a normal geomancer can walk in all the world's rifts at once, from anywhere on Earth. He could do extraordinary good, or terrible evil. But that's not for scientists to decide."

Adele groaned softly. Was that all she had been to Mamoru? An instrument of death? Was that all she was to the world now? She shoved her despair aside. She would not show emotion in front of this man. Her face fell into a numb stiffness. She held up the blue stone in her trembling hand. "Is this Tear some sort of crystal?"

"I have no idea, actually. No one knows for sure. There are many stories. A crystal. A statue. A weapon. A book. No one alive has ever seen it. There are no drawings. There are no written records of it."

"Do you believe Dr. Goronwy would have an interest in this relic?"

"I can't see why. Dr. Goronwy has excellent theoretical groundings, mind you, but his patrons are driven by results, not theory. And the only practical use of the Tear is to spark a catastrophic event that would kill millions." Selkirk took a civilized sip of tea and patted the cover of the book.

Adele leaned forward, gripping the crystal ever harder. "And you don't think his *patrons* would want that to win the war?"

"Oh. You're right." He settled back with a look of bemused surprise. "I suppose they might at that."

"If I showed you a map of the Himalayas, could you locate this village where they told you about the Tear of Death?"

"Certainly. I recall it very well."

Adele's blood chilled as she nodded to her guards. "Well, thank you for your assistance, Mr. Selkirk. I found our talk quite informative."

Selkirk registered surprise that shifted to disappointment that the conversation had come to a conclusion, but he covered himself well, rising to his feet and setting the cup and saucer down. "Of course. Thank you for the tea. Your generosity in light of certain matters is remarkable."

Under Major Shirazi's dark stare, Selkirk was escorted to the door, where he paused. "I just want to say, ma'am, that you understand that it's better that your daughter was killed, don't you?"

"How so?" Adele struggled to retain a conversational tone.

"What she was doing was extremely damaging to the Earth. She may not have known it. Perhaps neither did her teacher, but Goronwy knew. It was clear enough." He bowed to her in sympathy and proceeded out of the room with his guards.

Adele sat quietly.

Anhalt clasped his hands behind his back. "Your Majesty, I'm certainly no expert in geomancy. So this Witchfinder found a way to negate your abilities on some level, to send vampires safely into Britain. You have witnessed that; you know it to be true. But this next step, to believe that he can adapt that power into a way to kill every human on Earth? You don't give credit to what that man says, do you? Selkirk is utterly insane."

"Caterina said the Witchfinder was flying far to the east." Adele slowly opened her clenched fingers. The blue crystal lay there unaffected. Any other stone would have melted to silvery liquid under the pressure of her power. "Have *Edinburgh* prepared for a long journey."

CHAPTER 16

Simon stood across the room from a trunk and threw wadded up clothes into it, or at least at it. Shirts, pants, and underwear were scattered in piles around the foot locker and draped over its rim. He wore a once-smart navel uniform, now unbuttoned and wrinkled. A tossed shirt made it into the trunk, and the boy whooped in triumph. As he spun around with joy, he saw Greyfriar in the doorway. Simon's face lit with excitement, but then froze in dread.

He immediately understood the reason for Greyfriar's visit. "She can't. She can't!"

"Simon, I—"

The prince pointed at the disaster area around the foot locker. "I'm already packed. I'm leaving on *Saladin* tomorrow."

"I'm sorry."

"I knew it." Simon slumped. "I knew she'd never let me go." He kicked the trunk. "So where are you two off to now?"

"The Himalayas."

The boy gave a snuffling laugh to suppress a sob. He clenched his mouth tight.

"It can't be avoided, Simon. It's very important."

"It's always *very* important. And she's always the only one who can go."

"That's actually true this time. Adele has certain unique skills that—"

"Do you really believe that geomancy nonsense? Or do you just go along with it because you love her?"

Greyfriar grew stern. "You're right, I do love her. And it isn't nonsense."

Simon held out his hands in frustration. "Let's be serious. There can't be some magic out there that killed every vampire in Britain."

"Then what do you believe happened to them, Your Highness?"

"General Anhalt destroyed the clan chiefs when he crashed the *Bolivar* into Buckingham Palace. With their leaders dead, the rabble fled to the Continent." Simon sounded as if he was spouting rhetoric he had heard endlessly around Alexandria. He sighed and buttoned his tunic. "Vampires are animals. Once you spook them, get them on the run, they can't stop running. You should know that. It's not magic. It's war."

Greyfriar stepped into the room. "There were clan lords in Britain who weren't killed by *Bolivar*. Why would all the vampires flee the island rather than fight?"

"Disease." Simon pulled rumpled clothes out of the trunk. "Most of the members of the Imperial Academy believe the vampires are suffering from some sort of plague. Except for Sir Godfrey Randolph, of course. He talks about geomancy all the time, but he's always been a little odd, and he's the richest man in the empire so he can say what he likes. Any real scholar thinks we'll soon see the vampires dying off in droves and abandoning the cities."

"So you don't believe in geomancy?" Greyfriar studied the suddenly methodical movements of the prince as the boy folded his clothes and set them in orderly piles.

"Nobody does. Everyone laughs at it. Ley lines. Earth energy. It's ridiculous." Simon paused with a pair of striped trousers in his hands and stared off into the distance. His expression actually turned to worry. "She's going to go too far."

"What do you mean?"

"Adele was never a favorite of the old families, but now they openly talk against her. All this magic. These stupid stories about her waving her magic wand and vampires bursting into flame. She was held prisoner by the British clan, and now she believes she destroyed them? That's convenient." Simon shook his head, unable to say what he thought, and slammed the lid of the empty trunk. "She should just stop talking about it. She doesn't know how it is here. I do."

Greyfriar could hear the conflict in the boy's voice. He sat on the arm of a sofa. "She seems popular still."

"Oh, she is. The common people love her."

"What of the army?"

Simon put a thoughtful finger to his chin, weighing his answer, considering his position like an adult rather than a child. "Her support is still strong in the ranks. Some of the older High Command were never fond of her, but they keep their mouths shut generally."

"Because she's winning the war?"

Simon nodded. "Victory counts. They're willing to overlook her peculiarities and her allies as long as we're winning."

"Her allies? You mean me?"

"No." Simon laughed. "Everyone loves you. Everyone. I mean the vampire prince in Scotland."

Greyfriar paused in confusion, then said, "Oh, yes. Gareth."

"Yes. Him. Have you met him?"

"I have."

Simon saw himself reflected in the lenses of Greyfriar's glasses. "What do you think of him?"

"Not much."

"Traitors of any kind are disgusting, even if they're useful. Some people say he might be controlling Adele, that he's been controlling her since she was his prisoner. They say he was one of the bloodiest leaders of the Great Killing, and now he's using her to take power among his own kind."

"No. He's a beaten man."

"Man?" Simon's voice cracked with surprise.

"Vampire."

"Did he truly turn on his own kind?"

"He did."

"But why? If he's nothing but our prisoner now, what did it gain him?"

Greyfriar felt a coldness seep through him. He was suddenly aware of the scarf covering his face and the slight deflection of light through his glasses. "I don't know."

Simon sat down at his desk and placed a hand on a stack of folders. "What has he gained other than a castle in Scotland, which he had anyway? Is he the last of his line?"

"Yes. His clan is no more. Gareth is alone."

"Good," Simon snarled, but then glanced at Greyfriar. "Did vampires kill your family? Is that why you're the Greyfriar?"

"Nothing quite so heartbreaking and romantic, I'm afraid."

The young prince stared at the swordsman. "Then why did you become the Greyfriar? I mean, you were someone before this. Why did you stop being him and become you?"

"I'm sorry, Simon." Greyfriar unconsciously tightened the scarf around his face. "I can't tell you."

"You've told Adele."

"No, I haven't."

"Your family knows at least, right?"

"I have no family left alive."

"Oh, I'm sorry." Simon leaned forward as if in commiseration, as an adult would share a moment, but sounding uncertain and young. "Do you miss them?"

"I find that, with time, I miss my father a great deal."

"Me too. I wish mine was still here." The young prince tapped his fingers on the folders. He stared at them for a long moment, sliding them around to see the labels on each, from top to bottom of the pile. "When are you leaving for the Himalayas?"

"Tomorrow morning, if possible. Adele wanted to come tell you, but I asked her if I could instead. I've seen so little of you since we came to Alexandria."

"Thank you. What about General Anhalt?"

"He requested to come along. He does speak the local languages. But there are other available translators, and Adele is concerned about his health. She is more disposed to leave him here to help you."

"No!" Simon objected. "You have to take him. Adele tries to protect others too much. He needs to go."

"But there are times he can barely walk without a cane. Where we're going, that's very dangerous."

"It doesn't matter! He needs to go. Trust me. He would rather die in service than sit behind a desk of papers. Please. Convince Adele to take him. I have plenty of advisors here. But General Anhalt has only one purpose—to protect Adele. You understand that, don't you?"

Greyfriar nodded after a moment. "I do. I will speak with her. I would welcome General Anhalt at my side under any circumstances. One day, I hope you and I will share an adventure or two."

Simon offered an attempted smile. "You'll watch out for her, won't you?"

Greyfriar replied, "Of all people, Adele hardly needs anyone watching over her."

Simon put his foot up on the desk and gazed out a window to the harbor. He took a deep wistful breath. "I'm worried about her. So take care of her. I don't want to be emperor."

"Have no fear." The swordsman rose and reached out to the boy. "You're a good man."

"Thank you." Simon shook the gloved hand. "So are you."

Greyfriar didn't reply.

CHAPTER 17

HMS *Edinburgh* broke through the clouds into a dome of blue sky, the world below lost in a white fog. The early streaks of sunrise smudged the horizon like saffron paint over rice paper. The snow-capped tops of the Himalayas floated around them like icebergs on a misty sea. High winds blew plumes of snow off craggy surfaces flaring behind the monoliths like streams of white ribbons.

The scenery dwarfed the airship. It was a medium-sized ship, considered a brig because she sported only six masts. The sun glinted off her aluminum cage surrounding the dirigible from which the wooden hull was suspended. The masts extended from the dirigible, two along the top and two laterally from each side. A miraculously complex system of cables and shrouds connected the deck and the masts and the yards, and these were currently crowded with men taking in sail.

Greyfriar marveled at the magnificence of the panorama; it was so different than anything he had seen, stark and frigid. In all his travels, he had never flown so high. Ice crusted the handrail where he stood. Crewmen hammered at the frozen rigging to keep it clear.

Adele shivered beside Greyfriar, wrapped in heavy wool and thick furs, her face barely visible. Even the fierce winds that swept across the swaying ship would not deter her from such an impressive sight. On the icy deck stood her stoic Harmattan, pillars of red serge and steel undaunted by the vicious conditions.

Anhalt limped carefully across the frosted quarterdeck, leaning on his cane, to join them at the rail. The man's face was grey under his fur-lined hood, and his breathing was even more labored than Adele's. They both relied on breathers to ease their straining lungs in the oxygen-deprived air. The device was fixed over the nose and mouth, and a small brass canister nestled under the chin. Most of the crew carried them, particularly the topmen, who climbed the icy shrouds and lines overhead. Originally they were for use on the new higher flying ironclad steamnaughts, but Anhalt wisely made sure the *Edinburgh* was equipped with them in advance of this perilous journey.

Adele carried her camera on a strap around her neck, but found its limited scope ill-suited to capture the incredible majesty of the mountains under them. The lens was icing up too, making her fearful that it would shatter with no replacement. She raised it one last time and snapped a photograph of the ship's officers huddled on the wind-ripped quarterdeck.

Captain Hariri stood at the icy binnacle, where pneumatic tubes and speaking horns led to all parts of the ship, including the tops and the chemical deck below. He shouted into a speaking tube and ordered buoyant gas pumped into the dirigible at a rate that would be dangerous closer to the surface. The diminished air pressure at this altitude allowed him to overinflate, to drive the airship up into the thin atmosphere.

Fortunately, the *Edinburgh* only needed to stay this high long enough to traverse the first impenetrable range of the Himalayas. Hariri consulted an old map of the region; it was not a navigation chart, but it was the best he had. He watched the sails overhead as they grew stiff with ice and the brig sank back into the clouds. He could pour no more gas into the dirigible, even flying this high, without guaranteeing an explosion.

Mountain peaks loomed on every quarter. The clouds rose past them to form their ceiling. They were in a high mountain valley. Rocky cliffs broke over the highlands like cresting waves and in their shadow stretched deep narrow river gorges. The land far below was frozen under a thin blanket of snow. Crystal lakes glistened, fed by glacial streams with icy rivers that stretched like arms.

Adele exclaimed, "Such majesty. I've never seen . . . its like." Her words came in ragged gasps through the filter in the breather facemask.

Greyfriar pointed out the distant tiny shapes of goats perched precariously on the sides of a treacherous slope.

General Anhalt gazed about in awe, but labored for breath. "It's said that . . . gods live . . . in these mountains, bringing well-being . . . and prosperity. According . . . to the amount . . . of veneration. I suppose."

"I'm praying . . . very hard, trust me," Adele told him.

A down draft battered the *Edinburgh*, and everyone at the rail staggered as the ship dropped sickeningly. Greyfriar steadied Adele and grabbed Anhalt, who had lost his footing. If it weren't for the swordsman's steel grip, the old soldier would have sprawled hard to the deck. A mountain reared up beside them.

"Hold on!" shouted Captain Hariri.

The long masts extending from the dirigible overhead scraped against a cliff. Snow and rocks tumbled and the masts creaked. Yardarms snapped and sails shredded. Ice shattered off the rigging and pelted the deck in a shower of frozen knives. Greyfriar flung his cloak over Adele. Most of the glittering shrapnel bounced off harmlessly, crackling against the deck, but a few daggers struck crewman.

The ship swung wildly and bounced back into the vast chasm between the mountains. Orders were shouted and signal flags dispatched. Heavy thrashing sails were slowly brought under control and hauled back, lashed into place.

Adele kept her face calm, but she watched Captain Hariri closely as officers came and went with reports. Eyes constantly went upward. Finally, the captain stepped over to Adele at the rail and gave her a quick salute.

"Damage is minimal, Your Majesty. We should be able to continue. We can affect repairs when we put down."

Anhalt held the rail, bracing himself against more untimely jolts. "I survived two air crashes only to be nearly killed colliding with Mount Everest."

Hariri smiled at his old friend. "Then you will be happy to know that's not Everest. That is."

He pointed to a mammoth mountain off their port side. Its immensity shamed all others as it jutted up into the clouds. Necks ached as their gaze followed sheer rock and snow up into the swirling mist.

The *Edinburgh* steadied under their feet as the winds went from gale force to mere occasional gusts. Still it remained a bumpy ride, with the vessel shuddering against the mountains' breath. Every inch of her creaked under the strain.

Adele found the air a little easier to breathe. She reached into her pocket and removed a sheet of heavy paper. Unfolding it, she revealed a strange arrangement of lines, some intersecting on dots of varying size, some running off into lonely space.

Hariri leaned next to her, staring at the peculiar chart. "How much longer until we reach the village do you reckon, Your Majesty?"

"The sooner the better," muttered Anhalt to Greyfriar.

"It's hard to say." Adele ran her fingers along several of the lines. She tapped the chart. "I think we're here. We're close."

"Ah. I thought as much." Hariri rolled his eyes sarcastically. "Forgive me, but I can't make heads nor tails of your . . . map."

"It's geomancy. These are ley lines and those dots are nodes where the rifts come together. This chart was made by Selkirk himself when he traveled in this region years ago."

"Yes, you explained it to me before, but I must just trust you to direct the ship while I do my best to keep it from crashing into a mountain."

Anhalt snorted and Hariri gave him a sharp glance. Adele put a finger to her lips thoughtfully. "All right. It should be . . ." She pointed a few degrees right of the ship's bow. "That way."

"That way." Hariri nodded with a blank face. "If that's what we are resorting to, very well. *That way*, it is. If we may trust the directions given to you by your lunatic, I'm sure we will be there soon."

The ship turned two points to starboard. Adele folded her map and shoved it in her pocket. A man in the tops shouted down through a megaphone and signaled to starboard. Adele went back to the rail and looked over to see a fairly flat patch of land, dusted with snow. Near it was a small stone village surrounded by a meager wall, a speck of life in the wide desolation.

Adele turned around and grinned at Captain Hariri. The captain returned a gesture with his hand across his forehead, lips, and heart. He bowed to her.

"The plateau seems very small," Greyfriar said. It was perhaps only the size of several small farm plots. However, buoyant gases were already venting and sails furled. The ship dropped. Soon, her hull scraped along the snow, sending up a great wake of white. Field anchors dropped overboard to gouge the frozen land and slow the ship, but still, the *Edinburgh* crept forward toward the edge of the plateau. Mooring lines were tossed over the rails and scores of men went over too, sliding down the lines to hit the ground running. They seized the flopping cables in groups and dug in their feet with groans and curses at the ship and each other. Between the bite of the spiked anchors and the straining, muscled backs of the mooring gangs, the ship finally lurched to a full stop.

Adele took Anhalt's guiding hand and descended the gangplank after it slammed noisily to the ground. Greyfriar could tell it was she who was keeping Anhalt steady instead. They passed among the men who worked furiously to stabilize the *Edinburgh* in the winds that swept across it, pounding thick posts into the icy ground and lashing her down.

The snow was so dry it swirled about in sparkling granules with the least disturbance of boots. The air was dry too, and the cold sun broke through the cloud layer to coat the expanse with rich sunshine.

Lifting a hand to block the glare, Adele stared at the village in the distance. "I hope that's the right one."

This was the first real settlement they had seen in hundreds, perhaps thousands, of miles of endless mountains. They heard dogs barking. The village itself had nothing particularly striking about it. The buildings were smeared with mud and grime. There were small structures built against many house walls, which Anhalt explained were sanctuaries dedicated to local divinities. Lines were stretched between all the buildings and draped with colorful strips of cloth, prayer flags that sent supplications heavenward with each flutter of wind. Bright material of crimson and yellow streamed from houses.

A few people appeared at the low stone wall around the village, peering at the approaching strangers and craning their necks to see the airship in the distance. Greyfriar wondered if these people had had any contact with outsiders before. While most of the villagers hovered by an open gate, five men marched out toward Adele's small group of Greyfriar, Anhalt, Major Shirazi, and two Harmattan. These greeters appeared to be elders. They wore thick sheepskin coats and fur-topped boots. Greyfriar didn't fail to notice some of the villagers near the gate carried muskets. Antiquated guns, but he would think still effective. He could hear snatches of their language as those at the gate chattered excitedly among themselves.

Anhalt stopped when the elders were a few yards away. He bowed and said, "We seek shelter." He spoke Hindi, hoping that the trade language still found purchase this far in the mountains.

The elders replied back in kind. "You are welcome to the warmth of our fires."

Anhalt bowed to them again. He informed Adele of their welcome and then introduced the party as an expedition from Equatorian territory in India. He purposefully left out Adele's title. By the lack of response to even the name *Greyfriar*, it could be assumed the hero's exploits had not traveled this far.

The chief elder followed suit with introductions, calling himself Gyalo. He then waved the outsiders to follow him back to town. They were soon wading through curious crowds that lined the narrow streets and followed the foreigners, laughing, whispering, and gaping at them. The men almost all wore fur-lined hats and long, heavy coats. Full-cheeked women stood behind them. The stone houses were clustered together into blocks.

Gyalo led them to a building on the far side of the village where they finally left the bustle of curious onlookers behind. The interior was dark and smelled overpoweringly of something that Greyfriar couldn't identify. Despite the suddenly rancid stench, everyone kept their expressions neutral and pleasant.

Adele breathed out a sigh of relief as they entered a large room with a small fire burning at the center. Compared to the frigid outside, this place almost felt warm. She slipped back her hood and loosened a button on her coat. The floor was dirt and the walls, blackened by the smoke, were covered with intricate paintings of landscapes and gods. Gyalo invited everyone to sit on wooden frames covered with a cushion or two.

A woman, most likely Gyalo's wife or daughter, with her hair done in multiple tight braids, bustled about the fire and soon was dispensing some sort of hot liquid that Anhalt informed them was *po-cha*, or yak-butter tea. Greyfriar easily identified it as the source of the rank smell. Still, the thick tea seemed to be traditional and expected, so they all took a sip. From Adele's pinched face, it appeared to be an acquired taste. To Greyfriar, it tasted like any human food or drink. Bland. General Anhalt drank it almost eagerly, obviously familiar with the beverage.

Once the tea was finished, Anhalt conversed with Gyalo for a few minutes. He then leaned over and informed Adele that the elders were happy to have visitors. They took it as a good omen because they were preparing to celebrate a festival and would like the foreigners to participate.

"Festival?" Adele asked. "That sounds nice. I don't know that we have time to enjoy it. Could you ask him about the monastery? We need to know if we're in the village Selkirk talked about."

Anhalt repeated Adele's questions back to the elder. The leathery face hardened with suspicion. He spoke harsh words to Anhalt. Major Shirazi slid his hand toward his sidearm, but Adele kept her polite face directed at Gyalo.

Greyfriar had already begun to grasp elements of the language, and he could tell that Anhalt's calm reply offered great deference to the elder. In the face of the general's respect, Gyalo seemed embarrassed by his outburst. He continued in a more pleasant tone. Greyfriar could sense that Anhalt was drawing the village elder out with questions and amazed reactions, creating a bond of respect with Gyalo. He couldn't understand exactly what the two were discussing, so he settled back to wait patiently for the translation.

Finally the general nodded to Gyalo, then said to Adele, "Well, this is the right village."

Adele frowned at Anhalt's curious expression. "Is there something else, General?"

"Perhaps." Anhalt's lips held an odd bemused look. "He did inform me that the monastery is actually a fortress of demons. They are apparently very dangerous and will devour any human without provocation because they protect an ancient power. Gyalo considers us very foolhardy for seeking them out."

"Foolhardy?" Greyfriar intoned drily. "Us?"

"We appreciate his concern," Adele said with a cool glance at Greyfriar but had excitement in her voice at the mention of an ancient power, "but will he give us specific directions to the demon fortress?"

"He will do better than that," Anhalt replied, his expression turning serious once more. "He will show us the Demon King."

CHAPTER 18

The eager group of Adele, Greyfriar, Anhalt, and Shirazi trailed Gyalo through the village. All attempts to discuss the monastery had been rebuffed by Gyalo and the other elders. They didn't deny it existed; they simply had no interest in talking about it further. The festival however was another matter. Preparations were already stirring the whole village into a frenzy of excited activity. The elder spoke over his shoulder to the foreigners, explaining everything to Anhalt, who translated even as Gyalo continued to talk.

"The festival will begin in earnest tomorrow and will culminate in a ceremony at sunrise two days hence where they will execute their most dreaded enemy. The Demon King."

Gyalo led the outsiders to a stone hut in a rough courtyard. The windows had been mortared up, and the only entrance was a thick wooden door flanked by two formidable guards. He nodded imperiously to the sentries and swept inside with the foreigners on his heels.

The darkness inside made everyone falter a moment, except Greyfriar. He scanned the small entry room while Gyalo lit yak-butter lamps and led the way through an open doorway. The soft lamp glow fell on a hunched, naked figure bound with thick rope and by chains whose links were interwoven with prayer scarves. The Demon King's arms were yoked behind his back. A short length of chain ran from his neck to his bound knees as he knelt upon the rough dirt floor almost as if in forced prayer. The silver-haired head didn't even try to lift as they entered.

Greyfriar studied the prisoner and looked at Adele. They both knew that this demon was a vampire. If the old figure had ever been some sort of king, he was certainly brought low now. The prisoner's eyes were closed and his breathing was even, as if his discomfort was minimal. Despite his obvious age, the vampire seemed fit and muscular.

Gyalo boasted proudly over the prone vampire and kicked him

hard in the ribs. Now the prisoner opened his eyes but didn't react as Greyfriar expected. Instead of hissing in outrage, the vampire remained placid. Gyalo leaned down and snarled maliciously at the demon, who persisted with his serene countenance.

As Gyalo strutted around the prisoner, Anhalt translated the man's great pleasure in capturing the prize. "Apparently, the Demon King was no match for the villagers. Their might overwhelmed it weeks ago. The demon was wandering alone, as it sometimes does, seeking to steal into the village and prey on their elders or a child."

Gyalo took that moment to kick the vampire again, spitting out a string of vile words.

"It failed," Anhalt related. "The villagers were too fast, too strong. No one was killed as they captured it, and now its death will be a message to its brethren."

"Ask Gyalo how to they intend to execute him?" Adele said, but Anhalt already had the answer.

"He will be beheaded. Then the body will be cremated. They would feed it to the vultures but they're afraid it might turn the vultures into demons."

Adele winced, surprised at her sudden sympathy for the vampire. "How many has the *demon* killed here in the village?"

Gyalo replied with wild gesticulations. Anhalt translated. "He says that for generations the demons have been responsible for all of the sickness and death in the village, both human and animal. But when the king dies, the other demons will scatter, and all the village's troubles will end."

"How fortunate for them." Greyfriar's brows knitted together. While vampires might certainly have preyed on this village, Gyalo's ideas were superstitious nonsense. Vampires didn't drink animal blood and were unlikely to have caused illness; death, certainly, but not illness. Greyfriar's gaze slipped again to the bound vampire who remained quiet. The prisoner's chest rose and fell slowly. There were fresh scars and welts on his naked body, no doubt from frequent beatings by the triumphant villagers.

Gyalo escorted them all out and took them back to the town's central courtyard, where a platform was being constructed and decorated like a shrine with paint and colorful scarves. Off to one side was a thick chunk of wood about three feet high. There was a low depression in the top of the wood. A chopping block.

Adele leaned closer to Greyfriar and Anhalt. "We don't have time to worm our way into their good graces with our pleasant manners. I think it's time for something a little more impressive."

—◊—

Gyalo stared around the deck of the *Edinburgh* in the morning sun, as if he had walked onto another planet. Shirazi and the Harmattan were drawn up in respectful formation before the main causeway. Captain Hariri and his officers posed on the quarterdeck above in uniforms as sharp as they could manage. The village elder took in the complexity of the airship.

"Captain," Adele called out, "could you take us up, please."

Gyalo grasped the rail with the first bump of air. With wide eyes, he watched as the Earth receded from the hull of the ship. The villagers on the ground pointed and cheered. Gyalo waved. At two hundred yards, the capstan was locked. The *Edinburgh* hung in the buffeting wind like a gigantic child's balloon.

Adele pulled Gyalo from the rail, and said to Anhalt, "Let's step into my cabin and have a chat." She waved to Hariri. "Mission accomplished. You may reel in *Edinburgh*."

Within minutes, a steward brought pots of tea—Equatorian tea—and a tray of meats, cheese, and bread to Adele's cabin. Gyalo couldn't stop smiling.

Through Anhalt, Adele said, "Tell me about the monastery," as she poured tea.

"It was built many centuries ago by the wisest of shamans. They placed it far away from anywhere so they would be safe from the evil magicks of the world."

"What were they afraid of?"

"They were protecting something. You see, they had the Tear of Death."

Adele tried to appear calm. "I see. So this Tear of Death actually exists?"

"Yes. In the monastery. The wise shamans and lamas are gone. The Demon King and his horde guard it now."

"And what is it exactly?"

Gyalo nibbled cheese and set it aside, unimpressed. "Long ago, when the world was young, the gods shed a tear and it fell to Earth. Luckily it was found by a very wise monk who hid it away because he knew it was far too dangerous to be known by unenlightened men."

"Why?"

"It is a piece of the god of death. The only dharma it knows is death. It does not seek to teach. It only wants to kill everyone, everywhere." The old man smiled. "However, we are saved because it cannot act on its own. It can only do what men tell it to do. And all the men who were wise enough to know how to use it are gone. The only danger comes when men become demons. Demons have the heart to kill, but only men have the knowledge. Only when demons and men are one will the Tear of Death be used."

"And then what?"

"Then we all die," Gyalo replied simply. "The heavens and the Earth will separate. The path to enlightenment will be severed. The demons win once and for all."

"Where is this monastery?"

The elder looked confused. "It's high in the mountains."

"The mountains," Adele retorted, unable to hide her annoyance, "are vast. Something a bit more precise would be helpful."

Gyalo reached for more honey with a self-satisfied laugh. "There is no way to be more accurate. You simply look for it until you find it." He smirked as if they were foolish outsiders who didn't understand the rules of nature.

Adele, however, had no intention of searching aimlessly. There was one person in the village that knew precisely where the monastery was.

CHAPTER 19

The cold slap of the night made Adele pull her thick coat around her neck and plant a gloved hand on her hood. Greyfriar wore nothing more than his usual wool uniform, far too thin for a normal human in this frigid land. The icy wind flapped through his cloak, but he didn't care. The horns and drums had stopped. The bonfires had burned down to glowing piles of embers. The festivities were done for the night.

Greyfriar led the way through the dark, silent village to the stone hut where the Demon King languished. The two sentries huddled around a small fire, dozing. They both jerked awake as Greyfriar and Adele approached from the shadows. Greyfriar began a conversation with them in what sounded like serviceable Tibetan, rather than Hindi. The guards seemed relaxed by the foreigner using their language. Greyfriar shared a laugh with the two men before he drew long daggers from his high black boots and handed them to the sentries. They smiled and stood aside.

Once inside, Adele lit a small lamp. "What did you tell them?"

"The truth," Greyfriar said. "That I wanted to impress the beautiful woman by looking heroic in front of a demon."

"You're such a romantic." Then they were gazing on the bent form of the Demon King. He remained motionless as they entered, his eyes still closed. His prone position, after all this time, would have been excruciating for a human, and even a vampire would find it tiresome eventually.

"My name is Gareth." Greyfriar spoke in vampiric, a combination of guttural noises and hissing.

The grey head twisted suddenly to regard him but didn't react with any recognition to the name. The prisoner's nostrils flared as if trying to find the masked figure's scent, but failing. Greyfriar always smeared himself with human blood to mask his true species from his vampire brethren. However, the Demon King inclined his head as respectfully as

144

he could manage. "A clever disguise. I am Yidak. I'm sorry to meet you under such awkward circumstances. I'd prefer to talk to your true self."

The swordsman lowered his scarf and removed his glasses to show his cerulean blue eyes. The old vampire laughed with satisfaction before his gaze darted to Adele.

"How did you come to be captured by these people?" Gareth asked.

"I was on pilgrimage. Usually I do not stray so far out of the mountains, but a vision bade me do so."

"A pilgrimage?" Gareth queried with incredulity. That term couldn't be correct. Perhaps the old vampire was misunderstanding the word, or had adapted it to vampiric incorrectly. "What could you possibly have been on pilgrimage for?"

"To find you." Yidak smiled. "You are going to save me. And then perhaps I'll return the favor."

Adele's brow lifted at that. The old vampire's eyes were quick to regard her, so she softened her expression once more as if she wasn't understanding and allowed Gareth to continue the conversation.

Gareth rolled his eyes in derision at the Demon King's lunacy. "Let's not get too far ahead of ourselves. Why don't we start with you telling me about the place you come from."

The vampire shifted for the first time in his bonds, with the rattle of chains and the creak of tightening hemp. He struggled to crane his neck for a better look at Gareth. "You seek the monastery?"

"I have heard much about it. I am curious."

"Word of our retreat has traveled far it seems. From your accent, you made a long journey solely for curiosity's sake." The vampire took in Gareth's sword and pistols.

"The war has changed my perceptions about many things."

"War?" The silver-haired vampire stiffened.

"Yes," replied Gareth. "The humans decided to fight back. It's not going well for us."

Yidak's eyes fell on Adele. "And yet you stand beside your enemy. Or is she a meal?"

"She is neither." Gareth chuckled, while Adele bit her lip, trying desperately not to react.

"Intriguing." The vampire pondered the observation. Finally, he said, "Free me and I will welcome you to the monastery."

"I don't know that I'm in a position to do that."

"I suppose you could search for the monastery on your own," the vampire said without pretension. "You certainly have the lifespan to find it. She may not. It is not so easy to see as that. And even if you found it, you would not get in without much bloodshed. Yours."

Gareth looked at Adele. Her expression gave him no clue what direction he should take. She was allowing him to make the decision. These were his people. Gareth knew time was critical. The Witchfinder could be close.

"I'll consider it," Gareth finally stated.

The elder vampire observed Gareth's hands lift the scarf to cover the lower half of his face once more and placed the mirrored glasses over his blue eyes. Then the prisoner exhaled slowly and closed his eyes, his head hanging low once more. Greyfriar and Adele left him that way.

—∞—

The next morning at breakfast in their crowded room, Greyfriar watched the stunned surprise creep into Anhalt's expression as Adele told him of the offer from the Demon King.

"Please tell me you aren't considering it," the general began. His hand lifted to his forehead. "Oh God, you are, aren't you?"

Adele remained reasonable. "It would solve our problems. Let's face it, we could search these mountains for years before we found this hidden monastery. Goronwy is ahead of us and he has vampires to help him search. He may have found it already."

General Anhalt spoke in a low tone despite the unlikelihood of any English speakers nearby. "And how do you intend to prevent the Demon King's execution?" His attention went to Greyfriar. "I won't believe you would injure anyone in this village."

"And you would be right," Greyfriar informed him. "I will steal in and out with none the wiser. I will go unmasked so that, if I am seen, I will appear to be another demon come to save my king."

Anhalt regarded Adele. "And what about you?"

Adele couldn't keep the disappointment from her voice. "I will be with you and the rest of the men on *Edinburgh*. We should make ready to sail today before the festival concludes."

Anhalt breathed out a sigh of relief before adding, "Gyalo will be offended. He wanted us here for the execution tomorrow morning. He thinks our presence is good fortune."

"No, we need to be gone. If something does go awry, I don't want trouble between us and the villagers." Adele pulled her coat tighter about her. "It would be easy for them to blame the outlanders."

"Easy, and accurate," Anhalt said. "I will inform Captain Hariri to make ready to embark with all due haste."

Anhalt handed Adele a cup of tea. It was the honest-to-goodness Equatorian variety. She gave him a look of gratitude and shifted closer to Greyfriar for warmth. He opened his cloak and she slipped inside, nestling in the crook of his shoulder.

The general asked, "And this old vampire is content with leading humans to his home?"

"We'll soon see." Adele's breath misted in the air.

"He won't have a choice," stated Greyfriar coldly.

The general grunted with understanding. The pallor of his skin had resumed a more normal shade, but Adele could tell he was still in the grip of the altitude sickness. She debated asking Anhalt how he was faring, but she knew what his answer would be, and it wouldn't be the truth. However, the truth stood out in the hunch of his shoulders and the deep hollows of his eyes.

"I will rush Hariri along. We should be air-ready in a few hours." The old soldier gained his feet stiffly.

Adele rose also and placed a kiss on his cold cheek. He froze for a moment and then his hand brushed her arm with all the tenderness her father could never muster. That small gesture broke Adele's heart. She watched him depart and then sank back into Greyfriar's arms.

"He's struggling," the swordsman muttered.

Adele nodded. "I feel awful for allowing Simon to insist on this. But if I were General Anhalt, I wouldn't like to be coddled either."

"Would you like me to tell you he will be fine?"

Adele's throat tightened. "Yes," she whispered.

"Your Anhalt is a pillar of strength and when that falters he relies on sheer determination. This place won't be his end. Did you notice he no longer uses his cane?"

Adele turned to Greyfriar, her eyes shining in the firelight. "You're right. I'm ashamed to say I hadn't noticed. Maybe I only see the weaknesses in him because it's so unusual. The strengths, I expect." She smiled.

When Gyalo arrived to bring them to the final day of the festival, he was disappointed that Anhalt could not attend and shocked when Greyfriar launched into conversation in simple Tibetan. The delighted elder led his two guests out into the frigid wind full of horn blasts, drum beats, and the smell of charcoal. Colorful banners snapped in the wind as huge bonfires crackled. There was much singing and dancing from every corner of town and, unfortunately for Adele, much fermented yak butter. She had become somewhat accustomed to its smell, as it was in everything from food to people's hair, but the flavor took longer to accept. For the first time, she envied Greyfriar's inability to taste—that is until they served platters of delicious sweet rice cakes.

The villagers gave small gifts to Adele and she shared what little she had on her, sending for trade goods to be brought from the ship. Curious people bombarded her with questions and she did her best to tell them about life outside the walls of the mountains. There was much laughter and joy. Adele drew one of the children up onto her lap. The little girl played with Adele's scarf, so she removed and wrapped it around the child's neck, much to her delight.

Finally, it was late in the afternoon when Adele announced they had to be on their way. Gyalo pleaded for them to reconsider. The villagers crowded around, cajoling the strangers to stay. She and Greyfriar managed to work their way to the main gate and slip outside. As they approached the ship, trailing a mob behind them, the red tunics and rifles of the Harmattan deployed down the gangplank. Weapons were not brandished in a threatening way, due to Adele's urgent signals to Shirazi, but the presence of heavily armed men set the villagers back on their heels. Gyalo finally stopped arguing when Adele and Greyfriar set foot on the gangplank. They turned and bowed their thanks to the disconsolate elder, and then retreated on deck.

The solitude of Adele's cabin elicited a grateful sigh from her. Within the hour, the steam whistles sounded to signal impending take off. Now the chanting of airmen and the drumbeat of tramping feet filled the air, along with the roar of buoyant gases pouring into the last chambers in the dirigible. Soon the ship rocked as it lifted free of the ground.

Gareth turned from the bow window where final shafts of sunlight spilled in around him. "You should get some sleep while you can. We have hours before I need to make my way back to the village."

Adele didn't find the suggestion as appealing as it should have been. Despite the exhaustion of the village festivities and the copious amounts of the yak brew, the specter of nightmares remained with her. With the sudden darkness, the cold of the mountains seeped in through the wooden walls. She was loath to remove her coat, knowing the bed was as cold as the icy air about her. She rubbed her arms without conviction. "I don't have time to sleep right now."

Gareth shed his garb as casually as if it were a summer's day. His pale skin shone almost white in the gloom of the cabin. Adele marveled that there wasn't a scar on him, even after being burned to the bone by her geomancy last year. He had been reborn that day. His lean, corded body slipped into the blankets, and he reached out to her.

"Come to bed."

She found herself disrobing, flinging her clothes aside in her rush. A smile played on his lips. The cold gripped her bare skin and a gasp escaped her, but then she was under the covers and pressed close against his warm body.

Adele shivered. She couldn't help it, even though his arms and muscular legs wrapped tight around her. Through chattering teeth, she grumbled, "How can people thrive in this cold?"

"You've lived in the warmth of Equatoria your entire life. Your blood is thin."

Adele snorted. "Who told you that?"

"No one. I can taste it." Gareth's chest rumbled beneath her cheek.

Another shiver wracked her and she buried her head under the covers. "That's why I'm always cold."

"There are ways to warm you." Gareth's hand trailed down her spine. "A little exercise."

"Exercise?" Adele's eyes peered out. "Are you mad? In this weather . . . oh!" She bit her lip to stop the bubble of laughter.

"It would warm the blood . . . and the sheets." There was a fire already burning in his eyes.

Adele gave him a one-sided smirk. "That it would."

"Unless you're too tired."

Was that a challenge in his tone? "I'm never *that* tired."

He pulled her up toward him and kissed her, and the cold of the Himalayas finally melted away.

CHAPTER 20

Gareth took flight from the bow windows of the cabin. Adele watched him with a pensive expression as he slipped into the darkness. She also seemed slightly vexed that she could not accompany him on this venture. The woman's yearning for adventure was one of the traits that he loved, but sometimes it seemed as if she merely sought constant action to distract her from the weight of her world-changing decisions. Her small, pale figure vanished in the night, and when the sight of the yellow chemical lights of the *Edinburgh* were swallowed up against the colossal background of the mountains, Gareth felt a moment of loneliness.

The night wind buffeted his frame and it took a great deal of concentration to fight through the sky. He made constant adjustments to his density and repositioned his limbs, tacking and veering to keep from scraping against a mountainside. Snow was falling, not heavily but enough to create a wispy veil ahead of him. His internal sense of direction kept him angling for the village. The blowing snow was useful since he wished to come and go without being noticed. It would be best if they had no idea how their prisoner had escaped when they found the cell empty at sunrise. He hoped that the Demon King would not try to seek retribution against the villagers. If so, Gareth would have to step in and make sure he left quietly.

The faint lights of the village glowed deep in the valley even through the falling snow. The sound of horns and drums drifted up to him. Gareth sank lower, a dark shadow in the brilliant white of the night.

The bright glare of a bonfire in the central courtyard almost blinded him, but he could see a great crowd massed. Torches lit the shrine and the several figures who stood atop it. One was Gyalo, who held a torch, but the others carried a mixture of farm implements such as flails and wooden pitchforks, and there were a couple of old muskets too. All of the men had their weapons pointed into the center of their circle. When one of villagers shifted, Gareth saw that in the center of the ring of men was the execution block with the silver-haired vampire bent over it. His arms and legs were bound with rope. There was a steel band around his upper body, with a short chain to the shrine, keeping him bowed with his vulnerable neck over the block. Standing next to him, a burly man lifted a massive axe.

Cursing, Gareth dove.

He landed just as the weapon swung toward the neck of the Demon King. Gareth's arm stretched out across the path of the axe. The shaft slammed his forearm and his muscles fought to stop the blade just as it kissed the prisoner's neck. Gareth shoved the weapon and its wielder away, baring his teeth and hissing at the crowd.

Men fell back, screaming in fear. Gyalo stumbled away from the furious demon. In the crowd below, Gareth spied the young child with Adele's scarf crying in terror. Muskets fired and he felt two lead balls punch into him. Gareth wished for his sword as the men gathered their wits and came at him with blades and rakes. Such close quarter fighting was messy and dangerous. He didn't want to hurt anyone, but nor did he want to be harmed. He dodged and grabbed men and their tools, tossing them into the musketeers who were frantically reloading. His claws ripped through the loops of rope about the prisoner's arms and back. The iron chain kept the vampire's head down on the block, but as Gareth turned back to face the villagers, Yidak seized the links in a desperate attempt to free himself.

The mob surged toward Gareth, and he had no choice but to defend himself. Barely dodging a sword thrust, he took a rough-hewn bill hook deep in his side. He felt it as a heavy blow, but there was no pain. Grabbing up the brave farmer, who cried out in horror, Gareth used him to batter aside the others in front of him, trying to protect Yidak. Several sharp things impaled him from behind and he was pulled backward. He arched over and dropped the still screaming farmer.

Suddenly the implements holding him snapped in half, and he was free. Gareth turned to see Yidak standing beside him with the chain hanging loose around his neck. The vampire's still upraised arm looked poised to strike at the stunned assailants. They all fell back and stared in dread at the freed Demon King.

Gareth reached for the vampire. "No!"

However, Yidak was not intent on revenge. He leaned away as a sword struck at him three times. He avoided all of the blows with subtle twists of his muscular body. It took no effort at all, even though he had been held immobile for days. His next movements were fast, even for a vampire, his hands mere blurs. He didn't use his claws, and the flat of his hands sent men tumbling. Yidak grabbed a man in front and one behind him and, with a single sweep of his arms, their bodies flung up into the air only to slam down again on opposite sides. The two men dropped unconscious.

Abruptly a shrill screech split the night and all of the attackers covered their ears. It sounded so inhuman that even Gareth flinched. It took a second for him to realize the sound came from Yidak beside him. He had heard no vampire utter such a sound in hundreds of years. It was an age-old hunting cry.

Gareth quickly recovered and grabbed Yidak's arm. Leaping straight up into the air, he forced the other vampire to follow him. Yidak offered no resistance. They surrendered to the wind that swept them far from the dim fires of the village. Gareth released Yidak, and the old vampire followed him closely, like a shadow, matching Gareth's maneuvers in split seconds. The Demon King made no boasts of his deeds nor mocked those who had failed to exact their justice. It was as if he cared for none of those things. He was merely enjoying the freedom of the sky. They soared up along the mountainsides with utter abandon. Gareth found himself reveling in the experience too, simply because Yidak seemed transported by the moment.

The shape of an airship appeared through the swirling winds and Gareth ascended toward the *Edinburgh*. The old vampire regarded him with surprise. Gareth drew close to the hull and grabbed hold of the wooden planks. He turned to look for Yidak but found the old vampire clinging easily next to him.

"We will climb up to the stern windows," Gareth called out.

The other vampire looked surprised. "Are we attacking?"

"No. We are expected. I want no trouble from you."

Yidak smiled eagerly. He seemed oddly childlike with excitement. He motioned for Gareth to lead on. The two vampires crawled along the sloping hull toward the flattened stern. Hand over clawed hand, with feet shoved into the tarred gaps between timbers, they fought through the battering winds toward the yellow glow of the main cabin. Gareth hauled himself over the short balcony outside the bow windows. He gazed in to see Adele and General Anhalt in close conversation across the cabin. He tapped the glass with his claw. Adele leapt to her feet and ran for the window. Anhalt rose too and came forward, hefting a short-barreled shotgun, a deck sweeper.

Adele's peace of mind at the sight of Gareth changed to fascinated wariness as she noticed the naked form of the Demon King perched on the railing. She pulled open the window and drew Gareth inside, where he stumbled exhausted to the deck. He quickly dragged himself up and took Yidak by the arm. The old vampire cheerfully climbed through the window, staring around in fascination at Adele, Anhalt, and all the objects in the cabin.

Adele seemed assured that the Demon King was not an immediate danger, so she turned to Gareth with relief. Until she saw the shafts of wood sticking from his back.

"Bloody hell!" she gasped.

"It's fine." Gareth twisted his head to look behind him. "Mainly garden implements, I think."

"Garden implements," she repeated incredulously. She scanned the Demon King and saw he was unharmed. "Always standing in the damn line of fire."

"They'll be easy enough to extract." Gareth nodded at Yidak. "He was the one who broke them to free me."

"Thank you," Adele said to Yidak in English and Hindi, although she didn't know if he could understand. She made a conscious effort to keep her gaze on his face.

"You're welcome," he replied in English. He smiled at the shocked looks on the faces of Adele and Anhalt. "I speak many languages, and I sense you are more comfortable with this one."

"That will simplify things," Anhalt said, and without turning his gun away from their guest, he found a heavy-weather coat hanging on the wall and handed it to the naked vampire. Yidak studied the coat briefly, and then donned it with ease. He smiled at Adele, wrinkling the crow's feet at the corner of his eyes even more. She watched the old vampire slowly work the buttons on his new coat. She and Gareth exchanged glances of surprise. Yidak used his fingers with unvampire-like facility.

While the old vampire was admiring the long oilcloth coat, Gareth said to him, "We upheld our end of the bargain. Will you honor yours and take us to the monastery?"

"Sail west. I will direct you more fully as we grow closer. We have more than a day of flying before we draw near." Yidak then bowed low to Adele, to Gareth's surprise. None of his kind ever bowed to a human, no matter the act of kindness. What was the purpose? A show of supplication given that he was surrounded by superior force? All that graciousness could change once they came within range of his monastery and the odds evened up a bit. Yidak's eyes held either wisdom or cunning. Gareth wasn't sure which.

When Adele went quickly to pass orders to Captain Hariri, Gareth said to the old vampire, "You don't seem concerned to be a prisoner again."

Yidak shrugged. "There's value in every experience. I find the whole affair a curiosity. I find *you* a curiosity. You come all this way. You pretend to be a human at times." His eyes shined with a private joke. "You are unusual."

"So I've heard." Gareth's look of reproach showed clearly because Yidak's laughter roared through the cabin. Gareth straightened stiffly, feeling the wooden stakes shift inside him. "I am alone, but perhaps for a reason."

"Perhaps," Yidak replied. He gestured toward Gareth's back. "You should have your human tend to those. I will not try to escape. I am interested to see what comes next for both of us. I gave you my word in the village and I give it again now." His head nodded in deference. "Would you prefer to chain me?"

"No need." Gareth replied as Adele returned and she examined the wounds in his back. "If you do attempt to escape, she will kill you."

Yidak's expression faded to confusion for a moment. "*She* will?"

"You wouldn't reach the window."

From across the cabin, Anhalt nodded in agreement with Gareth's casual comment. Yidak looked at the general, and then stared at Adele with a curious smile.

Gareth rolled an encumbered shoulder and said to her, "Let's deal with these so the wounds can heal before we reach the monastery."

"We should lock our guest away," Anhalt said. "If Her Majesty is going to be distracted by surgery."

Adele pointed at a narrow door on the forward bulkhead. "He can spend time in the map room."

Yidak complied without argument, eyeing Anhalt, who held the door open, as he passed. The narrow closet was used to store maps and charts, none of which would be needed here because there were no useful charts of this territory. Yidak studied his new cell, then sat placidly on the deck, calm and unperturbed, as if preparing to meditate. Anhalt closed the door and Adele locked it.

"Well, he seems nice," Adele commented with pleasant sarcasm. Then she went straight to a cabinet and pulled out her usual supply of scalpels and clean linen as Gareth tore off what was left of his shirt. He felt nothing but the pressure from the implements. He caught Adele wincing in sympathy while he arranged himself face down on the deck. There would be blood, and he didn't want to ruin the bed. Wooden planks could be scrubbed clean.

"You look like a porcupine," Adele remarked in Alexandrian Arabic now, hopeful that even if Yidak was familiar with the language, he might not grasp the formal Egyptian dialect. With a grimace, she settled beside Gareth, laying out her instruments on a clean cloth. After a moment of silence, her hand touched his shoulder lightly. "You find Yidak interesting."

It was an observation, not a question. She knew him too well. While Adele went to work on the first wooden shaft that protruded from between his shoulder blades, he said, "I think he finds *me* more interesting, but you're right. He's odd. He had plenty of opportunities to savage his captors, but he refrained."

"Rare to find a vampire who can hold in his aggression." With a sharp tug Adele yanked out the first shaft, the sharp end of some sort of flail.

Gareth didn't react. "Vampires hesitate to kill these days for only two reasons. Fear and . . . well, only one. If they know they are out-matched, they will not engage unless their hunger is too great."

Adele grabbed the next broken haft with a steady grip. "Gyalo said they captured the Demon King over two weeks ago. He should be ravenous."

"And yet he held back."

"Interesting," Adele muttered, forcibly twisting the shaft to loosen it. She placed her knee on Gareth's back, grunting the words as she struggled to remove the last implement. "I don't know . . . if I'm looking forward . . . to what is waiting for us . . . at the monastery." With a spurt of blood, a curved blade came free from Gareth's back. Adele hooted in triumph. "Finally!"

Anhalt looked away with a sick groan.

"All done?" Gareth lifted himself up on an elbow.

"I need to dig out the musket balls. Roll over." With practiced ease, Adele probed the wounds with forceps and removed two lead balls from his abdomen. She took a towel and used it to soak up the blood drip-ping across Gareth's ribs. Soon the wounds stopped bleeding. Adele studied her work, then stood and went to a basin of water, turning it red. "You've lost a lot of blood."

Gareth couldn't deny the hunger was there, probably shining in his eyes. "I won't need much."

"You need to be at your best when we reach our destination. No telling what we'll be up against."

"I can't afford to weaken you. We both need to be functional."

Anhalt cleared his throat, and they recalled he was still present. The general looked merely uncomfortable, but he was probably horrified.

Adele gave him an understanding glance. "General, you may withdraw."

He indicated the door of the map room. "But I should—"

"Yidak isn't getting out. Please, go rest. We need you at your best too at the monastery, and the altitude will get higher."

Anhalt tried to appear untroubled, but without success. "Yes, ma'am." He went quickly out of the cabin and shut the door.

Adele slumped on the floor next to Gareth. "I forget that others are disturbed by our *unique* relationship. It's so natural to me now."

"I think you'll find that you are unique among humans in that way."

"That's not true. Your people in Edinburgh let you feed off them."

"I protected them from other vampires who would have killed them. They were . . . paying me, in a fashion. And, other than my realm in Edinburgh, a willing relationship is never the case between vampires and humans."

"But it could be," Adele shot back passionately.

Gareth placed a gentle hand on her arm. "Perhaps. One day. All vampires and humans will fall in love. It will be a golden age. We'll learn to cook for you, and you will open your veins so blood flows like wine."

She eyed him, hearing playful sarcasm in his voice rather than scorn. "Just feed. And take as much as you need. You drink so little all the time, it's a wonder you can function."

"I don't need as much as you seem to think. Do you want me to be bloated and lazy like my brother? I need to keep my lean muscular figure intact, as I am frequently portrayed shirtless."

Adele groaned. "You know, just once I'd like to be shown in a heroic light in those damn books." She poked him on the shoulder. "Which is why you have to finish your memoir and make me look good."

His humor vanished. "Someday."

"Soon," she insisted, baring her left shoulder. Her olive skin was almost a honey bronze in the gaslight.

Gareth's hunger flared again and he let it, pulling her closer, his lips brushing against her flesh. She shivered and her arms curled under his and across his back. He kissed a spot on her neck where it met the shoulder and bit her. Her body flinched slightly, but then settled in his tight embrace with a long exhale of pleasure. Surges of goose bumps traveled over her skin under his hand.

The rush of her blood across his tongue brought a flood of sensations. The foremost was always the power within her. It threatened to swallow him whole sometimes. Her essence rumbled like a volcano under the surface, hot and smoldering. The tang of spice showed she was fertile, and for a moment he wished they could be more than they were. However, children were an impossibility. For all their similarities, he and Adele were different species. Still, it was always a pleasant dream.

He heard her heart begin to pound harder and he pulled his mouth from her, but kept her in his arms as she sagged against him. Her breath was a shaking exhale.

His lips brushed her bare shoulder, licking a lingering drop of blood.

"Do I taste good?" she asked, her voice drowsy and her eyes half closed. "Or do I still have the flavor of the grave? Remember the first time you drank? You said my blood tasted like your death."

"You do taste of death and life," he whispered in her ear. "Because that is all there is in this world. But if it were up to you, you would choose only life."

"Your life . . . always," Adele murmured.

CHAPTER 21

The *Edinburgh* labored to climb against a gale that blew between the towering peaks. On the main deck Adele stood with Greyfriar, Anhalt, and Yidak. She and Anhalt were dressed in heavy furs, as usual, with breathers around their necks. The general wore his Fahrenheit saber and heavy sidearm on his hips, and also carried the wide-bore deck sweeper. Greyfriar was in his typical uniform with rapier and pistols. Major Shirazi and the Harmattan gathered nearby, with rifles ready in case their guest attempted to escape.

Yidak wore the same heavy weather coat, which he buttoned only to satisfy the modesty of his hosts, and he was bare footed beneath it. He studied the wild surroundings, bobbing his head in the wind as if he was sailing the updrafts himself. He wore an amazed grin.

"How far now?" Adele asked through chattering teeth.

Yidak craned his neck, peering about. He pursed his lips, replying in accented English, "Not long."

"You said that two days ago."

"Two days ago, it wasn't long either." He raised a finger. "But now it is very not long."

Adele turned away from the amused old vampire in annoyance. She took relaxing breaths and fell into herself. She once again reached out to the rifts. She had been seeking lines of power since leaving the village. She felt the tantalizing threads of energy slipping around her, far away and faint to her touch. She could only hope the monastery was built on or near a serviceable rift, as so many holy sites were. The plan was for her to enter the demon fortress, hiding from their sight, and locate the Tear of Death, if in fact it existed. If possible, she would bring it out, and they would be away on the *Edinburgh*. If it wasn't possible to carry it, she would obliterate the vampires in the monastery as she had done at Grenoble. The strain of the event would be great, but she hoped that the monastery was moderate in size, certainly not as large as the town of Grenoble, and she would only need to draw power from the Earth in a relatively small area. If all went well, they would have the Tear of Death and be away without any harm done to any of her men.

If all went well.

Adele felt Greyfriar looking at her because he sensed her reaching for a rift. She snapped back to the frigid deck and gave him a shrug of failure. He took a pensive breath and would have warned her off her plan, as he had done countless times over the last few days, except that Yidak was standing within earshot. Adele then noticed the old vampire staring at her too with great interest. He obviously sensed her geomancy, as did all vampires. She held his gaze boldly, as if to say that the power he had sensed could fall on him if he crossed her. Anhalt poked Yidak in the side with the shotgun and motioned for him to take his attention off Adele and put it back on the geography. The vampire laughed as if this was a skit.

Greyfriar suddenly twitched nervously. He glanced at Yidak, and then over the side. He cursed out a warning.

Adele pushed beside him. In the valley below, a weird swarm of blackness erupted out of the cliff face. The mass shifted and changed shape like a flock of swallows, rising with the wind, twisting toward the little airship.

"By the way," Yidak said, "we're here."

"Damn you." Greyfriar seized the old vampire and pressed the edge of a dagger across his throat. "I'll kill you."

Anhalt shouted over his shoulder, "Major Shirazi! Form square! Captain Hariri! Stand by for action!"

Within seconds, steam horns sounded across the ship and men ran for cannons or leapt into the ratlines to scale into the tops. The dark vampire swarm continued to lift toward them. The ship's guns rumbled out. Shirazi took Adele's arm. "Get below, Your Majesty."

Adele ignored him. She stretched out her hands, desperately reaching for the power of the rifts. She touched faint embers, but they were too weak. She needed a great rift to bring fire on the approaching horde, to ignite them and send the lot drifting back down as burnt husks. With a curse, fighting her fear, she sank deeper into the Earth. Threads of power trickled just out of reach. With the most tantalizing pressure, slivers of fire grazed her fingertips. She stretched, trying to grab them or hook a fingernail around them so she could drag a rift toward her. The music of the Earth was beautiful but muffled, and she only smelled the scent of ice and snow.

She felt the hard deck beneath her feet again. Greyfriar had Yidak in a death grip, but his attention was on her. Anhalt watched too. Adele shook her head at Greyfriar in alarm. The red-coated Harmattan scrambled to form a square around her. The front rank of troopers knelt, and the back line stood with bayonets out and up.

Yidak reached up gently to Greyfriar's wrist. With a subtle motion, Greyfriar's blade flew away from the old vampire's throat. In an instant, Yidak leapt into the air, vaulted over the soldiers and sailed beyond the side of the ship. Greyfriar was already pulling his pistol while Anhalt had barely registered the rapid action. Adele stretched her hand out toward Yidak. She hoped she could summon power enough to at least burn him out of the sky.

The old vampire stared at her with a nervous narrowing of his eyes, and he screeched into the wind. The horrific sound pierced Adele's ears just as a wave of bodies roared up above the rail. Inside the dense mass, individual vampires could be seen staring with cold blue eyes. The flock thundered past with a terrifying flutter of cloth like the beating of hundreds of wings.

Adele recovered from the stab of the vampire's cry, but felt something grab her arm and Greyfriar was shouting, "No!"

Startled soldiers fired an irregular volley into the swarm of torsos. The ear-numbing report from several cannons reverberated under their feet. Murderous shrapnel shot tore ragged holes in the undulating vampires.

Then the horde was gone, arcing away under the curve of the dirigible and splitting into smaller clutches. The twisting flock rolled away from the airship.

Yidak remained alone, floating just off the side. His head turned to watch the throng of vampires slipping away through the sky. A gun boomed and glowing green shot tore into the old figure. Yidak tumbled wildly through the air. Anhalt broke the smoking breach of the shotgun and reached into his coat pocket for new shells.

"Stop!" Greyfriar grabbed the shotgun by the barrel and pointed it at the deck. "Don't attack him."

Anhalt looked at the swordsman in shock, then at Adele. She was surprised too. In the distance, she could see the vampires dropping back the way they had come like blurry lines of charcoal smoke in the sky.

"Cease fire!" Adele shouted, although all fire had already stopped.

Soldiers and airmen looked at their commanders and at each other for answers. The attack had come and gone in seconds. It couldn't be over, however. That wasn't the way of vampires.

"Don't." Greyfriar extended a cautioning hand at Adele because she was still poised to burn Yidak. The old vampire drifted haltingly back toward the ship, grimacing in pain. "He's no danger."

"How do you know that?"

"His cry. He was calling off the attack. That's why his pack turned away at the last second."

Yidak fell onto the rail and crouched with gasping breaths. He looked at the gaping hole in his coat. Underneath, his abdomen was raw and the flesh steamed. Yidak winced at Anhalt. "A little closer and it might have taken my heart."

The general kept the deck sweeper aimed at the Demon King. "This is a Fahrenheit gun. Those pellets burn, don't they?"

"They do." Yidak huffed loudly. "I'm not used to pain. Remarkable. When does it stop?"

"I don't know," Anhalt replied.

The old vampire sucked air with painful hisses. His eyes shifted to Adele and Greyfriar. "I told you, I am not your enemy. I welcome you." He extended his hand down off the ship. "There is what you seek."

Adele moved to the rail next to Yidak, with Greyfriar close at her side. She peered over, but saw nothing except mile upon mile of grey rock and white snow. And then suddenly, there it was. About halfway down the valley wall, nestled into a steep cliff face, almost as if it were a gecko on a mosque wall, was a miraculous structure. It seemed to hide against the mountainside. White walls gave it the appearance of fallen snow, masking it from view. A collection of large buildings surrounded a multitude of smaller ones stacked up along the cliff face, but it was hard to see where the rock and snow ended and the monastery began.

Then Adele noticed what appeared to be narrow, irregular stairs carved into the mountain itself, providing what must have been a treacherous and dizzying approach to the monastery from the valley much farther below. In certain spots the stairs gave way to hemp bridges that looked treacherous. She wondered how anyone but vampires could call it home. It was difficult to reach without wings.

"So," Adele said cautiously, pushing down Shirazi's pistol that was still aimed at Yidak's head, "we can land our airship at your monastery?"

"I won't allow your soldiers or your ship." The old vampire forced a smile. "I value peace with you, but I'm not stupid. You may land your ship at the foot of the Ten Thousand Steps." He pointed at Adele, Greyfriar, and Anhalt. "You three will be my guests. Whatever you seek, I will help you find it."

Adele took a deep breath and she could hear Major Shirazi's teeth grinding with fury because he knew she was preparing to agree to go with the Demon King into his fortress. The major snorted angrily and muttered under his breath, "Why even have a bodyguard?"

—⁓—

From Adele's vantage point at the bottom of the Ten Thousand Steps, it certainly seemed that the name sold it short. The endless stairs were little more than flattened steps carved from the mountainside. Each step was barely two feet wide, worn slick and smooth, with a rough mountain wall on the one hand and the abyss on the other.

Adele gave a final glance at the center of the small plateau where the *Edinburgh* sat moored. She took a picture of Major Shirazi noticeably annoyed at the railing. Once they were out of sight, Captain Hariri would take the airship down to a more hospitable berth, where he would await Adele's recall signal. The frustrating distance from useful rifts meant that her original plan of sneaking into the monastery had gone by the boards. She could not hide from vampires here. They had no hope now but to get inside through the good graces of their enigmatic host.

They climbed with Yidak in the lead. Adele saw iron rings driven into the stone wall, but the rope guide that may have been there once was long gone. Countless prayer flags fluttered overhead. She couldn't help but wonder at who had planted these flags. It couldn't have been the vampires, and humans wouldn't come all the way up here for fear of the *demons*.

Step after weary step passed. Leg muscles burned. Lungs seared for breath. The wind pounded as if someone was trying to shove them off the edge. Adele watched Yidak's back straight ahead of her. He seemed unaffected by the effort. Gareth removed his scarf and smoked glasses. The pretense of Greyfriar was no longer needed. Just behind her, Anhalt rasped painfully through the breather. She tried to keep the pace moderate, but she knew this was torture for him. He grasped his leg frequently, grunting with effort. There was hardly space on the steps to look back, so it would have been perilous to turn around and try to help him.

Hours passed without notice. The only measure of time was the sound of feet scraping on stone. There was no space to sit and rest, but every so often, Adele called a halt and they would crouch and drink water from canteens. Clouds drifted by beneath them and, through the gaps in the white, she saw dark patches that must have been the ground somewhere miles below. To step off into space would have been meaningless. There couldn't be any sense of falling, only misty nothingness. And then the exhausted metronome of footsteps would continue.

Adele was shocked when they came around a bend in the cliff and suddenly the monastery rose in front of them. She was so light headed, she almost forgot why she was walking. Glistening ice-covered walls sparkled in the sun. Even this close, it seemed to be levitating in the white sky. The sprawling complex reached up the side of the mountain, level after level of long straight windows and columned arcades. A few domes and spires created some visual relief from the unrelenting cold white slabs.

The rock steps led Adele and the others to a towering red wooden door. She paused to take one picture, but she was running low on film because she hadn't wanted to burden herself with unnecessary weight.

Yidak lifted his face toward the wall and within moments the door creaked open. Shadowy figures stood atop the ramparts staring down. They wore robes of dark crimson. Adele flexed her fingers, searching for a dragon spine in the Earth beneath her. A faint trace beckoned from the east. She doubted the rift would be strong enough to unleash fire if this turned into a trap.

They passed into a windy courtyard. From out of a tall sparkling building above, a figure drifted down along the glinting snow. Adele gasped. "He looks like a samurai."

This vampire wore a long pleated skirt, a hakama, tied at the waist. He had a wide-sleeved jacket, a haori, over it. The color was a simple grey and black. Even more amazingly, he had a long katana sword shoved into his belt. *Another vampire with a sword.* His suspicious gaze swept over the party behind Yidak. He minced no words and demanded in vampiric, "What happened? You have been gone for too long."

Yidak smiled soothingly. "A slight misunderstanding with the villagers on the plateau." He gestured to Gareth and company. "These travelers were kind enough to smooth things over. As recompense, I invited them to stay with us. And speak English, as they prefer it."

The samurai's glare did not ease as he scanned Yidak in his torn coat, and then studied the strangers. Gareth tensed and Anhalt's hand went to his weapon.

Yidak said quickly, "May I introduce Gareth. And his companions, Adele and General Anhalt. This is my right arm. Takeda."

"These strangers," hissed the samurai vampire in serviceable English, "helped you?"

"Yes, they did." Yidak chuckled, then glanced at General Anhalt. "Mostly. It goes to show that even as old as I am, I can still be wonderfully surprised by the world."

Takeda's deep blue eyes, penetrating and full of mistrust, fell upon Gareth and his weapons. The tension between them rose and, for a moment, Adele feared they were preparing to fight. But the moment passed and Takeda nodded. "You have my sincere gratitude for returning him to us."

Yidak laid a wrinkled hand on Takeda's arm, and gestured toward Gareth. "He uses tools. He fights with weapons." The old vampire then nodded at Adele with a wink. "That woman *allows* him to feed from her, and she tends his wounds. They consider themselves *friends* perhaps."

Takeda's eyes widened.

Gareth said, "Both of these humans have saved my life many times over, even knowing what I am."

Takeda snorted with derision. "They're buying his power."

Yidak shook his head. "No, I think not, but come, I am tired. Let us go inside."

Takeda waved his arm and two other vampires scurried from the shadows. In their arms they carried bundles of red and yellow. Yidak carefully unbuttoned the coat and slipped it off. The wounds from the Fahrenheit gun had healed. He handed the coat back to Anhalt with a word of thanks. He then turned and raised his arms. The two new vampires, one male and one female, draped the Demon King in silk brocade and stepped back, bowing to him with their hands clasped in reverence. The elder vampire adjusted his colorful new robes. Suddenly he went from eccentric, old stranger to a figure of dignity and respect. Yidak smiled at Gareth and Adele, and motioned for them to follow him into the monastery.

Takeda bowed deeply to Yidak. "Welcome back, Your Holiness."

CHAPTER 22

Adele jerked away from the grip of her nightmare. Her chest rose and fell painfully and her heart pounded. The fires of the dream rifts that had just been scorching the world and burning Gareth to bones faded into the thin, crisp cold of the mountains. The disturbing music of the Earth lingered.

Sunlight streamed around the edges of heavy yak-skin rugs that draped the windows. Her breath misted into the air above the makeshift bed. Gareth was not beside her. Turning her head, she saw him standing with General Anhalt next to the low fire pit in the center of the plain room. The smell of smoldering yak dung rose from the brick ring, but so did heat. Adele hurriedly slipped from under the dense pile of hides; luckily she was sufficiently dressed. She jammed into her boots and, dragging a thick blanket, scurried next to the glowing pile.

Gareth moved behind her and wrapped his arms tightly around her shoulders. He spoke in Arabic. "Are you all right?"

She nodded, not bothering to mention her dreams again.

Anhalt bowed his head toward a clay pot of simmering water on the glowing coals. "There will be tea soon, Majesty."

"Thank you, General." She glanced back at Gareth. "Do you think they have herds here?"

"If you mean humans, I don't smell any."

"Why would they have animals for dung otherwise?"

"I don't know. I don't smell animals either."

"I dreamed I heard musical instruments, but I think I still hear them. Maybe the altitude is affecting my ears."

"You aren't dreaming, but it isn't music. It's vampiric language."

Adele furrowed her brows. "It is? It was so melodic. Are they singing?"

"I don't know." Gareth sounded irritable at not having answers.

Anhalt poured tea. "Have you been able to locate this Tear of Death?"

"No." Adele moved to the edge of the low fire pit, enjoying the radiating heat from the bricks. The thick dung smoke wasn't rank enough to drive her from the warmth. "I have a limited connection to the rifts here, but I didn't sense anything unique."

"Is it possible," the general asked cautiously, "that this entire mission is for nothing?"

"Yes. However, the risk of *not* coming was too great."

"Of course, ma'am." Anhalt strapped on his sword belt. "If what Selkirk said about this object is true, I rather hope it is for nothing."

"I do too," Adele admitted. "But it isn't a fruitless trip in any case because we've found this clutch of unusual vampires. *Another* clutch of unusual vampires."

Gareth went to peer out of the window. "I've told you, my kind is going mad. But at least these lunatics haven't talked about me as their guide for the future."

Adele paused, listening. "Now I hear bells. Do you?"

"Yes." Gareth moved to the door. "Let's have a look around. I'm tired of waiting."

Sunlight blasted through a blue sky, but the air was dangerously frigid. The sound of small bells bubbled without a source, as if an invisible herd of sheep wandered the courtyard. Several vampires lifted off the rooftops and slipped into an open window in the largest temple above. Within minutes, Yidak and Takeda dropped down to the dirt square and approached.

The Demon King bowed to Adele. "Did you rest well?"

"I did, thank you. It was surprisingly warm, for which I am grateful." She waved her hand in the air. "Do you have herds? Animals, I mean. Your fuel?"

"No, no. However the bells you hear are those of goats ascending the Thousand Steps."

"Goats?"

"And men. A group of travelers are coming. They're coming to appease us." Yidak laughed. "To placate the mountain demons."

Takeda appeared less amused. "Humans make pilgrimages here and do certain duties for us."

Gareth asked, "Do you feed from them?"

"Oh yes," Yidak replied. "They come every few months."

"You only feed every few months? Do you prey on local villages in between those times?"

"If there are injuries that require nourishment, we may visit some of the villages. Normally the pilgrims serve. We have trained ourselves to go for great lengths of time without feeding." The Demon King tilted his head, listening to the bells. "I admit I'm glad they're coming because I'm a bit weak from my recent misadventures below. And Takeda has told me there are wounded from a recent attack."

The samurai cast a grim frown at the old vampire. "Is it wise to speak of it, Holiness? These visitors may be in league."

Yidak waved his aide-de-camp's suspicions away. "No, no. I don't think so."

"You were attacked here?" Adele asked quickly, causing Takeda to glare at her impertinence. "What happened?"

"We're not completely sure." Yidak wrapped his long fingers around his belt. "We've been attacked in the past by some of the Chinese clans. Chengdu particularly fears us."

Takeda continued to stare at Adele. "This attack was not from Chengdu. Nor any Chinese clan. They had an airship, as you do."

"An airship!" Adele looked at Gareth and Anhalt with alarm.

Yidak said, "We can assume there were humans with this pack of foreigners. Takeda has no idea who they were or what they wanted. They came out of nowhere. Takeda led our monks in battle. Several of the enemy were killed, but none talked. They were driven off and have not come back, wisely."

"How many of you are there here?" Adele wondered.

Yidak regarded her with a sly smile as Takeda stood ready to interrupt his overly communicative senior. But the Demon King was discreet. "Enough. And skilled, you may be assured." He gathered his robes. "We have some simple food for you and your general. And we should be able to acquire a goat or two for you when the pilgrims arrive later today."

After Yidak and Takeda departed, Adele stood in the courtyard listening to the bells wafting up along the mountainside. She turned to Gareth. "Vampire packs attacking and an airship. That has to be Goronwy looking for the Tear of Death."

"But he failed. That's good news."

"Yes." Adele rubbed her hands together and whispered, "Finally, we're ahead of him. Now we just have to find this . . . thing, whatever it is, and take it out of here from under the noses of hundreds of warrior vampires and back to Alexandria where we can protect it."

Gareth said, "And hopefully not trigger some apocalyptic event just by moving it."

Adele stared crossly at him. "That too. Thank you."

Anhalt put his shotgun over one shoulder and muttered, "Yes, that *is* good news."

—⚏—

It was late afternoon when the pilgrims finally arrived. There were twenty-five men in heavy traveling robes and thick fur hats. Their weathered faces turned down in reverence as they topped the Thousand Steps. The men were undaunted by the vampires who crouched on the monastery wall watching them. However, they entered the gate slowly, stopping very few seconds to kneel and toss dirt on their heads. The goats bounded ahead of the men who led several yaks loaded with supplies.

When the pilgrims gathered in the center of the lower courtyard, Yidak came to greet them. One of the visitors fell prostrate on the ground before the Demon King. Yidak reached down and lifted the man to his feet, and they conversed. The vampire gestured toward the building where Adele had been granted quarters. She and Gareth and Anhalt stood in the open window watching. The pilgrim eyed them, then bowed to Yidak and walked toward Adele. He then bowed to her, speaking in some dialect she didn't understand.

Anhalt said, "Do you speak Hindi?"

The man nodded slowly. "Yes. A little. The Demon King bids us gift you several goats, which we happily do. We also have salt and milk as you need it. Is there any other service we can provide you?"

Through Anhalt, Adele said, "That's very kind. May I ask what relationship you have with the demons?"

He replied simply, "We feed them."

"Why do you come all this way to let them drink your blood?"

The old pilgrim looked confused. "If we didn't come, they would come to us. And to others."

"Why you?"

"Because someone must. And my father did. And my son will."

"Do you not want your temple back?"

"Oh no. We were not meant to be here. This is a home meant for demons." The pilgrim turned away, calling back over his shoulder. "We will prepare a goat, and bring it to you."

Adele watched the old man stride back to his group and said to Anhalt, "I don't mind telling you, I'm starving. I could devour one of those goats raw."

The general let the heavy rug fall over the window. "Amazing. I never thought I'd see such . . . commerce between humans and vampires. Other than traitorous interactions such as Lord Aden had with Cesare in return for cheap coal from the north."

Adele returned to the fire, already anticipating a warm meal. "It's not terribly different from Gareth's relationship with his subjects in Edinburgh. But you're right, it's fascinating and heartening to see it work elsewhere."

Gareth paced a dark corner of the room. "Lord Aden was driven by greed, and he was exploited by Cesare. The arrangement here is fueled by fear. Those pilgrims are afraid if they don't give their blood to Yidak's clan, they'll be killed for it. That's hardly a shining beacon of co-existence."

Adele sighed in exasperation. "I don't know how to tell you, but even among humans, relationships are driven by greed and fear. I think this place is amazing. Aren't you stunned by Yidak and his monastery of vampires?"

"No." Gareth tugged irritably on his gloves. "It's no different than how my kind lives everywhere. I'm sure they came here, killed the humans, and took their places. We've been doing it for centuries, but we've succeeded only in fooling ourselves. Humans still know we're savage monsters. We'll do well to find your Tear of Death and get away from this place." He went for the door and slipped out into the cold.

Adele's shoulders sank and she put her hand to her suddenly aching forehead. She wasn't sure if he was wrong or not. Perhaps he was blinded by his own history. Or maybe she was goaded to optimism for the constant fear that there might be no future for the two of them. She sank to the floor, cold and hungry and dejected.

Anhalt also stepped to the door, but he merely leaned out and scooped up a handful of fresh snow. He packed it into the earthenware pot and set it on the fire.

"Is he right?" Adele mumbled. "Is there really no way for our species to connect? Am I being foolish?"

"I have no idea, Majesty." The general shaved tea from a black brick. "I have known you to be foolish a few times in your life."

She sighed loudly.

"But," he continued, "I have never known you to be false, nor to pursue empty goals."

Adele smiled up at her old friend and reached out to take his hand. General Anhalt bent at the waist and kissed her fingers. Together they quietly waited for the water to boil, their breath misting in the air.

CHAPTER 23

Gareth stalked up the wide steps out of the central courtyard. Nearly twenty vampires, male and female, descended past him in an organized assembly. They all wore crimson robes, and bowed to him in a unified motion. One of them whistled sharply at the pilgrims gathered in the shelter of an alley. Several of the men instantly detached themselves from the group and came forward without obvious emotion. The blood red vampires opened their ranks to allow the men to enter, and then closed back around them. The orderly group climbed the steps again and went inside a temple. Soon they would begin to drink the blood of their guests.

Gareth rose into the air over the carved temple spires. Many vampire eyes watched him with interest. He spun away and plunged out over the edge of the plateau. He vanished into the vast mountain emptiness, leaving the monastery behind. Hanging in the sky, arms outstretched, he felt the terrible wind batter him.

Gareth fought to suppress a rage. It all seemed like nonsense. These lamasery vampires here in Tibet. Those rebels in Europe spouting his own chaotic choices back at him as if they had meaning. His attempt to write a book lauding the life story of a monster who had killed thousands of humans. And most of all, the Greyfriar, that childish spawn of his own mock humanity.

Even Adele frantically flailed for some proof that the future made sense. The problem was that it did make sense, just not the sense she wanted. Humans would exterminate the vampires. It would take time and blood, but it would happen. There was nothing to stop it. Vampires were on the wrong side of history.

Perhaps it would have been better if Adele had just let her power run amok from Edinburgh last year. Instead of merely eliminating the vampires from Britain and Scotland, she should have swept them from the whole Earth.

Gareth slammed against a wall of rock. He clawed desperately to keep from being scraped along the mountainside. Foolish, he cursed himself. He had lost attention and the wind had taken him. Recovering his density, he dropped heavily onto an outcrop below. He fell hard, tumbling in the dirt where he lay still and tried to silence his bloody thoughts.

Fading sunlight glistened off a strange finger of ice in front of him. A thin stream of water had found its way out of a mountain crevice and created a small pool on this rock ledge. It was all ice now. The tiny trickle of water had frozen solid in the endless act of weathering away the great Himalayas.

"Are you injured?"

Gareth leapt to his feet and spun around. Yidak stood calmly nearby with the wind ruffling his red and gold robes.

"You announced yourself to the mountain quite hard." The old vampire gestured to the huge peak rising over them. "The wind can be unforgiving, even for those of us used to it."

"I'm fine."

"Good, good. You strike me as someone who's been hurt worse in your time."

Gareth wanted to be alone. He craved only the roar of the wind in his ears. He crouched on the edge of the escarpment overlooking miles of empty air. He heard Yidak squat next to him. They hunched together, silent, like a pair of vultures waiting. Time passed. Gareth finally gave an annoyed huff.

Yidak asked eagerly, "Yes?"

"Don't you have a pilgrim to drain?"

The old vampire laughed loudly. "I fed. And we don't *drain* them. They all walk out of here quite well because we want them to come back. And you're free to use them. They count you as a demon too."

"How fortunate for me."

"Yes." Yidak pursed his lips thoughtfully. "Demons are plentiful in Tibet and generally get what they want."

"We're plentiful where I come from too." Gareth paused with a crooked smile. "Well, we used to be."

"What happened to them?"

Gareth considered springing into the air to escape the chatty Yidak, but instead said, "Adele happened. She killed every one of my clan, except for me."

Yidak started to laugh, but instead narrowed his eyes in wonder. "Then what you said to me on your airship was true? She could kill me?"

"Yes. Easily."

"Hm." The Demon King turned to contemplate the purple and blue mountains with their small patches of snow glowing red in the last touches of the sun. "Why doesn't she then? Why doesn't she kill all of us?"

"I don't know."

"Don't you?"

Gareth moved abruptly across the ledge to stare into the frozen pool at his feet. "Because of me."

"Oh! She loves you. That is an old story."

"If you say so."

"Good, because I do." The old vampire smoothed his robes. "But could she leave you alive while killing all of us?"

"Perhaps."

Yidak nodded wisely. "I think there must be a reason other than just her love for you, another reason she doesn't kill all of us. What do you think it is?"

"Why don't you ask her?"

"Will she kill me for asking?"

Gareth shot him a callous glance. "Why don't you ask her?"

The old vampire smiled and idly rocked back and forth. "Tell me of your people, Gareth."

"I told you, I have no people," Gareth snarled. "They're all dead. What more do you need to know."

"They weren't always dead. Where are you from?"

Gareth sighed and gave up trying to fight off the conversation. "The British Isles. Have you heard of them?"

"Of course," Yidak said with a touch of sarcasm. "I haven't lived up here my entire life. Are you from London?"

"No. I was born in Scotland. That was my father's country."

"Who was the chief of your clan when the last war began, the great war against the humans?"

"My father. He called himself Dmitri."

"Was your father a good king?"

There was a long silence before Gareth sank to his knees beside the frozen pool. "I'm sick of talking about me."

Yidak crossed the frozen dirt. He lifted a stone and tossed it onto the ice. It broke a small, jagged hole and fell into the dark water. The old vampire straightened. "What do you see?"

Gareth pressed a clenched hand to his head. "If you're pretending to be a wise man, you're failing."

"There is something there to learn if you can." Yidak gave a deep sigh at Gareth's lack of interest. "The monastery was built long ago by wise humans who wanted only to teach. By the time I came here after I left Samarkand when the vampires rose there, only one or two of the monks still remained. I enjoyed my talks with them, but they eventually grew old and died."

Gareth looked up. "You came here to hide from the Great Killing?"

"*Hide* seems cowardly, but yes. The war seemed like a poor path. I wanted no part of it, but that wasn't an option if I had stayed with my people. So I came here to be away from it. I suspect you fought, didn't you?"

"I did."

"Your father favored the war then?"

"No!" Gareth leapt to his feet. "He was against it, but he couldn't convince the other clan lords. They were all sure that we had to strike or we would be driven to extinction. So many of us believed it that my father began to doubt his own ideas, even though he was right. But he wouldn't run away from his people, no matter what." Gareth glared intensely at the old vampire, waiting for a reaction, but Yidak seemed not to notice.

"Did you share your father's doubts about the war?"

"I was young and eager for blood."

Yidak shrugged with acceptance. "So you fought well."

"I did." Gareth wasn't boasting. "I showed no mercy."

"Do you hold me in disdain because I didn't fight?"

"No. I actually admire you," he admitted grudgingly. "My father believed the same as you, but if he had done as you have, he might still be alive. He would certainly have lived the rest of his life with sanity." Gareth noticed that the hole in the ice had already glazed over. "So all of your people here at the monastery refused to fight in the Great Killing?"

"No, not all. A few came with me at the beginning. Some came deeper into the war. Others have joined in the last century since the war ended."

"What about Takeda?"

Yidak grinned with delight. "I thought he would interest you. He fought in the war, in Japan mostly. He quite enjoyed it. After the war, he continued to fight for many of the clans across central Asia, raiding the frontier, crushing attempts by the humans to gather themselves. He was even the war chief of the great clan of Chengdu for many years although he was a foreigner to them. He came here several decades ago."

"Why?"

"Why don't you ask him?"

Gareth almost smiled, but managed to suppress it. "Does he just carry that sword as a trophy?"

"No. He wields it. He taught himself to fight with all manner of human tools. You should test him."

Gareth eyed the old vampire, seeking some sign of lies or mockery. There appeared to be none. "Is he the only one?"

"No. Many of my monks use weapons, but none so fervently as Takeda. Most prefer fighting with their claws, as they have always done."

"Then these praying monks of yours are actually a trained pack? You've formed your own clan. Do you raid human territories?"

"We do not. We fight only in defense. We have no interests outside this monastery. The clan lords do not understand we have no political ambitions, so they fear us. They come against us. And if they survive, they usually have no desire to return." The old vampire stopped and tilted his wizened head, listening and scenting. "We should return to the monastery."

"Is someone near?" Gareth tested the air too, but detected nothing.

"Perhaps. Something isn't right. With Takeda's story of a recent attack and my own recent adventure, it's best not to be caught out alone."

Yidak prepared to rise from the escarpment, waiting for Gareth to join him. Gareth lightened, and the two were seized by the wind. They beat their way back toward the monastery.

When finally the faint scent of fire and a few dim lights were apparent below, Yidak reached out toward Gareth. "Tomorrow, come to me. I would like to talk more. I have things to show you that should interest you. And perhaps your humans too." With that, the Demon King dropped like a stone to the roof of a dark temple. In a second, he crawled into a cleft in the dome and disappeared.

With an uneasy sense of confusion, Gareth descended through the blustery wind and eagerly sought the warming glow of Adele's light.

CHAPTER 24

Huddled around the fire, Adele finished a generous portion of stewed goat. General Anhalt was gnawing a bone with great relish. Gareth finished telling of his time with Yidak as cups of tea were downed.

"No mention of the Tear of Death?" Adele mumbled around a mouthful of goat.

"It didn't come up." Gareth gave her a wry glance. "Would you prefer they cook a larger animal for you? One goat doesn't seem to be enough."

"I could eat ten goats. I haven't had fresh meat since we left Alexandria."

Gareth took a long scent of the stew warming over the fire. He shrugged indifferently at it.

She wiped her mouth with the sleeve of her heavy robe. "Maybe you can keep Yidak and his people occupied while I snoop for the Tear of Death."

"There's something strange about this place. I don't like it."

"Do you think Yidak will try something against us?"

Anhalt offered, "It's Takeda you need to worry about. *He* doesn't trust us."

"How do you know?" Adele asked.

"Because I wouldn't trust us if I was him."

"The general is right," Gareth said. "Takeda is clearly the war chief here. Yidak is more curious than suspicious."

"Yidak is interested in the world beyond his claws," Adele said. "He's like you."

"Or he's crazy." Gareth peered outside into the activity of the late afternoon.

Anhalt rested his feet against the brick fire pit. "If the old Demon

King wants to know about you, tell him. Befriend him." He nodded toward Gareth. "Feed his curiosity. Give him a reason to spend time with you. Talk. Ask him questions."

Adele raised her teacup to the general in a toast. "I agree. Yidak may well spill every secret this place has if we seem interesting enough to him." She smiled at Gareth. "Remember how badly you wanted to talk to me at the British Museum when we first met? He may be just like that."

"Or he may be crazy," Gareth repeated.

Adele brushed off his concerns and stood. She went to her rucksack and pulled out her camera. As she inserted a film plate, she said, "I want another photograph while we have a minute. Let's go outside where it's brighter. General, will you help us?"

As they trooped out into the bright day, Anhalt took the camera, briefly inspecting it while Adele stood beside Gareth with the towering monastery in the background. She put a firm arm around his waist and looked toward the general, who peered through the viewfinder.

"Are you ready?" Anhalt asked.

"Smile," Adele told Gareth, who tried to comply. "Fine. If that's the best we can do, go ahead, General."

Anhalt clicked the button and held out the camera as if it was a complex machine he was fearful of breaking. Adele took it and pulled out the plate. She waited the requisite time and flipped it open. She smiled broadly and held up the picture. The photo was brighter than the one she had taken in London. Both Adele and Gareth looked present-able. "That's more like it! Well done, General. Gareth, you look very handsome."

Anhalt peered over her shoulder and gave an impressed nod at his photography skills. Adele slipped it into her pack, along with the camera.

"Now I've got a decent picture of us." She tightened the belt on her fur-lined robe. "Let's go and find Yidak. It's time to become the Demon King's close friends."

The eerie music of vampiric speech rose in the air again. When it stopped, tiny metallic noises followed. It was the sound of tools working methodically, likely the pilgrims tinkering on something. That noise ceased, and the vampiric stirred again.

Gareth looked to be confused, brows knit, mouthing phrases silently as they slipped past him in the cold air. "It's the same phrasing as before, but the voice is different. I can't make it out aside from a few common words."

Adele hooked her arm through his. "Let's find out."

Anhalt grunted uncomfortably as he followed.

Adele held up her hand. "Please, General, I beg you to rest while you have the chance. Don't argue. You are in pain."

Anhalt couldn't muster the energy to contradict her. "By tomorrow, I will be in fighting form." He bowed and returned to their room with a grateful look.

Adele and Gareth paused to take the bearings of the vampiric chanting that seemed to Adele to be coming from everywhere. They climbed steps to a large temple topped by a high minaret, the same one Gareth had seen Yidak taking refuge in. Many vampires hovered overhead but didn't intervene. The sounds of vampiric burst from deep inside the temple.

The interior was dark, but Adele could make out cracked and fading paintings on the walls. Once-bright colors depicted strange beings with long sharp teeth and ferocious eyes. She and Gareth passed between thick columns carved with indecipherable bas-reliefs. The chanting grew louder and harsher. Many voices cut through the air like swords and the cacophony amplified the natural grunting and hissing of vampiric. It was nearly impossible to understand the words.

They reached a thick-beamed doorway that opened onto a large chamber. Vampires crowded in the center of the space, all facing outward. Adele expected them to be chanting like monks in prayer, but they were all silent. Their mouths were closed, as were their eyes. They were listening.

She saw a strange shape against one wall. Some sort of machine about the size of a hand loom. It consisted of a wooden frame easily ten by ten feet, but instead of spools of wool, there were six metal cylinders suspended on the front like rollers. Each cylinder was about two feet long and six inches in diameter and they were all spinning. A figure sat in front of the machine working levers and turning handles. His feet pumped pedals on the floor like an organist. The vampiric chanting seemed to be coming from this strange loom.

The organist suddenly stopped. The garbled chanting ceased as the rotating cylinders slowed. The room grew silent but for a ringing afterglow. The vampires in the center looked as one to see who disturbed their reverie.

Yidak turned from his seat before the machine. He regarded Adele and Gareth expectantly. All the other vampires in the room were staring coolly at her.

"Welcome!" Yidak called out. "You heard our memories."

Adele gestured to the machine. "What is that thing?"

"Our memories." The Demon King laid a hand on the wooden frame. "Your kind might call it a library."

She couldn't take her eyes off the apparatus. The levers and pedals were connected to interior cords that ran over a series of wheels and pulleys, which, in turn, drove spools on which the metal cylinders rested. Yidak reached down to the floor next to his bench and picked up another of the metal cylinders. He shuffled across the chamber and extended it to Adele. He was eager for her to examine it. It was light, made of a thin metal like copper. Adele ran her fingers over the surface and felt dimples, holes, and scars in the metal. She handed the cylinder to Gareth, who studied it and rolled it between his hands.

Yidak chortled. "That is the lives of our people."

"What are you talking about?" Gareth asked with an edge in his voice.

Yidak signaled for them to follow him. He returned to the machine and settled onto a wooden bench in front of it. The vampire pulled his voluminous sleeves up and set his hands purposefully on a lever and handle. Bare feet pressed onto the row of pedals. Pumping his legs, he manipulated the controls before him with dexterity equal to Gareth's swordplay or skill with a pen on paper. The copper cylinders rotated and the guttural hissing of multiple vampire voices filled the air.

Despite the harsh sounds clawing at her ears, Adele moved closer and peered through the machine's frame into its workings. Each spinning cylinder was being brushed by a metal stylus of some sort, which was fixed on a moving arm that carried the stylus back and forth across the pitted copper surface. That interaction created a mechanical replication of vampire speech. It was amazing. Although created from rough materials and without beautiful decoration, it functioned with all the elegance and complexity of any clock or automata device Adele had ever seen.

Bobbing her head to better study the interplay inside the mechanism, Adele called over the screeching, "Who built this?"

"I did," Yidak replied simply.

"No." The grinding disharmony of the chanting set Adele's nerves on edge. "Who built it? Who *made* it?"

The old vampire turned his head in confusion. "I did."

Adele straightened and felt light-headed. The hissing was cutting through her brain. "The pilgrims, you mean?"

"They bring the materials. And they forge those for us." Yidak indicated the copper cylinder in Gareth's hand. "We don't have that skill. Yet."

Adele leaned heavily on the frame of the machine, blinking her eyes and feeling a creeping headache from the merciless barrage of noise. She wiped her perspiring forehead. "I don't think you're understanding the question."

Yidak released the handles and sat back. The cylinders ceased rotating and their screeching silenced. Adele nodded in grateful relief.

"I don't think you're understanding the answer," the old vampire said to her. "I built this. Yes, some of the more delicate work was done by human hands, if that's what you wish to hear. But most is my work. When I was young, I befriended several generations of craftsmen around Samarkand. They were divinely skilled at clocks and music boxes, all manner of machines that produced chimes and sounds." Yidak ran his claw over one of the cylinders. "Over the centuries, I found ways to mimic my own tongue. So we spend our days chanting our memories and recording them. Each of these cylinders is the story of one of my monks, dictated by them, saying whatever they feel is important. We come here to listen. It may sound odd because we have trained ourselves to hear multiple voices at one time. There are many of these cylinders, created so that our kind may remain, even if we are gone one day."

Adele realized her mouth was open in amazement. She glanced at Gareth, who was staring at the cylinder. "That's incredible."

The Demon King nodded in agreement.

She ran her hand over some of the cords inside the strange loom. "I never thought this could be possible from a vampire."

"It's not." Gareth shook his head.

Adele looked at him through the machine's workings. "But it plays your language. We heard it. You said vampires didn't have any sort of script or writing."

"We don't. I don't know what these marks are."

"How else do you explain it?"

"I can't," Gareth snapped. "But he's lying."

Yidak smiled with gentle patience and motioned with his hand. The group in the center shuffled past soundlessly out the door.

Gareth said to the old vampire, "Even if you could make these things, *why* would you do it?"

Yidak met the stern gaze. "Why are you so surprised? You use human tools and weapons."

"This is so far beyond that. *This* is impossible for us." Gareth raised the cylinder again and crushed it easily in his gloved hand. "Impossible!"

Yidak grew briefly perturbed at the mangled copper in Gareth's clutch. Then he took a deep breath and studied the younger vampire with concern. "Why are you so angry, Gareth? Is it because you are no longer special? Is it because you know there was another way, but it has been lost?"

"We're wasting our time trying to be human," Gareth said in a harsh voice.

"Time is all we have." Yidak looked slowly at the painted walls surrounding them. "But I don't want to be human. I want to see what *we* can be. Or at least, what we could have been."

Gareth dropped the bent metal tube to the floor with a sharp clang. It rocked back and forth slowly and noisily. He looked at the machine. Adele held her breath. The bewilderment in his eyes was almost painful. Then Gareth spun on his heel and went out into the night.

CHAPTER 25

Adele started to follow Gareth, but there was something compelling in Yidak's face that made her stop. Curiosity? Doubt? Vampires typically expressed emotions as a mask; beneath them was always either hunger or fear.

Yidak spoke with what sounded like actual concern. "He seems so angry."

Adele hesitated to reply. She didn't want to say anything about Gareth to this stranger. She had a limited notion of the reality of the vampire world, other than it was dark and brutal and advantages were always exploited. Still, there was a real desire in Yidak's eyes to understand.

"Many are," the old vampire continued, "when they come here. I think we can help him."

Adele grew suspicious and the vampire noted it instantly because he smiled.

"Don't worry," he said. "I have no dark motive. There is no war here between us."

"Right," Adele agreed. "Here, you've already won."

"I suppose it looks that way to you." Yidak laughed. "You must look harder." He gestured to a small arched doorway in the rear. "Won't you sit with me?"

Adele glanced anxiously toward the door where Gareth had gone.

Yidak repeated, "He will return in a moment. Trust me, please."

Her curiosity won out. She followed the Demon King across the stone floor. Beyond the arch was a small room, again decorated with flaking paints of gods and demons.

Yidak sat and indicated a chair for Adele. "I can have tea brought, if you wish."

"No, thank you. Gareth is right that it's very unlikely you made that machine."

"Yes, it is, but you don't doubt it. And Gareth only says he disbelieves because it frightens him, not because he thinks it's untrue."

"Why would this thing scare him?"

Yidak interlaced his long fingers in a monastic pose. "As I said, most of my little clan came here for the same reasons he did. They felt like outcasts and heard rumors of a place of sanctuary. I think Gareth is searching, but he's helpless."

"Helpless?" Adele grew annoyed with the pedantic old vampire schooling her on Gareth. He had no notion of what Gareth truly was. "I've never known anyone less helpless than Gareth. He's reinvented himself many times."

Yidak shook his head. "No, he has covered his face many times with this mask or that."

Adele shifted angrily, scraping her boots across the floor. "You don't know him."

Yidak settled back in his chair. "I actually know him very well because I have seen many like him. He is different, but I know his type. However, I don't know *you* at all. He did say you could kill me with a thought."

Adele stayed purposefully quiet, trying to bring her anger under control.

Yidak clicked his claws on the arm of the chair. "You are a geomancer."

She stared with alarm, reaching out immediately and gathering whatever distant energy from the Earth she could. It wasn't much, but heat rose around her.

Yidak shifted uncomfortably, inching back as if from an open flame. "Don't be shocked. In China, geomancers are plentiful. Every winter the clans there kill as many as they can. Can't afford to let them grow too numerous or powerful. Are you powerful?"

"Yes."

The Demon King regarded her with peculiar respect and a hint of concern. "You have nothing to fear from me."

"I know."

He laughed awkwardly. "Does he drink your blood?"

Adele flushed and power crackled through the air. Yidak pulled back with a pained hiss, but didn't flee or strike out. His question was completely guileless. He wasn't goading her. He was curious. She reined in the energy.

Yidak exhaled with wide eyes. "How do you not burn him?"

"Oh, so you don't know everything?" Adele snorted a little more spitefully than she intended.

"No. I know nothing. But I want to know everything. You see my dilemma?"

Adele said, "I only harm those I wish."

"So with all that power, you've never hurt him?" Yidak stared into her eyes. "Why didn't you kill all of us if you had the chance?"

Adele clenched her mouth and looked away. She suddenly wanted to flee, but something felt cowardly about it. She smelled charred flesh and knew it was only the memory of Gareth's terrified face burning away as she fought the very power she had unleashed, or that Mamoru had forced her to unleash.

"Was it just for him?" Yidak pressed. "You betrayed your kind for him? Was there something more? Or are you even sure? Are you afraid you missed the chance you had to be the savior, and that you will never have that courage again?"

It was all Adele could do to whisper, "Don't provoke me."

"I am not your enemy."

"It's hard to tell. You look like my enemies."

Yidak lowered his head and exhaled. His posture grew calm. His voice was unhurried. "Very well. Let's discuss something we both care about. I can help Gareth."

"So can I," she snapped, recovering her breath.

"I am not competing with you. I am merely offering a path. There is a ritual in this land called *chöd*. I think Gareth would benefit from it. With time, the acolyte calls upon the demons he fears most to come and devour him."

Adele shuddered under the glares of the monsters painted on the flaking walls, as if a hundred Yidaks watched her. "You never stop fighting your demons or you fail."

"On the contrary. It leaves only your purest self behind. Your fears and failures. All gone. You abandon everything you have. There is nothing braver than casting yourself into the void and being scattered to nothingness. It is the experience of choosing the end that is the greatest act of self-determination."

Gareth's voice penetrated the darkness. "I've already done that."

Adele twisted to see Gareth in the archway. His face was still intense, but the anger had passed. Her legs quivered when she stood and went to him. He took her hand.

"Adele destroyed me," he said.

"Don't," she began.

"No, it's fine." He kissed the top of her head. "More than a year ago, her full power was turned loose. It tore me to pieces. I watched my flesh burn away, and felt my bones blacken. There was nothing to be done. It was enough that I knew I had done what I could to insure she would survive. So I accepted it and died. However, she brought me back. She risked her life to bring her powers back under her control, and she used them to restore my life. After that ordeal, when I opened my eyes, I saw her face." He turned his blue gaze on Adele. "I never want to go another day without seeing her face."

She embraced him. She felt his heart beating through his chest.

Yidak rested his chin in his hands and wide eyes flicked between Adele and Gareth. "Well. That's . . . well."

"Well said." Adele remarked.

Gareth slipped an arm around Adele's waist.

Adele stiffened in alarm. "He's speaking Arabic. Just as if he was in court in Alexandria."

The old vampire smiled as he pushed himself out of his chair. "Not so elegant as yours, I fear, but I used to hear it often in the old days. I thought it would make you more comfortable. Come, I'll show you our memories again."

He strolled past them, and Adele thought she heard a faint chuckling from the Demon King.

—◊—

General Anhalt opened his eyes. Something had awakened him. He heard the gentle crackle of the fire. His back was against the warm brick fire pit and he was wrapped in a thick rug. He hadn't intended to fall asleep; he wanted to be awake when Adele returned. He hated to look unprepared to her. He threw back the rug in a futile pretense that he was simply resting.

Takeda stood a few feet away, holding the general's glowing Fahrenheit saber. Anhalt's hand instinctively flashed to his sword, but only found the empty scabbard. He came up on one knee, fumbling with the flap of his holster and drawing his service revolver. The vampire let his gaze drift from the green glow of the sword to the gun. He betrayed no sense of alarm.

Anhalt feared the vampire's presence meant something ominous. Perhaps Adele and Gareth had been seized, or even killed. And now this creature had come to finish off the foolish visitors. The general tightened his grip on the pistol.

Takeda weaved the saber through the air, watching the emerald haze left behind. "What is this?"

Anhalt aimed at the vampire's head. At this range, it was a solid bet he could hit the thing, which could well kill Takeda or at least buy time for a second shot. The vampire stared past the muzzle into Anhalt's eyes.

Takeda said, "I am not here to harm you, or you would be dead."

"That does make sense." Anhalt didn't lower the pistol. "But you took my sword."

The vampire nodded with eyes closed. "Forgive me. That was improper." He slowly held the saber to Anhalt with blade down and hilt forward.

Anhalt reached out his left hand and delicately grabbed the sword by the pommel guard, careful not to brush the vampire's fingers.

Takeda kept his hands away from the katana in his belt. He nodded toward the pistol. "Humans are so distrustful."

"Attempted genocide has that effect." Anhalt used the sword to push himself to his feet. The revolver didn't waiver. "This is a Fahrenheit blade. It will burn even you." He carefully slid the saber back into the scabbard. With the vampire's gaze following him, Anhalt leaned over and took the shotgun in one hand. He brought the heavy gun to bear and holstered the pistol. He sat carefully on the edge of the fire pit with the shotgun pointed at Takeda's chest.

The vampire said, "A larger gun gives you more confidence?"

"I wouldn't mind a cannon, but this will serve."

"May I lower my hands now?"

"No." Anhalt had begun to believe that his earlier fear was misplaced. The general lost his concern for Adele and Gareth but was still worried about the vampire's visit. "What do you want?"

Takeda bowed slightly, acknowledging Anhalt's direct question. "I want to know why *she* is here."

The general felt the hard steel of the trigger guard and the smooth wood of the grip. He wondered if Takeda was trying to catch the humans in a lie if Adele had already given some story to Yidak. He could have been independently seeking answers to pass on to the old Demon King. Or he could have been trying to protect his leader, who was not always attentive to his own security. Anhalt almost smiled at the last thought. "That's not for me to say."

"Only my kind comes here, looking for something or trying to hide from something. But *he* did not bring her here. This is clearly *her* mission. That vampire is merely her tool. Why has she come to this place?"

Anhalt stayed silent.

"You are a soldier." Takeda studied the general, who wore common clothes with a heavy coat and no indication of his service or rank. "How many of my kind have you killed for her?"

"Quite a few. Not enough, however, or the war would be over."

"So are you losing the war?"

"No. We're winning."

"You must have improved yourselves since the first war."

"We have. Our weapons are better, and our will is stronger."

Takeda asked, "You are content to exterminate us?"

Anhalt shifted slightly to ease the pain in his leg. Takeda noticed. The general adjusted the shotgun to remind the vampire that the big gun was leveled at his chest. "Tell me, how many of my kind have *you* killed?"

"None recently."

"But during the Great Killing?"

"Oh. Many." Takeda smiled, his teeth showing. "Many."

"You seem pleased by it."

"At the time, I had no qualms with it. But you understand that, don't you?"

Anhalt admitted, "I do."

"Take solace though, General. I have also killed my own kind." Takeda looked around the chamber at the meager pile of their possessions. "And what of your . . . man, Gareth? He has the look of one who has spilled human blood."

"I'm told he has."

"But you forgive him, and treat him as a comrade. Why?"

The general pursed his lips with a slight smile. There was something he found compelling in this vampire that he didn't feel for Yidak. Something in his manner that Anhalt recognized. Takeda, no matter what else he may have been, was a soldier. It was a commonality, even if the creature was a potential mortal enemy. For that reason, the general had to guard against saying too much.

Takeda nodded with acceptance of the silence. "What about that woman? How odd that both you and your blood-soaked colleague follow a woman. It wouldn't be strange for my kind, but I thought humans held females to be weak."

"Not all humans." Anhalt grinned now. "Of any of us, that woman is the one you should fear most of all."

Takeda grew grim. "Then why shouldn't we kill her now?"

"One, because you probably couldn't. And two, because she is also the one human who might save you from extinction." Anhalt exhaled and lowered the shotgun into the crook of his elbow. "All right, put your hands down. You're making me tired."

The vampire stood unsure for a moment, then he lowered his arms. "I can still smell your fear, despite your pretense of unconcern."

"I'm sure you can. I am afraid. You could slay me quite easily." Anhalt set the shotgun aside. "But this isn't some sort of pretense. It's called living with the fear. We've changed in that way too. Your kind still terrifies us, but now we fight all the same. I'm having some tea. I assume you wouldn't care for any." The general turned his back and shifted pots on the fire. He hoped the vampire didn't notice the slight tremor in his hands.

Takeda strolled toward the glowing coals. "I would, actually. I will try it."

Anhalt paused only briefly in his preparations before carrying on. While settling the tea, he saw a face peering between the edge of the yak rug and the door. It was a young face, and the general felt no threat from it. He stared at the blue eyes and they quickly darted away.

The general said, "You may tell your young friend to come in."

Takeda didn't turn to look. "Hiro. Stop lurking and step inside."

The thick rug shifted slightly and a young, male vampire came in on his hands and knees. He looked warily up at Takeda and then down at the floor, refusing to meet Anhalt's eyes.

"Stand up," Takeda chided. "Don't crawl."

Anhalt bowed to the young male. "Hello. I am Mehmet Anhalt."

The boy rose slowly, unsure whether to respond.

Takeda said, "Speak."

The young vampire blurted out, "I am Hiro."

"Very pleased to meet you." Anhalt pressed the water vessel deeper into the hot coals. "Would you care for tea, Hiro?"

The boy looked confused by the question but stepped forward. "What is it?"

"It is a drink," Takeda said. "You won't like it."

Hiro frowned. "Then why drink it?"

"I like it," Anhalt told the boy.

Hiro tilted his head. "Then I want to try it. Is it hot? Is it hotter than blood?"

General Anhalt froze briefly, eyeing the young vampire. "I don't know. But it is hot."

"Why?"

Takeda grunted with annoyance. "Why must you ask so many questions?" The samurai reached out and cuffed the boy lightly on the back of the head. "You do not need tea. Go."

Hiro looked disappointed, but he slowly wandered for the door. He gave Anhalt another silent glance of deep interest, then slipped outside.

"We are not spying on you," Takeda said. "Hiro's curiosity is abnormally extreme."

Anhalt smiled at the fact that the vampire felt the need to explain and excuse the lad. "I understand completely. He doesn't seem too different from young men I know."

"You have children then?" Takeda asked, trying not to sound too eager.

"No." The general poured two cups of tea. "Is Hiro your son?"

"No," Takeda responded. "He is not my blood, but he is mine, for better or worse."

Anhalt handed the small cup to Takeda who took it with great concentration on exactly where to place his fingers. He was clearly trying to be sure that he didn't accidently crush it. The general lifted his cup and held it out. The vampire looked at it, unsure what to do. Anhalt tapped his cup against Takeda's. "Cheers."

Takeda lifted the cup to his lips. He smelled the liquid and then drank the contents in a single gulp. He stood as if waiting. Finally he lowered the cup.

"Well?" Anhalt asked.

Takeda smacked his lips without conviction. "I'm sure it's very good."

CLAY GRIFFITH AND SUSAN GRIFFITH   195

The general smirked and sat on the edge of the fire pit. "Your name is Japanese. Is that where you're from?"

"Originally yes. I was born on the island of Hokkaido."

"And Hiro as well?"

"No. He is from the great clan lands of Chengdu. To the east."

"Isn't Hiro a Japanese name?"

"We take whatever name we wish. Sometimes we take many names. I think Hiro took that name because I am Japanese."

Anhalt swirled his cup, watching the dark tea leaves swim in the liquid. "How did he come to be here? He seems far younger than anyone else I've seen."

"Hiro came because I brought him after I killed his parents. He had no one else."

General Anhalt gave the samurai a curious glance. "Does he know that?"

"He does."

Anhalt grunted with interest, but Takeda didn't seem disposed to go into greater detail. The general lifted the pot and found the vampire extending his cup. Takeda took the refilled tea and went to the door where it was colder. He settled cross-legged on the floor.

Anhalt watched the samurai shifting his katana to the side. "How did you come to use that blade? I've never known a vampire to do such a thing, except for Gareth."

Takeda ran his fingers over the hilt of the sword. "I killed so many men who used them. Yet they seemed confident in the ability of these things to protect them. They were wrong, of course, but they never stopped believing it. I found it fascinating."

"Most of your kind would think it's pathetic."

"Most of my kind don't think. At all."

Anhalt laughed. "We have something in common then."

The vampire smiled with a conspiratorial nod. He swirled his tea around, similar to the way Anhalt had done. "You have led young men like Hiro into battle? So you have experience making children into adults?"

"I have led many men into battle, some barely children, yes. But I only have detailed experience with a particular young man who has been my charge, off and on, throughout his life."

"How did you acquire him?"

Anhalt laughed. "I didn't *acquire* him. As a soldier, there were two children whose safety has been my duty. A young man named Simon and the woman you see with me here, Adele."

"Ah. I see." The vampire nodded thoughtfully. "Duty."

"Their well-being is not *just* my duty; it is my honor. What you would do to protect Hiro and to serve Yidak, I would do the same for Adele, and for Simon were he here. You understand that, don't you?"

Takeda stared at the old soldier for a long time. His blue gaze studied the brown eyes of Anhalt. Then he raised his teacup as if to click it against Anhalt's.

"Cheers." Takeda drank.

Anhalt swallowed the last of his tea and set about brewing more.

CHAPTER 26

Caterina prowled the halls of the Tuileries. The sun was warm and it suppressed activity around the palace. Most were asleep, but she was restless. Apparently so was Lothaire because he was not in his usual resting place. Likely he was with the children. So she headed for the nursery, feeling the urgent need to be among her family. Caterina turned the corner into the corridor where she saw Fanon standing in the hall. He had been a long trusted retainer of the clan and the war chief for centuries. He was old now; he had been one of Lothaire's primary mentors and a ferocious fighter during the Great Killing. Normally his steady presence was comforting, but now Fanon jerked oddly to attention when he saw Caterina. His gaze fell to the floor.

"Fanon, I'm surprised to see you here." She regarded the old soldier, but he refused to meet her eyes. "What's wrong with you?"

"Nothing, Majesty."

Caterina assumed that Fanon was simply uncomfortable or ashamed to have lost his position as war chief after so long, particularly to someone like Honore. It wasn't unusual for the eldest child to become war chief, but Honore was not qualified, even his mother had to admit that. Then she heard voices. One of them was her oldest daughter, Isolde. The other was not Lothaire.

It was Lady Hallow.

Caterina exchanged a quick accusatory glance with Fanon. He offered a brief embarrassed look. She snarled and broke into a run. She swept through the nursery door, searching the room frantically for any disturbance. In the far corner, near a broken window that overlooked ruined gardens, Isolde and Hallow sat knee to knee in deep conversation. They looked up in surprise at Caterina's dramatic entrance. Isolde was wide eyed with excitement. Hallow was her usual calm self and raised a warm smile for the queen.

"What's wrong?" Caterina asked. "Why are you here, Lady Hallow? Is something wrong with Honore?"

"No, Your Majesty." Hallow's voice was like a smoothly running stream. "I'm visiting with Princess Isolde. Didn't Fanon mention I was here? I left him in the corridor."

"Why are you here? Why are you visiting my daughter?" Caterina felt small hands on her legs. Her youngest peered up, insistent for attention. She lifted the babe into her arms.

Isolde beamed. "I'm going to fight." The girl was a little younger than Honore, but nearly as tall as her mother already, and dark like the queen.

"Fight whom?" Caterina searched the room, spotting her inseparable twins sitting quietly against the far wall. She turned back toward Isolde, who approached with a manic grin.

"Humans."

Caterina pushed the baby's gnashing teeth away, trying to focus on Isolde's senseless comments. From across the room, her son shouted, "Can I go too?" followed by his sister arguing that she should fight instead because she was more vicious. Isolde yelled at them to be quiet; no one had asked them to fight.

Caterina went to the door, wrestling with her baby. She called for two human servants who cowered nearby. "Feed him!"

The pale couple shuffled forward and took the wriggling child so Caterina could spin back to her squabbling family.

"Quiet! All of you! No one is fighting the humans."

"I am!" Isolde barked. "Lady Hallow said."

"Did she now?" Caterina glared coldly at Hallow. "Well, Lady Hallow doesn't make *all* the decisions in this family yet."

"Honore needs me—"

"Isolde, silence!"

The young female gaped back at Hallow for support against her tyrannical mother. In return, the pale wraith said, "Your Majesty, the Dauphin has requested Princess Isolde begin her war training. There is a raid on Poitiers being planned. Fanon will be beside Her Highness at all times. You trust him, don't you?"

Caterina felt a coldness in her stomach and struggled to keep her voice calm in front of her children. "She's too young."

"I am only doing my duty. I am Prince Honore's adjutant."

"And I am the queen."

"I will remind him."

Caterina froze in rage at the temerity of her reply.

Isolde whined, "Please, mother! Let me fight! I want to help. I want to be like Honore, not like father."

"How dare you!" Caterina rounded on Isolde, but she looked into the fiery eyes of a young female vampire rather than her daughter. Rage drained away to be replaced by gloom. A sense of sadness for Lothaire swept over her. His children were everything to him, but they only knew him as the sedate old father content to raise them. They had never seen him as he was.

Isolde retorted, "I am going to fight. Honore needs me and he's running the clan. If you don't let your older children fight," she jabbed a finger at her younger brother and sister, "you'll watch Equatorians bayonet *them* in the streets of Paris this summer. Right, Lady Hallow?"

Hallow remained unmoved, watching Caterina with a despicable triumphant expression buried beneath her bland face.

Caterina managed to say in a rough growl, "You may withdraw, Lady Hallow. And you will never set foot in this wing of the palace again without my express permission."

Hallow gave the queen a curt bow and put a brief hand on Isolde's arm as she passed. Hallow departed and there was a rustle as Fanon fell in behind her. Isolde followed, but Caterina seized her wrist.

"You do not have leave to go."

The young vampire glared into her mother's face. Then her eyes darted toward her young siblings. "You have them to control for a while longer, but not me."

Caterina tried to hold onto her daughter's arm. Isolde jerked her hand free and stalked out without looking back. The manservant appeared in the doorway and dropped the baby on the floor before staggering away. The child's face was smeared with fresh blood. He held his arms up to Caterina. She slowly picked him up. The twins whispered to one another, eyeing their mother suspiciously.

Caterina held the baby tight and he pressed his warm head against her shoulder as he drifted off into well-fed sleep.

—✎—

Caterina walked slowly across the bridge and south into the narrow labyrinths of the Left Bank. She tried not to think too much about the coming meeting with Lady Hallow. She had sent a servant with a message to her son's advisor, pleading of a troubled heart and a concern for family. The queen indicated that she understood Hallow was now a part of the clan, and that she had resisted that notion for a long time. There had to be a reconciliation between the two powerful women. They both knew the men involved, Lothaire and Honore, were not truly the ones making the decisions. The clan would go the way Caterina and Hallow chose, so they should work together.

It had pained Caterina to talk about Lothaire that way, but she knew it was honest, and she knew Hallow would perceive it as such. So the queen asked Hallow for a private meeting to work out a compromise. They had much in common, and the clan wouldn't survive their continued strife. Caterina stated she would wait in the catacombs and hoped Hallow would see fit to join her.

Hallow would understand and value secret one-on-one conversations. They were her métier as a political creature. Hallow perceived the queen had little ground to negotiate; she would consider this meeting to be a prelude to Caterina's surrender.

That was what Caterina wanted. She needed Hallow to believe that so the meeting would take place and Caterina could kill Hallow. This stain had to be removed from the clan and from the family.

Caterina had lost her skills at being secretive. Still, she wandered the streets, up and back, doubling over the same terrain for a long while. She looked for familiar faces or shapes, trying to discover if she was being followed.

Only after the third passage down the same narrow lane did she notice a figure overhead. It had been there before. She couldn't make out the face in the sun, but the figure was smaller, likely a young female about the size of Isolde.

Caterina sprang up, kicking off old stone walls and swinging onto a failing slate roof. If this spy was one of Hallow's, it was best to just turn her out and forget about the meeting. Caterina stood openly staring at the floating figure above, daring her to present herself.

The figure sank toward her, drawn up, hunched as if embarrassed at being seen. The face came clear. It was the young female from Gareth's group of child malcontents. Nadzia.

"What are you doing?" Caterina demanded. "Spying on me?"

"Um. I suppose so." Then Nadzia quickly added, "But not in a bad way."

The girl was so innocent, Caterina almost smiled at her pluck. "Did Gareth tell you to watch me?"

"No! He's never told us to do anything. It's what I do. I watch and report back to Kasteel."

"Why?"

"To gather information."

"Why?"

Nadzia thought for a moment. She stayed silent.

"Are you watching me to see if Gareth has returned?"

The girl's shoulders slumped. "Yes. Kasteel is worried that we won't ever see him again, that we failed him. We've been observing you and the king whenever you leave the palace."

Caterina was disturbed and a little angry that this was the first time she had observed the watchers. They were better than she expected, or perhaps in the chaos of Paris it was impossible to notice anything so minor.

"Well, on your way, Nadzia." Caterina saw the girl smile broadly when the queen called her by name. "I have heard nothing from Gareth. You may inform Kasteel. And please don't follow me any longer."

Nadzia bit her lip, hesitant to speak, but couldn't stop herself. "Majesty, you have many enemies in Paris."

The queen bristled at the boldness. "Do I? How would you know?"

"We listen." The girl was embarrassed to be speaking to the queen like this. "It's clear. There are few who support you and the king."

Caterina tried to appear unaffected, glowering at the messenger. "Thank you, I'm sure. I aim to set that straight even now."

Nadzia blurted out, "Don't do anything dangerous! We can help you. Lord Gareth is very fond of you. We will do as you say."

Caterina impulsively reached out for the frantic girl, anxious over her desperate outburst of support. "No, no, stop. I don't need your help. You're children—"

"We're not! We helped save Lord Gareth and the empress from the packs of Bruges. We've fought and killed."

Caterina squeezed Nadzia's hand. "I don't want you to fight and kill for me. Why don't you go home? Don't stay in Paris. It isn't safe."

"I have no home. Kasteel and the others are my family now."

"Then go back to them. Do not involve yourself in my affairs. Do you understand? It is too dangerous for you."

"Yes," Nadzia said quietly.

"Good. Go." Caterina released the girl's hand with unexpected sadness. "Don't follow me!"

Nadzia nodded and lifted into the air. The two kept their eyes together. Caterina felt a twinge of regret when the girl drifted out of sight beyond the rooftops. She wished she could have sat with her and passed the time as she once had done with Isolde.

Before Hallow.

CHAPTER 27

"I am Gareth, the son of Dmitri. I was born south of Kiliwhimin in the Great Glen of Scotland. My father taught me to hunt humans and drink their blood. That is what I am."

Gareth stopped speaking. It was rare for him to say even that much in vampiric.

Yidak stared at a smooth cooper cylinder, deep in thought. In his wizened hands, the old vampire held simple tools, short metal rods with flattened tips. His eyes cast upward as he fought to recall something. "Could you repeat it, please? Your accent is odd to me."

Gareth restated the phrases about his birth, the opening lines of his nonexistent book. Yidak tapped the curved copper with his instruments. After a few minutes of work, he studied the dimples and scratches while speaking silently to himself. He then proceeded to alter the marks before sliding the cylinder onto one of the spools of his strange loom. He sat on the bench and readied his hands and feet, muttering hopefully, "We shall see."

Adele moved to Gareth's shoulder, eagerly watching the machine. Gareth flexed his gloved hands anxiously, pretending to be calm. Yidak started the cylinder spinning and worked several levers. A hissing voice spilled out, "I am Gareth, the son of Dmitri. I was born south of Kiliwhimin in the Great Glen of Scotland. My father taught me to hunt humans and drink their blood. That is what I am." Gareth gasped in amazement. It wasn't his voice, but those were his words in his native language.

Adele grabbed Gareth's arm, jostling him back and forth. "I understood that! It was just what you said. He recorded what you said!"

Yidak wiped his forehead, peering quizzically at Adele. "You understand our tongue? Knowing you, I'm not shocked, but I am surprised you can figure out what he's saying. He speaks oddly. Hard to believe a vampire's vampiric could be rusty."

Gareth watched as the pockmarked cylinder slowed to a stop. "Why go to all that trouble? Why not simply write on a piece of paper?"

"Why should we write in a human language?" Yidak ran a loving hand over the cylinder. "This is vampiric as we hear it. Any of us can understand it."

"As long as we have that machine," Gareth added.

Yidak smiled, not grasping or recognizing the sarcasm.

"Gareth," Adele whispered with excitement, "he is creating a vampire script. Those marks are a written language."

"No, Adele." Gareth shook his head with academic surety. "He's only making scratches on metal so it will create sounds that seem to be vampiric. It's not a written language."

"Yes it is. Don't you see how incredible this is?" The scowl on his face told her otherwise. "Do you think humans created their first written language overnight?"

"No. He's mimicking a human technology to imitate our language. He doesn't really know what he's doing."

"Don't be arrogant." Adele's annoyance was plain. "This is something no one, including you, thought was possible. What he's doing here is astounding."

Gareth stared at the old vampire, watching him continue to chisel small marks onto the cylinder. For a brief moment he considered Adele's words. Chips and grooves in copper. Was that a written language? Was that vampiric script? It was something that had never existed. Vampires were an oral culture. They wrote nothing. They made nothing. They preserved nothing. This was impossible.

Adele lifted the camera out of her satchel. "May I take a picture of the machine?" At Yidak's confusion, she added, "It's one of the ways humans make a record of what we see. For the future."

Immediately, Yidak came forward to examine the camera, excitement making his wrinkles more pronounced. "It is so small. Where are the cylinders?"

"There are none. Here, let me show you. Stand by your machine."

Gareth sighed in mild exasperation, but it was merely out of habit. His heart was hammering at the thought of what he was witnessing. He even felt a twinge of shame for doubting, like a precocious child who discovered he wasn't the unique prodigy he thought.

Adele nudged Yidak a little to the side so he wasn't blocking the view of the machine. Then she lifted the camera, jostling for a good angle and more light in the dim room. Only when she was satisfied did she press the shutter release. The small click elicited the sound of whirring gears from inside the camera. She opened the back and removed the plate.

Yidak hovered impatiently. "Is that it?"

"Almost." After she had counted off a minute in her head, she flipped open the plate and pulled out the picture. She held it up.

"There I am!" Yidak laughed. "It's like a painting but not as attractive."

"Yes." Adele slipped the photograph into her bag. "Humans won't believe a vampire could do such a thing without the proof. That machine will change the world." She suddenly turned to Gareth. "That's what your book needs as well. You should use my photographs. They'll see you as you are."

Gareth offered a cautious purse of his lips. "I'm sure your people would *love* to see me as I am, with their empress. Perhaps a picture of me drinking your blood?"

Adele snapped the lens cap on the camera with an angry huff. "Why do you always have to go to the worst case scenario?"

"Because in *this* case, there is only a worst case."

Hiro appeared in the entrance to the temple chamber, wringing his hands. His eyes strayed curiously to the camera. "Holiness, Takeda requests you."

The Demon King excused himself and went out. Gareth and Adele followed into the bitter night. Yidak rose into the air and joined Takeda, who clutched the minaret on the temple roof.

"I'll find out what the issue is," Gareth told Adele. He lifted to join them. When Gareth set foot on the cracked tile roof, he crouched and listened. Both Takeda and Yidak were staring off into the wide mountain valley to the south.

"There," Takeda hissed and pointed.

"Ah yes. I see."

Gareth followed their directions, and he saw it too. An airship. Many miles away. It wasn't the sleek, little *Edinburgh*. It was a large European ship, but the sails were tattered and several of the masts were mere stumps. It was not a derelict; there were faint lights aglow.

When Gareth's attention returned to his surroundings, he saw Takeda staring down at him. The samurai said, "That is the same ship we saw when we were attacked. Is it familiar to you?"

"No," Gareth replied sharply. "But it is clearly a bloodman slave ship."

Both Takeda and Yidak eyed him, as if he was leaving something unsaid. The old vampire asked his lieutenant, "What do you think?"

"I say we take it, Holiness," Takeda replied. "It lurks here for a reason. We must destroy it."

"I agree." Yidak grew strangely cold; all the trappings of the peculiar old holy man fell away. He raised his head and sent out an ear-splitting shriek. Action erupted all around in response. Shapes scrambled over the ground and crawled along the buildings. The monastery became a moving carpet of living beings.

Gareth turned to go back to Adele, but Takeda grabbed his arm. "You're coming with us."

Gareth pulled free and snarled, "I am, but let me see to Adele."

Yidak replied without mirth, "If she is as terrible as you say, she'll survive a few minutes without you."

Down below, Adele fought to keep her place amidst the roiling mob, now with Anhalt behind her. Gareth caught her eye through the crowd and a quick nod was sufficient between them to tell the story. The pack, in their dark red robes, went airborne and swept past the temple in the heavy wind. Takeda bellowed commands to his swarming forces, hanging onto the tip of the minaret with one hand.

The samurai slid back down to the temple roof and regarded Gareth. "Stay close to the west face. Don't allow yourself to be silhouetted in the sky. And take off those gloves." Then he pointed down at Hiro, who waited on the ground staring up as if he would burst with expectation. "Hiro! You are coming with us too."

The young vampire bent at the waist and clenched his fists with uncontained excitement.

Gareth pulled off his gloves and tossed them down to Adele before he rose into the air with Takeda. He saw Yidak remain behind, but he had no more time to think as he fell into the tail end of the swarm. Arms and legs surrounded him. It had been more than a century since Gareth had traveled in a murmuration of vampires like this. He ran into the monks all around him, eliciting angry curses and snarled demands he stay in his place. A strong grip took his arm. Takeda glared and adjusted Gareth's position within the group before doing the same to young Hiro on his other side. Gareth took deep calming breaths, desperately craving open air and room to stretch his arms out. He needed to drop out of the mob and fall into the soft clouds beneath him. He wanted to fly alone.

He had no choice, however, so he kept his hands moving, touching the figures around him, and trying to anticipate their movements. Vampires banked and slammed against him. He hurriedly adjusted to follow the drift. He forced his senses to explore the changes in the air around him. The nature of the swarm altered the flow of the wind. Changes in course by the pack were translated to him in small bursts of air created by the arrangement of the individuals. The press of the bodies all around him brought terrible memories that Gareth had suppressed. It took him back to the glory days of the Great Killing. He could smell blood and hear the pleading of the victims.

Suddenly Gareth slammed against a wall of rock. Again Takeda grabbed him to keep him from tumbling across jagged stones. All around him, the monks settled onto the sheer wall, and crawled forward in one fluid motion, scrabbling hand over hand, hundreds of shadows wriggling over the mountainside. The humans on the airship shouldn't be able to see them coming. And even if there were vampires with the ship, keeping close to the black mountainside should allow Takeda's forces to draw near before they could be spotted.

The monks pushed off the rock face into the open air. Gareth did too, a split second later. He fell into place, banking into the wind, swooping down with the pack and then back up, hundreds of bodies moving as one. Every motion spread across the dark horde as it undulated in the air. With a sickening feeling, Gareth surrendered to the surge that ran through him. His heart pounded at the prospect of striking the airship in force. The pure furious power of a charging pack resonated through every nerve.

Then, below him, Gareth saw thousands of odd blue spots. Tiny pinpricks of light were moving in the upper edges of the swirling mist that filled the valley.

Eyes.

A huge swarm of vampires erupted from the cloud tops. Gareth had just started to shout a warning to Takeda when he heard other cries of alarm interrupted by the resounding thuds from colliding bodies. He could feel impacts as they crushed into his pack like hammer blows.

Bodies cascaded around Gareth, slamming him into a cartwheel. Screams of shock and anger cut the air. Takeda shouted orders lost in the tumult. Gareth caught himself and felt sharp fingers slash across his chest. He tried to counter but he was pounded to the side. Crashing into the rock, he kicked back out into the melee. Gareth caught one of the attackers around the head and snapped his neck. He let the body drop and barely dodged claws plunging at his face. He seized the arm and pulled the vampire close, noting the look of shock. Gareth buried his teeth in the enemy's neck and tore. Blood spewed and another dying body fluttered downward.

Vampires swirled around Gareth. Clutching arms and gnashing teeth collided everywhere. Torn robes. Flailing bodies. He felt dull thuds against his back and legs and arms. Gareth attacked, smashing faces and ripping across eyes. He struck and moved, killed if he could, but dealt damage in all cases.

A hand clamped on Gareth's shoulder and spun him around. As he wheeled out of control, he clawed for the arm that held him. Takeda dodged the blow and grabbed Gareth to stop his spin.

"Fall back!" Takeda screamed into his face. "Gareth! Fall back!"

Gareth fixated on a small trickle of blood that made its way around Takeda's nose. The samurai took Gareth bodily and tilted him down. In the hazy blackness below their feet were thousands of glowing blue specks rising into the starlight. Gareth fought the urge to drop amidst the oncoming army and wreak what havoc he could. Instead, he bit his lower lip and nodded. Gareth swept upward. He saw Takeda coming behind him with Hiro trailing. The boy's face was a mask of terror.

The walls of the monastery came into sight. The air around it was thick with struggling bodies. The enemy seemed to crash against it like a wave, and the once unstoppable surge broke into smaller battles. The monks now fought in organized defense. They struck the enemy with murderous artistry. Yidak was visible racing along the walls. He seemed to move in slow motion, and Gareth feared for the old vampire. At first. Every sweep of the Demon King's arm or leg, every strike of his hand, sent an enemy flying or crashing senseless to the ground, yet it seemed with hardly any effort at all.

Gareth worked his way back to the wall, dropped onto the backs of the enemy, raking with claws and snapping bones. Takeda fought too, moving with speed that even Gareth could barely follow, protecting Hiro as much as hitting the enemy. Every spot the samurai struck left an enemy tumbling or bloody. He and Takeda landed on the broad top of the outer wall. Hiro stumbled down beside them and turned gamely to fight, but he was bloody and gasping for breath. Takeda drew his katana and weaved steel around him. Limbs and heads dropped with audible thuds.

The enemy was retreating. Thousands of vampires backed away from the monastery into the swirling air beyond the precipice. With no more targets close at hand, Gareth gathered himself and rose into the air to hasten the enemy's withdrawal. A hand pulled him back down. "Don't be stupid. Let them go."

Gareth shook Yidak off, barely seeing him, eager to feel more muscles rend and bones shatter beneath his claws.

"Gareth!" The old vampire grasped Gareth's head between his hands. "Listen to me!" In a blink of an eye, Yidak spun away and struck a stray enemy who dove out of the chaos. His hand impacted the attacker's chest. The vampire froze for a moment, then collapsed insensible or dead. Yidak turned calmly back to Gareth. "Are you listening now?"

"Yes." Gareth grimaced with the hunger to cause carnage still pounding through him. The figures flitting across the night sky all around them taunted him. They should all be dead for their temerity. He wiped blinding blood from his eyes. "Yes."

"Good." The old vampire patted Gareth's cheek. "They are retreating. They have no desire to contest us here in our home. We have no reason to fight them out there in the open. There are too many of them."

"They lured us!" Takeda hunched, gasping for air, with his bloody sword dragging along the stones. He looked down at Hiro who huddled next to him. "They lured us with that airship. And we fell for it. I fell for it!"

"Why did they break off?" Gareth asked. "They had the advantage."

"They know better," Takeda snarled. "They know what would happen if they came in here."

"Gareth!"

He turned to see Adele and General Anhalt rushing through the wounded on the ground. Her glowing khukri sizzled with dripping blood. Anhalt carried the heavy shotgun, keeping Adele covered. She reached up frantically.

Gareth willed his shaking hands to be calm. He knelt and grasped Adele's arm. When he drew her up, she suppressed a cry from the power of his grip. He set her on the wall next to him with a murmured apology.

Adele inspected him, shifting torn clothing aside, running her fingers over his flesh. All the while, she whispered, "Oh God. Oh God. Look at you."

"I'm fine." Gareth took her hands to stop her.

"Actually," Yidak said with a fatherly smirk, "you are not. You are fairly butchered."

Takeda wiped the red katana on his sleeve and returned it to his belt. "You fight like you are alone. You think the only one who can save you is you. In a war, that is how you die."

That sounded like the type of advice Gareth had received from General Anhalt at some point in the frozen trenches of Europe. He finally saw that he was a host of bloody gouges. Deep welts crisscrossed his chest. He fingered a huge flap of skin that hung loose from his stomach.

Yidak stared out along the wide valley, where thousands of eyes shone in the dark. Figures floated in the air and shapes crawled across the mountainside. At the distant end of the valley, the airship still floated with a large swarm of vampires circling it. They were not attacking; they were protecting.

Takeda stooped and grabbed the hair of the last vampire Yidak had dropped. He twisted the head around to see the face. The eyes fluttered; alive but badly injured. Then Takeda spat. "Chengdu. This one is from Chengdu."

Yidak continued studying the shadows. "It wasn't Chengdu who attacked while I was gone."

"No." Takeda answered. "It wasn't nearly this many either."

Yidak moved with a grunt of effort. Gareth and Takeda both reached out to take the old vampire's arms. Yidak smiled gratefully. "We appear to be under siege. Not the first time, but I would like to know what they want now."

Takeda lifted the unconscious vampire. "I'll find out."

Gareth looked at Adele. It was time for the truth. He urged her to speak.

"I can tell you what they want," Adele announced after a deep breath. "It's the same thing I want."

Yidak gave her an odd glance before drifting down from the wall. "I would appreciate hearing about it, if you don't mind. Takeda, before you chat with the prisoner, survey our people and let me know the toll. Arrange an organized watch."

Under Takeda's fierce glower, Gareth lowered Adele from the wall and dropped behind her. He nearly stumbled to his knees. She grabbed him, but before she could demand to care for him, he shook his head. He took her hand, assuring her that he would recover but that there were more important things to attend to now.

CHAPTER 28

Bodies littered the courtyard. Wounded vampires struggled to move. Many were tended by friends. There were also a number of the black-garbed Chengdu fighters, and those still alive would not be for long, as Yidak's monks moved swiftly to execute them. The old vampire led the way, pausing to speak to followers or lay a supportive hand on a slumped shoulder.

The hunger in some of the bright vampire eyes that followed Adele unnerved her. They climbed the steps to the large temple and passed through the chamber with the memory machine. Yidak brought them into his smaller room in the rear. They all settled heavily into chairs. Gareth slumped with exhaustion.

Yidak said to Adele, "You and your general should go nowhere without me or Takeda with you until I tell you otherwise."

"Why? Do you think they'll attack again soon?"

"I'm concerned about my own people. There are many wounded and they will need to feed."

Anhalt was reloading the shotgun. "What of those pilgrims?"

"I have had them moved to a safe place as well."

Adele found the old vampire's concern for humans fascinating, and a little touching. Yidak ran his hand along his silk sleeve. Then he looked up at Adele, waiting expectantly.

"The Tear of Death," she replied to his unspoken query.

Yidak stared blankly, so Gareth translated into Tibetan.

The old vampire sighed. "Ah. I wondered as much, but I didn't think anyone from so far away would have known about it."

"Do you know about its power?" Adele asked.

"The old monks said it was powerful." Yidak shrugged. "But I have never seen it do anything but lie in the dust. If you had told me that you sought it, that another was looking as well, we might have come to some arrangement. Instead of the disaster we have now."

"I'm sorry." Adele's words fell weakly in the cold room.

"Trust, trust," Yidak muttered and scrubbed his disheveled hair. "There's no point in giving it to you now because you can't get out with it."

"Your Majesty," General Anhalt said, "could you not take it and slip out unnoticed by the vampires?"

Adele answered, "I'm not leaving you behind. Besides, I couldn't make it all the way to the *Edinburgh*. And summoning them here now would be leading them into a meat grinder."

Yidak leaned forward. "Can you not simply destroy the fighters from Chengdu? I felt a taste of your power. And I've been told you killed every vampire in Britain."

Adele felt a chill from the question. Yidak could be testing her claim to have deadly power. Gareth stirred in alarm, but for a different reason. He was fearful she could die from the strain. Her geomancy here was limited, largely useless against the besieging army outside. Still, she didn't want Yidak to think she was powerless or she might find herself on the menu for his hungry followers.

"No," she replied calmly, trying to control her emotions. She was aware that vampires could often smell when someone was lying. There was truth in her next statement. "Not without also killing your people."

The old vampire nodded with acceptance. "Well, while we wait, would you care to see it?"

"It?" Adele stood with excitement. "The Tear of Death?"

Yidak pushed himself to his feet. "It's just below us."

Adele stared at the floor, instinctively searching for hints of power. If this object was extraordinary, and so close, it shouldn't have escaped her notice. Perhaps it was just an artifact that held only myth and nothing more. She wondered again if this entire journey was a pointless farce, a quest for a magical mirage.

Yidak shuffled out into the large chamber and went to a wall covered with faded paintings of beasts and monsters. He rubbed with his hand until his fingers caught something. With a click, a seam appeared in the wall. He pushed a huge slab of stone back.

The old vampire started down a set of steps without speaking. Adele followed with Gareth behind, slightly more steady on his feet now. Anhalt came last, shotgun broken at the breech to prevent an accident. Only the sounds of human footfalls and their heavy breathing could be heard. It was soon pitch black, which Yidak didn't notice. Adele pulled her Fahrenheit blade so the glow would keep her from taking a misstep on the icy stones. Yidak turned, eyed her and the blade, and continued down. Adele lost count of the steps.

Finally she saw the shadow of a doorway ahead. Yidak stepped through a narrow arch into a wonderful, horrifying room. The surrounding walls bristled with incredible sculptures. Humans and creatures intertwined and swirled in the strange half-light from the khukri. The sculptures were carved deep into the rock walls, making the life-sized figures virtually freestanding. Human arms reached, beseeching and craving. Demons surged out with claws ready, tongues lolling, eyes hollow and shadowed.

Adele breathed out in amazement at the dense forest of tortured limbs and bodies. It was as if she stood in the midst of a battle between humans and demons, frozen at the height of the brutal struggle. Gareth too was consumed with fascination at the creations of human hands. He seemed to have forgotten his wounds as he peered at the motionless mob from just beyond their grasping fingers and snapping jaws.

When Adele turned back to Yidak, he was holding an object out to her. It was a common black phurba, a triangular dagger. She peered at it. "Is that a key? To open the container of the Tear?"

"This is the Tear of Death."

The phurba was unremarkable in all ways. It was not even decorated in any noticeable fashion. Adele put her hand near it.

There was nothing. No energy. No power.

Gareth warily watched her. Anhalt came close, his face etched with worry.

"I don't mean to be insulting," Adele said, "but are you sure?"

The old vampire cackled. "I was told about this object long ago by an old human monk. He said it was carved from a single teardrop of the God of Death that fell to Earth. It had the power of death, so it needed to be hidden and kept from the hands of humanity, who could not be trusted with such a thing. I remember he seemed to be afraid of it. He said none of the human monks who were here then would dare to touch it. Here. Take it." Yidak shoved the phurba into Adele's gloved hands like it was a squalling baby.

She froze. There was nothing.

The dagger was carved from a single piece of black stone. It had no metal and it was heavier than it appeared. She took a deep breath. If nothing else, she could determine the nature of the rock's structure and its point of origin. She took off one glove and grasped the phurba in her bare hand.

The world vanished and she was alone. The sounds of the Earth grew silent. No colors. No smells. She could feel nothing. Hear nothing. The emptiness was so extreme she couldn't even sense herself in the blank space. She flailed around her, trying to touch anything. Surely there was a rift somewhere for her to gain her bearings. She had to feel or smell or hear something. She felt as if she were being smothered. On the ragged edges of her awareness, she thought she saw something black and huge. It was slow but only because it had nothing to fear. She felt herself fraying as if the blackness was unweaving her. And then, there was nothing. Even she was gone and only darkness remained.

Adele gasped loudly, like breaking from the surface of the sea. She blinked as she returned to the normal world. Gareth crowded in front of her, holding the phurba. Yidak observed with interest.

"What happened?" Gareth asked.

"Nothing." Adele's gaze swept over the unassuming facets of the phurba, which seemed to hide the void. She stared up at Gareth. The cold blue of his eyes warmed her.

He asked, "Then it is powerful?"

"I don't know." Adele felt tears that she didn't understand. They dribbled down her cheeks. Something deep and empty pulled at her. "I don't know . . . I don't know," was all she could say.

Adele stared into the crackling fire pit. "I don't understand. I've never felt anything like it."

Gareth dropped more fuel on the fire to keep the shivering Adele warm. "I'm glad we left it behind."

"I don't want it near me." Adele pulled her thick fur collar tight. "But I need to understand it, if I even can. What did Mamoru teach me? I'm not sure I know anything."

Gareth joined her on the edge of the fire pit. "He taught you enough to be a weapon. That's all. You've told me that he actually kept knowledge from you so it didn't conflict with the purpose he had planned. Any true knowledge you have came from your own studies, not Mamoru."

Adele put a hand to her forehead as if feverish. "I can't fathom what Goronwy must know that I don't. How could he use it? How powerful is he?"

"Does it matter?" General Anhalt handed her a cup of her Edinburgh whiskey. "You have the weapon now, so he is powerless. What good is his knowledge to him?"

"It matters. I have no idea what that thing is, or what it does." She slammed her hand on the bricks. "My knowledge only extends to what I can touch."

Gareth said, "You can touch the entire Earth."

Adele seemed to ignore him as she tore into her rucksack, pulling out her mother's notebook. She dropped to the floor and bent over the book with a furious expression. "I need to think. I need to think."

Gareth stepped away because he sensed she wasn't asking for comfort. She wanted room to flail mentally, and perhaps physically. He tapped Anhalt and motioned toward the door. The general looked concerned for Adele, but Gareth wordlessly assured him. The two men shoved the heavy yak hide aside and went out into the cold.

CHAPTER 29

Gareth strode across the courtyard. Vampires hurried all around him. Others crouched motionless on walls and rooftops, watching the swarming horde outside the walls. Wincing with pain, General Anhalt struggled to follow up the steps as Gareth flew for the central temple.

Inside, Yidak sat at his machine, arms and legs moving in concert. The rows of copper cylinders spun, filling the room with a multitude of jumbled memories. Gareth took Yidak's arm, interrupting his manipulation of the knobs and wheels. The old vampire sat back and looked up at Gareth expectantly while the cylinders spun down into gibberish.

"What are you doing?" Gareth demanded.

"I was listening." Yidak nodded a congenial greeting to Anhalt, who finally hobbled in. "Why do you ask?"

"Why aren't you doing something?" Gareth leaned on the machine. "We're under siege. We have to do *something*."

The old vampire stood. "You want to slip away to find the enemy's leader and kill him. That would fix Adele's problems, wouldn't it?"

Gareth had considered that very thing. He hadn't expected to have it thrown back at him with a sense of mockery. "What's wrong with that plan?"

Yidak smiled and went to the door. "I suspected as much. It's simple and quick and proper work for a lonely hero."

They all went back out into the cold, with Anhalt exhaling in dismay while rebuttoning his coat and lifting his collar around his throat. Yidak paused on the cracked steps piled with snow.

"Look out there, son," he said. "There is hardly a rock without eyes. The air is full. You could not slip away without being swarmed."

"He does make a good point," muttered Anhalt, glancing at the crawling vampires on the surrounding mountains.

"I'm very good," Gareth stated flatly.

"I have no doubt," Yidak replied. "You may be the best I've ever seen. And I can't stop you from trying, but you would die."

"What else then?"

"Nothing." The old vampire went slowly down the steps and across the square, with crunching steps on the icy dirt. Each vampire he passed bowed or reached out a kind hand to him. "We will wait."

"Wait for what?" Gareth cried. "For the enemy to charge in here and crush us?"

"You think like a human," Yidak said. "There is time."

"No, there's not. Adele and General Anhalt and your pilgrims need food, and there isn't much. What about your own monks? How long before your meager herd is drained?"

Yidak refused to be shaken by Gareth's use of *herd*. "That could be a problem, but it is not one yet. Give me your hand."

"Why?"

"Don't ask why to everything. Give me your hand."

Gareth raised his hand, swathed in a dark leather glove. Yidak pressed his gnarled talon into Gareth's palm. Yellowed claws barely reached the tips of Gareth's long fingers.

Gareth stood quietly with their hands together. Finally, he said, "What is the point of this?"

"You don't see it?"

Gareth stared at their hands more intently, waiting for inspiration. There was an obvious size difference, but that seemed unimportant. And clearly Yidak's claws were always extended while Gareth's were retracted into sharp fingernails. Or it would've been clear if he hadn't been wearing gloves.

He was wearing gloves.

Gareth hadn't been Greyfriar for days, perhaps weeks; it was difficult to follow time here. Yet, he still wore gloves out of habit. The cold didn't bother him, he simply felt comfortable wearing them around Adele.

Gareth feigned ignorance, preferring to believe that couldn't be Yidak's point. "I don't see it."

The old vampire grinned with kindness. "You've been human for a long time now, haven't you? With your gloves and mask and firearms. You're good at it. You write and read. You watch clocks and count hours."

Gareth pulled his hand away angrily. "You do the same with robes and chanting and your idiotic library." His stomach clenched as he instantly recalled the first night he had shown Adele his own library in Edinburgh Castle. He had pulled her to the room with giddy pride, knowing he could appeal to her human love of knowledge. He showed her the trunk containing the pitiful few books he had gathered from vampire-wrecked northern Europe and stepped aside for her approval. The look on her face had nearly killed him. Her eyes betrayed a stunned disbelief that this measly collection was what he had been lauding as a *library*. He realized later that he had misread her expression. However, in that moment he stood exposed, having granted her alone access to the grandest of his secrets, the most prideful aspect of his hidden life, and her unintentional shock showed how false it was. It only served to drive home just what he was, despite the masks and swords and great library consisting of seven thin volumes.

Yidak showed no such embarrassment at Gareth's insult. Rather, he was confused by the pain that washed over Gareth's face.

The old vampire said, "You hate our kind, don't you?"

Gareth started to refute the question as ignorant and simplistic. Yidak had no way of knowing his heart, his life. There was no way the old vampire, hiding away on his mountain, could understand what Gareth had gone through. Instead, he merely said, "Yes."

"Why, Gareth? What did we do to you to make you hate all of us?"

The wind howled around him. "We killed my father."

Anhalt shouted against the gale, "But Cesare killed King Dmitri."

Gareth stared into the distance at the swarm of countless vampires. "Cesare just put an end to his dying. I murdered him when I joined the Great Killing. I knew he was right about it, but I did nothing.

"That night, one hundred and fifty years ago, when the packs first struck, I saw the fear in his eyes. I ignored it. For years, I thought he had been frightened because I was going off to war, as any father would be. Only later did I realize the truth. He knew the path we were embarking on; he knew it was a disaster, and there he was, casting his beloved son out into the terrible world he couldn't prevent. My father never recovered from the shame. The more territory we took, the more humans we slaughtered, the more my father retreated into the howling wildness of his own mind." Gareth ran his gloved hands over his arms. He could still feel his father's strong fingers clutching him. He could hear the cracking voice bidding him goodbye on that starry winter night and see his reflection in those frozen blue eyes. "That was the last time my father truly saw me."

Yidak quietly interlaced his claws over his red and yellow-robed stomach. "What are you doing *now* to save him?"

Gareth barely heard the nonsensical question. He was still trying to recapture the memory of that last night with his father.

Yidak lifted into the air and hooked onto the decorated eaves of a temple. "That is why you're lost. He may be dead, but his memory is not."

Gareth watched Yidak crawl up the roof and vanish. He gave Anhalt a quick glance to excuse himself from the general's company. The man nodded with understanding and limped back toward their quarters. Gareth strode off across the crowded monastery grounds. He felt leather stretch tight across his hands as he clenched his fists.

—⟩⟨—

Adele stood in the center of the frightful room of the Tear of Death. Her glimmering khukri sent long shadows of stone arms and torsos writhing around her. The black stone dagger lay at her feet. It looked so simple. It didn't glow or quiver or throw off waves of powerful energies. It didn't call seductively to her nor whisper threats. It merely sat in the dirt as it had for centuries.

She had contemplated the thing for the last twenty-four hours, wrestling with her uncertainties as well as the worries about Goronwy's army scuttling just outside the walls. There was something horrible about the phurba. It couldn't be understood or controlled. There was nothing inside it.

Utter emptiness.

Adele knelt beside the phurba and set her glowing khukri on the ground. She dug into her pockets and brought out two objects. One was the sharp metal tool that Yidak used to inscribe the copper cylinders. The other was a heavy mallet she had acquired from the pilgrims. She slowly placed the awl over the center of the stone artifact. She waited for some reaction, half expecting the phurba would suddenly spring to occult life to defend itself. It did nothing.

Adele touched the tip of the tool to the stone with an audible click. She took a deep breath and raised the hammer high over her head.

"Adele," came a soft voice from behind.

She spun around, instinctively raising the sharp tool as a weapon. Gareth stood in the doorway. Adele lowered the awl with a twinge of embarrassment. Under Gareth's steady gaze, she felt suddenly childish. Perhaps it was worse than childish. It made her wonder if she was acting out of pure fear. Or perhaps jealousy. She was down here alone in the dark without anyone else's knowledge.

Adele said, "I am going to destroy the Tear of Death."

Gareth glanced over his shoulder and stepped inside. "Does Yidak know you're here?"

"No." She gripped the awl tighter. "I assumed he would try to stop me."

Gareth knelt next to her in the dirt. "Here, give those to me. I'm far stronger."

Adele hesitated, then handed the instruments to him. He placed the sharp point of the tool in the center of the stone dagger. Then he raised the hammer and brought it crashing down on the butt of the awl, snapping the steel shaft in half with a sharp crack. There was no mark on the phurba.

Adele cursed. Gareth immediately pressed the jagged tip of the awl against the stone and pounded it again. The steel pick caromed off to the side. The black dagger remained unaffected.

Gareth looked at the blunted shaft of the awl. "Do we have anything stronger?"

Adele shrugged. "Not here. Maybe if we dropped it in a blast furnace, but we're far from that. How did they carve it in the first place if it's so hard?"

"What about your geomancy? Can you destroy it from inside?"

She stared at the black stone again. It didn't seem like a small object any longer, but a hole into the endless night sky. Nothing but untouchable emptiness. "When I went inside it, I couldn't sense anything. There were no facets to touch. There was nothing I could change."

A scuffling sound from the door brought both Adele and Gareth to their feet. Yidak stood in the dim archway with an unreadable look on his face. The Demon King said, "You cannot simply destroy your fears."

"Oh shut up," Adele muttered. "You're starting to sound like Mamoru." She spat the name like a curse.

The old vampire strolled forward. "You must fight them as best you can." His eyes went to the awl in Gareth's hands. "Oh. I was looking for that." He took the tool.

Adele said, "Did the old monks ever tell you about a way to destroy this thing?"

"No. I'm sure it never occurred to them as something that should be done."

"Well, it occurs to me."

"Obviously." He held up the broken awl.

"I had to do something. Goronwy won't wait for long. He wants this thing and he knows it's here. He'll send his packs to get it."

Yidak smirked as he regarded Gareth. "A human giving orders to vampire packs? I suppose it's not too unbelievable."

Adele stepped toward him. "You have no idea of his power. And I'm telling you, if this thing falls into his hands, the results will be catastrophic."

"Catastrophic for whom?" Yidak glanced at the stone artifact lying helplessly on the floor. "I could likely make my problems go away by delivering the Tear of Death to your enemy out there."

Adele narrowed her eyes at the old vampire, her fists tightening. "Is that your choice?"

Yidak stared back evenly at her. "Let's go back up, shall we? The weather is changing. If your prediction is right, we have much to plan."

Adele didn't move for a long moment. Her breath clouded in the faint emerald glow. Gareth stood next to her, ready to fight no matter what move she made. She stooped toward her khukri and noted that Yidak twitched slightly before recovering his immortal calm. She motioned toward the doorway with the blade.

"Shall we?" she said.

Yidak hesitated, then turned his back to her and walked out. Adele and Gareth followed, leaving the Tear of Death lying in its place.

CHAPTER 30

Caterina waited in the catacombs. Hundreds of dead eye sockets stared at her from every wall. The passageway to the outside gaped in front of her and a smaller tunnel for escape opened behind, should something go terribly wrong. She wasn't stupid enough to box herself into a corner. Caterina stood motionless, with her hands clutched penitently in front. A shape appeared in the passageway. Hallow cautiously entered the chamber of bones.

"Lady Hallow," Caterina said, not trying to hide her nervous voice. "Thank you for coming."

Hallow's eyes darted around the skeletal remains before settling back on the queen, satisfied. "I'm grateful you called on me. I knew we could make peace for the good of our clan."

Caterina noted the *our* with a frozen smile. "You and I have been at cross purposes since you came to Paris with the Witchfinder. In some sense, Honore was already lost to us thanks to Cesare, so your attachment to him was no surprise. However, I now see you have intentions on my entire family."

"Majesty, I—"

"Please let me finish," Caterina interrupted forcefully. She still didn't move, keeping Hallow's attention locked to her. "I don't care if the human armies are coming. I don't care if we have to abandon Paris and flee. I won't have you interfering with my children. Do you understand me?"

Hallow adopted a calm, sympathetic demeanor. "I do, Majesty. It isn't my intention to vex you. I know you understand the threat that we are under."

"Yes. And if you had skill in meeting it, your old clan wouldn't consist of a large pile of bones now." Caterina slapped the wall of skulls behind her. "Your intellect failed in Britain. Cesare is dead. Flay is dead. Gareth alone survives."

Hallow couldn't hide the flinch of pain before letting it change into a sneer of anger. "You have no idea what you're facing. You have no clue how to combat it. We are on the edge of the apocalypse and all you care about is that I am stealing your children from you. You are pathetic. Your husband is a soft failure and you are a shrill idiot. Your son, Honore, isn't much of a leader, but he's something at least. I suspect Isolde might serve better, but I'll find that out in time. Frankly, I couldn't care less what you think of me, or of anything. The time when your opinion matters is fast coming to a close. Now, are we done here?"

Caterina extended her claws. "You are."

Hallow regarded the queen, sure that Caterina would never attack physically. Her threat was baseless, just another pathetic ploy. The tall consort shook her head at the immobile queen and spun on her heel.

Caterina struck in that moment, fueled by the memory of her daughter treating her with scorn. Hallow shouted in alarm, flailing at the queen with strength but no skill. Caterina felt blood on her hands when suddenly she was seized around the waist and pulled back from her target. Her arms were pinned and she was forcibly pressed against the wall of bone. Shouting curses, Caterina saw Fanon behind her with a look like he wished to die. But still he held her firmly. Several mercenaries stood behind him, grinning at the sight of the queen being manhandled.

"I'm sorry, Majesty," Fanon mumbled as he fought to contain her. "Hallow suspected you would try something desperate. I've been waiting in the tunnel beyond for hours now. I wish you hadn't done it."

"Take your hands off her!"

All eyes turned at the strange female voice. In the entrance of the passageway stood a group of vampires. Caterina recognized Kasteel and Nadzia, who stood with claws out, glaring toward the queen and her captor. Behind those two were a clutch of their rebel comrades.

"What are you doing?" Caterina ground out through clenched teeth. "Get out. You will be killed here."

Nadzia raised her claws toward Fanon. "I said take your hands off her."

Fanon grunted in confusion, while the mercenaries behind him laughed.

Kasteel stepped into the chamber, crunching over loose bones. He stared at Hallow. "I've killed vampires. Many of them."

Hallow had recovered her composure from Caterina's attack. Blood soaked into the neck of her silky gown. She stared at the rebel in disbelief, and glanced at Caterina to scoff at Kasteel's childish boast. Then Hallow laughed. It was genuine amusement, not a pose or a misdirection. Her slight frame shook as she doubled over with silent, shuddering laughter. When Hallow finally looked up, her porcelain face was ruddy and tears welled in her eyes. She could barely speak.

"Oh my," Hallow gasped. "Thank you. I haven't laughed that hard since the Age of Enlightenment. Truly, I am delighted by all of you."

The rebel leader glowered at the still-chuckling Hallow. "The revolution that began in Britain continues here. For Prince Gareth!"

Hallow froze with a look of shock at Kasteel's cry. She pressed against the skeletal wall, suddenly disconcerted and shaken.

Nadzia leapt for Fanon. She caught the old fighter in the face with a surprising blow. The deep gashes broke him from his shock and he released Caterina to engage the girl. They slashed at one another. Nadzia was far faster and more nimble, but Fanon was much stronger. However, speed and agility had its limits in the small chamber. The old fighter would eventually corner her and beat her down.

Meanwhile, four mercenaries stormed at Kasteel and the rebels behind him. It was a blur of violence as the rebels were driven back into the passage. Suddenly more mercenaries appeared, charging down the passageway, falling on the overwhelmed rebels from behind. Clawed hands raked, cutting shoulders and backs. The rebels struggled to turn and meet the attacks from both sides.

Stunned, Caterina realized she had been trapped. She couldn't allow her own stupidity to doom these innocents. She lifted herself off the ground and ran headlong between Nadzia and Fanon. They both saw her and disengaged to avoid injuring her.

"Run!" Caterina shouted at Nadzia as she threw her arms around the stunned Fanon. "All of you! Run!"

The rebels broke. Some smashed their way through the fighters in the passageway to make for the outside. Kasteel cut across the bone chamber to grab Nadzia by the arm and they ran for the rear tunnel. Fanon tried to pull himself free from the queen but she fought with all her strength. Hands fell on Caterina's shoulders and Hallow attempted to drag her away from Fanon. Caterina drove her elbow into the pale female and propelled her into the wall with a rattle of bones. Fanon freed himself from the queen's grip and ran alone into the tunnel after Kasteel and Nadzia.

After he disappeared, Hallow seized one of the mercenaries nearby before he could take off in pursuit of the rebels. She pointed at Caterina. "Keep her from me! The queen's gone mad."

Caterina didn't run; there was no reason. There was nowhere she could go, and there was nothing more she could do to help Kasteel and Nadzia. She saw three rebels lying at the mouth of the passageway. Two were dead; the other was badly wounded and moaning softly. Caterina knelt beside the wounded rebel and put a helpless hand on his shuddering chest.

Hallow stared at her with an impassive countenance, safe behind her mercenary, until Fanon returned after several minutes. He crossed to where Caterina waited by the injured rebel. The queen rose at his grim visage, unsure what he intended. Without pausing, Fanon dropped and executed the wounded vampire with a sharp snap of his neck. Caterina stood with mouth agape.

Fanon turned back to Lady Hallow. "They escaped."

"What?" Hallow snarled. "How is that possible? Why didn't you run them to ground?"

Fanon eyed her with suppressed anger. "There are many passages. I returned here so you didn't come to any harm at the hands of the queen. Why didn't you tell me that Her Majesty would have forces here?"

Hallow worked to recover her composure. "I didn't know. I didn't realize how great a traitor she is."

Light crunching footsteps announced one of the mercenaries returning along the front passage. He was spattered with blood. "We killed two. We are in pursuit of the rest."

Lady Hallow stepped away from the skulls. "We have the most important one." She pointed at Caterina. "Fanon, escort the queen back to the palace. The war chief will want to hear about tonight's events."

One of the mercenaries sneered at the queen until Fanon shoved him into the wall with a growl. Then the old soldier faced Caterina with downturned, apologetic features. "I'm sorry, Your Majesty; please come along."

Caterina kept her head high and started out. She stepped over the bodies of the dead rebels and walked down the tunnel of skeletons toward the uncertain mercy of her son.

—⚍—

King Lothaire sat in a large chair that might have been a throne if he had any pretentions at all. He balanced the baby on his knee and watched the proceedings with an air of incredulity. He glanced at the empty chair beside him. Honore and Hallow huddled with Isolde in one corner, quietly conversing. Fanon and several of the mercenaries waited at the door, silent and ready.

Dust-moted shafts of sunlight stabbed onto the figure of the queen standing in the center of the vast musty chamber. Caterina was careful to maintain a superior indifference to this insulting and undignified spectacle. She reminded her husband with every gesture and inflection that she was the queen and should have been in the empty chair beside him rather than standing alone in the dreadful sun.

"Well," Lothaire intoned in a voice that reverberated in the immensity of the garish red and gold room, "it seems to me no harm was done."

Hallow looked at the king in shock. Honore scowled with fury, and even Caterina couldn't suppress a laugh at her husband's typical attempt at dismissal.

"Are you insane as well as weak?" Honore snarled. "I am the war chief and Hallow is my future bride. Queen Caterina is a criminal."

"Criminal?" Lothaire wagged his head back and forth with uncertainty. "That's not clear."

"She lured Lady Hallow under false pretenses, and then set on her with some private militia." Honore raised both hands with an air of indignation. "She is endangering the clan at our most critical time."

Lothaire again glanced at Caterina, hoping his wife would speak up, defend herself. She had to help him. Instead, she stayed quiet.

Hallow filled the silence. "If I may, Majesty. I do not believe these thugs belonging to the queen were merely her private army. I have information that there are cadres of rebels."

Lothaire looked genuinely confused. "Rebels? Rebels against what?"

Hallow said, "They seek to destroy the clans entirely."

The king rubbed his chin as if Lady Hallow were telling him that their kind didn't drink blood. "I'm sorry. I don't understand what you're trying to say. The clans are what we are. How can you rebel against that?"

"Exactly, sire," she said. "They're completely mad. Which is not surprising since they apparently have some connection to Prince Gareth."

"Prince Gareth?" Lothaire sat forward with disturbed interest. "What do you mean?"

"Gareth has influenced some of our people. It's dangerous and must be crushed. Particularly if some of our own leaders are involved in spreading his murderous lunacy."

The king grew stern even as he returned to jostling the cooing baby. From the frost that gathered over the king's demeanor, it was clear he would brook no discussion of Gareth's *lunacy*.

Hallow realized she had overstepped, a rare miscalculation on her part. She regrouped. "Fanon, you fought the queen's thugs. What did you notice?"

Fanon hardly stirred, clearly uncomfortable to be a part of this quarrel. "They were skilled. Some of them more than others."

Lothaire looked at the old soldier with disappointment, sad that Fanon was on the wrong side. "Did these ruffians threaten Lady Hallow?"

"They did, sire. It was their clear intention to kill her."

"Did the queen threaten Lady Hallow?"

Fanon paused. He took a deep breath. "I did not hear it."

Hallow spun on the soldier, but she didn't openly accuse him of lying. Fanon was too long with the family for her to make another error treading on the king's affections.

Honore was not so shy. "We know mother tried to kill Lady Hallow! We're not stupid. Everyone in Paris knows mother wants to kill her."

"Honore, shut up!" Lothaire screamed, then restrained himself as the baby jerked in fear. "Sorry. Sorry. Shhh." He returned his now-suppressed aggression to his son. "Forgive me if I require more evidence than the word of Lady Hallow before I believe the queen is a murderer or that our entire culture is collapsing. I've heard enough."

Honore said coldly, "I want something done about the queen!"

Lothaire stood with menace, set into oddly frightening relief by the child he clutched to his chest. His brow furrowed in anger. "Here's what I'll do for you, son. Her Majesty the Queen is confined to the palace."

Lothaire's eyes begged Caterina not to argue. She relented and stayed quiet.

The king continued, "And Lady Hallow, you and your mercenary packs are banned from the palace. We'll have Equatorian troops in our laps in a few months, so we can't let the clan lords see this petty conflict continue." When Honore opened his mouth again, the king raised his free hand. "No, Honore! That's all. If you want to test yourself by trying to raise the packs against me, do it now! Otherwise, we are concluded."

Father and son stared at each other across the bright length of the gallery. Hallow took Honore's arm, willing him to be quiet. The Dauphin strained at the leash, but couldn't overwhelm her firm stare. Honore clamped his angry jaw shut.

Lady Hallow bowed to King Lothaire, and then again to Caterina with a strange smile before gliding to the door. Honore followed her, fuming like a humiliated child, and then Isolde. Hallow paused to give Fanon a quick, unnerving glance and left the room. After a moment, Fanon made an embarrassed bow to the royal couple and led his men out.

Lothaire's exhalation echoed in the empty room. He hefted the squirming baby and trudged down the sun-speckled floor. Caterina stood waiting. When he passed, he stopped and stared into her eyes. The belligerence melted away. She could smell the blended scents of her husband and baby. He leaned close and kissed her on the cheek.

"Caterina, my love," he said in a cracked, fatigued whisper, "if you ever try to kill her again, please succeed. This sort of thing is exhausting." With that, he cradled the baby and departed.

Caterina laughed with slumped shoulders. She shuffled to the empty chairs at the far end of the room. She lowered herself into her usual seat. With a deep chord of sadness, she looked at Lothaire's chair, and she realized just how unbalanced it felt to sit here alone.

CHAPTER 31

Gareth was muffled in white. He strained to hear and smell the world around him. Clouds had risen out of the valley and rolled over the monastery. He couldn't see beyond a few yards and the wind was so calm scents weren't carrying. The mist swirling before him offered nothing to see but folds and crevices shifting from white to grey. Suddenly dark shapes pierced the clouds. Gareth flexed his hands and realized he still wore gloves. He removed them quickly and shoved them in his belt.

Hundreds of black-clad vampires settled noiselessly to the misty courtyard. Their feet had hardly touched when the monks rushed out from around Gareth. He quickly sprang from the overhang of a small building. Claws out, he tore at the invaders. His sweeping feet shattered knees and legs. He seized and wrenched, nearly tearing arms from sockets.

Gareth wore his rapier and pistols, but it was more efficient to lay hands on the enemy. He always prided himself on his combat skills, but he was a lumbering brute in comparison to the monks. Yidak's forces were works of art in motion. Their claws raked multiple targets even as they dodged and ducked without effort, riposting at the exact moment needed. In turn, the fighters from Chengdu hardly landed a blow and often stood staring as their abdomens were torn apart or their throats ripped open. The monks were soon drenched from the spraying blood that filled the air.

Gareth used his advantage of strength, which was great even among vampires. He bulled his way through the fight, absorbing many blows and feeling the pulls of flesh tearing. His stamina preserved and powered him so he could thrash through the enemy like a cyclone.

Amidst all the butchery, silence reigned. The only sounds were feet scraping over dirt, pounding impacts of hands against muscle, grunts of injury, and the flapping of the monks' wet robes. The fighters on both sides were male and female, which was common among vampires, where females were just as vicious as their male counterparts. Gareth had never quite gotten used to the fact that women were banned from the battle-field in human culture.

Eventually, as the struggle pressed on, the telltale sound of rasping breath rose. Gareth had no idea how long he had been fighting—five minutes, five hours, five days—but the Chengdu packs still flooded into the monastery. Dark shapes dropped through the clouds in an endless deluge. The monks fought on, but they were a second slower to turn and took an instant longer to deflect an attack. Robed monks staggered and dropped along with their enemies.

A high-pitched screech cut across the muffled tumult of battle. Gareth recoiled at the sharp sound. Yidak called on his men all over the monastery to drop back. The monks had been divided into smaller oper-ational packs and stationed across the grounds. Each pack had specific buildings or temples as their base. The buildings were intended to cover their backs and heads, to limit the space that the enemy had to attack. Now it was time to pull the Chengdu packs deeper into the narrows and winnow them.

Gareth pulled his rapier to use the combination of claws and blade for clearing space for the monks around him. With the sword in hand, he found his Greyfriar fighting style returning. He drew on grace and motion, rather than pure strength the way *Gareth* would fight. His movements became a liquid series of feints, lures, and strikes. As the robed monks battled their way back toward sanctuary, they stole glances at the remarkable skill of the foreigner.

Gareth backed toward the building where he and Adele had their room, which was the base for his small pack. He stabbed out at a fighter who lunged for him, then kicked the dying thing away. He slipped inside the room already crowded with monks. It seemed strange to see their homey little space full of blood-drenched vampires.

Soon the windows and door were choked with figures battering, clawing, and biting at one another like animals. Monks blocked the two windows and single doorway, struggling to keep the surging invaders from pouring inside. The monks cut down the Chengdu fighters, who were dragged out of the way and replaced by new attackers who were likewise savaged. Other monks took advantage of the thin respite to gather their breath or kneel bleeding on the floor.

Gareth was shocked to see Takeda among the crowd. The samurai was a statue of blood. His katana was a length of dripping liquid. Hiro crouched near him, also covered in red. The boy wasn't nearly as terrified as before. The set of his eyes showed that Hiro was growing hardened to the task of his kind.

"What are you doing here, Takeda?" Gareth asked immediately. "This isn't your refuge. What's happened in your quadrant?"

"We were cut off from the main temple, so my forces retreated here."

Gareth froze. "Damn it! That's where Adele is. I knew I should have been with her."

"This was *her* plan." Takeda weaved through the wounded as some rose to replace more injured brothers defending the entrances. "She's inside the hidden chamber. Can't she defend herself?"

"I don't know. I'm going to get her."

"No! Wait for Yidak's next call. We can't protect you out there."

Gareth started for the door without a response.

"Are you insane?" Takeda cried. "Do you think you can fight your way alone?"

Gareth turned back and snarled with building rage. "Yes." He pulled both pistols and shoved the monks aside. He raised the heavy revolvers and opened a murderous barrage on the vampires who crowded into the door. Some fell to the ground; others reared back for a stunned second. Gareth slammed into them, muscling through the mob. Within seconds, he had disappeared from view through the roiling mass of vampires.

—⚏—

Adele sat cross-legged in the pitch dark. Her eyes had adjusted well enough that she could make out the sinewy hints of carved figures around her crying, struggling, and killing. In the thick silence, she imagined the faint creaking of stone arms shifting and jaws widening in terror. The Tear of Death lay before her on the floor, a blot of black in the darkness. She was close enough to touch it, but she would not.

Adele strained for sounds from above. The only thing she heard was the soft breathing of General Anhalt, who was positioned in the far rear corner. He was partially hidden among the tortured statues, cradling the Fahrenheit shotgun. Adele tried to filter out his sound and focus outside.

Buried deep in the mountain, Adele had no way of knowing if the Chengdu packs had attacked, as she had believed they would. She felt the enveloping clouds would provide Goronwy the cover he needed to unleash his forces on the monastery with some hope of surprising the monks. Takeda had been suspicious of Adele's idea, preferring to believe the enemy would starve them out instead of risking a fight. He hadn't understood, as Adele did, that Goronwy wanted the Tear of Death very badly and needed to return to France before the spring offensive could dislodge his new patrons from Paris. Takeda also refused to credit the idea that his old army of vampires would take orders from a human. However, he had given Adele's theory enough benefit to distribute the warrior-monks around the temple buildings in the fog to await a possible assault. She had come here to guard the Tear.

A scratching sound came from above, followed by a faint click. Adele strained to listen, her tilted head wondering what she had truly heard. There was nothing now.

Then she heard a sliding whisper, perhaps someone descending the steps. Maybe Gareth was coming to collect her. The cloud cover had lifted. The assault hadn't happened. She had been wrong, but she was content to face Takeda's smug silence.

Adele tried to focus on the dim outline of the doorway and the faint horizontal lines beyond it that indicated the steps. She fought to control her breathing and to stay as quiet and motionless as the statues around her. Even without a nearby rift, she managed to slip into the shadows. After several minutes with no more sounds, she let her shoulders droop and relax.

Something obscured the lines of the stairs and Adele froze. The blurry space of the doorway filled with moving darkness. Thin black contours like fingers slid along the sides of the door and objects protruded into the room.

Vampires. Three of them. They were not clad in the typical black garb that the Chengdu fighters had worn, nor were they Yidak's monks. These three wore European clothes. They hugged the doorway and cautiously peered into the chamber. Their vile faces bobbed from side to side. They crouched low, studying the sculpted walls and ceiling with no interest other than the fear that the figures might be real.

Only now did Adele worry about how these three had found their way down. Not so much how they discovered the hidden passage; vampires were so sensitive to smells and air flow, it was likely simple for them to find the seam in the wall. Rather she was filled with the fear that the monks had been overwhelmed, and Gareth along with them.

One of the creatures jerked his gaze in Adele's direction as if he noticed her. She regained her calm and deepened the shadows around her. The vampire twisted his head in confusion, but then his attention went to the floor. He pointed at the Tear of Death, and hissed at his companions. They came forward in a spidery crawl, scenting with their mouths open, all of them staring at the phurba.

One of the vampires jerked his head up, glaring into the back corner where Anhalt stood in the darkness. The other two followed suit and mouths full of sharp teeth opened wide in brutal smiles at the sight of a lone human.

"No," Adele said calmly and appeared before them.

The vampires barely had time to register shock at her appearance. The roar of a shotgun sent one careening across the floor. Adele's khukri swept up and sliced through a second, leaving a sizzling gash along his torso. The claws of the third grabbed her arm. Adele gutted him, then seized the vampire by the hair and drew her dagger across his throat. She kicked the body away and dropped to the floor as Anhalt leveled the shotgun over her and fired again. The first creature had been trying to rise with a chest full of Fahrenheit shot, but now it was smashed into the wall with half its head missing. The general dutifully reloaded and dispatched the other two.

"Thank you, General," Adele said, and they dragged the bodies into a far corner.

Anhalt saluted and returned to his spot to resume his watch. Adele took a long, calming breath and settled back to the floor near the phurba. She sheathed the khukri and darkness returned. She pulled her gaze away from the dim outline of the cadavers and returned it to the phurba. What was happening in the cold far above? Adele wanted to run up the steps and find Gareth, be sure he was alive. However, she knew she could do little in such a swarm. She had to protect the Tear of Death, even with her life. Sadly, even with Gareth's life.

There was a faint breeze against Adele's cheek, no doubt from the open door above. If only Gareth would appear to tell her the fight was won, that these three vampires had slipped through, but no others. It was over. He would reach down to help her stand from the frozen floor. He would say—

"I can see you, Princess."

Adele leapt to her feet. She spun around, seizing her khukri and pulling it with a hiss of steel. Wavering green light filled the chamber and cast garish shadows throughout the jungle of limbs and faces around her.

Against the far wall, an arm moved, dappled with shadows. A leg uncurled into the light. Sinewy arms stretched from inside the tangle of screaming stone faces and grasped the extended stone claws of demons. A female shape detached from the entangling statues and slipped soundlessly to the floor some twenty feet from Adele. She wore dark breeches and a robe of navy silk. Long black hair draped her shoulders. Her pale face lifted to reveal searing blue eyes. The demon who had come to life smiled.

Adele stared at the shape before her. Shadows quivered because her hand on the glowing khukri was shaking. She recognized the face. It was altered, but she knew it as clearly as she would know her own gravestone.

Adele breathed. "Flay."

CHAPTER 32

Adele plunged her essence into the Earth, seeking the power she needed. The heat was distant. Normally the fire would roar like a furnace and sing like quicksilver at her touch, but here it was so deep it seeped like tar. Her mind seared from the strain to drag it up into her trembling hands. She felt as if her muscles were tearing. There was no hesitation, no fear of the power. Terror controlled her as she filled the chamber with a silver cataclysm. The bodies of the three vampires across the room collapsed into dust.

Adele drove the Earth into a frenzy, stretching out her arms to their painful limits, dragging up ever more terrible fire to surge over the impassable flames already pounding the air. Tendrils of white flame swirled around her enemy. Adele screamed aloud with the brutal joy of incinerating Flay.

Bright spots exploded in Adele's eyes and a wave of vertigo swept over her. It seemed as though she had drained the Earth because she had certainly drained herself. She took a faltering step, then stumbled to her knees. The silver fire guttered. Collapsing onto her hands, Adele gasped for breath, but her lungs were raw. Sweat dropped wet to the floor beneath her. The room grew dark and quiet.

Adele heard the whisper of feet on stones. She glanced up through strands of damp hair.

Flay stood there in the ashes of her brothers. Unharmed. The vampire's expression was one of shock. She held out her hands and studied them, flexing her fingers. She looked around the room with the growing satisfaction that she was still standing. Then she stared at Adele with a mocking smile.

From the rear of the room came the sound of movement. Anhalt leveled the shotgun and an explosion of green reverberated. In that instant of brightness, Flay was no longer in the center of the room. Before the glow faded, she was already backhanding Anhalt to the floor.

"No!" Adele's hand gripped her khukri. In the emerald haze of the glowing blade, Flay's face was suddenly right in front of Adele. The khukri slashed, barely catching the flesh of the vampire. Adele tried to come around again, but Flay had already delivered a blow to her head that staggered her to her knees. A foot slammed onto Adele's back, crushing her against the cold floor.

Adele tried to push herself up against the incredible pressure. "Gareth killed you. You're dead."

"He was confused, Princess." Flay's nails dug into Adele's scalp, twisting her head so the empress had to look into the scarred visage of the vampire. Flay raised a clawed hand and whispered, "It's *you* who are dead."

A shuddering impact drove Flay off her feet. She crashed into the stone carvings at the back of the room.

Gareth launched himself at Flay. She was incredibly fast, slipping under his powerful blow and latching onto his arms and back. He spun as she raked him with her claws and sank her teeth into his shoulder. He smashed back against the wall, causing her to grunt from the pressure, snapping stone arms and legs off the statues and making sharp stakes from the shattered limbs. Gareth grabbed Flay's wrist and wrenched her loose. He threw her over his head and slammed her onto the floor.

Flay surged up at him. Her sharp teeth clamped onto his thigh and claws dug into his midsection. She gouged his stomach, re-opening the gash that hadn't healed perfectly. Her hand plunged into his gut. Gareth cried out.

Adele forced herself to her feet and she lumbered across the room. She saw Flay's back. Her glowing khukri drove between Flay's shoulder blades. The chemicals hissed and wisps of smoke curled from the wound.

Flay's head spun around. She spit a chunk of Gareth's flesh into Adele's face and smashed her elbow into the woman's head. Adele fell to the side, tasting her own blood, with the chamber spinning around her.

Flay laughed and returned her attention to Gareth, lifting him off his feet with one hand still buried in his abdomen. He slashed at her, blood boiling from his mouth. With a furious roar, Flay thrust him into the wall and impaled him on the sharp, jagged arms of the wailing statues. His head turned up in a silent scream to match those frozen around him.

"There!" Flay stepped away. "Hang there in the arms of your beloved humans." She reached awkwardly behind herself, taking hold of the khukri and yanking it from her back. She slumped with a grimace of pain, eyeing the blade's fading hue. She flung the dagger across the chamber.

With faltering arms, Adele crawled toward the dim green light of the khukri. She felt pressure around her ankle and she was dragged back through the grime. A heavy foot cracked her across the cheek and she thought her neck had broken from the impact.

Adele still reached out a hand. Fingertips dug into the seams in the floor. With aching effort, she pulled herself forward again.

"Just accept it, Princess." Flay walked in front of her. "I only have to decide whether I'd rather have you see him die, or vice versa." The vampire knelt. One of her blue eyes was nearly closed from the scarred flesh on one side of her face. Flay had once been beautiful in a cruel way, but now only the cruelty remained. "I've decided. I can no longer abide your stench in my nose." Flay raised her hand and looked beyond Adele's still struggling form. "Gareth! If you can spare a moment. Watch."

Gareth struggled. He tried to wrench himself off his bloody perch. His hands slapped the irregular surfaces around him, but he couldn't get leverage. The jagged limbs on which he was impaled were lodged tight between his bones. He roared and forced himself forward, feeling bones break within him, but still not enough to free himself. His eyes watched the horrible scene as if willing it not to be true.

"Flay! Stop!" A new figure came crunching into the room with the heavy tread of a human. Flay winced from the effort of withholding the blow to Adele. Her face contorted in rictus agony. Then she relented, spinning around, showing impossible resignation to the will of another, and to the will of a human at that.

Adele managed to turn her head so she could see an old man with white hair and a long beard. His greatcoat was unbuttoned and she saw a metal device that looked like a cross between a maritime sextant and an astrolabe hanging from his belt. Adele recognized it as the geomantic scryer that had belonged to Selkirk; she had seen it once on Selkirk's belt when the geomancer came to her in the Tower of London. Goronwy stood over the Tear of Death with the calm of a researcher studying random test tubes. He showed no joy of miraculous discovery, just the gratification of careful experimentation come to fruition. The old man went to one knee and scooped the phurba out of the dust.

Goronwy, the Witchfinder, held his prize in hand.

Adele tensed, unsure what to expect next. However, nothing happened. The man tested the weight before slipping the artifact into a deep pocket of his heavy fur coat.

Goronwy spared a quick glance at Gareth and smiled with casual politeness. "I remember you. Prince Cesare's brother. I'm surprised you survived Britain." Then he regarded Adele with much more interest. "Well no, I'm not. Not with her by your side. So that is Adele of Equatoria?"

Flay growled, "Kill her now."

"Pshaw." The old man waved off the vampire. "She is a great geomancer, I'm told. I knew it was you when we heard another airship was in the area. How did you hear about the Tear of Death? From my old friend, Dr. Selkirk, I'd wager."

Adele kept her eyes locked on Flay, but said to Goronwy, "You have no idea what that thing is. It will eat you alive if you try to use it. You're not prepared."

"Oh, I think I am." He patted the pocket where the phurba nestled. "I've already mastered the technique I need on a small scale. Now with this catalyst, I can extend the effect wherever I choose. I'm very excited by the potential of this artifact. Very excited."

"I realize there are things you know that I don't. I can't understand what you did to create those talismans. But I can walk the rifts in a way that no other can. You can't understand the Earth on that level, and I'm telling you that geomancy on the scale you're contemplating has dangerous repercussions. What I did in Britain, and what you are doing in Europe, is doing damage to the Earth. Cracks are forming in the rifts."

Goronwy just laughed. "It is you who don't understand. Nothing was ever accomplished by being afraid of knowledge. This artifact has much to teach me."

"Come with me to Equatoria," Adele said through clenched teeth. "I'll set you up with a research institute that you couldn't dream of in the north."

"Oh, that's very generous, I'm sure." Goronwy raised an affected eyebrow. "I have all the support I need in Paris. My patrons there are expanding their reach. Just on this mission, we've hammered out an alliance with Chengdu that could continue to bear fruit for both clans in the future. It certainly benefited me in the short run. Plus, I don't wish to work for imperialists."

"You idiot. They're using you. Once they have what they want, they'll kill you."

The Witchfinder shifted his gaze to Flay. "I don't think so. The vampires and I are completely on the same page."

"You're on the wrong side of the war. We're fighting to free your own people."

"The fabric of lies for all aggressors, my dear. You invaded clan territory without provocation. You destroyed the British clan, which was a very progressive and useful employer for me. Luckily I managed to find new patrons. But I have to put an end to your aggression first."

Adele's skin crawled at the simplistic admission. "How?"

"This." The Witchfinder touched his pocket again. "I don't particularly want to use it, but since I can, why not? You must be stopped." A long horn sounded from outside. Goronwy shuddered with surprise. "Well, this has been pleasant, but we have to go. You could be very useful. Let's bring her back to Paris, Flay. I want to *consult* with her."

Adele fought to her knees, ignoring the nausea that wracked her, searching for her khukri. She had to kill Goronwy, here and now.

Flay stalked to the Witchfinder's side. "She's right. You have no idea what you're doing. Kill her!"

The old man pressed his lips together in disapproval. "Stop it, Flay. I didn't save your life back in London so you could disobey me. We've been through it all before. Do as I say, please, or I can make it very unpleasant for you." He shook one fist, creating the sound of crystals rattling inside his grip.

Flay scowled but then pointed at Gareth. "At least let me kill *him*."

Goronwy huffed with impatience and turned toward the door with alarm. "No time! Our friends from Chengdu are losing ground up there. We were lucky to convince them to join us in the first place. I'd rather not create ill will to complicate future diplomacy. So, if you'd be so kind, bring the empress to the airship. Now!"

Flay snarled, but dutifully streaked toward Adele who still struggled to reach her faintly glowing dagger. The vampire kicked the woman in the stomach, knocking her over onto her back. Flay snatched up Adele by the collar.

Goronwy prattled on. "Flay, if there's one lesson I want to teach you people, it's that you can't learn from the dead. I want to know what makes her different. Experiments will enlighten me. Hurry now. Bring her. She'll be a useful asset to the Parisian institute."

The vampire dragged her prisoner toward the door. Adele's gaze cast back to Gareth thrashing on his bloody perch. Their eyes met in a moment of fear. She flailed and took hold of Flay's cold wrist. She called up a rush of boiling heat. Silver smoke encircled them both, but no flesh seared.

"Stop squirming." Flay shook Adele, bundling her roughly from the hellish chamber and up the steps out of Gareth's sight. "You can no longer hurt me."

"I'll never stop trying," Adele managed to grind out. She continued swiping at Flay's arm. She also struggled to get her feet under her, but it was impossible. Exhaustion gripped her as hard as Flay. They emerged into the upper temple chamber and Adele noticed a pile of wood and metal wreckage against one wall. Yidak's memory machine had been destroyed.

"Flay!" Goronwy called out in alarm.

The war chief dropped Adele on the floor. The empress's breath whooshed out, but she immediately pushed herself up onto her knees. She caught a glimpse of Flay rushing past Goronwy to intercept two figures who stood in the outer archway. Flay ducked a flash of steel that swept over her head. As Takeda spun to strike her again, Yidak barked a quick command for the samurai to see to Adele across the room, and the old vampire moved in seamlessly to engage Flay. Takeda ducked a savage blow without looking as he passed.

Yidak fought Flay in the doorway. They weaved and struck, blocking and feinting. Claws flashing. Flay hit the Demon King hard several times. Yidak scored strikes on her as well, but as the fight continued, the old vampire's expression betrayed uneasiness. His blows couldn't stagger her. He clearly had never faced a foe as skilled as she. They continued to spin and slash, silent and fast, clothing snapping with their motions. They leapt from floor to wall to ceiling, but their precisely placed feet made no sound as they fought.

Takeda knelt next to Adele with concern. His robes were torn and bloody. His voice creaked with weakness. "Good, you're alive."

Adele tried to speak. She desperately pointed at Goronwy. Flay and Yidak moved with frightening preternatural speed, even to Adele's skilled eye. However, the old man approached the combatants without alarm and reached out his hand. A large red crystal on a thin chain dropped from his fist. Adele could sense the power coming off of it despite the distance. Yidak shuddered, jarred by the energy of the crystal. That slight hesitation was enough. Flay tore into him with both hands. She shredded his face and grabbed him by the chest. She picked the Demon King off the floor and brought him down against her upraised knee. Yidak cried out and went slack.

Takeda roared and charged Flay with his katana drawn back over his shoulder. She let Yidak tumble from her grip, her back still turned to the onrushing samurai. Goronwy slipped around them toward the doorway, the crystal still dangling in the air. Takeda staggered as its power battered him, but he still swung at Flay's exposed neck. She instantly faced him and her two hands clapped the sword between them, bringing it to a sudden stop. Takeda stared in disbelief for a second before he too found himself savaged by Flay. He stumbled. The katana fell with a clang to the stones. Takeda dropped, still trying to strike at Flay, but only ripping her silk robe.

Goronwy knelt next to the groaning Yidak. He dropped the talisman onto the old vampire's chest and Yidak screamed in agony. The proximity of the crystal also tore through the battered Takeda as he vainly struggled to reach his mentor.

There was another horn from outside, and Goronwy stepped over Yidak with a grunt of annoyance and continued quickly for the daylight. "Flay! Come!"

Flay started back toward Adele, but noticed movement overhead. Shapes slipped through cracks in the high dome of the temple, crawling along the ceiling. Five of Yidak's monks hissed their anger when they saw their leaders writhing below. They drifted down to the floor around Adele.

Goronwy's voice came from just outside. "Flay! We have what we need. Attend me!"

Flay's eyes locked on Adele from across the chamber. With a sneer of fury, Flay turned and followed the Witchfinder out into the light.

The monks looked down at Adele with blank stares and grimaces of pain. They pushed and bobbed as if they tried to go to Yidak and Takeda, but they couldn't fight into the searing power of Goronwy's talisman.

Adele heard the faint sound of buoyancy gases roaring outside. With the vampire monks hissing impotently, she half staggered, half dragged herself across the floor to Yidak and Takeda. Smoke rose from the old vampire's chest and he had lapsed into a quivering palsy. The crystal leaked geomantic forces like a cracked steam engine. Takeda now lay nearly senseless beside his master, but he still fought to reach the talisman.

Adele's hand fell onto the crystal and she snatched it up. This was a geomancy she understood, and had mastered. She closed her fist around the talisman as if she could crush it with brute strength. Her vision sparked and everything spun. Weakness battered her body. Still, with a grinding effort, she forced the energy back through the crystal all at once. The stone glowed bright between her fingers and collapsed into a hot liquid that drizzled to the tile floor.

Adele fell over. Yidak coughed and clutched his burnt chest. The monks now raced forward to their master. Adele's arms felt like rubber. Her boneless fingers couldn't grasp anything. She gritted her teeth, feeling blood dripping along her cheek. Her face lay helpless against the floor.

Gareth put a hand on her back and leaned close to her face.

Adele grabbed him and held him for a second to be sure he was real and not an illusion. His chest and arms held numerous jagged wounds where he had ripped himself free. She groaned, "Anhalt?"

"He's alive." Gareth pointlessly wiped blood from her face with his bloody hand.

Adele wanted to hold him, protect him, heal him. Instead, she hissed out, "Stop him. Please, stop Goronwy."

Gareth didn't speak as he reeled to his feet. He paused to look at Yidak, but the old vampire waved him on with an agonized smile of relief. Adele then heard him padding heavily toward the door.

CHAPTER 33

Gareth broke from the main temple, dragging in a lungful of frigid air to stir himself. He ignored the dreadful grinding of bones inside his chest and stumbled for the nearest open rampart, where he launched himself into the air. Blood from his wounds dripped slowly to the Earth. The sky was full of Chengdu fighters, but few paid any attention to him. The battle had come to a confusing close, and they were wandering off, unsure if they had won or lost, trying only to survive the continuing attacks by Yidak's monks.

The clouds had thinned. Goronwy's airship sailed south for the end of the valley. It was unable to escape by climbing over the surrounding peaks. Every bit of wretched canvas was stretched on the yards, trying to gain speed.

As Gareth came in range, humans at the rails opened fire. Long orange tongues flashed from muzzles. A few bullets whizzed close. A ragged volley of cannon fire belched from the ship's flank with an exhale of black smoke. He veered away from the projectiles barreling toward him just as the bellow of the cannon finally rolled over him. Gareth rose to put the hazy sun behind him and he dove for the masts. His claws raked through a mainsail. The wind quickly battered the rips into great flapping holes, and the ship lurched and slowed.

Something slammed into him from above. Flay. The power of her strike drove them both tumbling through the jungle of yards and shrouds until they crashed against the deck. Their impact cracked the rotting planks. More of Gareth's ribs snapped. He shoved her off him. Bloodmen wheeled toward them but held their fire, most likely for fear of hitting their war chief. Flay had always been sinfully fast and strong, but there was something more furious about her now, almost animalistic and regressive.

She rolled to her feet and came at Gareth without pause for breath.

Barely blocking her strikes, he maneuvered for room. Gareth shifted to the side, and as her arm went past he drove his claws into her side. She countered with a blow of her own, nearly taking his arm off. Blood splattered the deck.

Leaping up into the air, Gareth planted his foot on the back of her neck and shoved her forward and down. Across the deck, the bearded old man watched the battle with fascination, fingering the chain of another talisman. Gareth used his momentum to fly at Goronwy. His arm lifted to claw the old man down and end this.

A bloodman stepped suddenly between them and took the blow meant for Goronwy. It ripped him in half. The body knocked against Gareth and threw him off balance. The Witchfinder stepped up and looped the talisman's chain over Gareth's head before stepping back with a smile.

Instinctively Gareth expected excruciating pain. It didn't come. In fact, he felt nothing. The surprise on Goronwy's face told him it wasn't what the Witchfinder expected either. He couldn't have known. Adele's geomancy had changed Gareth forever.

Gareth went to strike at Goronwy again, but Flay grabbed him from behind. Her claws opened the flesh on his shoulder. She grabbed his exposed collarbone and flung him aside. He smashed into the rail, scattering the sluggish human crew. Three of them went screaming over the side. Gareth snapped upright as two vampires grabbed his arms. With a cry of rage, he slammed them together, then catapulted the stunned forms overboard.

His strength was fading fast. He had lost too much blood. He needed a few minutes to feed and regain his vigor, but the nearest human was now scrambling away across the deck.

Flay rushed Gareth again. He leapt aside, creating the space he needed to land a blow on her spine. She crashed into the deck. Gareth pulled the talisman from his neck and wrapped it around hers.

Flay laughed through bloody teeth and pushed herself to her feet. "Did you really think that would work?"

Gareth moved warily as she did. "It was worth a try."

"You and I are no longer affected by the wielders of the Earth." Her robe was shredded and Gareth caught a glimpse of the huge scars that cut across her flesh almost like a cage. "So the playing field is even once again."

Gareth didn't understand, but he didn't reply. He was already moving. Flay was the only thing he had ever feared, even when they fought on the same side. Now she was even more dangerous. The hatred on her face wasn't just for him. She stared at everyone, including Goronwy, with the same contempt.

Gareth vaulted over a capstan toward the Witchfinder. Goronwy was the priority. With him dead, humanity would be safe. Adele would be safe.

Flay, instead of rushing Gareth again, tore a carronade from its lashings and heaved it across the deck. The small cannon struck Gareth's hip and sent him sprawling into a morass of torn rigging. The iron cannon crashed against the side of the ship, taking out the rail. It teetered on the edge, tangled in the cables and shreds of sails that littered the deck.

Gareth staggered to his feet, his leg almost a dead weight. Blood saturated his hip. He didn't feel the tangled ropes about his legs until the cannon tipped over the side and the lines tightened. It pulled him off his feet and yanked him along the deck through the shattered rail. He saw the sky below the airship and a lake-studded plateau far below. His claws dug furrows into the planks, clutching jagged wood as the weight of the cannon tore at him. He reached a hand back, trying to slash at the ropes tangling him. Suddenly Flay was there swinging one of the heavy teak spokes she had snapped off the capstan. He couldn't protect himself.

A bright light exploded in front of his eyes and then darkness enveloped him. The world melted. Then he was airborne. He plummeted. More light shoved its way into his dazed brain. He fought the hurricane of wind, reaching for his tangled legs.

Then there was another jarring explosion and the world went from white to dark. He was surrounded by a choking blackness. Gareth snapped back to awareness as he realized he had fallen into the lake far below the ship.

Fear almost paralyzed him. He thrashed at the water. The sun above him was a watery circle that was fast disappearing from view. The mass of the cannon still lashed to his legs dragged him down into the darkness.

Gareth screamed and watched his breath disappear in a wave of bubbles back up to the surface. He tore at the ropes binding him, taking chunks of his own flesh in his desperation. But he finally kicked free. Hands clawing through water, he fought his way toward the shimmering light far above him. His chest ached to breathe. His vision narrowed to a mere pinprick of light and he reached for it.

He breached the surface with a massive gasp. He had time for only one gulp of air before he sank again, his clothes heavy and his arms leaden weights. Terrified, he struggled again to rise. When he broke the surface once more, his arms flailed about. No matter how hard he struggled, he couldn't free himself. He couldn't lift up out of the water.

The sodden bulk of his coat pulled at him with nearly the same drag as the cannon. He shrugged it off, slipping beneath the icy water again. He floundered his way back up, managing another shallow gasp of air. This time he caught a glimpse of a distant shore in all directions, and he despaired.

He would never make it. He was near the center of the broad lake. His head arched back in a desperate attempt to keep his nose and mouth above the water. Within seconds, the depths grabbed him again and swallowed him down toward the darkness.

Water slipped into his lungs. He panicked, twisting in pain, his eyes bulging. He silently shouted. He thought of Adele waiting anxiously for him to return. He reached once more for the surface, but it seemed miles away.

A shadow crossed in front of the light above him. The water churned as something entered the lake.

Had Adele followed him? He tried to see her, but his vision faded and his limbs hung limp in the water. Darkness surrounded him.

Then a gush of water coughed past his lips. He was on his back with an arm tight around his chest. He was being dragged across the surface of the lake toward the shore.

He tried to speak. "Ad—," he choked out. He struggled to turn and look at her.

"Don't move," came a masculine voice. "Just lie back or you'll drown both of us."

Takeda.

"How . . . did—?" Gareth broke off into wracking coughs as his lungs expelled more water. Only then did Gareth's foggy brain realize the samurai was swimming. He had never known a vampire to swim. They were terrified of the water, with good reason. "How are—?"

"Enough talk!" barked Takeda sharply. "Stay still. I've never done this with another."

Takeda's swimming was barely that. He slapped at the surface with his free arm. Instead of being vertical in the water, they lay flat upon it. Gareth attempted to relax—a difficult feat. The thought of the cavernous empty deep yawing beneath them stirred his fear. Water continued to rush over his face. Waves pushed by the wind and Takeda's frantic motions agitated the area around them. Gareth desperately tried to keep water from slipping into his open mouth as he struggled to breathe and remain calm.

He felt Takeda's legs kicking powerfully under him. It was a similar motion he had seen Adele use when she was soaking in her vast pools in Victoria Palace. The expanse of the bath meant she had to nearly swim across to him. Often she had tried to coax him in with her. Always he denied her. Now he wished he hadn't.

An indeterminable amount of time passed. Takeda's strength waned, his breathing only ragged gasps. The air misted constantly in front of him. Ice had formed on their exposed skin and hair.

Soon they were sinking as much as moving. Gareth knew that they would both drown if he didn't do something. He pulled at Takeda's arm holding him tight.

"Let me help."

"Do you . . . know how?"

"Obviously not. But show me." Gareth felt the grip relent. Immediately, he sank.

"Lie flat on the water." Takeda's orders came quick and strained. "Kick. Stretch your arms out. Push the water past you. Keep kicking."

Gareth tried to emulate the samurai. It was a frantic explosion of churning water. Too quick. Too fast. He slipped deeper into the lake.

"Slow down. Don't panic!" Takeda shouted to be heard over the splashing tumult. "Take a deep breath and hold it. Fill up your lungs. It will keep you on top."

Gareth sucked in as deep a breath as he could muster and to his astonishment, he didn't sink as far or as fast as before. Takeda grabbed Gareth's shoulders and steered him in the direction of the shoreline, which was much closer than it had been before. Hope flared in Gareth and gave him the strength to strike out for it.

"Slowly, or you'll exhaust yourself," Takeda warned him.

"Too late . . . for that," rasped Gareth. Still, he forced himself to reduce his frantic paddling to rhythmic slaps. He stopped talking, as the exhalations of his breath only served to make him sink. He gulped in more air and held his breath. His head spun from the exertion and the odd way of breathing. His body felt more numb than usual.

It seemed like hours later when stones scraped Gareth's hands and knees as he reached the shore. He dragged in painful breaths, collapsing on the lapping bank. Takeda crawled up alongside him. Neither spoke for several minutes.

Finally Gareth croaked, "Thank you."

Takeda nodded wearily, his topknot flopping over slightly from its tight gather. "The Tear?"

Gareth shook his head. He desperately wanted to resume the pursuit of the airship. It was possible he could catch it. Blood still gushed from the numerous wounds. The weakness in his limbs left him no strength to rise from the shallows. Takeda literally heaved him out of the water and onto dry ground.

"You have to feed or you'll die," Takeda commented, looking at the horrific wounds.

"At the monastery," Gareth muttered in a voice that seemed far away even to his ears.

"Too far. There's a shrine close by. Human pilgrims visit it frequently. Come. We may be fortunate."

Gareth staggered to his feet with Takeda's help. "How did you learn to swim?"

Takeda grunted, taking most of his weight. "There is much time in the monastery, enough to learn new things."

"And you chose swimming?"

Takeda shrugged.

"I must really learn that skill." Gareth gave a weak laugh. "It could come in very handy."

"Shut up and walk."

Takeda was right about the shrine. A lone pilgrim was there, placing incense and food at the stones. The moment he saw the two bedraggled figures, he raced to help them. It wasn't until he was easing Gareth to the ground that he realized what they were.

Takeda grabbed the pilgrim's arm tight before the human could flee the demons in terror. He nodded in Gareth's direction. "Help him. He will die without a blood tribute. We won't kill you."

The pilgrim's gaze jerked from Takeda's fierce countenance to Gareth, who looked more like drowned cat than an otherworldly demon at the moment. A smile attempted to cross his lips as reassurance to his frightened meal, but it probably came out more like an evil grimace.

It had less than a comforting effect on the poor man, but still the pilgrim nodded. Blood darkened Gareth's clothes and stained his pale skin. He lay limp on the ground. However, his eyes blazed with hunger. His thirst for survival fanned the hunter inside him as the man came closer. The pilgrim lowered his head baring his neck from under thick folds of wool, but Gareth grabbed his wrist and sank his teeth into the man's flesh. He was embarrassed at his own desperation.

The warm thick rush of blood tasted like heaven. He closed his eyes and focused on drawing as much as he needed to replenish what he had lost. There came with it the rich gamey taste of yak and an odd array of spices. The man's fear made the blood rich. Gareth could have drained him dry, and there was a part of his instinct that bade him to do so, but civilization and reason reasserted itself in time and Gareth released him after a minute.

The pilgrim swayed light-headedly at the sudden loss of blood, his skin now as pale as Gareth's.

"You have brought honor to your family." Takeda told the pilgrim, then found some food and drink in the man's belongings and prompted him to eat.

Gareth closed his eyes as vigor slowly returned to his body. He could feel his extremities again.

Gareth roused from a drowsy slumber. He saw that the sun had gone behind the crest of the mountains. He had fallen asleep, but not for long. Takeda crouched next to him, staring quietly into the distance. "Takeda, what about you? Did you feed?"

"No." The samurai regarded Gareth, studying his wounds again. "I have nothing that rest won't take care of."

The pilgrim glanced between them, packing his meager belongings. They were speaking in vampire, which gave the man little clue as to what fate awaited him.

Gareth said to the man in Tibetan, "As soon as you feel strong enough, you are free to return to your family. I thank you for your kindness. You have saved my life."

The pilgrim's expression went from fear to shock to relief. He bowed before both of them repeatedly. After draining his flask dry, he said a final heartfelt prayer at the shrine and ran off for home in the dusk.

Takeda shifted away from the pile of holy rocks, unsettled by the power of the pilgrim's prayers. "Rest a while longer. We'll start for the monastery when you are able."

"I'm ready now." Gareth sat up. "I need to get back to Adele." His last vision was of her bleeding form. She was so much frailer than a vampire.

Takeda scowled at him. "Your wounds could reopen."

Gareth fixed him with a hard stare. "There's no time. I've failed already. We have to pursue Goronwy. If he uses the Tear of Death, it will spell the end for Adele and all of humanity." He half expected for Takeda to shrug his shoulders and ask why that should be of any concern to him. It was something Cesare would have countered with.

But Takeda nodded grimly and helped Gareth the rest of the way to his feet.

"Do you think the monastery is safe?" Gareth asked.

"Yes. Once your Witchfinder departed, the resolve of Chengdu fled. We were routing the stragglers when Adele found me and bid me follow you."

"She's all right." A weak smile slipped across Gareth's lips.

"Yes."

"She was worried for me, eh?"

"Good thing, too. You would have drowned."

"You could have drowned as well. What you risked—?"

"Perhaps that was the reason I trained all those years. A test of sorts." Takeda shrugged. "Otherwise, why else would I have chosen swimming to learn of all things? Yidak would call it karma."

"Not many vampires would've taken that risk to save another."

"We have much in common."

"We both use swords. What else do we share?"

"You still have to believe you're unique." Takeda huffed a silent laugh at Gareth's ignorance. "That's fine. We all did when we came here. I did too, until years ago when I led Chengdu's packs in an attack on the monastery. I saw this place and met Yidak. I realized I served the wrong master so I abandoned Chengdu for Yidak."

"How long have you been here?"

"It seems like my entire life, but it's only the useful part of it."

"Are you ever going to leave?"

Silence hung in the air. Gareth looked over to see Takeda pondering, as if the question had never occurred to him before. The samurai merely sat quietly, staring into the sinking sun.

It was at least another hour before Gareth felt strong enough to take to the wind and let it do the work of carrying them home. From a distance, he saw Adele pacing the ramparts, wrapped in a thick coat, waiting anxiously. The hard lines on her face only relaxed when Gareth and Takeda landed beside her, though they reappeared as she took in his miserable state.

Gareth was too exhausted to speak. He noticed her own blood-streaked form, but didn't see any critical wounds. She was bandaged, and, though pale, she moved with more strength than he at the moment. As they limped toward their room, Takeda filled her in, using sparse words and descriptions. It wasn't until the last point that Gareth saw her wince in pain. The relic remained in Goronwy's possession.

"Damn," she whispered. "Heaven help us all."

CHAPTER 34

"They should have been here by now. It's been two days." Adele held the stone that she had used to send a signal to Captain Hariri.

Gareth wanted to placate Adele's concern, but his own level of anxiety had been steadily rising. "I'll go look for them."

A scowl of irritation showed that she couldn't go with him, but she said nothing. She knew the mountains were treacherous to impossible on foot, and she would only slow him down. "Take Takeda with you."

Now it was his turn to be annoyed. "I'm fully recovered."

"I doubt that, but that's not the issue. We don't know why they're late. Nothing short of a disaster would have stopped Hariri. I don't want you walking into trouble alone."

She was right, of course. His strength had not been enough to defeat Flay or Goronwy, nor retrieve the Tear from them. "If he's willing."

He was willing, as was Hiro. The three of them departed from the monastery walls within the hour.

"Do you know their last location?" Takeda made room for Hiro between them as they lifted into the air.

Gareth wore Greyfriar's costume again, although he only looped his long scarf around his neck. "Close enough."

Takeda said nothing more as they flew through the towering mountains of black granite. Keeping their bodies flat and actually increasing their density to fight against the crushing gusts, they tore along a valley to the east. Gareth pointed down and they descended toward a distant plateau where the *Edinburgh* should have been moored. The ship was nowhere to be seen. Gareth caught the faintest hint of blood and smoke in the gusting winds. That did not bode well.

They veered north, trying to follow the scent. It wasn't long before they saw wreckage strewn across the plateau. Bodies lay partially buried under a fine dusting of snow. A cold sweat gripped Gareth as they followed the trail of debris from high above.

Finally he saw the airship far below. It lay almost on its side, the masts digging into the ground. A deep furrow cut almost a hundred feet behind it. The dirigible was still intact. Suddenly there was a volley of gunfire. Takeda veered off, as did Gareth. Hiro dove down to the ground and they followed him, dropping out of sight from the sharpshooters. Hiro stuck his finger through a bullet hole in his tunic.

Gareth wrapped his face and pulled up his hood. He was completely Greyfriar once again. Even the timbre of his voice was quite different. "I'll walk in so as not to alarm anyone with a large gun. Stay behind me. Far behind me."

They trod over the frozen ground for more than a mile until the zeppelin came into view through a narrow crevice. Greyfriar studied the area around them to make sure there weren't snipers positioned. He slipped up to the last outcropping before the open plateau where the airship lay.

"Put down your guns! It's Greyfriar! I'm coming in." Despite the faint sound of rifle bolts clicking, he stepped into the clearing. He had his hands up. "There are two with me!"

The figure of Major Shirazi climbed onto the rail. Light flared off his spyglass. "Come ahead!"

Greyfriar muttered to Takeda and Hiro, "Be so good as to not mention I'm a vampire, would you? These fellows don't know."

The two vampires exchanged looks of incredulity and Greyfriar strode forward to the beached airship. He climbed up onto the tilting deck, followed by the more cautious Takeda and Hiro. He shook Shirazi's hand and accepted comradely greetings from the Harmattan, while the major stared past him at the two vampires with undisguised hatred.

Captain Hariri emerged from the causeway and limped toward them. He was greatly relieved to see Greyfriar, but he too looked at the vampires with nervous suspicion. He didn't wait for Greyfriar's obvious question. "A pack came at us. We were lucky to spot them before they hit. Managed to get airborne to run for it. It was no good. They crippled us. We lost maybe a third of the men." He glanced angrily at Takeda and then back to Greyfriar. "Friends of yours, eh?"

"Yes, from the monastery." Greyfriar took in the rust-colored bandage on the captain's leg. "How bad is the ship?"

"They slashed sails, cut rigging, and smashed a good number of the yards. And crashing didn't do us much good either. The poor girl is a mess."

Greyfriar slammed his hand against the rail. "Can she fly at all?" If not, they were trapped here in Tibet while Goronwy roamed free.

Hariri scanned the chaotic deck and the huge dirigible overhead with its dented aluminum cage. He took a deep breath. "She'll float, aye, but I don't know how she'll sail. She won't get far without major repairs, I can tell you that."

"As far as the monastery?"

The captain laughed and wiped his brow. "Up those slopes? It would be a feat worthy of a wizard." Then he realized the swordsman was serious.

Greyfriar met his stunned gaze with mirrored glasses. "You have demonstrated magical flight before."

"In gales as strong as these? And settling this ship on the precipice that monastery sits on?" Hariri shrugged with a sardonic frown. "Maybe."

Greyfriar moved his gaze slowly over the soldiers and the ship's captain. In a low voice, he said, "Make ready then. Your empress needs you."

A grueling six hours later, the *Edinburgh* struggled to lift off the ground. As it cleared the dirt, the ship listed dangerously. Thick cables and metal stays groaned, threatening to part and leave the hull of the ship dangling helplessly from the dirigible. Men scurried with heavy bars to pry several cannons from their carriages and manhandle them over the side. Hariri ordered venting gas to balance her out.

The wind gusted. The entire crew held their breath and watched the canvas fill. The spars held, and the *Edinburgh* swept about the mountain's waist. Every draft of wind threatened to force the ship to career into the rocks. Still, the little vessel put her shoulder down and got to work, her destination the monastery.

Greyfriar made his way forward, following the pitch of the ship as it was buffeted by the wind. Takeda followed, and they stood at the bow looking down the length of the deck. The armed soldiers stared at the vampires, while fingering their rifles. Takeda and Hiro ignored that and followed the concert of airmen in motion with unique fascination.

"Exhilarating, isn't it?" Greyfriar grinned at Takeda's overawed expression.

"I have never seen its like. Yidak would be astounded."

There was a cracking sound behind them. Greyfriar spun around to see the jib boom splintering back over the bowsprit. Cables parted one by one. Spritsails tore loose in the wind. The ship came about wildly to starboard. The deck shifted beneath their feet as Captain Hariri and the bosun competed to shout profane orders that would hopefully bring the *Edinburgh* into the wind. A phalanx of airmen scrambled out along the bowsprit, unmindful that nothing was between them and the Earth far below but a few frayed cables. Shouts echoed as men struggled to make fast the shaking jib boom before it took the entire bowsprit with it.

Hiro surged forward onto the gunwale, desperate to help. A heavy mainstay snapped loose with the sound of a cathedral bell. The metal buckle flailed through the air and bashed Hiro in the head causing a gush of blood. He staggered, but still fought to brace the bowsprit even while loose rigging flew wildly around him.

Greyfriar had a sudden terrifying flash of falling while entangled in the ropes, but he still pulled the last airman off the failing mast. The tangled spritsails ballooned in the wind, dragging the ship around toward the mountainside. He grabbed Hiro before the boy was dragged over the side in a mass of cables.

"Let it go!" Greyfriar shouted. "Let it go!"

"They need it!" Hiro argued.

"Cut it away!" Hariri called from the waist. "It's pulling us over!"

Crewmen rushed forward with axes. They chopped splintered

timber and cut snaking cables. The jib boom roared past, nearly decapitating the lot of them. Takeda took one of the axes and lent his formidable strength to freeing the ship from the tangled morass. When he cut through the mainstay cable that Hiro was holding, there was a crashing tumult as the bowsprit cracked off the ship. Greyfriar and the boy tumbled back onto the deck. The ship righted itself and veered away from the treacherous jagged cliffs. Hariri came forward and put his hand on Greyfriar's shoulder, studying the damage with dismay.

Hiro stared in disappointment. A rivulet of blood flowed from the gash on his scalp, but he didn't notice it, he was so caught up in the excitement. Crewmen rushed to clear the aftermath, but two of them stopped, and almost without thinking, clapped Hiro on the back in a gesture of gratitude. If there was one thing these men appreciated, it was shared danger and a love of their ship.

The boy weaved to the rail and leaned over. "Can we still land without that?"

"Captain Hariri has sailed with less." Greyfriar turned to Hariri. "Right?"

"No. Never." Hariri made his way back to the quarterdeck, where he gave orders to furl sails except for the small topgallants. The topmen looked like spiders climbing out along the yards over the treacherous open air. Below them, a cruel death waited.

Takeda's eyes widened. He dropped a firm hand on Hiro's shoulder before the blood-soaked lad could dart up into the tops to join them and disrupt their work. "They cannot fly, but they risk such precarious work."

"This coming from the man who dove into the water to save me," noted Greyfriar.

Takeda shrugged, but then grinned. They held onto the rail as the ship labored through another tremulous tack. The monastery came into view, a vision of silver against the dark mountain. The *Edinburgh* slowed, but not near enough to Greyfriar's experienced eye. They swept toward the monastery at far too swift a speed.

Hiro moved to the crushed rail and waved to the vampires on the ramparts, signaling all was well. Greyfriar saw Adele in the courtyard with Anhalt and Yidak beside her. He chuckled when Adele shouted orders and vampires raced to comply, Yidak included.

"Where do you intend to land it?" Takeda wanted to know.

Greyfriar looked almost roguish. "Right in the main courtyard, I should think."

Small bow chaser cannons bellowed on the foredeck and grappling hooks flew out with cables snaking after. Steel hooks embedded into the mountain and the walls of a temple. More lines blasted out to create an intricate spider's web around the little ship. The first lines frayed and tore free from their anchors. Men tossed cables down to the ramparts, and the vampires grabbed them, putting their strength to the task of slowing the *Edinburgh*. Takeda and Hiro leapt off and descended rapidly to the walls. They grabbed lines and heaved back on them. The ropes creaked with the strain.

The cries of hundreds struggling to bring the mighty ship to a halt before it crashed into the white slope of the monastery rose like a prayer. The ship's forward momentum eased and the dirigible cage bumped against the pillars of the main temple with nothing more than a light bounce.

Adele let go of the rope she manned with Anhalt and Yidak. The old vampire had a broad grin on his face. His bellow of laughter rang across the square. The crew of the *Edinburgh* whooped with triumph and the vampires joined in, feeling a sense of accomplishment.

It was an odd sight, Greyfriar thought. Never would he have imagined vampires and humans working together. The monumental accomplishment had kept either side from thinking about their enemy. There was only the task at hand.

Adele waved vigorously up at Greyfriar, the smile on her perspiring face beaming. Yidak followed her gaze and lifted his own hand in victory. Greyfriar leapt onto one of the anchor chains and slid down with his cloak flying behind. He touched down and seized Adele around the waist.

Captain Hariri limped down the lowered gangplank with Major Shirazi and the Harmattan marching in formation behind him. Hariri looked very tired and very cold. He shared an unnerved slump of his shoulders with all the men. They watched the vampires surrounding them with barely controlled panic. Hariri bowed to Adele, trying to take some comfort in her well-being and the fact that she seemed safe among these creatures. Shirazi stood by his troopers, all their rifles ready with bayonets gleaming. One hand rested on his pistol and in the other was a small grenade called a shrieker, which emitted a high-pitched sound harmful to vampires.

Adele smiled at the grim major and then clasped Hariri's arm with comforting familiarity. "Captain, now that was a feat worthy of a legend!"

"Thank you." Hariri laughed cynically. "It was. And with the ground crew we had to assist us, no one will believe it. Perhaps we shouldn't try to convince them."

"Someday they'll believe," she assured him. "How long before she's ready to sail out?"

Hariri offered his best put-upon face. "Many days, if at all, Your Majesty." Before Adele could protest, he continued quickly, "There's spare timber, cable, and canvas in the hold, but I have lost men, both dead and wounded."

"We will help you," Yidak exclaimed almost joyfully. "Show us what we need to do, Captain, and we shall do it."

Hariri couldn't respond. He only stared nonplussed at the old vampire. Shirazi snorted in angry derision, watching the empress for her response.

Hariri rubbed his stubbled chin. "No matter what we have for labor, repairs will be makeshift at best. It will be a difficult and slow journey home."

"We don't have time for slow." Adele leveled a commanding stare at her captain. "You will make use of Yidak's people in whatever way you can; do you understand?"

Hariri bit his lip with concern. He glanced toward Anhalt, looking for some guidance. The general offered a confident smile that urged him to trust the empress's judgment without question. Hariri accepted the advice begrudgingly, and bowed to Adele.

She asked, "Can you get us over the mountains?"

"You mean the mountains towering all around us? The highest mountains in the world?" The captain sighed.

"We'll make for Delhi," Adele stated with a firm set to her jaw. "That's the nearest imperial port. We can acquire a new ship to pursue Goronwy."

Anhalt asked with surprise, "You're not returning to Alexandria?"

"No, General. I intend to run down Goronwy. In the air, if I can. If not, I'm going to Paris to kill him and retrieve the Tear of Death."

CHAPTER 35

The next few days passed slowly for Adele. All she could think about was what Goronwy could be doing while they were stuck here. She wanted to spend every second studying and re-examining the blue crystal, for all it had been worth so far. Instead, she stabbed a heavy needle fiercely and sharply through thick canvas, dragging rough cord behind. Around her hunched the shoulders of numerous vampire monks all doing the same work as she, repairing sails as best they could. They sat in the limited lighting inside the main temple with the material stretched between all of them, each laboring awkwardly over a section. With each stitch, Adele's impatience grew, but she tried to focus on the sewing. Finally her mending was done. Her fingers stung and her back ached. She reached for another section to continue working, but the vampire beside her said, "We are almost finished here. Go outside and see the sky."

Adele nodded gratefully, pushing herself to her feet, feeling the stiffness in her limbs from sitting for hours on end. With shuffling steps that gradually became more limber, she headed out. The light blinded her for a moment, but then she drew a deep breath of the cold air, free of the smoke of the burning candles inside. She headed down to the ship with her camera looped over her neck.

Adele climbed onto the deck of the *Edinburgh*, relishing the scent of freshly sawn wood and the sound of hammers, as well as singing. She marveled again watching humans and vampires working together. The crew found that their mortal enemies learned quickly for the most part. A few demonstrations of the tool or the work, and it was quickly replicated. It didn't mean there weren't incidents and resentment, but overall it was more than Adele could have hoped for.

Her attention fell to the new rail under her hand. Intricate carvings weaved their way around the wood, delicate geometric shapes. Stooping in amazement, her fingers traced the beautiful artwork. It held the precision of Greyfriar's hand, but joyous wonderment as well. When she lifted her head, she understood why.

She saw General Anhalt kneeling alongside Hiro. The boy was working at the end of the rail with a narrow chisel, shaving infinitesimal bits of the plain wood to form his designs. Then Adele saw his handiwork everywhere: on the rails, gunwales, and hatches. His focus was so complete he didn't notice her until she walked over to him.

He looked up at her, his face perspiring despite the cool temperature. "You like it?"

Adele looked wonderingly at Anhalt. "Did you teach him this?"

The general shook his head. "I taught him nothing. He said he wanted to help improve the ship. He's been spending all his time doing it. I'm just looking at it in amazement."

She said to Hiro, "It's beautiful."

The ship's old carpenter approached them. His kindly face puffed with pride. He actually placed a hand on the young vampire's shoulder. "He's a fine apprentice. A bit artistic for my taste, but you cannot deny he makes *Edinburgh* fit for royalty, Your Majesty."

Adele nodded. "It's about time she looked like the queen she is." She bowed to the young vampire. "You do us honor, Hiro. Thank you."

The boy's blue eyes shone and he bent back to his task. Adele thought he looked a bit tired, and she was about to tell him to take a break when Shirazi's stern voice came aft as he instructed a vampire on the use of a planer. "For spit's sake, use both hands like I showed you!"

The vampire who crouched near the major lifted her head, making no effort to hide her scowl, but still she grasped the tool with both hands as the soldier demonstrated again with irritation. Shirazi came to his feet and saluted.

"Your Majesty, the ship is nearly ready to sail."

"Excellent, Major," she said. "Where is Greyfriar?"

Shirazi craned his head upward. "In the tops. Shall I send for him?"

"Not at all." Her hand reached for the shrouds stretching up to the masts high above.

Major Shirazi immediately called for a crewman to swing over a bosun's chair. Adele waved the contraption aside, refusing to be hoisted like some dainty maiden. She wore pants under her kaftan and the same thick boots as most of the men. The crew in the rigging hardly batted an eye as the empress pulled herself up onto the ratlines alongside them. Adele found bright prayer flags tied to the shrouds and fluttering in the wind. They brought a warmth to her chest to see them on her beloved ship.

In the dizzying heights of the port foremast, she found Yidak assisting Greyfriar in fitting a replacement yardarm. Yidak's face was a mask of concentration, listening to instructions, bearing the heavy weight so the topmen could fix stays and cables. Soon the rigging looked as good as new, at least to Adele's eyes.

It was only then that Yidak noticed her and beamed a wide grin. Greyfriar's posture showed he was not so pleased to see her in the tops, but he didn't bother chastising her.

Adele brushed her tousled hair from her face. "How many more left to refit?"

"We have one more mast to swap."

Hariri clambered along the rigging to land lightly on the newly placed spar, testing its strength with a few daredevil jumps. The spar bounced but held. "Solid work."

Yidak clasped his hands together in humility. "Your men taught us well. The work is hard but very satisfying."

"Perhaps you were meant to be a sailor."

"Who is to say a man must be only one thing in life." Yidak glanced for a moment at Greyfriar.

Greyfriar let out an amused sigh at the old man and immediately took a line to swing to the stump of the mainmast. "We have work to do."

Yidak winked at Adele, but then looked at something behind her. She turned to find, with a shock, a vampire floating beside her.

He bowed his head to Yidak. "Something is wrong with Hiro."

The good humor faded from all of them. Adele quickly descended, but then she felt Greyfriar wrap his arm about her waist. She immediately let go of the rigging and then they were airborne. She heard Hariri shouting to his men, but they were swiftly out of earshot as Greyfriar seized a rope in midair and pretended to slide down to the deck, while he really dropped under his own power. Yidak flew close on their heels.

They alighted on the deck. Hiro lay unconscious, with a group of vampires around him. Some of the crew gathered on the fringes. Takeda was kneeling in the center of the crowd, cradling the unconscious boy in his arms.

"He just collapsed," exclaimed the carpenter to Adele.

She pushed her way to the boy and dropped to her knees beside Hiro. His breath came too fast and short. His face had gone pale and clammy. The bruise from his old head wound stood stark purple and yellow against his white flesh.

Takeda looked at her with terrible pain in his eyes. "What is it?"

"I'm not sure. That head injury looks bad. They're insidious things. You could be fine one moment and not the next."

Greyfriar sank down and put his ear against the boy's chest. He winced with alarm. "His heart is failing. He's dying."

"He needs blood," Takeda said. "He hasn't fed since before the battle. There were so many wounded, he refused."

Yidak's face was drawn tight. "The pilgrims are gone. They had been tasked too hard. I sent them away."

Adele pushed up her sleeve, revealing rows of slowly healing bite marks. Greyfriar's hand snapped out and stopped her. "No. You've lost too much already. Hiro will need more than you can give."

"I can give just enough to keep him alive."

General Anhalt stepped into the circle. "No, Your Majesty. I will do it." He already had his arm bared and a knife poised. With a swift cut, he opened a small wound. Kneeling close to the crumpled form, he placed the dripping arm over the boy's mouth that was gently eased open by Takeda. "Rub his throat gently. It will force him to swallow."

Hiro's throat convulsed and the blood dripped in. After long minutes of this, the boy's eyes fluttered and he weakly seized Anhalt's arm, pulling it closer, wrapping his mouth around the gash. The general flinched but didn't pull away. A hand fell on his shoulder and he looked up with assurance that he was all right. It wasn't someone trying to stop him; it was Captain Hariri baring his own arm.

"My turn. I have more blood than I need, my friend."

To Adele's astonishment, a few men stood behind Hariri: the ship's carpenter and one or two of the crew. It wasn't many, but the fact that any were willing to volunteer was unbelievable. She heard Greyfriar's sharp intake of breath beside her. His hand gripped hers tightly. She felt a swell of amazement and pride. She would have never thought this possible outside of Gareth's enclave in Edinburgh. One by one the humans offered their blood to Hiro, even while most of their shipmates looked on in distaste.

The boy awakened and he gazed up with wide eyes. "What happened?" he muttered, suddenly embarrassed to have everyone crowding around him. He realized he held a human's bloody arm. He released it as if it was forbidden.

Takeda held the boy tighter. "It's all right, Hiro. You collapsed. You need to feed."

"My head hurts," Hiro whispered.

Another airman crouched down and bared his arm. "Might as well drink, lad. You still look like a ghost. Hope you don't mind a touch of rum with it."

Hiro hesitatingly took the man's arm and placed his mouth over the cut as the warm blood flowed. His strength was returning, and the vibrant blue eyes of hunger faded. His sated gaze went to Takeda with eyes drooping drowsily. "I feel better now."

Greyfriar again put his ear to the boy's heart and came away with a relieved nod.

Yidak gently laid a hand on Hiro's head. "You need to rest." He regarded the humans around him, his expression almost confounded by their generosity. "I don't know what to say. Thank you."

Many of the men of the *Edinburgh* took off their caps, shifting a bit, uncomfortable under the direct gaze of the fierce vampire. "Was nothing," intoned the carpenter, stepping up to place a hand on the boy's chest and laying the small worn chisel there.

Adele only had one more undeveloped piece of film, and she used it here.

—⁂—

The *Edinburgh* stood in the thin morning light, ready to sail. Her crew scampered about her rigging making last-minute checks. Her hold was filled with fresh water and enough dried meat to serve for the jump to Delhi. Adele stood on the quarterdeck with Greyfriar and Yidak on either side of her. Anhalt and Takeda were together in the waist, chatting about strategy or weapons, Adele wasn't quite sure, but watching the two soldiers talk so easily made her smile.

Bright red and yellow robes milled among the dull colors of the crew. Many of the vampires had wanted to see what it was like to be under sail on a ship even for a short while, so Adele had encouraged them to come on board. Hariri ordered the lines to be cast off. The deck shifted beneath their feet as the sails luffed. The binnacle was a hive of activity. Canisters flew and clunked inside the tubes on their way to and from the tops and the chemical deck. Hiro darted from one rail to the next, watching the ground fall away and craning his neck to see the men crawling above.

For a moment, Adele was transported back to the time when she and Simon flew on the *Ptolemy*. Simon's excitement had been uncontainable. She had been so worried about formality back then, worried about people's opinions and her uncertain future. She had barely taken the time to enjoy the moment. Despite the peril, she wished she had brought Simon with her now so he could have experienced this incredible adventure. He and Hiro would have gotten along famously.

The ship shuddered as the wind shifted abruptly, trying to drag them back to the side of the mountain. Greyfriar held Adele steady as she staggered slightly. Then the *Edinburgh* was free of the monastery ramparts and her prow pointed for the open air. She continued her rise into the saffron light, making the sails glow with an inner heat, the sunrise reflecting off the dirigible's metal casing.

Yidak's smile was a delight to behold. He was much like a child himself in many ways. Or maybe he was just able to embrace the remembrances of youth, when one's spirit was open and willing to accept new experiences and chance changes. Life seemed a series of amazing events for him.

The old vampire turned and embraced Adele, his robes draping around her. "You have brought new life to our home and our hearts. Things will never be the same again."

"Is that a good thing?"

"Why wouldn't it be? No one can hide forever."

Adele held him tight. "And I'm so sorry that your . . . memories were destroyed."

"Destroyed? No matter, I recorded a cylinder on how to build it. Oh wait. Well, I probably remember." He threw back his head and laughed. "I'm going to miss you. Who would have thought I could say that about a human?"

Adele dug into her pocket and pulled out a small stack of photographs. She shuffled through them and exclaimed with delight. "Here!" She showed Yidak the picture of his memory machine that she had taken.

The old vampire held the photograph with both hands, staring at it with wonder. "Yes, that's it exactly." He leaned over to see the other photos and slid them around with his claw. He tapped one. "May I have that?"

Adele saw it was the picture of her and Gareth that Anhalt had taken. It was still the only photo she had of the two of them. Even so, she nodded graciously and gave it to the old vampire.

"I knew that *you* would have a miracle in your pocket." Yidak beamed at the photograph, looking at it and then at the real people. Back and forth several times. He clutched the pictures joyfully. Then his hand reached out to Greyfriar. "Walk with me."

The two stepped to the rail beside a pile of tackle that had yet to be stowed. Yidak peered over the side. "Look down there."

Greyfriar leaned on the intricately carved wood. Several hundred feet beneath the airship was a lake shining in the sun. He shuddered. It was the same body of water that had nearly drowned him. When he turned back, he saw Yidak holding a heavy wooden block. The old vampire tossed the object over the rail.

"Hey!" Hariri shouted from the binnacle. "What in the hell are you doing?"

Yidak put on an apologetic face. "Oh. That was garbage, yes?"

"No!" The captain threw up his hands, cursing in Arabic.

Yidak turned back to Greyfriar with a conspiratorial chuckle. "This is more important than whatever that thing is used for. Look. Look down again."

Greyfriar saw that the block had struck the middle of the lake. It raised chills along his spine.

"What do you see?" Yidak asked.

"Ripples on the water where you threw Captain Hariri's block."

The old vampire shoved Greyfriar playfully. "Yes! Exactly. Now do you understand?"

"I understand gravity. More or less. Is that what you mean?"

"No. Do you remember when I threw the stone into the ice, that first day you were here?"

Greyfriar thought back. He had almost forgotten the forlorn spectacle he had presented then. The brooding vampire prince lost in his own shadows. "Yes. And so?"

"This is the same."

"No, it isn't. I didn't see ripples then."

"Yes, but they were still there. They are always there whether they are hidden or not. They will be there forever." Yidak stared into his mirrored eyes and leaned close to him, whispering, "Son of Dmitri."

Greyfriar took the Demon King's hand. "Thank you. I think I know what you mean."

"Good." Yidak pushed away from the side with a laugh. "Someone should."

As they returned to the center of the deck, Hiro darted forward and collided with Adele, hugging her tight. She leaned down and placed a kiss on his cheek.

"Stay here," he demanded. "Must you go?"

"I wish I could stay, but I must go and see to the safety of my people."

"Can I come with you?"

"*May* I come with you," Adele corrected him instinctively, as she had done to Simon a thousand times.

The boy turned to look at Yidak pleadingly. "May I go with them?"

Yidak shook his head sadly. "Not this time. Perhaps there will be another chance."

Greyfriar nodded. "We'll come back. There's still much we can learn from each other."

Takeda and Anhalt climbed the companionway to the quarterdeck to join them. The samurai pulled the katana from his sash and turned to face the Gurkha, bowing at the waist. "For you."

Adele drew in a sharp breath.

Anhalt took it reverently in his hands. "You bestow a great honor on me, Takeda."

"This blade never leaves the side of its master. May it watch over you."

Anhalt bowed, holding the sword out as he did so. He fumbled with his own sword belt with one hand, unbuckling it, and held up the belt and his Fahrenheit saber. "For you. It's seen me through a lot of troubles."

Takeda bowed again, receiving the sword and scabbard with both hands. "Perhaps one day we will meet when we won't need to carry weapons."

Anhalt grinned. "If I last so long, I'd enjoy that."

"Men such as you last forever." Takeda wrapped the belt around his robed waist and buckled it on. He grasped the hilt of the saber and smiled at the touch of it.

CLAY GRIFFITH AND SUSAN GRIFFITH   275

Yidak's hand lifted in farewell to Adele and her companions. "You are always welcome here."

Greyfriar's hand rose also. "And you are welcome outside."

"Good. Someday I will make that journey. Just to see what becomes of you." The old vampire reached into his robe and pulled out a copper cylinder. He offered it to Greyfriar. "This is your memory. It isn't much. But it is a start."

Greyfriar took the cylinder carefully, running a gloved finger over the marks on the copper surface. "Thank you."

Yidak bowed. "You are welcome." Then he raised his head and let out a cry as he rose from the deck.

All around the ship the monks in their colorful robes lifted into the air. They floated beside the *Edinburgh* in a glorious armada of yellow and red. The vampire monks swirled about in a vibrant display. To Adele, they looked like a second sun cresting the mountain in their bright mantles. They circled the ship twice, wheeling in exquisite formation, and then descended to the Earth as the *Edinburgh* lifted higher into the sky.

Greyfriar pulled Adele closer and whispered, "Back to the real world."

"Wasn't that the real world?"

"Depends on the two of us, I think." He stared at the vanishing vampires drifting back to their hidden home.

CHAPTER 36

The coming of spring was a time of sadness among vampires. They relished the cold and dark of winter. This spring seemed especially morose in Paris. As the riotous scents of fresh growth swirled and clumps of color appeared along the decrepit avenues and tumbled buildings, the warmer weather brought the human army stirring in their camp in Nevers. The Equatorians stretched their stiff limbs, shouldered their weapons, and assembled their columns to march north. Equatorian airships appeared overhead to launch bombing sorties. After the vampires concentrated their forces in the air over the city and numerous ships were torn from the air, the sorties stopped.

No vampires offered opposition to the Equatorian ground forces, even while endless swarms of packs from around France streamed into Paris. So within mere weeks of breaking winter camp, the distressing clank of Equatorian machines drifted over the southern limits of the city, fueling the already frantic atmosphere around the Seine River. Smoke rose from human campfires in nearby Fontainebleau where the Equatorians had established a base that sprawled for miles south of Paris.

From her home exile at the Tuileries, Caterina had no knowledge of why Lady Hallow filled the city with packs while allowing the human army to march virtually right up to the Seine River. When Hallow had been banished from the palace, the power simply went with her. She and Honore ruled from their nest across town at the Hotel de Ville. The pack leaders and clan lords swarmed there. The Tuileries became a backwater, forgotten and ignored.

Caterina smelled the end coming before it arrived. The balmy evening breeze brought warning of Honore and Lady Hallow. The Witchfinder was with them, along with a fourth scent, a strange frightening harshness that Caterina almost recognized but couldn't place. Everything told her to flee, gather the children and get out of Paris. Leave everything behind because there was nothing here any longer.

However, Caterina was the queen. To run meant that the world had crumbled. She refused to believe they had come to that place.

Honore and Hallow entered Caterina's private room without requesting permission. The queen stiffened with pointless indignation. Behind them came the Witchfinder, with a confident expression that no human in the north should have. He was almost insulting in his calm demeanor. The Witchfinder paid no more homage to the queen than her son had. Caterina waited for the disturbing fourth, but no one else entered the room.

"Mother," Honore said, "the time has come."

"Has it?" Caterina put her balled fists on her hips.

"I'm taking the clan. The packs will support me. The clan lords will stand by and do nothing. Father is finished."

The queen eyed her son with unrestrained rage. "So you're going to kill him? Is that the monster you've become?"

"Yes." Honore seemed to vibrate with nervous energy. "There's no other way to save the clan."

Now Caterina turned her attention to Hallow. "This is *your* doing. He isn't cunning enough."

Lady Hallow remained calm. "It's the king we want. We have no qualms with you, despite your attempt to assassinate me."

Caterina laughed, but the sound froze in her throat as another figure slid into view. A shudder shook her body at the sight of Flay in the doorway, a horrible specter of her former self. The old war chief of the merciless Cesare stared coldly into the room. The shadowy shapes of more vampires crowded behind her.

Lady Hallow continued, "Your Majesty, you will testify before the clan lords that Lothaire aided the traitor Gareth. In return, we will forget your indiscretion with that mob of dissolute children to take my life. Then we will schedule the king's execution and the assumption of Honore to the throne."

"Are you insane?" Caterina let her claws slip from her fingertips. "You can kill me then. I will never say anything against Lothaire."

Flay shook her head with a disgusted glare. "Just kill them both."

Hallow barked over her shoulder, "Quiet, Flay! We need *proof* that the king is a traitor. We want the queen to provide that proof. Honore must assume the throne in a completely proper fashion."

Flay cast a quick, savage glare at the pale female, then slipped back into the hallway.

Honore smiled at Caterina with failed charm. "Mother, please. Do as we say. It's for the best. Father isn't suitable for this crisis. When I'm king, I'll take care of you."

Caterina felt sick. Surely she hadn't borne this pathetic creature. "I can't believe you're Lothaire's son. Look at you. You're weak. And a liar. I could understand if you simply wanted power. But you're doing this because you're afraid of *them*. Those outsiders. I can't even hate you, Honore. I just never want to see you again."

Hallow said, "We can arrange that, Majesty."

The Witchfinder exhaled in annoyance. "Oh please, Hallow, just do whatever it is you're doing. I'm behind on my work. I've hardly slept preparing Paris in case Empress Adele comes to call."

"She will," Flay murmured from the shadows.

Goronwy ignored the vitriol in her tone. "Perhaps. I've spent *my* valuable time insuring that the empress can't burn you all to cinders like she did my former employers in Britain. I should be at Notre Dame positioning my crystals, not here listening to children bicker over who does what. So will the lot of you just sort it out?"

Hallow waved her hand toward the queen. "Flay, take her."

Honore blocked Flay. "Don't lay hands on her!"

The old war chief reacted on instinct and seized the Dauphin's arm with her claws. Snarling, she brought Honore to his knees. He shouted in frightened alarm and Hallow gasped.

Caterina ran for a window and leapt out. She caught the wind, propelling herself around the corner. She clutched the wall tightly, crawled down, and swung inside one of the countless open windows. She knew there was a wide gap in the floor in this chamber. She dropped through it into another room, then quickly pressed into a crack in the plaster. She slid between the interior walls before falling to her knees and wriggling into a long unused back corridor. There were very few holes in the Tuileries she didn't know because she had chased her children through all of them.

Inside the nursery, Lothaire sat with the toddler and the two whispering twins when Caterina shoved her way through a gap in the ceiling. They all looked in amazement as the queen rose, shedding chunks of plaster and splintered wood. She ran for Lothaire, trailing a cloud of dust.

"Run!" She grasped her husband's arm and pulled him to his feet. "You must run."

Lothaire clutched the baby with one arm and tried to steady his wife with the other. "What's wrong? Are the Equatorians in the city?"

"No." Caterina wrestled the small child away from him and put him down on the floor with a gentle shove toward the twins. "Please, Lothaire, just run. They're coming for you."

"Who's coming? Caterina, please calm yourself."

"Honore has turned against you. He and Lady Hallow want you dead."

"What?" Lothaire instinctively comforted his wife. "Are you sure? Tell me what happened?"

Caterina continued to pull him toward a window. "Flay is in Paris. I saw her. She is with Hallow and the Witchfinder."

"Flay! You must be mistaken. You're delirious. Calm down."

"They're all in league. All of Cesare's old cohorts. They want Paris. If you can stay alive, they'll never be able to do it. Please run!"

"What about you? What about the children? I can't just run away."

Caterina cupped her husband's cheek in her palm. "They want me because they think I will betray you. They won't hurt the children if they have any prayer of me cooperating. I can buy time. So go. Across the river. Quai du Voltaire. Left from Pont Royal. The next block down. There is a blue door. Find Kasteel. He can hide you and get you out of Paris."

"Out of Paris?" Lothaire drew himself up. "I won't abandon my family."

"Your Majesty." Honore stood at the door with mercenary fighters behind him. "Stand where you are."

Lothaire stepped in front of his wife. "Is it true, Honore? Have you given the clan to those outsiders? To Hallow? And Flay?"

"They're *my* retainers. I'll be king."

"No." Lothaire raised his claws. "This can't happen."

Honore smirked. "Do you want to fight me? You're old and fat."

"Don't," came Flay's warning voice from outside the window. "Hallow wants a public execution, not a murder in the shadows." She lit on the sill and grinned at the royal couple, who stood just under her terrible figure.

"Run!" Caterina shouted to Lothaire as she pulled a surprised Flay to the floor, wrapping her in a tight grip. The mercenaries rushed forward, while Caterina caught a glimpse of Lothaire plunging out the window.

The queen now snarled and lashed out, battering Flay against the floor. She was fueled by the image of Lothaire dying at the former war chief's claws. Caterina tightened her arms around Flay's chest, wishing she could crush the monster to death. Flay threw her head back, cracking against Caterina's forehead.

Many hands seized Caterina. She fought back, straining to hold Flay, trying to bite her in the throat. Fingers ripped through the queen's hair and tore at her face. She screamed as her grip was pulled away from Flay. The war chief cursed and smashed her fist against Caterina's jaw. She kicked the queen in the stomach and pushed herself free. Caterina continued to fight against the many claws that strained to hold her.

"Damn you." Flay staggered upright. She pointed at several of her mercenaries. "Why are you standing there? Go after the king, you imbeciles!"

When some of the hands released Caterina, she nearly broke free. Strong arms clenched around her throat. Feet crashed into her knees, knocking her to the floor, and she was pressed under ruthless arms and legs. The twins had stopped whispering and the baby wailed.

Honore pulled the mercenaries off his mother, cursing and shoving them away. Then he nearly lost his hold on the queen as she surged toward Flay, snapping again with her teeth. Honore wrestled his mother under control. She glared up into his face and slapped him. Then she suddenly felt spent and collapsed with a sorrowful exhaustion under her son's stunned expression.

Flay smiled at the charming family tragedy while she pushed loose strands of hair from her face. "Bring your mother along, Dauphin." The war chief spit blood on the floor of the nursery and left the room.

CHAPTER 37

The *Raksaka* was a sloop of war that had been chosen for speed. Adele had commandeered it at Delhi, leaving her beloved *Edinburgh* behind. General Anhalt was dispatched back to Alexandria with all haste to support Prince Simon in case there was a disaster in the war brought on by Goronwy. Captain Hariri took his most fit men for the sloop, pressed others from the imperial air service, and they set out for Europe.

There was no reasonable belief they could catch Goronwy's airship, so they flew for France in as direct a line as possible. Crowding on all the sail the sloop would take, Hariri mercilessly drove the sleek airship. They saw vampires frequently, but rarely in force and they were able to avoid contact in all cases. It took nearly a week before they cruised through the vicinity of Grenoble, where they saw more Equatorian airships. The sloop turned toward the advance positions of the imperial forces at Nevers.

Air traffic over Nevers was lighter than expected, and the presence on the ground more scattered. Sirdar Rotherford had already broken winter camp. The countryside was churned up in a wide swath leading away toward Paris. The *Raksaka* sped north too.

Adele leaned on the quarterdeck rail. The heavy furs of Tibet were gone. She wore her typical traveling clothes with a thick cloak. It was cold at a thousand feet, but spring was coming quickly in France and the brutal weather of the Himalayas was a distant memory. With a spyglass to her eye, Adele scanned the ground. There were men all around her on the deck and in the tops with glasses pressed to their faces as well, keeping watch for vampires. Greyfriar joined her to find her muttering as usual.

"This isn't right," she said. "Look down there. Mile after mile and no signs of any battles. Just muddy tracks. A few wagons tossed aside, but that's the only damage I've seen. It's as if the army is moving as fast as they can walk. The vampires aren't fighting." She looked at Greyfriar. "Is that reasonable?"

"No. They should be swarming your people with every step. That should be a trail of dead below us, human and vampire. I don't understand it either."

"We haven't seen a single vampire since we reached France. Where are they?"

"I don't know."

"Something is wrong. It has to be Goronwy. It has to be the Tear of Death."

"Majesty!" shouted Captain Hariri as he came from the binnacle. "Word from the tops. Smoke ahead. I'll take us up to get a better look."

The sloop rose through thin, wispy clouds. Adele and Greyfriar made their way forward and positioned themselves along the prow for a clear view past the jibs. As the horizon fell away, Adele saw many rising columns of smoke. It wasn't from a battle. They were coming up on the Equatorian camp.

With increased altitude, she could clearly make out the army spread across the ground ahead. They were in a series of orderly camps, well laid out and defended, occupying several miles of territory encircling the southern end of Paris. Trenches and earthworks surrounded it, with pikes and razor wire for protection. There were small cities of tents with cooking fires. In the center was what appeared to be a battalion of Galahad walkers, the workhorses of the Equatorian army; large mobile suits of armor powered by chugging chemical engines, carrying ferocious firepower. Several small airships were docked at makeshift landing towers south of the base. And along the forward line, white puffs rose from heavy artillery busy lobbing shells toward the southern suburbs of Paris.

Adele asked Greyfriar, "Can you tell how far we are from the city?"

He scanned the area around the airship, trying to use his unerring sense of direction. "Twenty-five miles perhaps." He tightened his grip on a cable and climbed quickly onto the gunwale, peering forward. "Adele. Look at this."

She took his hand and climbed next to him into the shrouds. With an elbow wrapped through the ratlines, she leaned out over the side and put the glass to her eye. She gasped. "Is that Paris?"

"Yes," Greyfriar replied.

North of the Equatorian camp, the green landscape lay as yet untrampled by imperial boots. Scattered houses and small villages appeared as overgrown lumps in the virginity of the spring countryside. However, on the horizon swirled a mass of blackness. It looked like a huge dome of a cathedral, but it moved. It was alive. Paris was covered by a swarm of vampires so thick in the sky that the city itself couldn't be seen through the creatures.

"That's far more vampires than the clan of Paris could muster," he mused. "I think that's where they've all gone. It looks as if every vampire from across France has come to Paris. I think Flay is using them as a screen to protect the Witchfinder from your army. No matter how powerful that human is, he's still just a human. A bomb or a cannonball could kill him and ruin everything."

Adele continued to stare at the roiling mass above the city. "Tell Captain Hariri to bring us down at the camp."

The *Raksaka* sank quickly, firing a signal gun and running up flags to alert the ground crews to stand by. The docking was mercifully fast and efficient. When the ship was tied down and the gangplank set, Adele and Greyfriar followed the Harmattan down into a waiting crowd of soldiers and airmen. Far more amazed faces and fingers pointed at the Greyfriar than at their empress. Adele smiled, amused that so many didn't recognize her in common clothes since they had only seen her dressed for official portraits.

A line of vehicles blowing chemical steam came roaring across the airfield. Each truck carried soldiers with long pikes on their running boards. The lead vehicle fluttered the scarab flag of the sirdar. They screeched to a halt, throwing clods of dirt. Field Marshal Rotherford emerged from the back. With a phalanx of officers and pikemen quickly gathering around him, he strode toward the airship. His head bobbed, trying to see Adele through the crowd, exchanging words with his adjutants, who hustled along with him. Finally, he burst into the clearing around the empress and stopped dead in his tracks.

"Your Majesty?" Rotherford bowed deeply. When he straightened, his face was full of alarm. "When they said a ship was approaching flying your standard, I didn't believe it. We were not informed from Alexandria. This is a very dangerous position, Majesty. It is most unwise for you to be here."

"Sirdar," Adele presented her hand to him as she started toward the idling trucks. "Let's go to your headquarters. We must talk."

—⁂—

General Rotherford looked up from a plate of sugared oranges. "Surely I misheard you, ma'am."

Adele drained her wine from a crystal goblet. The general had managed to put on a magnificent spread on very short notice and very far from home. In the midst of a war camp, under the shadow of the enemy, he had produced marvelous roast lamb, as well as fresh fruit and vegetables and a very excellent wine from the Rhone Valley. Adele ate heartily despite being on edge. She hadn't had such food in months, and she tried to tell herself she was only following Greyfriar's old ranger dictum of always eating and drinking when the opportunity presented itself because you never knew when you might be caught away from sustenance. A young adjutant refilled her glass as soon as she set it down.

"Thank you," she said to the boy, who nearly fainted from the words of the empress. He staggered out quickly. "Sirdar, I said you must withdraw. Immediately. Leave the heavy equipment. Speed and distance are all that matter. I don't know that you can move far enough to be away from danger, I don't know if there's *anywhere* far enough away, but I can find an area nearby, I hope, that will provide you with some protection." Adele shoved a stuffed grape leaf in her mouth. "I should be able to find a place free of rifts, or at least as free as possible. The farther from a rift, the less Goronwy's power should be. Of course there may be no place safe from him." She drank more wine. "Hopefully it won't come to that."

Greyfriar slouched silently in a camp chair in the corner. The general's private tent was large, with several separate rooms and a wooden floor. It was much more luxurious than General Anhalt had managed in the frozen camp beneath Grenoble last year.

Rotherford leaned on his elbows, glancing from Adele to several of his generals who were dining with them. He took a pensive breath. "Majesty, I am on the verge of taking Paris. Our meteorologists say that the weather the next few days is optimal to launch the assault. I have begun the artillery barrage, as you can no doubt hear. The enemy is running scared. The animals have pulled back into the city so I'll be able to slaughter every vampire in France in one fell swoop." The general laughed.

"Sirdar, you are facing an adversary for which you have no defense. There is a power in Paris that can strike you down before you can come within arm's reach. You must withdraw or you could lose every man in your army," Adele raised an eyebrow, "in one fell swoop."

Rotherford rubbed his chin irritably and drummed his fingers on the arm of his chair. He considered his response while watching Adele eat lamb rolled in bread, like something purchased from a street vendor in Cairo, rather than using the expensive silver cutlery he had had carried across France.

He leaned forward, laying his hands on the table. "Ma'am, you will forgive me if I tell you that I refuse."

Adele stopped chewing in surprise. "I will not forgive you, sir. Nor will the mothers of all the hundreds of thousands of men who will die because you refused to listen to me."

Rotherford stood abruptly, causing Greyfriar to swing his feet off the camp table and half rise from his chair. The general froze, watching the swordsman, before straightening slowly. The sound of his hands twisting his baton of rank was audible.

"I take my orders from the general staff in Alexandria."

Adele finished her wine. "I could relieve you of your post."

Rotherford's eyes flicked to Greyfriar. "None of my officers would obey such an order that runs contrary to the good of the empire."

The empress set down her goblet quietly and dabbed her mouth with the general's fine linen napkin. She fought to keep her voice calm. "You are insubordinate, Sirdar. In fact, you are advocating mutiny and treason."

Rotherford shouted, "And you are talking witchcraft! I am a soldier! I live in a world of reason. I will not be hostage to your lunatic fancies. I will win this war for you, ma'am, but if you insist on inserting yourself into the affairs of rational men with your voodoo, I can't answer for the length of your reign."

Adele folded her napkin with slow deliberateness. Rotherford couldn't decide whether he needed to watch her or Greyfriar, whose mirrored eyes were locked on him with a terrible intensity, despite the fact that the swordsman was once more draped casually in his chair.

She stared at the other officers, who were pale. "Do you gentlemen concur?"

The other generals sat still. They exchanged furtive glances. One stood, General Mirambo, whom Adele knew to be honest and brave, and said, "Yes, ma'am." Then the other two rose and nodded agreement.

Rotherford rapped the baton against his thigh with satisfaction. "There you are."

"I admire your loyalty, but not your wisdom." Adele pushed back her chair with a ferocious gaze that raked across the nervous officers. Her limbs felt numb despite her anger. She was stunned by her own control. "I don't have the physical power to force you to accept my . . . recommendations. So I'll say thank you for dinner, Sirdar. I pray you are right."

The officers all bowed as Adele swept from the tent with Greyfriar stalking behind her. Outside, the young adjutant leapt to his feet, swinging open the doors to the sirdar's vehicle. Greyfriar took Adele's arm as she climbed in.

"You took that calmly," he said. "Aren't you going to fight? Where are we going?"

"I don't have time to argue with that idiot, and there's no way to prove what I say is true." Adele had already accepted that she couldn't win the battle with Rotherford. As always, it seemed, she had to win the battle in spite of him, in spite of all those who would stop her. "We're going back to the ship to get ready. We have to enter Paris now."

Greyfriar turned in the direction of the great city and its churning dome of vampires, although it was invisible below the horizon. "Inside that swarm?"

Adele looked at the face of the young man who held the door. His eyes were wide with amazement at being so close to the empress and the Greyfriar. She could hear the door handle trembling under his white-gloved hand. She leaned close to Greyfriar and whispered, "If we don't, this boy will die, and millions more like him."

They settled into the back of the truck, and it roared off toward the airfield. Adele turned to see General Rotherford standing in the door of his tent with a satisfied smile on his doomed face.

CHAPTER 38

Adele kept looking up even though the skies were clear of dark shadows. She reached for a nearby rift. It flinched when she touched it, shivering as if in fear or discomfort for both of them. She sank into the folds of the uneasy Earth. Any vampires they encountered would be unable to see her.

A group of humans shuffled past, eyes averted from Gareth's tall form. Their fear radiated, terrified that they would draw the vampire's hungering gaze. They slipped into a ramshackle house and closed the door. Few humans lingered in these outer boroughs of Paris, which would soon see the tread of Equatorian forces, and no vampires walked the streets. Adele knew that wouldn't last as they moved toward the city center where the creatures swarmed overhead.

Adele took a step forward and suddenly the Earth vanished beneath her. She gasped and staggered as a vast blackness yawned under her feet. She tumbled to her hands and knees, her stomach bottoming out as if she were falling into a deep chasm. There was nothing to stop her. She would fall forever, unable to touch anything. She couldn't save herself.

Then she was looking at Gareth. He had her in his arms, with a look of terror. He was carrying her back the way they had come.

"Stop." She shook her head. The warmth of the rifts returned to her. "It's all right."

Gareth slowed but didn't relinquish his hold on her. "What just happened?"

"I lost connection to the rifts. All of them. Some sort of dead zone. Nothing to see or touch or hear or smell. Goronwy must have warded the city against me somehow. Damn effective." Adele indicated he should put her down, which he did reluctantly. Her knees still felt a bit weak but they held.

"You mean you can go no further?" he asked.

"No. It just means I won't have my geomancy."

"That's the same thing. You can't just walk into the heart of Paris disarmed. I'll find Kasteel and the others. We can take the Witchfinder. You return to the *Raksaka* and stay out of harm's way."

"Don't." Adele's hand rested on her mother's khukri. "I may not be at my best, but I'm hardly at my worst. It's no different than being in Britain. It won't cripple me."

Gareth knew there was no point wasting time in argument. "We still have to get across the city under that mass." He pointed above him at the swirling vampires. "Paris is littered with catacombs. Let's see if we can get underground."

Adele nodded. "A fine idea. Where's the nearest one?"

Gareth started north again. "If we can cross six more blocks without incident, there is a location in a house. Few know of that entrance, but Lothaire and I scouted hundreds of tunnels in our youth. Be on your guard. It's possible we'll encounter vampires down there."

They passed over the void line again and it was all Adele could do not to grab onto the nearest wall. The sense of an abyss beneath her made her skin crawl. No matter what she told Gareth, the effect she felt was worse than she experienced in Britain. Once again, Goronwy's geomancy showed itself to be frighteningly powerful. She worked to feel the ground under her boots, using that touch to reassure her that the Earth was still there. As she went, the sensations returned to a semblance of normalcy. Her boots were dusty but nothing more. Her rational brain battled through what her geomancy told her, and she could see the real world around her again.

Adele stayed close to shadows and overhangs as much as possible. Gareth guided her toward a tumbled townhouse. They climbed the steps and shoved open the door. There were no locked doors in Paris. Vampires could enter any house and take what they wanted.

Luckily it was empty. At one time the home would have been grand, but the wallpaper was ripped off and furniture lay smashed for fuel. A rank smell filled Adele's nose. Gareth led the way downstairs and found a narrow alcove, almost a closet. He pushed aside a mass of detritus until a small hatch was revealed on the floor. There were no handles but Gareth extended his claws and caught an edge.

"Stand back."

Adele grimaced at the waft of stale air that came up with it. Gareth dropped down into the hole first and took stock of the area.

"It's clear," he called up.

Taking a deep breath, Adele sat and swung her legs over the edge, lowering herself down. She felt Gareth's arms about her, taking her waist and setting her beside him.

Adele could only see utter blackness. She asked quietly, "Are we alone?"

"So far as I can tell."

Gareth took her hand in his and guided her steps. The horrible stench returned, but she didn't ask him about it. Her blindness brought disturbing thoughts. Her memory flashed on the terrible time she had crossed the Thames River via an underground tunnel. The thought of the teasing claws of the feral vampire that had found her in the damp darkness made her shudder against her will.

"Can we strike a light?" Infuriating fear welled up in Adele. The dark shouldn't be bothering her, but it had control at the moment. She struggled for breath in the stale air.

"It would be safer if we didn't."

"I know but—" Adele whispered, almost like a child.

"Wait here."

Gareth left her side. His warmth fled quickly and Adele wrapped her arms around herself. Several minutes passed and Adele tried to still her hammering heart. She felt as if she were sinking into endless black ink, being slowly swallowed whole. She reached out her hands in desperation and whispered frantically, "Gareth?"

When there was no answer, she took a step, then another, picking up speed. She slammed her knee into something hard. Her hand sank into a soft, crumbling mass. She reared back.

Something grabbed her. She let out a shout.

"It's Gareth. It's all right."

Adele gasped and clung to him. Then she punched him on his chest. "Don't do that."

"Sorry. I found this." He extricated himself from her grip. There was a spark of a flint and a small flame rose on an oil lamp. Warm light filled the tunnel. His form flickered into view and he smiled, but concern displaced his momentary triumph. "Are you all right?"

"It's just the dark," she muttered, though it was far more than that. The dead zone that Goronwy had created was eating away at her mind. She was losing touch. "You know where you are going, right?"

"It's been a long time, but so long as no humans have done any new construction or there hasn't been a collapse, I know exactly where I'm going."

"Let's think cheery thoughts, shall we," she said.

They walked through the dark warrens of the past. Decaying foundations and crumbling stones. The limestone walls appeared to sweat in the glimmering lamplight. Water hung from the ceiling in crystal droplets, occasionally striking them as they walked. The Earth smelled of the dead, full of decay and blossoming mold.

Abruptly, Gareth grabbed her hand and stopped her. He had heard something. Then she heard it too. Hissing. Vampires. She reached for her weapon, but Gareth prevented her from pulling the blade from its sheath. Slapping the lamp down to the ground, he thrust her into a dark alcove. His fangs pierced her neck as he draped her body with his. Her eyes went wide in surprise and her gasp was loud in the echoing chamber.

A group of vampires appeared. One laughed and another muttered, "Nice catch. Care to share?"

"No," Gareth snarled at them. His bloody lips moved across Adele's neck. Her breath sounded ragged in the suffocating air.

"Don't blame you. We'll find our own." The vampires crept away.

Gareth waited until they were well gone before he released her throat.

She pushed herself unsteadily off the wall. "Any excuse for a kiss."

He grinned before rolling up his sleeve. He used a claw to slice open his forearm.

"Here! What are you doing?"

"We need to mask your scent. It's an old trick I use as Greyfriar. The reverse can work for you, I think." He drizzled blood into his palm and smeared it over Adele. "Those fellows came looking because they smelled human. If you smell like another vampire rather than a meal, we'll encounter fewer. And I don't have to bite you every few moments."

Adele stood stock still in horror as he covered her in his blood. She swallowed hard. Her neck throbbed with a burning heat. "It's not like I don't mind the biting. It actually shocked me back to the real world for an instant."

He looked at her sadly. "I'm sorry. This is the best way to keep you safe. Better this than being hunted down here."

Adele gave a sharp nod as Gareth wiped his hands on her clothes. "Let's keep going. I want to get out of these catacombs."

Hours passed, or at least that's how it felt. Adele's feet scuffed through the debris on the floor. They reached a crossroads where another group of vampire stalked. Adele froze. Gareth placed his broad frame between her and the hunting pack. They hissed a greeting and moved on.

When they were farther up the tunnel, Adele exhaled. "How could they not know I was human? Blood doesn't cover it all."

"My blood masked you well enough. Any human scent they caught, they would've assumed was merely from an old meal. It won't fool them up close, but it's enough for now. Besides, we're here." He pointed up at an iron ladder.

"Thank God," Adele breathed.

Gareth went first and pushed the iron hatch above their heads. It swung open with very little dust. That meant it had been used often, or at least fairly recently. Vampire faces peered down at Gareth, and Adele had no time to hide. She pulled her Fahrenheit blade, bathing her in a green glow.

"Lord Gareth and the Death Bringer have returned to us," Nadzia announced from above.

CHAPTER 39

Gareth assisted Adele out of the tunnel. The room was dark, but at least moonlight filtered through the window. The smell of the Seine drifted in. They were in the house on the Quai Voltaire. Kasteel's loyal rebels crowded around, looking curiously at Adele and her blood-smeared face. She didn't offer any explanation.

Gareth left the matter as well, focusing instead on a figure forcing his way forward through the small crowd.

"Lothaire!"

His friend had heavy shadows around his eyes and deep creases in his brow. Something was wrong. It took a great deal to unsettle Lothaire's easy manner, even in times of strife.

"Gareth! I hoped you'd come. They seized Caterina. They're going to execute her!"

"What? She's the queen. Who would dare?"

"Hallow! And Honore, but he's in her thrall. He's lost to us." Lothaire's voice cracked and his voice fell silent save a choked-off sob.

"Why was Caterina taken?" Adele wanted to know.

Lothaire's gaze snapped up. "She defended our family. Was she to stand by and let Hallow go after all our children? She did what any mother would do! She tried to kill Lady Hallow."

Gareth's voice was desolate. "And she failed."

Nadzia hung her head. "We were there. I was afraid for the queen so I convinced Kasteel to come. We lost several members, but we couldn't help her." She turned to Lothaire. "I'm sorry."

The king gave Nadzia a comforting half smile, but slumped onto a bench. "Gareth, you must help me save what's left of my family. You know what Caterina is to me."

Gareth exchanged a look with Adele. They couldn't spare the time. Goronwy was their only priority.

However, Adele asked Lothaire, "When is the execution?"

"This morning," came another voice, and Fanon appeared on the stairs amongst the rebels.

"Fanon." Gareth greeted the old soldier he had known from the Great Killing. "How do you know this?"

"Because I was Honore's bodyguard." Fanon dropped his head in shame. "I was close to the Dauphin and Lady Hallow. But the execution is merely a ruse to draw the king out of hiding. They have no interest in the queen. I came here at her request to beg His Majesty to stay underground and not—"

"No," Lothaire interrupted. "Trap or not, we've stood by and let Hallow slowly take control of the clan. Finishing the corruption of Honore that Cesare began. Bringing the damned Witchfinder into Paris. And now it turns out that disgusting human has Flay on a leash. Flay! I'll not have my city fall to the likes of them!"

Gareth said, "But if Fanon says this whole affair is a show, why walk into their trap?"

Lothaire turned his pained gaze on his old friend. "I would like your help. I will do it alone, if necessary. But I ask you as a friend, and as a friend of Caterina's. Please. I have no belief that Hallow or Flay can be trusted to be reasonable. I can't bear to see Caterina mistreated. I'll give up Paris before I lose her." He gestured to Adele. "Could you leave *her* in the hands of your enemies?"

Adele touched Gareth on the arm. "There's no time for us to do both." Her attention was on the rebels gathered around them. "But we are not alone."

He understood her implication. With the city choked with vampires, and Flay at their head, these rebels were a petty force. Splitting them seemed like suicide. "Are you sure?"

She nodded. "Lothaire and Caterina are your friends. They were willing to help you when you had no one. You can't abandon them."

Gareth turned to Kasteel. "I need you."

The rebel chief went ramrod straight. "We're yours."

"Good. Thank you." Gareth pointed at Nadzia. "You will take ten and go with Lothaire."

Lothaire turned to Fanon. "And I have a mission for you, old friend. Do you know where my children are being kept?"

"I do."

"Then go and bring them out. In case, we lose control of the clan, I want them safe from Flay. Even if Caterina and I don't survive, I task you with protecting our children."

Fanon nodded. "Done."

Nadzia pointed at several of the group and they moved to stand with the king. The young female seemed pleased to be with Lothaire.

Adele said, "Then that leaves us with finding Goronwy."

Fanon looked up. "I know where he is."

Gareth laughed. "Fanon, you're magnificent."

"When he returned from Asia, he moved out of Versailles and into the city."

Adele muttered a curse. "He's inside my dead zone. He knew I was coming."

"Is he in the palace?" Gareth asked.

"No. He took the old church on the island."

"Notre Dame," Adele whispered. "The cathedral sits on a major rift. It will make it easier for him to extend his power anywhere around the world."

—✺—

With the rising sun, Adele and Gareth led their small crew of fifteen back out into the city. They paralleled the Seine, but stuck to narrow alleys that afforded Adele some cover. Kasteel and his rebels traveled above them, slipping through the black cloud that swarmed over their heads. Eventually they turned for the bridge that would take them to the Île de la Cité. The wide avenue ahead of them made Adele pause. The air above undulated with vampires. Gareth grabbed Adele a bit roughly and dragged her after him.

"Keep your head down," he commanded. "Act like a meal."

She gave him a sour look but immediately obeyed, hunching her shoulders and stumbling after his quick pace. Shadow after shadow swept the ground around them. Some loomed large, as vampires swooped down to inspect the duo. The small of Adele's back twitched, knowing that hundreds of eyes watched them.

They stepped onto the bridge. It was a terrifying open expanse littered with corpses. Adele's heart drilled in her chest as a great cloud darkened their path. The frantic collisions of their countless voices awakened echoes of the chanting of Yidak's Tibetan monks. The memories of those near musical recitations slicing the clean, frigid air and its similarity to the wild gurgling of violent animals she heard here in Paris nearly brought tears to Adele's eyes.

"Don't look up," Gareth snarled, jerking her nearly off her feet. His gruff demeanor seemed to send the right message to the vampires circling them.

"Leave your meal and join the pack," came a hissing voice from behind.

"I will as soon as I see to my duties," was Gareth's sharp retort. He didn't stop walking.

More growls sounded nearby. Gareth pulled Adele close against his chest, his arm pinning her there. "This one knows where the rebels may be hiding. The Dauphin will want to *talk* to her."

"Then I will take the human there." A vampire landed in front of them and reached for Adele.

Gareth swiped with his claws, ripping open the vampire's forearm. "The glory will be mine. I found her."

As the vampire jerked back his bloody arm, Gareth took a warning step forward, dragging Adele with him. With the sharp tone of a general expecting to be obeyed, he commanded, "Go back to your duties."

The vampires obviously didn't recognize Gareth but hesitated at his authoritative presence. They fell back, then lifted and veered eastward.

Adele and Gareth raced the last few yards off the bridge and into a stand of trees with enough budding foliage to hide them from vampire eyes in the air. Gareth's grip eased and he drew Adele into his arms.

"I didn't hurt you, did I?"

"No, I'm fine," she answered breathlessly. "You do the dominant male quite well."

Kasteel and his rebels dropped through the branches. "That was close."

"I'm glad you didn't engage them," Gareth said. "Well done. There are far too many."

Kasteel beamed at the praise. "It won't be any easier at the cathedral. It's crawling with them."

"Of course it is," Adele muttered.

"This way," Gareth ordered, already in motion. "We're almost there."

They ran toward the towers of the cathedral. The buildings they passed were once magnificent structures, but no more. Gareth took them through another natural area where the city was being reclaimed by tall, gnarled trees and a carpet of grass. To their right was a massive dilapidated structure with overgrown courtyards barricaded behind crumbling walls.

To the south, Adele heard the bellow of Equatorian gunfire grow more intense. It wasn't just the howitzers now. She recognized the heavy shoulder guns of the Galahads. The armor battalion was marching. The invasion of Paris had begun.

The living cloud veered suddenly. Thousands of vampires flew together in a chaotic and ever-changing pattern, transforming in an instant into wild geometric abstraction across the sky. Twisting and turning into a dense swarm and then spreading thin, they swooped down beyond the river.

Gareth and Adele approached as close as they dared to Notre Dame with Kasteel and his rebels, staring across an open square at the behemoth. The ground was covered with the dead, the fruits of mass vampire feeding. The magnificent façade of the cathedral should have brought a sense of awe, but it only filled Adele with dread. Kasteel had been right. From the gothic gables and flying buttresses clung multitudes of dark shapes. The cathedral was crawling with a thousand living gargoyles.

"Damn," Adele cursed quietly. "We won't make ten yards."

Gareth looked around to gain his bearings. "Which is why we are going back underground."

"They might have fighters down there also," Kasteel pointed out.

"Perhaps, but they can't swarm us down there. We stand a better chance."

The thought of returning to the silent ground chilled Adele, but Gareth gave her no time to contemplate the matter. He used his claws to pry up a rusting manhole cover. Damp muskiness rolled out of the inky pit. Gareth jumped down the shaft. Adele gulped several deep breaths while the rebels filed after their leader.

She grabbed the iron rungs and climbed down. The Earth swallowed her like a giant snake. Her foot touched the bottom. The small ring of light from above illuminated her and she hesitated to step out of it.

Then it hit her. Nausea flowed into Adele and her knees weakened. Horror gripped her. Her gut contracted, pushing acid up into her throat. She struggled to keep her balance, fighting the vertigo that tried to drive her into a senseless spiral.

A hand reached out. She knew it was Gareth.

"You're shaking," he said.

As Adele was drawn into the darkness, she gasped, "It's beginning."

CHAPTER 40

Queen Caterina stood on a scaffold in the northwest corner of the Place de la Concorde. She felt very alone although Flay and Lady Hallow were beside her and thousands surrounded the platform staring up at her in the light of the early morning sun that filtered around the Tuileries Palace to the east. It was already a warm day, which made her feel sluggish, as it would to all of them. There was little breeze but it brought the constant, distant booming of the human guns to the south. Vampires thronged the grounds and swarmed the buildings and trees. They perched on vine-covered statues, crawled over the smashed fountain and the cracked Egyptian obelisk in the center of the square.

Flay eyed the crowd. "Where's Fanon? I don't like that he isn't here. I don't trust him."

Hallow smiled serenely. "Don't worry about him. The packs are loyal to me."

"To *you*." Flay snorted with derision.

"This day will end badly for all of you," Caterina said. "It's already warm and this mob is annoyed that you couldn't do this at night. No doubt you had to hold it to accommodate the Witchfinder. Humans love sunlight." She laughed, which unnerved the crowd. The queen seemed awfully self-assured to be under the thumb of her pointless son and his sinister advisors from the dead clan of Britain.

Hallow ignored the queen and murmured to Flay, "Watch for Lothaire. And keep yourself under control. This is a dangerous game we're playing up here."

Flay sneered at her.

Caterina added, "Do you think Lothaire a fool? He knows this is a ruse to draw him out."

"He'll come." Hallow surveyed the crowd. "He won't allow you to be humiliated. Nor can he take the chance you could be harmed because

I hate you or Flay is an unbalanced lunatic. He loves you. I know how he'll act."

"How would you know that? You've never had anyone love you."

Hallow gave a slight twitch, which was the only sign that Caterina had struck the target.

A figure in long regal robes appeared in the crowded sky. Flay tensed, but it was only Honore. The mob followed the Dauphin's arrival as one until he settled lightly onto the scaffold. He faced the crowd with his arms out and a pompous grin of triumph. Caterina tried to catch his eye, but he purposefully avoided looking at her. After absorbing enough attention from the clan, Honore swung around to Lady Hallow.

"This had better work," he hissed. "I can't stand here like a fool all day."

"Don't fret, Your Majesty. We'll have your father and the end of the war before noon."

Flay whistled sharply and two of the mercenaries rose onto the platform and took positions beside the queen. The scarred war chief eyed Caterina with the precision gaze of an executioner, evaluating the resistance of her body and exactly how much effort it would take to tear open the queen's chest and crush her heart. Judging from the bland expression, Flay didn't imagine it would require much.

Hallow stepped in front of Caterina. "This is the last time. You will either denounce the king's traitorous relationship with Gareth now, or we will pass sentence on you for attempting to kill me."

"How many last times will you give me?" Caterina feigned surprise. "You won't do anything because you can't."

Hallow didn't smile. She nodded to Flay, who was laughing at the comment but then snarled a command. The two mercenaries seized Caterina's arms and roughly pulled them taut. The queen grunted from the pressure. Flay seized the collar of Caterina's worn gown and, with a single motion, tore the front of the dress away leaving the queen's breasts and stomach exposed. The action caused many in the crowd to laugh and jeer, winning back the moment for the new regime.

Honore showed a flash of anger before turning away with embarrassment. It wasn't the nudity that was hurtful—many vampire females went bare-breasted—but the blatant expression of insolence for Caterina as queen upset her son. He snapped at Hallow, "This event was for the king. Not to humiliate my mother."

"Start speaking, Honore," Hallow said. "The clans are waiting. The king will be here."

"How do you know? I'm not sure that you're right."

"We've come too far to quarrel now." Hallow remained calm, and even a little subservient. "Do as I say and I will make you the king who sets the humans back hundreds of years. Cesare couldn't dream of what I will do for you."

The Dauphin let his gaze linger along Hallow's elegant form as he tightened his fists. "Is that so?"

Hallow gave a faint smile of promise. "The sooner you start, the sooner you can finish."

Honore spun back to the crowd and raised his hands above his head for silence, although the crowd was relatively quiet. "I come to you today on a mission . . . an unfortunate mission. I must denounce the queen. She attempted to assassinate Lady Hallow, whom you all know is my chief advisor. I must lay this tawdry affair before you, the clan lords."

A line of old vampires stood near the scaffold, whispering to each other. None of them could bring themselves to look at Caterina, but the oldest of the crowd, a walking fossil named Lord Marais, croaked out, "We leave the fate of the queen to you, Dauphin. What of the king? Where is Lothaire?"

"Hiding!" Honore stood at the edge of the scaffold, towering above the ancient lords. "He's a failure. He has done nothing to stop the Equatorians, who are practically wading across the river. It is time for a change."

Marais said, "Since we hope there are no more refugees from Cesare's clan to blow into our city and take positions of power, we assume you will confirm us all in our possessions without any sort of quarrel." He left the final word hanging, letting Honore know that he was risking civil war if the status quo wasn't respected.

"Of course, Lord Marais. The old lords such as you are the backbone of our clan. I look forward to decades . . . years at least, of the same loyalty you gave my father." Honore turned around to Hallow and, with a clever grin, whispered, "Hopefully better, the old traitors. They are the first for Flay to visit when this is over."

"Quiet," Hallow said, with the same officious look on her face.

"They're old and deaf as stones."

"Do as you please, Dauphin," Lord Marais called out, "but do it soon. It's hot. You have our permission to set the royal couple aside."

Flay growled deep in her throat. It wasn't in response to Lord Marais's statement. In fact, she was hardly paying attention to the farce at the front of the scaffold. The war chief turned her head, listening to the distance. Caterina realized the human guns had stopped. The nonstop sound of cannons that had dominated the city for the last few days was gone. In the silence that no one else noticed came a rumbling and grinding of metal.

"Damn it," Flay stared toward the south, clearly agitated.

The thuds of new explosions sounded from across the river. They were smaller blasts than the big guns of the last week, but closer. The popping of rifles filled the air too. The clan lords began to show alarm at the smoke rising across the river. Some in the crowd slipped away.

From high overhead came the high-pitched whine of incoming artillery. Smoking canisters arced through the blue sky from the south, flying for different parts of the city. Several descended toward the Place de la Concorde. Vampires scattered as the canisters crashed on the cobblestones. They didn't explode, but smashed into pieces. Dull grey metal balls skittered wildly through the feet of the confused vampires. The spheres burst open with brain-stabbing squeals. Shriekers.

The square erupted in chaos. Vampires clutched their ears. Others launched themselves into the air, trying to escape. Honore doubled over from pain. Hallow put a hand to her head and staggered.

The mercenaries holding Caterina loosened their grip. The queen pulled her arms free. She felt a blow to her back and she fell to her knees. Her head was jerked up hard.

"Enough of this." Flay towered over Caterina with eyes narrowed against the shriekers.

Honore grabbed her around the waist and pulled her away from the queen. "Take your hands off her! You dare hurt my mother? I'll have you execu—"

The prince stiffened as Flay spun in his grip. She grinned as her claws grasped him by the throat and tore. A wash of his blood covered her. The Dauphin stumbled and fell to the scaffold.

Caterina's scream broke through the fading wail of the shriekers. She fought to rise. Something grabbed her arm. She turned to strike and saw Lothaire. Others raced past them and closed on Flay, with Nadzia shouting, "Take the queen and run!"

"Honore!" Caterina tried to pull away from her husband. She wanted to touch Honore's hand that lay on the wooden planks, stretched out toward her.

"Come!" the king yelled. "Honore is dead."

One of the mercenaries gathered his wits and reached for Caterina. Lothaire seized him with the sound of snapping bones. He clawed the brute's face and kicked him aside.

"Can you fly?" he asked. "Caterina! Can you fly?"

The queen lifted off the platform and he followed.

Hallow stayed on her feet with great effort. "Flay! The king!"

Flay looked up at the royal couple rising away through the chaotic swarm over the square. She then regarded the rebels who had surrounded her. Claws came out. Flay ducked multiple strikes. She spun and raked. Dodged. Snapped a neck. Crushed a rib cage. Shattered knees. Sliced open muscles.

Nadzia weaved through Flay's blows and struck her. The war chief immediately stepped up, expecting the girl to retreat. Instead Nadzia closed in and ripped Flay again. Flay fell back with her hand covering a bloody wound just as a rocket slammed into the square, sending fire and shrapnel everywhere. Staggered, she looked around for the young female who had hurt her, but she and her last comrade were gone. Eight rebels lay dead on the scaffold.

Hallow stumbled to Flay's side with blood dribbling from her ears. "You must find the king and queen and kill them."

In the distance to the south, human screams echoed. The weapons' fire grew more ragged and disordered.

Flay grinned. "And it begins. The Witchfinder strikes."

Panic filled Hallow's porcelain features. Her pristine veneer cracked. "We can save this situation. Call your mercenaries. After you kill Lothaire and Caterina, find Isolde. We need an heir to put on the throne. Do as I say!"

Flay laughed. "Your day is over, Hallow. The queen is right. Your schemes and plans are pointless. I'd advise you to hide, because when I come back I'll kill you." She raised her head and screeched a call to war. As she lifted into the air, vampires rose around her. Most of them were her mercenaries, but there were Parisians and other French clan members who came to join her. They had no one else to follow.

Flay and her new pack drifted south toward the battle that raged in the ivy-cloaked suburbs and into the toppled edges of the city. Through the frantic bodies of diving vampires and the thick haze of gun smoke, the khaki hordes of Equatoria dropped in their tracks. Rank after rank staggered and fell. The thundering lines of steel Galahads ground to a halt and tilted uselessly to the side, venting steam. Over the faltering clatter of gunfire came more human screams, even from the distance where the vampire packs had not yet struck.

The scale of death she witnessed below unnerved even Flay. No one should have such power, certainly no human.

CHAPTER 41

All-encompassing black surrounded Adele and drowned the chatter of gunfire from the south. She drew her khukri and beat back the ebony maw with its green chemical burn. They were inside an old sewer pipe. Water from the spring thaw sloshed around their feet. Her steps were slow and measured, as if she were struggling through a black mire.

Gareth led them to a crack in the curving wall. He pulled more of the bricks aside, letting them tumble to the wet floor. Kasteel and the others moved forward to help. Soon the crack widened to a hole big enough for Gareth to wriggle through. He disappeared inside and Adele had to fight down her terror as she squeezed in after him. She held her blade aloft, but its light didn't quell the rising dread inside her as she inched through a long passageway. It didn't help that she knew vampires crawled right behind her. Old fears died hard.

Gareth dropped from her line of sight and then his hand reached back for her. She tumbled into a cavern with a low ceiling. It looked like a pile of dirt at first, but then she noticed exposed tiles and a brick arch.

"How did you find this place?" Kasteel emerged from the crevice.

"Lothaire and I used to explore the underground." Gareth gave the young rebel a purposeful glance. "When we lived in holes in the ground."

Kasteel laughed nervously.

"Does it connect to the cathedral?" Adele was already pushing forward despite the darkness.

"We're in front of the cathedral, but these halls stretch to it. I used to think they were the crypts of the old church."

On they went through the lost city. Despite the crumbled debris, many rooms were intact. Occasionally they had to use their hands to claw open a wider entrance, but the group of vampires worked in tandem. It didn't take long to clear a path.

Finally, Gareth looked upward as if searching. His fingers dug into the low ceiling and a rain of dirt fell over them all. Gareth stood and the top of his head cracked against a barrier. His hands pressed into the underside of something solid. A flat stone. Gareth braced and pushed. It didn't give. Kasteel joined him, imitating his mentor, and the stone shifted slightly. The two vampires drove against it, pushing upward with their legs. They gained a few more inches of space. The stone tilted. Gareth bowed his back, holding the heavy object in place. Together, he and Kasteel forced it to the side.

Gareth went up silently and, a moment later, Kasteel followed. Adele looked up into a vaulted ceiling stretching far above her. Gareth reached down and pulled her up. The rest of the rebels emerged from the hole into Notre Dame.

The echoes of clattering machine gun fire from across the river had grown more sporadic, so the envelope of silence inside the vast chamber shouted their arrival to the rafters. Shadows shrouded the ceiling. And the shadows moved, writhing like rats in the hold of a ship when a hatch is opened. Adele stifled a cry, pointing up. The shadows fell toward them.

Kasteel stepped in front. "Go! Find your Witchfinder!" The rebels flew up to meet the incoming vampires.

Gareth and Adele ran up the nave, across the open marble floor. The sounds of battle filled the church with screeching, the rending of flesh, and the ring of claws.

More vampires appeared in the shattered stained glass windows. They crawled inside and launched themselves. Three slammed into Gareth, smashing him against the wall. One turned to Adele, but Gareth pushed free and laid a hand on him, yanking him back. "Keep going!"

Adele didn't hesitate, racing for the choir. She had no idea where Goronwy was, but the church was surprisingly small, and he had to be in contact with the ground. That left only the eastern end of the church. Racing past the painted figures of holy men, Adele prayed she was in time. All she could think about were the men dying on the battlefield. Were any alive to save?

She rounded the altar sanctuary and had to shield her eyes from sudden brightness. The Witchfinder knelt in the midst of a vast field of crystals. He was adjusting his scrying sextant. Needles of light shot through each of the crystals, sending color slicing through the dusty air. As the web sparkled, Adele saw that the crystals were not just on the floor but were set into the walls too, like vibrant stars. The intense glare sent spikes of vertigo through Adele and she had to clutch the wall, gasping to catch her breath.

Goronwy looked up at her. His lips held a smile. In his right hand, he clutched the Tear of Death.

"Ah, Empress. I'm glad you got to see this." Goronwy let the scryer fall on its long strap around his neck. He casually reached into his pocket and pulled out two crystals. He tightened his fingers around them so there was a brief flash of light and then he carelessly tossed them aside. He stepped over a small array of blue crystals set near the center of his sprawling indecipherable quincunx. "Flay assured me you'd come. She was quite worried about it. That's why I had to block you from the Earth, which I'm sure you've noticed. She was worried you would just slaughter all of Paris as you did in Britain. She claims that's your catch-all for solving problems. No matter now." He held up a finger. "Do you hear that? Nothing. The gunfire has stopped. Your army is dead. I've already won the Battle of Paris."

Adele fought down nausea, focusing on the figure of the old man before her. The deathly quiet from outside chilled her. She summoned her courage again. "I'll kill you."

Goronwy frowned in disappointment. "That's all you can say with this miracle around you? Flay was right. Look at this. I was somewhat limited in space so I anchored crystals on the walls and on the ceiling. As long as they're tied to lodestones fused to the rift, they function admirably." He pointed with the phurba to several stones on a column. "I believe those stones correspond to the rifts through Alexandria. The Tear of Death is remarkable. I can feel it working through me even now. I thought I had exercised power before, but I was wrong. I'm not absolutely sure how fast it will move, but its *influence* is already traveling down the rifts I've mapped, southward through the territory your armies have occupied. It will cover the Rhone Valley, through Marseilles, and into the Mediterranean. It should reach North Africa by tonight. When the people in your empire wake up to find everyone in the capital dead, well, it should give them pause before continuing this war."

Adele stopped studying the crystal alignments all around her and shifted as if to come toward him. From an alcove behind the Witchfinder, red eyes stabbed through the shadows. Adele's gut plummeted. Snarls and the rattle of chains reached her ears. Something lurched forward until a chain snapped taut. The limited light showed an inhuman face, bleached near white and hairless. A feral vampire. No, two of them. Savage throwbacks that even vampires feared. Flay had always used them as hunting hounds. Swallowing bile, Adele rushed forward.

Goronwy stumbled away, scrambling to the alcove holding the ferals. Adele paid him no heed and ran to the edge of the map. She kicked out to dislodge the crystals, but they didn't move. The stones were not simply lying on the floor; they had been fused to the Earth.

Adele heard a sharp click. Goronwy pulled a large iron pin from a bracket on the wall where chains were secured. The chains crashed limp to the floor.

"Kill her!" the Witchfinder shouted.

The lithe muscular forms of the ferals sprang for Adele. The naked creatures moved like lightning. She barely dodged the first, slicing the second with her khukri as it went by, eliciting a satisfying screech of pain. Nails scraped stones and the creatures both slid to a stop beyond her, their claws and fangs elongated more so than normal vampires. These hunters knew nothing but slaughter. She dove for the small arrangement of blue crystals just like the ones in the vampires' talismans. They had to be what was silencing the Earth around her.

A bony long-fingered hand clutched her leg and dragged her back, claws digging into her calves like needles. She spun around, her blade flashing for the creature's throat. It anticipated her move and ducked its head. She flipped the khukri in her hand and stabbed downward, striking its exposed chest. The feral howled and released her.

The other creature clamped down behind Adele, its teeth latching onto her shoulder. She felt its mouth begin to drain her blood. She flung herself backward, looping a leg behind its knee, hoping to drive it to the ground under her. The starving creature was so focused on its meal that it didn't realize what she was doing. It stumbled and fell back onto the crystal map on the floor, but it still didn't relinquish its hold.

Adele struggled to free herself, but the clawed hands held her tight. A scream left her throat as her flesh tore and more blood gushed into the vampire's mouth. It would not end like this! Across the room, the other creature rose to its splayed feet, blood dripping from the wound in its chest that glowed with residue from the Fahrenheit chemical.

The feral under Adele made horrible, contented noises as if suckling at its mother's breast. This only goaded Adele more. She stabbed downward and behind her. The angle was awkward, but she was desperate. The thing bellowed as the blade seared through its flesh. Its mouth ripped from her shoulder in a spray of blood.

With a cry of her own, a mix of pain and rage, she rolled off it. Slipping on the slick floor, Adele struggled to get back to the blue crystal pattern only inches away. A feral leapt onto her, sending them both skidding. One of the sparkling blue crystals was torn from the floor by furious claws struggling to recover from their slide.

Beneath Adele, the Earth awakened and gazed on her. She shouted rapturously, her spreading senses aware again at last. Here in the center of the city, the rifts were sluggish but left alive, otherwise Goronwy himself would have been killed; he was only human, after all. She reached for them.

The creature above her howled in triumph. Fangs plunged into her shoulder again, but before the hunter could even taste her blood, Adele drew the power of the rift into her and let it sing. The feral flew upward, shoved toward the vaulted ceiling by the force of geomancy exuding from Adele. It screamed as its body burned in a torrent of fire. Its skin blackened and cracked as the flames sucked every bit of moisture from it. It shattered into ash as it hit the ceiling, falling slowly back to the floor like drifting snow.

Adele struggled to her hands and knees, looking for the other feral. There was no hesitation left in her to use the fire and it rose in her. The creature attacked with claws extended. Suddenly, Gareth rushed into the area, charging the remaining feral as it leapt for Adele. Gareth's face twisted in rage, baring his own fangs. He grabbed the snarling creature around the head and tried to snap its powerful neck. Adele couldn't stop the rush of energy pouring from her. It engulfed both of them. She looked on in horror.

The vampire in Gareth's hands burned with a raging fire and crumbled. Gareth however stood untouched by the rift's silver flames. Adele gasped in relief. His eyes met hers, and as he took in her blood-streaked form a flash of anger rose in him. He crushed the scorched skull in his hands. Adele spun around, looking for Goronwy. The Witchfinder stood gaping.

"So that's all you have, bastard?" Adele strode toward him, her knife glowing, ribbons of blood dripping down her arm. "Vampires at least have the decency to fight face to face. But you're a coward and a monster."

"Tell that to the clan of Britain you slaughtered."

Adele didn't stop moving forward, fighting dizziness, pulling the power under her feet closer, letting it fill her. Gareth was a dim shape beside her. She wasn't thinking about anything save stopping the horror that the Witchfinder had sent out.

Terror swept over Goronwy's face, giving ground before her fury. He clutched the Tear of Death to his chest like a child protecting a toy.

A stained glass window shattered. Flay dropped to the ground in a shower of colored shards. Immediately she sprang from her crouch to strike for Adele, and cursed in rage when the blow landed on Gareth's shoulder instead, as he streaked between them. Her claws ripped through him, spraying the holy place with more red. Gareth slashed at her face, forcing her to retreat.

Adele grabbed Goronwy by the throat. Unexpectedly, he dropped to his knees, dragging her with him. He stabbed the Tear of Death into the floor, directly through the heart of a rift. The stone slab underfoot shattered with a loud crack. Tendrils of inky smoke rose from the floor and encircled them. Adele reached down and took hold of the Tear of Death along with Goronwy. Abruptly her vision darkened as if the hands of night covered her eyes and ears. She fought to retain the world around her, but the great eye of the Earth had gone blind. Only darkness prevailed. Adele couldn't move; she barely felt the hard stone of the Tear beneath her fingers. The world melted away as the rifts dragged them into their embrace.

Adele's skin flushed hot and her stomach convulsed. The rifts should have been vivid and warm, but here the veins of the world were ice cold. She felt the sickening black aura of death oozing out of the Tear, spilling over itself in an endless torrent. The tarlike substance clung to Adele as she moved. It burned where it touched her skin.

Goronwy dragged his angry gaze from the Tear of Death up onto Adele. His eyes were wide with maniacal fervor, almost in rapture at the power rushing through him.

A corrupted rift at Adele's feet convulsed. She could exert no control over it. The thing was alien to her. It struck her side and searing pain blossomed.

With a trembling hand, Adele struggled to hold the phurba. The terrible power that pulsed through it like enflamed blood threatened to smother her. She wanted to let go, to cleanse herself from the corruption that wriggled over her. She craved distance from the horror and blackness. She needed time to breathe and think, to see the light again. If she stayed here, she would go mad.

A wave of pitch splashed over Adele's legs, chilling her to the bone. Agony seeped into her, coursing through her, eating away at her like a disease. Her body shuddered with a sickening flush. The black substance crept up to encase her like a growing cocoon, trapping her and swirling around her, higher and higher.

Still she held onto the Tear of Death.

CHAPTER 42

Gareth sidestepped a furious strike by Flay. His arm slammed across her throat and he swiped behind her legs at the same time. She went down hard, but kicked out at him in an effort to keep him at bay. Her feet were bare, with sharp nails. They ripped through cloth and flesh.

Gareth shoved her leg aside and drove his fist at her face. She turned in time and his fist crushed the stone under her into dust. Her roll took her under the shattered windows. She crouched, spitting obscenities at him.

"You will not touch her," Gareth hissed back. Neither Adele nor Goronwy had moved from their spot kneeling motionless on the floor with hands clutching the Tear of Death. Not knowing what was happening to her in there tore at him, but his focus remained on Flay.

"I'm already touching her. My pack is out there now mopping up what's left of her army, the pathetic few that the Witchfinder didn't already kill." Flay's eyes darted about, seeking a path around Gareth to Adele. "I'll kill both of you before we're through here."

"Yet you continually fail to make that promise a reality." Gareth wanted to keep her attention on him. "I'm rather tired of killing you too."

"Yes, you were close last time but, as usual, you were so concerned with *her* you didn't make sure I was dead. The Witchfinder found me and revived me with his blood, and then he protected me when the princess murdered your family and clan, with your approval. And he made me immune to her, so there's nothing in the world that can stop me now."

"We're both slaves of humans it seems," Gareth chided. "What an irony."

"Except that I'll kill mine when I'm done with him." Flay surged up. Gareth stood his ground in front of Adele, deflecting her attacks but at great cost. A weakness began in his muscles as every strike drew more blood. A smirk of triumph spread across Flay's face and she drove at him harder.

As her torn jacket shifted, the brutal scars along her torso caught Gareth's attention. He blocked a clawed hand that would have disemboweled him, then gouged his claws deep into a long scar on her chest. He touched something solid under her flesh, but it wasn't bone. He slammed a fist into her face, jerking her head brutally to the side. His fingers dug into her chest and took hold of a crystal.

Flay's eyes snapped wide and she became a wild animal in his grip. He bore her attacks as he pulled his arm back, ripping the crystal from her flesh. She screeched and retreated. Furious hatred rose in her, but Gareth also saw fear in her eyes for the first time.

This blue crystal was the same as the talismans the vampires in Bedlam had worn. This was what protected Flay from Adele's power. And judging from the many scars, Goronwy had sewn multiple crystals into Flay's body. Gareth tossed the bloody crystal aside and sprang toward her. If the loss of one stone didn't slow her down, perhaps more would serve.

Flay leapt aside, clinging to the wall of the cathedral. Gareth crawled after her. She spun back to him as he neared, propelling off the stones and colliding with him. They fell back to the floor. She smashed his head into the stones. His vision blurred.

Gareth grabbed her head and dug his claws into her face, his forefinger pressing at her eye. Flay snapped at his throat, her sharp teeth inches from tearing it to shreds. His other hand raked for a long scar on her abdomen. Her fear at his cunning returned and she thrust herself away, her foot shoving him across the floor.

Flay sprang for Adele, whose eyes were open and staring into dead space. Gareth raced to intercept her, reaching Flay just as her arm rose to strike the defenseless woman. He slammed into the war chief and shoved her through a teetering iron fence into a tomb beneath a towering cross. He bent her back over the reclining form of a dead man carved in cold marble. Gareth tore again into her stomach, burying his hand up to the wrist. Flay raged under him, kicking him away. He staggered back, his hand dripping red with her blood. In his palm, he held two crystals.

CLAY GRIFFITH AND SUSAN GRIFFITH   315

"Damn you," she gasped. Her flesh smoldered with silver smoke. A crack emerged on her cheek. She wrenched a tall golden crucifix from the floor and slammed it into Gareth, who rushed forward again. The cross connected with his head. He smashed against a column and slumped to the floor. His vision of the church wavered.

Flay rained blows on him with the heavy crucifix. The metal splintered, Gareth's bones fractured. He couldn't get his feet under him. He blurrily saw her raise the crucifix again. His arm lifted to deflect the blow. Flay stabbed the jagged holy symbol through Gareth's shoulder like a lance, pinning him to the floor.

Flay's skin split in deep fissures down her limbs. She spun about and dropped heavily to one knee. Fighting her way back to her feet, she searched frantically across the littered floor. Her flesh continued to burn. Then Flay cried out and pounced on two of her missing crystals. She jammed the stones back into the raw gash in her stomach as she staggered toward Adele with a strangled laugh. The remnants of the silver smoke wreathing her face vanished.

Gareth braced himself against the crossbar of the crucifix and forced himself to his feet, wrenching it from the floor. He staggered to intercept Flay, leaving a trail of his own bright blood that streamed down the golden shaft protruding from his back.

"Flay!" he screamed to bring her focus back on him.

Movement caught his attention in the air. Several figures swept through the stained glass window that Flay had burst earlier and settled to the floor near Adele. Lothaire took in the situation with a grim study of the area and placed himself in Flay's path. Caterina stood beside him. Nadzia and another rebel spread out on their flanks.

More footsteps came from behind and Kasteel appeared with the remainder of his rebels, all torn from battle. He rushed for the wounded Gareth, who shook his head and directed them into position to surround Flay. The rebel chief hesitated, but joined the ring closing on the reeling war chief.

"All your packmates are gone," Kasteel called to Flay. "They all rushed south to feed off the dying."

Flay tried to straighten but couldn't. She eyed Gareth as he staggered to Adele. Kasteel steadied him on his feet. Gareth slowly pulled the golden crucifix from his shoulder hand over bloody hand, and threw it aside.

Flay clutched one hand against her open stomach. She stared at the vampires around her in confusion while blood dripped off her chin. "How are you all standing there? Why aren't you burning?"

Caterina held out her arm. When she opened her clenched fist, a blue crystal dangled on the end of a chain. Lothaire reached inside his shirt to reveal another one of the talismans. Likewise, the rebels all produced blue stones as well.

"Fanon," Caterina said, "was very helpful to us."

Flay gave a disgusted snort of laughter and turned slowly to Gareth. "You can't trust anyone. Well, I actually owe the princess a debt. Before she came along, I had no place in the clans because I was merely a commoner. Now, thanks to her, the only clan that matters is death. And I'm the one who can lead it. I will reshape our kind. We are born for war and I am born to be our empress. I'll have her one day. *You* can't stop me."

"*I* don't have to stop you, Flay. I'm not alone anymore."

Flay's eyes darted from Gareth to Kasteel to Adele and back to Gareth. "But I am the future." She threw herself into the air and flew out the shattered windows.

—〰—

A silent, black nest of snakes coiled about Adele. Her nausea flared again, but she focused elsewhere. Like dark flesh, the polluted rifts slid near her. She felt their wet touch as they probed her resistance.

She sensed Goronwy in the distance, visible through the cascading sickness. He stared at her with a horrible grin on his face. He raised his hands, as if conducting the motions of the black rifts. The putrid things struck her again, slapping her hard to one side. Adele tried to shove them away, frantic to maintain freedom of movement. The oily surface was sharp. It cut her hands like razors.

Adele sent a burst of energy into a dying rift stretching back to Goronwy. But before it could strike him, a black eel-like arm slammed down, smothering it.

Goronwy laughed and pointed at her. For a moment nothing happened and the Witchfinder looked confused. Adele tried once more to waken a rift from its drowning mire, jolt it into life to attack the Witchfinder. Sluggishly, it obeyed and heat flared bright and yellow in the swathe of darkness. Goronwy gestured again, desperate now. A wall of black lifted and protected him, snuffing out the light once more. More unctuous coils roared past him toward Adele, wrapping around her body.

Her legs were pressed together and squeezed. She felt her flesh being sliced. A scream was silenced by a rubbery knife edge covering her mouth. Every nerve shrieked. Tendrils of darkness crushed the breath from her and sliced through her like razors. She knew the dark expanse was going to take her.

From inside the roiling black, traces of light reached Adele. Goronwy had directed his pollution to follow a specific direction along certain rifts to destroy her army. That left a few clean rifts glimmering nearby, untouched yet by the Tear of Death's spreading mire. Adele felt that faint warmth. The hints of healthy scents wafted among the death, even as the sick rifts grew thicker, splitting open with the life essence they were siphoning away as they crawled southward.

With a surge of excitement, Adele reached out, stretching for the cleanliness beyond. The heat responded to her. She felt it rising in her body, filling her mind with fire. The sweet smell of hyacinth crowded out the stench of Goronwy's pollution. Fire collected inside her. She drew in more, building the flames, holding them, and feeding them until they flowed inside her like magma. The Witchfinder had no idea what power was, but he soon would. Adele prepared to unleash the full force of the rifts. She would pour power into the sodden diseased veins to the south and cauterize them. She would sear them from the land. The sharp rifts shuddered as if sensing the terrible power building within her.

In an instant, Adele remembered Gareth. And Kasteel's rebels. And

Caterina and Lothaire. They were all within range of her wrath. The explosion of power would be so catastrophic it could melt even the protective talismans.

And what of the rifts themselves? She recalled the terrible cracked and scabbed veins of Britain. She had done that. She had crippled the Earth, just as Goronwy was doing.

Adele couldn't do it again. She couldn't be the Death Bringer any longer. She didn't have the right. There had to be a way that didn't require utter destruction.

Through the swirling morass, she saw Goronwy's face. He was close. They were only a few feet apart; they always had been. The distance was an illusion of the unreal setting because Adele saw now that they still both gripped the Tear of Death.

Adele knew that if she released her hold on the ancient weapon she would be cast adrift, lost in the blackness, cut off forever from a chance to recover the warmth above. From Gareth and everything she loved. And more, the dark would continue to spread with its slow, inexorable progress. It would kill everything.

Her dark eyes became silver orbs as her gaze locked onto Goronwy. Adele's voice echoed across the narrow expanse. "You wanted to see true power. This is it. Is it what you imagined? We've got to stop it before we can't. You must help me!"

"It's mine. I created it. It's mine." Goronwy twisted his head as stygian worms curled around his throat. He leaned into the caress of the black tendrils, mistaking it for affection or worship, lost in his own rapture. He had no experience to prepare him for this. He assumed that the powers he summoned would obey him. He grinned at her, at the Earth, as if he knew something. "The Tear listens only to me. I know what you did to the rifts from Edinburgh. Now I have that knowledge!"

"You have nothing." Adele tightened her fingers around the Tear. "This thing isn't obeying you. It was only defending itself. Don't you see? It's a cancer. Neither of us can control it. This power is a terrible delusion. You told Selkirk that I was being trained to destroy the natural order. And you were right! What you've done here is the same thing.

We are changing the tapestry of life with dire consequences. Neither of us have that right. We can't remake the Earth as we will. I understand it now. Why don't you?"

"I do know." Goronwy's fervent smirk was ice cold. "And I can't wait to study the aftermath."

"But this thing won't stop. It will spread across the world and kill everything. Then it will finish with you."

"You're jealous. You're not half the geomancer that I am."

Adele saw that there was no reasoning with the Witchfinder. He was surrounded by chaos but thought it was order. He believed he had authority only because he hadn't tried to exert it.

"I've tired of you," he said. "I thought you could teach me something, but I'm far above you."

Goronwy shook the Tear of Death as if to awaken it to the danger she presented, to cajole it to finish her. The rifts continued their frenzied work, forming their seething pattern around him as well as her. His confidence clouded and he looked suddenly sick. Concerned eyes shifted side to side at the blackness crawling over him as if finally seeing evidence of his own twisted geomancy. The rifts curled around, cutting deep into his flesh, smearing him with unnatural pitch.

"No!" he roared in pain. "Obey me!"

Fear burrowed out of Goronwy. The rifts knew nothing about him. He shouted in growing panic. His mouth gaped in stunned awareness of his own frailty, of his powerlessness. The corrupted dark slipped into his open mouth and streamed from his eyes. He locked on Adele, obviously seeing her calm as some sort of mooring in the cyclone.

"I don't understand," he slurred in disbelief. "I studied."

Adele knew well the terror in Goronwy's eyes. It echoed the first time she had waded out into the rifts alone. She had found herself lost, fearful she would never find her way home.

"Help me!" The Witchfinder seized her with both of his hands. His grip was frantic but weak.

Adele looked at the Tear of Death. Only her hand held it now. In seconds, the blackness tore into Goronwy's body. It sliced into him like saw blades. Adele tightened her hand on his clothes and on the Tear, as if that would create a connection of some sort, but the foul power would not be denied. It pulled the Witchfinder away and cast him into a tumultuous current. His face appeared briefly in the morass with a distinct look of terror and incredulity before he disappeared screaming into a surging sea of black pitch.

Adele held the Tear of Death. She was alone in the huge expanse of nothingness. Oddly enough, she missed the mere presence of another, even if it was the vile Goronwy.

The horrific skin of death spread. The warm rifts in the distance grew cold. The bright nodes where rifts crossed blinked out. The dark stain spread ever so slowly, but without any resistance. The inky tendrils curled around Adele, not violent or sharp, but now sickly seductive. She could feel the chill seeping from the Tear of Death into her and then back out.

The blackness wasn't trying to penetrate her. Rather, it was flowing through her eagerly. The Tear was using her as a conduit. It needed someone. It needed an anchor to the real world to continue its work, but it only needed one. A more powerful one. Now it had her.

Adele suddenly realized that, as the dark rifts passed through her, they were leaving hints of the lives lost. She felt melting glimpses of fear and hope like snowflakes of souls. She hardly felt each individual, but a growing storm of awareness gave Adele a taste of all the people falling.

She wondered if this was what Gareth experienced when he drank the blood of humans. He often said how he absorbed tantalizing hints of their love and hate. The wonderful and horrible touch of strangers suddenly made intimate. But Adele couldn't allow it. It had to stop, no matter what the cost to her.

She thought of her brother, Simon, unaware in Alexandria, waiting for a chance to enjoy a life that might end soon. General Anhalt no doubt stood beside him, who had struggled for so long and would accept death with resignation and dignity. Sanah who lived life as a poem and would understand a bitter ending, if given the chance. There were thousands, the thousands upon thousands living in Equatoria. Beyond that, millions throughout the world who were going about the day, whether grand or wretched, whether frightened or comfortable, completely unaware of the coming hammer blow. Adele was their only source of salvation. No one else would help them. They were in a nightmare but didn't know it.

Adele knew what to do. She had to deprive the monster of its connection to the rifts. She must release her hold on the Tear of Death. To do so would cast her small lonely frame out on the same storm into which the frightened Goronwy had been abandoned. The sightless, silent void would become her only home.

The blackness engulfed her hand on the Tear, pressing her fingers tight against the frozen stone. It fought to hold her. It was frantic to keep her. Adele suddenly felt that the Tear of Death was trying to remind her that if she willingly cast herself out into the blindness she would die. She would float forever lost. Her fear came from it.

Adele pried her fingers away from the phurba. The throbbing dark couldn't hold her. She felt the cold stone rip away, along with a layer of skin, and she was free. Her hand burned in agony. Immediately the tides caught her and dragged her to the infinite horizon. Exhaustion numbed her body. Out of instinct, she reached out, grasping for something solid.

The Tear of Death appeared before Adele. It was the safe, calm shore her mind craved. She could easily swim for it and pull herself out of the riptides. She didn't have to drown alone in the dark. Adele stared at the black stone.

Then she pulled her hand back. She smiled. She understood now. She had all the time she needed to find her way. It was the Tear that was lost and alone in the fading tendrils of black. Adele swam, easily and forcefully, with no specific direction in mind. All directions were proper. The power surrounded her, called to her, but she knew she didn't have to answer. She had the power to resist. It was her choice. Adele's breath escaped her in a sobbing exhalation.

The energy surrounding her warmed, and a slight scent reached her.

It was sweet. The eye of the Earth opened to stare at Adele, greeting her warmly. It was over. The rifts ceased their agitation and instead wrapped about her, draping her body with warmth and healing light. It held her close, gentle and soothing. The conduits of life swirled around her hand. It glowed bright white. She couldn't feel her hand at all now.

She searched into the distance. The remnants of blackness dripped from the rifts south across Paris, where the killing stain had spread. Also gone were Nanterre and Montreuil. But then she heard and smelled life in Rouen, Nantes, and Dijon. She sought farther still to the warmth of Lyon and Marseilles, and traveled all the way to Alexandria. Tears fell over her cheeks. Tears of relief. Simon was alive. As horrible as the cost had been, the potential was so much worse. The rest of humanity was safe.

Adele opened her eyes. Strong arms held her. She was on her knees hunched over the stone floor of Notre Dame. Gareth knelt next to her, holding her up, his face a mask of worry.

"Adele!"

She could only nod at him. The warmth of the rifts vanished, leaving her cold. She leaned against Gareth, trading one source of warmth for another. Her eyes found her hand. The raw skin was covered in a sheen of ice crystals and her fingers were blue. Gareth took her frigid hand. Her fingers bent slowly and painfully.

Nearby, the Tear of Death lay on the stones. It had been pulled from the Earth and it sat near Goronwy's body. He was contorted, with terror in his open eyes.

"He's dead," Gareth told her.

"I'm sorry." Adele's voice sounded strange, hoarse and far deeper than normal. Everything about her ached.

He took her against his chest. "The both of you were just lying there, holding that thing. Goronwy collapsed and then you pulled the Tear from the floor and flung it aside. But then there was nothing. I was afraid—"

"I wasn't. Finally." Adele gave a soft laugh. Then she focused on his face, so torn and blood-caked. She tried instinctively to rise with a croaking exclamation, "Flay!"

"Gone." Gareth soothed her. "For now."

Adele almost asked why he hadn't given chase, but she knew the reason.

A shuffle of footfalls made her start, but he continued to hold her. "Don't worry. It's only friends."

Kasteel, Nadzia, Caterina, and Lothaire, along with the surviving rebels, stared at the twisted body of the Witchfinder. Their gazes tracked fearfully to Adele.

She regarded the line of bloody faces. Then she turned wearily back to Gareth, his sapphirine eyes studying her anxiously. She didn't even have the strength to touch his torn cheek. "We did it. We stopped him. All of us together."

Gareth lifted her in his arms and bowed his head against her cold cheek. "Yes," he whispered.

EPILOGUE

Adele walked once more in Greyfriars kirkyard. The air was soft and warm. Daffodils quivered around the moss-scarred tombs. Birds sang in the budding trees. It was a beautiful picture.

The gravel crunched under her feet and she saw ripples of energy spread with each step, as if she were strolling through a shallow stream. When she reached a spot near the Flodden Wall, fear welled up in her, numbing her legs and arms. Even so, she walked toward the tomb where Mamoru waited. She knew she shouldn't go. Only shame and death waited there. But she couldn't stop herself.

As she made her way between gravestones, she saw her body lying on top of the tomb. She drew close and looked down at her figure, sleeping peacefully, as if unaware that something terrible was about to happen. She wanted to wake herself and warn her, tell her to get out of here. Maybe there was still time to run. At least hide behind a nearby grave so Mamoru wouldn't see her.

The body on the tomb opened her eyes and smiled up at herself. "Don't worry. I understand."

Adele blinked and saw Gareth. He sat at a desk, framed in a window. Sun shone red around him and nearly shaded him into a black shape. The familiar roofs of Paris were visible behind him. The timeless patience in his posture gave her comfort. His head drooped. He was asleep.

Adele smiled. She felt rested and calm, just as she had seemed on the tomb. Mamoru hadn't appeared at all. She took a long breath and felt a fresh bed sheet ripple over her. Gareth leapt to his feet and the chair clattered to the floor behind him.

"You're awake?" He leaned over the bed.

Adele started to stretch, but aches shot through her legs and shoulder. Still, it was merely pain. She could heal from that. "Where's the Tear?"

Gareth pointed toward the windowsill, where a small lump rested wrapped in cloth and tied with twine. She reached out for it, so he handed it to her. She held it for a moment, feeling the hard edges under the rag. She was careful not to touch any part of the stone that might show through. While her fingers tingled, she didn't feel the terrifying disassociation that the Tear of Death caused when she touched it with bare skin. She would have to find a safe place for this object; a place only she knew. Perhaps there was a chamber in the Great Pyramid where she could hide it, and then seal it in. Until then, Adele would keep it close no matter how frightening it was to her.

"You've been asleep for two days," Gareth said.

"Have I?" She sat up into the sunlight. "Have you been here that entire time?"

"Where else should I be?"

It brought a renewed sense of peace to her. She looked past him toward the window. "What's happened out there?"

He knelt in front of her. "The city is back under Lothaire and Caterina's control, more or less. Hallow has disappeared. Flay is gone, but she took nearly half the packs with her." He lifted her face and looked deeply into her eyes, searching for something. "The Witchfinder's attack wasn't absolute. They're estimating nearly seventy-five percent casualties in Rotherford's army and among the humans for many miles south of Paris. Survivors of your army are retreating. Lothaire guaranteed their safety back to Lyon. Not that he could've sent more than a few hundred against them in any case."

Adele groaned with the memory of climbing into the tower of Notre Dame after Goronwy's death and surveying the vast field of death to the south.

"Don't blame yourself, Adele. You tried to convince the generals."

She looked up in alarm. "What about Captain Hariri and his crew?"

"They're alive. As are many more. Thanks to you."

"Not just me. I couldn't have accomplished anything without you and Kasteel and the rebels. Millions of humans have you and your dis-

ciples to thank for their lives, although they'll likely never know it."
Adele sank back against the pillow. "That will be no comfort for the
families across the empire when they find their sons and husbands and
brothers have been killed." She pressed his hand into her cheek. "We'll
have to return to Alexandria immediately. Simon and General Anhalt
can't be left to deal with this disaster. The sooner I can get a ship back
the better."

"Yes." Gareth seemed hesitant and nervous.

"What's wrong?" Adele asked, searching his face. She attempted to
move to the side of the bed, intent on standing up.

"Nothing is wrong." He calmed her with a gentle touch. "You need
to rest, to heal."

"Just tell me what's the matter. Has something else happened while
I lay here in a stupor?"

Gareth smiled at her and shook his head. "No, nothing has happened. I'm merely wondering if it is possible that we could delay our
departure for Alexandria for a week?"

Adele paused. "We could, I suppose. Why?"

Gareth twisted his head as if making a decision. "I'd like to work
with Kasteel. Just for a brief while, you understand. Help him. A week
at most and we can go."

Adele sighed in relief. "Of course. Stay here. It's important that you
do. Take what time you need. I can go ahead to Alexandria. What I have
to do there is no work for the Greyfriar in any case." She smiled back at
him. "So you think there might be something to Kasteel and his rebels?"

Gareth shrugged. "I don't know. But I *want* to know."

"Good." Adele walked slowly to a table, where she found some fresh
bread and several green pears, obviously brought in by Gareth in case she
awakened. Her stomach rumbled. "Teach them well. Your Holiness."

"Hardly. I have no idea what I can do, but . . ." Gareth let the words
drift away. He stared out the window. "I won't be a week at most, trust me."

"Take the time you need. I'll miss you but I'll be very busy. The
nation will be mourning the men lost here. And I have a great deal of

work to do on geomancy. I just can't leave it to develop on its own; look what happened with Goronwy. I've got to plan and organize."

Gareth went back to the desk and held up a small sheaf of papers. "I have something for you to read on the voyage."

Adele paused with a chunk of bread in her hand. Her eyes grew wide with excitement. "Is it . . . ?"

He handed the sheets to her.

With a wide grin, Adele looked at the top page full of his recognizable handwriting: *My name is Gareth. I am the son of Dmitri. I was born south of Kiliwhimin in the Great Glen of Scotland. My father taught me to hunt humans and drink their blood. That is WHAT I am.*

She turned to the next page to see a crumpled photograph of her and Gareth arm in arm. It was the picture she had taken in London and then ripped apart. Gareth had apparently collected the pieces and saved them all this time. He had pinned the two halves, creased and worn, together on the page to reform their first photograph as a couple. The picture still showed her looking haggard but happy standing beside Gareth in his unnatural state.

Below the repaired picture were the lines: *But this is WHO I am. This is who WE are.*

Gareth took the page from her hand and held it out to stare at the photo. "Here is the evidence you sought all those months prowling our kirkyard with your camera. This is proof of what you've wrought and it's only a hint of what you're capable of. It's not about the Death Bringer or the Empress of the End. It has nothing to do with your magic. It's you, Adele. You will change the world because you accept the impossible."

Blinking back sudden tears, Adele threw her arms around him. Through the window behind Gareth, Paris was coming back to life. Humans emerged from hiding while dark shapes flitted over the city.

ACKNOWLEDGMENTS

Thanks to our readers who wanted more Vampire Empire.

And thanks to Rene Sears—editor, colleague, and friend—who helped us to give our readers more Adele and Gareth.

ABOUT THE AUTHORS

Photo by Vivian Cronin

C lay and Susan Griffith met at a bookstore thanks to *Uncanny X-Men* #201. They got married because of a love of adventure stories featuring heroes who both save the day and fall in love. Soon they were writing stories together. After years cowriting television scripts, comics, short stories, and novels, they remain happily married. When not writing or talking about writing, Clay and Susan are watching classic movies, playing Warcraft, and struggling to entertain the cat.

They still have that copy of *Uncanny X-Men* #201.